desert world
REBIRTH

LYN GALA

DSP PUBLICATIONS

Published by
DSP PUBLICATIONS

5032 Capital Circle SW, Suite 2, PMB# 279, Tallahassee, FL 32305-7886 USA
http://www.dsppublications.com/

Desert World Rebirth
© 2015 Lyn Gala.

Cover Art
© 2012 Justin James.
dare.empire@gmail.com
Cover Design
© 2012 Mara McKennen

ISBN: 978-1-63216-955-6
Digital ISBN: 978-1-63216-956-3
Library of Congress Control Number: 2014920707
Second Edition June 2015
First Edition published by Dreamspinner Press, January 2012

Printed in the United States of America

This paper meets the requirements of
ANSI/NISO Z39.48-1992 (Permanence of Paper).

This book is dedicated to everyone who has stood by me through difficult times—from the beta group who helped with both books, to wonderfully supportive Facebook and LiveJournal communities, to my very supportive mother. E.L. Doctorow once said that writing is a socially acceptable form of schizophrenia, so I definitely should thank all the people who put up with my brand of insanity and continue to love me despite it.

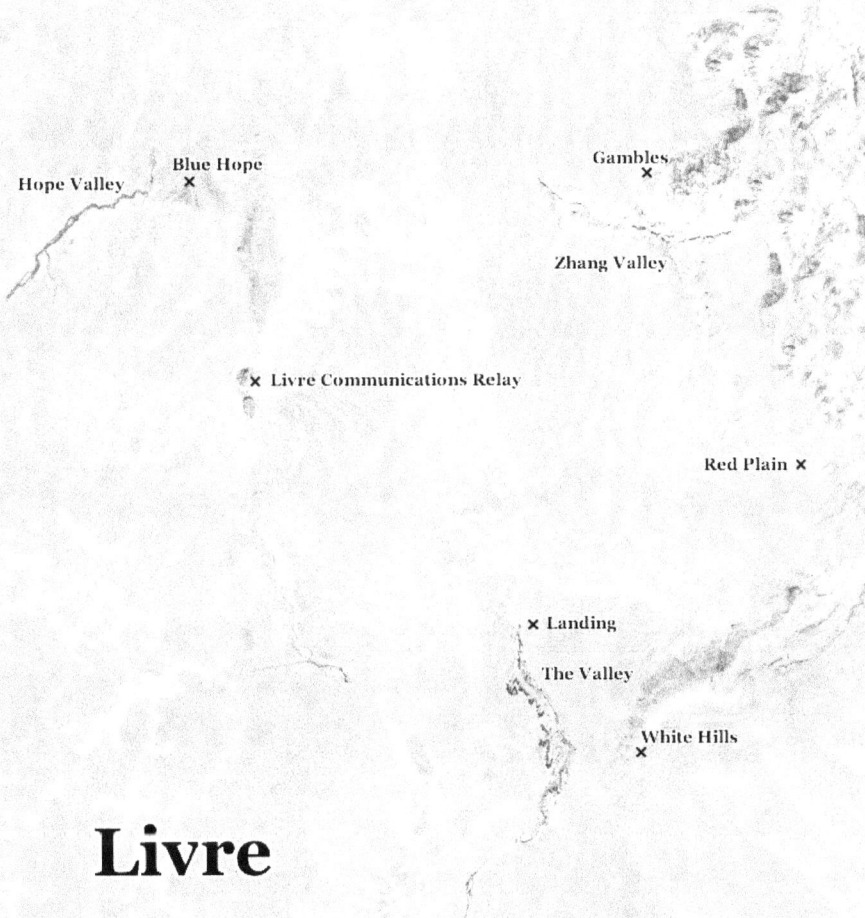

Hope Valley

Blue Hope
×

Gambles
×

Zhang Valley

× Livre Communications Relay

Red Plain ×

× Landing

The Valley

White Hills
×

Livre

chapter
o n e

SHAN HEARD the door chime and nearly jumped out of his skin. Three months living in the relay station set deep in the Livre desert, and he still wasn't used to some of the technology. Door chimes, for one. Another difference would be the sheer amount of space he lived in. In the church, he had privacy, time to search his thoughts. However, there he was always aware of Div shuffling somewhere in the house or softly praying, his Latin drifting through the air. Livre houses were generally small, built to stand up against the desert wind. Here, silence reigned. The early settlers had built the station before the inner worlds had largely abandoned Livre to survive—or die—on its own.

Shan walked through the storage room to one of the five living spaces. Through the thick window, he could see a shadowed form moving in the bright Livre sunshine. Maybe he'd been living alone too long, because his mind went to Ista and to all the men and women who had tried to kill him... to the wealthy and beloved landowner Ben, who had shown his true colors when he raped Temar. Shan could forgive the murder attempt more easily than Ben's willingness to rape. But considering Ben, Ista, and most of their coconspirators were dead, fearing that they'd turn up here suggested that he *had* been alone a little too long.

Pushing aside irrational fears, Shan opened the door and smiled as he saw Temar standing in the light, his sand veil hanging around his neck.

"Temar!" Stepping forward, he caught Temar in a quick hug. "I thought you were off working your glass this week." Temar often stopped by, running the long dunes to visit once or twice a week, but he'd already warned Shan that he wouldn't be able to visit this week.

A flash of pain crossed Temar's face, and he dropped his head so his shaggy blond hair hid his features.

"Temar?" Shan asked, his voice quieting.

Temar gave a shrug.

"Do you want to come in?" Shan took a step back to give Temar some room. He didn't want to push him, not after what Ben had done. So even if Shan's cock sometimes ached with need, and if he sometimes lay in bed stroking himself while thinking of Temar, Shan wouldn't physically crowd the man. He'd give Temar space to heal on his own.

With a small nod, Temar came into the station, passing through the room with the metal and plastic chairs and tables with the perfect lines and symmetrical bolts that Shan still found a little alien. When he and Temar had left the door open to pursue Ben, not even the wind and sand of the desert storm had left a mark on the sterile room. Shan was used to the curves of windwood, the uneven gaps formed by the twisted branches, and the way a truly great craftsman could make a piece curve with the human body. Every craftsman had his own style. Roget Ally from Landing created chairs and tables with small branches that intertwined so perfectly that the pieces of wood appeared to wrap around each other, as though in love. In comparison, these perfectly uniform chairs brought down by the drop ships that first carried settlers to Livre had no life.

Temar headed through the storage room, into the computer control room, and then through a door into the one living space Shan actually used. He dropped down onto the couch and pulled his sand veil off, fingering the edges.

"What happened?" Shan asked, settling into a chair near enough that he could reach out to offer a comforting hand if needed.

For some time, Temar seemed to struggle with his feelings. Most times, Temar wasn't an emotional man. The shyness clung to him, muffled his reactions, but right now, Shan could see the pain etched deep into his features. "Dee'eta hates me," Temar finally confessed in a miserable voice.

Shan doubted Dee'eta Sun's feelings were as simple as hate. "Why do you say that?"

Leaning back, Temar stared up at the perfectly flat metal ceiling. "She can barely look at me. Three weeks into my apprenticeship, and my glass-master can't even look me in the eye when showing me how to use the paddles to shape the piece. It's the most uncomfortable place I've ever been." Temar tilted his head and looked Shan right in the eye. "Ever," he repeated. Given that Temar had once been trapped in Ben's bed, a victim of both rape and a criminal justice system that had failed him, that was saying something.

Shan had been on the council that had sentenced Temar to a term of slavery after his vandalism had caused more damage than he could ever repay. Of course, he'd been following his sister's attempts to play detective when it had happened. It hadn't been fair, but Cyla had gone to an owner who trained her to work and Temar had gone to Ben, who had raped him and blackmailed him into not reporting it to the council. At least Shan could hold on to the fact that he had argued against slavery. Vehemently argued. Dee'eta didn't have that luxury. She had to look at Temar and know she'd played her part in sending him into that hell. "This can't be easy for either of you," Shan said, not entirely sure how to broach the subject of Dee'eta's guilt when it had been Temar who had suffered the most.

"No, not really," Temar said, his voice defeated. "I spent my entire childhood dreaming of an apprenticeship with her, and now that I have my dream, it's not…." Temar sighed. "It's not any good, Shan."

"Is that why you left?"

"I screwed up. I cooled the punty too much, and when Dee'eta tried to transfer the glass, it slipped off and broke."

"That happens with apprentices," Shan reassured him. "When I apprenticed for Div, the very first sermon I gave I mixed up John and Paul and said something very stupid about the Book of Matthew. Luckily, I was so scared that I was preaching in a monotone that had put everyone to sleep by then."

Temar looked at Shan seriously. "Did he yell at you?"

Shan smiled. "In a way, I suppose he did. With Div, yelling was done in this really soft, disappointed voice that made you want to crawl into a hole and pull the sand in over you." He missed Div. Leaving the priesthood had been the right choice, no question. And when the councils had offered him a chance to finish his long-abandoned mechanics' apprenticeship by studying the relay station systems and reading a hundred years' worth of technical manuals, he'd jumped at the chance.

He still missed Div, though. He missed talking to him over breakfast and that odd look Div gave him when Shan had done something desperately foolish. That was how a father should act—not that Shan had a lot of experience with good fathering.

"Dee'eta didn't yell," Temar said in a defeated tone. "She gave me one glance, and then she started lecturing on how to recycle scraps."

Shan was confused. "So you didn't leave over that, did you?"

"I did." Temar practically leaped out of his seat and started pacing. Shan was more than confused now, but he held his tongue and waited for Temar to explain. Both Shan's brother Naite and Temar had suffered terrible abuse, but unlike Naite, Temar opened up if you gave him enough time and space to get the words together. But this time it took longer than normal. He stalked the room, his fingers running over the smooth, rolled metal edges of the tables and shelves. He was a tactile man, and sometimes touching a well-made piece of glass would soothe him enough to start talking. Shan gave him that space.

Temar stopped at one of the few pieces of furniture Shan had insisted on bringing out—a windwood chest with intertwining branches that Roget Ally had made for Shan's mother before she died. It was the only part of his father's farm he'd saved when the man's land and house were sold to pay his debts. Temar crouched down and let his long fingers dance over the intricate work and smooth joints. "How can she teach me if she's so afraid of me that she can't even tell me when I'm wrong?" he asked in a tired voice.

"She's feeling guilty," Shan said.

Temar turned and gave him an incredulous look. "Do you think I don't know that?"

"I know you know it," Shan said, "but maybe you—" Shan put his hand over his heart. "You and Naite know the pain of being hurt, but you need to know there's a pain and guilt to being not hurt." The moment he said that, he knew it sounded incredibly rude. It sounded like he was dismissing Temar's trauma, which wasn't his intent.

Standing up, Temar crossed his arms over his chest. "I know that, but do you really think I'm so weak that I'm going to collapse in tears if you rip me a new asshole for ruining a beautiful piece of work?"

"Me? No. I know you're stronger than that," Shan said in all truthfulness. He'd seen Temar's strength, and he knew it would take a lot more than a few words to bring the man down. Temar was worth waiting for, in part because of his strength.

Temar shook his head. "Naite is the only one who treats me normally."

"Not surprising. After the council assigned him to three years of slavery with you, he's going to go out of his way to make sure that he doesn't change, because he won't want to let himself act servile, even if he's serving. He knows the danger of letting a slave-sentence get to you too much."

"Not that he's actually a slave," Temar said in a disgusted voice. He leaned against the wall and closed his eyes.

Clearly something was wrong there, and that shocked Shan down to his core. Naite was a cantankerous, difficult man. Growing up, Shan had wanted to kill him more than once, but Naite had already been suffering their father's abuse. Well, they'd both been abused, but Naite had been the one raped while Shan had suffered only the cold disinterest of a man who had neglected and ignored him while seeming to shower all his love on the older Naite. However, it was Naite who understood Temar better than anyone else on the planet. Shan would have expected Naite to support Temar, not make him feel worse.

"What's going on?"

Temar pressed the heels of his hands to his eyes as though trying to block out some memory. "He ripped me open, left me about as raw as a sand-rat-chewed wound and stalked off."

Shan's breath left him. "He… what?"

Temar made a little huffing noise that was either frustration or amusement—Shan couldn't tell. "He told me I had a right to sell the balance of his contract, but I didn't have a right to ignore him after asking him to manage Ben's farm."

"Your farm," Shan corrected him.

"Well, apparently, I'm letting Cyla treat it like her farm, and Naite informed me that if I didn't get my head out of my ass and make my idiot sister stop acting like a sandcat, I wasn't going to have anyone to work the crops but him."

That did sound like Naite. When people weren't living up to his expectations, he could be a sandstorm, blowing in and destroying entire villages without slowing.

Temar sighed. "And the worst part is, he's right."

Shan leaned back in the chair and studied Temar. His shoulders were pulled in, and his whole body looked as tight as a person could get without having a heart attack. It bothered Shan that he'd driven out in this mood, because the sand dunes were unforgiving if you made a mistake, and Temar wasn't all that experienced on a bike.

"So," he said carefully, not wanting to make things worse, "you're upset that Dee'eta can't treat you normally, and you're upset that Naite is treating you normally?"

Temar had a self-deprecating half grin on his face as he shrugged. "I didn't say I was feeling logical. I can be annoyed with both of them and you all at the same time."

"With me?" Shan sat up straight, not sure when his faults had come into the conversation.

"With you," Temar echoed. "Are you attracted to me or not?"

Shan's mouth fell open, and he had to consciously close it and gather his thoughts before he could answer. Even before he'd blurted out his whole stupid infatuation while drunk, he'd been less than subtle. Apparently. Shan always thought he'd hidden his interest well—he'd certainly lived in denial. However, since leaving the priesthood, more than one person had clapped him on the back and congratulated him for finally having the strength to openly court Temar. Shan had to assume he'd been a little more obvious than he'd thought. "You know I am," he said as calmly as he could.

"So, you haven't changed your mind now that you're not a priest and you can sleep with anyone you want?"

"No." Shan studied Temar more carefully, sure the man had some hidden agenda for this question. "Have I ever shown any interest in anyone else?"

Temar crossed the room slowly. Since leaving the priesthood, Shan hadn't taken anyone to his bed. He hadn't wanted anyone in his bed, no one except Temar, and he'd been very open about both his interest and his willingness to wait, so he met Temar's uncertain gaze. Temar had such beautiful eyes—blue eyes that reflected more emotions than Shan could ever hope to understand.

Temar settled on the end of the couch. "Why don't you ever touch me?"

"I hugged you! When you came, I hugged you, so I know I touch you," Shan snapped. He had enough flaws of his own without Temar inventing reasons to be upset with him.

Moving slowly, Temar rested his hand on Shan's knee. "Why don't you ever really touch me?" he asked again. The warmth of Temar's hand soaked through the fabric.

"I do," Shan said, only this time his voice wavered. This was the sort of touch he generally did avoid.

"No, you don't. Shan, I know that you liked me before, but you were a priest, so it was safe for you to like me without thinking anything would happen. If you aren't interested—"

"I am." Shan cut him off, bringing his own hand up to rest on Temar's. Temar had long fingers and small hands, and Shan's big, scarred paw just about covered it. They were the hands of a mechanic, not a priest.

"Then why don't you touch me?"

For a second, Shan chewed on his lower lip and tried to control the growing hardness in his pants. He did want Temar. Too much. "I don't want to push things too far too fast."

"Shan, I need a little more pushing. Actually, I can do the pushing myself, but I need a sign that you're okay with me pushing."

Shan looked at Temar, but he didn't see any doubt or fear in his expression. He'd expected Temar to want to move slowly, to heal from his time in Ben's custody. Hell, Naite had been clear that it had taken years for him to get his own balance back after being abused, and Shan couldn't expect more of Temar.

After that uncomfortable conversation, Shan had firmly counseled himself about patience and the dangers of lust. That had been more than ironic. Naite wasn't exactly celibate, and he'd lectured Shan about not having sex. God could have a sharp sense of humor. Shan had even considered asking Temar to marry him before taking him to bed, wondering if the commitment would ease the fears. It would ease Div's mind to know that Shan was still taking the church's teachings so seriously. But now that he was looking into Temar's eyes, fear didn't live there; frustration did. "I take it I've been moving too slow?" he guessed.

Temar nodded. "I was starting to think you were trying to find nice ways to let me down easy. I thought maybe, like Dee'eta, you were too afraid to hurt me."

Shan tightened his hold on Temar's hand. "I don't want to hurt you, ever. But I want you. I want you more than I should."

"Then why aren't you showing any interest in having a relationship?" Temar asked. Shan's gaze drifted down to his own pants, where his hard cock pressed up against the seam. Temar chuckled. "Okay, so you're showing some interest," he added with some amusement, "but in my defense, that's the first time I've seen that."

Suddenly Temar pulled his hand away from Shan. "Wait. Is this about you not wanting to show me a hard cock? Do you think that I'll confuse what Ben did with sex?"

Shan's sexual frustration was interfering with his ability to form coherent thought at this point. "You don't have a lot of experience...."

Temar gave a rough bark of laughter that didn't really match his normal shy manner. "Unless you have a few lovers Naite doesn't know about, I have more than you. He insists you're a big coward who doesn't want to admit that you're clueless."

"You talked to my brother about my sex life?" Shan demanded, hot anger rising up to vie with the sexual heat that was already making his skin warm. His anger couldn't maintain itself, though. In three months, he hadn't done more than offer a quick hug, so Temar had some cause to get a little insecure. "Of course you did. That sounds exactly like Naite, only without the profanity that he would have thrown in."

"He did have a couple of choice words. But without Naite, I wouldn't have had the nerve to do this. I would have sat home and given you time to move on because you clearly didn't want me." Temar set his jaw and glared at Shan, clearly not willing to apologize for going to Naite. "I love you, but I'm starting to doubt whether this is right for us. For you."

"It is," Shan insisted. Leaning forward, he captured Temar's hands and held them between his palms, their warmth mingling. "I admit that I haven't had many lovers. I took my vows seriously, and before the priesthood...." Shan thought back to himself as a young man, gawky and awkward and fumbling in the dark with a boy named Nuesis, and with two different women. Both of them kept warning him not to put his cock in them because pregnancy was serious and a man who got a woman pregnant had his life tied to her until the child was grown—neither of them liked him enough for that. "I don't have a lot of experience. But the main problem is that I would rather wait until you're ready than risk ruining the friendship we share."

"I'm ready," Temar said gently. "I'm more than ready."

Shan grimaced. "I should also mention that I'm not exactly good with relationships."

With a smile, Temar ducked his head. "Naite mentioned that."

"If we're going to do this, could we not mention my brother anymore?" Shan begged. There were certain topics guaranteed to send his cock into full retreat. Ben was one, and Naite was another.

The smile remained as Temar brought his hand up to rest against Shan's cheek. "Deal. But no more waiting. It's giving me a neurosis."

The heat was gathering in Shan's body, making his throat dry and tight, so he simply nodded. Temar slowly smiled, shifting forward on the couch so that he perched on the edge. It had been a long time since he'd done this, but Shan's body remembered. He remembered the slide of skin against skin, the aching need to touch, the hunger. Reaching out, he slid his hand under Temar's shirt so he could feel the hot skin hidden underneath.

Temar's hand came up to stroke Shan's arms, his fingers reaching up under the loose sleeve. "I'm not sure what you want," Temar murmured before he ran his fingernails down Shan's arm hard enough to make three tiny trails of white on Shan's olive skin.

"I'm open to anything," Shan said, and he meant it. He was nervous about it because his experience with men was limited to some touching and sucking, but this was Temar.

"Funny enough, me too," Temar said with a smile that Shan couldn't resist. He leaned forward and caught Temar behind the neck and pulled him close. Temar came off the couch and put his knee on the edge of the chair, leaning close so Shan could press his lips to Temar's. He smelled of sand and salt and soap, and Shan groaned.

Temar pulled back a few inches. "Problem?" he teased.

"Yeah," Shan said. "And I'm too old to do anything about it in a chair."

Temar laughed. "You're not that old."

"I'm old enough not to give up a good bed for a small chair," Shan countered. Temar must have agreed, because with a smile he stood. Shan didn't realize Temar had caught hold of his shirt until the fabric pulled tight.

"Then the bed it is," Temar said, tugging on the shirt to urge Shan up. Shan's cock was painfully hard as he pushed himself up and followed.

chapter
two

ALL SORTS of fears churned through Shan's guts as Temar followed. He didn't have a lot of experience, he didn't want to hurt Temar, and he didn't want to screw this up. He liked Temar too much to make a mistake now, after everything they'd been through together. Workers would often disappear into the fields at night, but this was something more than a night of lust. This was something infinitely more dangerous than that. Shan hadn't used the word with Temar yet, but he loved the man, and the fear of making a mistake constantly gnawed at the edge of his awareness. Temar reached the bedroom and stopped. Whatever demons Temar carried, they didn't rule him. His cock pressed against his pants, making a good-sized bulge, and his pupils were black with lust, dilated until the blue looked like a ring.

Shan's smile grew as he moved close, his hands sliding over Temar's shoulders and arms. "Anything you want," Shan whispered the promise.

"On the bed would be a good start," Temar said. "You're too tall."

Shan chuckled. "I can do that." Backing away, he moved toward the bed, pulling his shirt off and dropping it on the floor before he sat on the edge.

"Better," Temar said. He stalked forward, his body tightly controlled as he stepped between Shan's legs. Shan spread his legs and looked up, waiting for some sign of what Temar wanted from this. Bringing both hands up, Temar cupped either side of Shan's face and then leaned close for another kiss. His lips moved against Shan's, and Shan's hands came up to rest against Temar's hips. Temar's lips tasted of mint and salt.

Holding him as the kiss grew hungrier and more aggressive, Temar slid his hand around to the back of Shan's head, and Shan thrust up almost involuntarily, his body aching for this. Starving for this.

Temar's other hand tightened on Shan's shoulder, and he flinched in pain before Temar gentled his touch, fingers stroking over the abused spot. "Sorry," Temar whispered.

"I want you," Shan said. "I want you so much."

"Then you should have asked earlier," Temar said, a touch of condemnation still in his voice. A voice in the back of Shan's head warned that Temar had been more hurt than he'd admitted, but Shan couldn't fix that now. He could only show Temar how much he wanted him. He slid his hands under Temar's shirt, feeling the wiry muscles tense and relax under his fingers. Shan might not have been sexually experimental in his youth, but he knew what felt good. He reached up and ran a thumb over Temar's nipple.

Temar arched his back and groaned. "Yes," he said, the hissed word drawn out to impossible lengths. Shan's balls drew up, his cock hardening even more in the prison of his jeans. Panting, lips parted slightly so that Shan could see the pink tongue inside, Temar yanked off his shirt and threw it to the side before pressing both his palms against Shan's shoulders, pressing him back to the bed. Shan yielded, grateful that Temar was taking the lead in this. Shan would follow, because in this one area, he feared leading into dangerous territory.

Instead, he lay back, fisting the sheets and struggling against a need to come in his pants. He hadn't ever let a man enter him, so his fears whispered warnings about being too tight, too small, and damn old to start learning new tricks. Luckily, that whisper lived in the distance. Shan's skin burned for Temar. His cock ached, and if Temar wanted to have full sex, a good 99 percent of Shan was on board with that plan.

When Temar's curious fingers finally found the zipper of Shan's jeans, each tooth of the zipper yielded with an audible click. Shan sucked in a breath as the pressure over his cock eased. His white underwear bulged up through the open zipper, his cock making it clear that it had no doubts. Letting go of the sheets, Shan caught Temar's forearms and held tightly as he arched his back in need. He'd been denying himself for so long, this desire frightened him. It was as if the embers of lust he'd hidden under the ashes of the priesthood had suddenly found oxygen and burst to life.

Temar settled onto Shan's legs, trapping them, but then he didn't do anything else. He sat, studying Shan's bare chest and his hard cock, pressing obscenely up. Shan squirmed, cravings gathering in the pit of his stomach until he wasn't sure he could control the need for more. His palms itched as he fought an urge to grab himself and start stroking his sweat-slick hand up and down his shaft.

"Anything," Shan repeated hoarsely.

Temar's smile was slow and silky as he inched his way backward to the edge of the bed. Shan frowned, not sure why Temar seemed to be retreating. He'd opened his mouth, on the verge of asking what was wrong, when Temar leaned down to mouth Shan's cock right through his underwear. Shan shouted, the sound ripped from him as his cock twitched painfully. He needed to come. Oh, God, he needed to come. Temar sucked, the fabric making the sound almost obscene. Throwing his arms out, Shan fisted the sheets and cried out again.

"Temar," Shan gasped out. "Temar," he said a little louder. He needed to tell Temar to stop before he came in his pants. He needed to say it, but his words scattered like grains of sand in the wind. "Temar," he gasped out for a third time.

Temar pushed himself up so he was straddling Shan. "Good?" he asked.

For a minute, Shan could only breathe fast and try to regain his sense of balance, because the world was tilting and he was about to slide right off the bed. "Too good," he finally agreed.

"Too good?" All the surety Temar had shown a moment before vanished, leaving him looking slightly confused and maybe even concerned. Shan caught Temar's hand in his.

"I'm going to come in my shorts if you do that again," he confessed. Shan ran his fingers over Temar's pale skin. Tiny pinprick scars hid under blond hair—the sort that Shan himself had earned from welding, but he imagined working with hot glass would have the same dangers. That was the perfect description of his Temar—beautiful and strong and able to endure the heat of a glass shop, even if he looked ethereal and fragile. Shan's cock was burning with need, but he was not going to be a selfish lover. Unfortunately, he wasn't sure exactly what to do. When Shan looked up, Temar smiled down at him.

"That sounds like it's a good thing," Temar said.

"Very good, unless you do that again, and then this is very over," Shan warned. Temar's smile grew wider. Temar trailed his longer fingers down Shan's arm, stopping at a scar above his wrist. He frowned, and Shan could almost feel the unspoken question. "When I was seventeen and working for Holmes, I burned it on an exhaust,"

Shan explained. When he had first changed from an apprenticeship in mechanics to one in the priesthood, he'd thought it would be safer. Clearly God had made a jest out of that belief. Temar's fingers continued down to the back of Shan's hand, tracing the lines of veins. Shan watched.

Moving slowly and carefully, Temar closed his hand around Shan's wrist and brought Shan's hand up to his chest. Shan spread his fingers against the pale chest and looked up into Temar's blue eyes. After a few seconds, Shan started slowly tracing tiny circles over smooth, soft skin. Temar's eyes drooped in pleasure, and Shan allowed his hand to wander up the side of Temar's neck and face. This slow, intimate exploration of another's body was foreign to him.

Temar's eyes slowly opened. "Anything covers a lot of territory."

Shan swallowed, his mouth dry as dust. It *did* cover a lot of territory, but he'd wanted Temar so long, and that want grew stronger the longer he knew Temar. The man's strength and goodness had survived so much darkness.

"Anything," Shan repeated. He could see the desire in the curve of Temar's neck and his half-closed eyes as Shan ran fingers over his chest, pausing to tease a small, dark nipple. Temar sucked in a harsh breath when Shan pulled at the nipple. Emboldened, Shan moved his hand down and ran his finger along the smooth skin above the waistband of Temar's pants. Shan had to slow his own breathing and concentrate to get the zipper down.

Temar's cock pressed out through his underwear, the tip visible and a tiny spot of moisture like a dark target on the white fabric. "I'm really not sure what I'm doing here," Shan confessed in a whisper.

Temar caught his hand and kissed the palm. "I'm not either. But it feels good."

"We're both going to die of blue balls at this rate." Shan gave a little huff of laughter. Here he was with his first lover after leaving the priesthood, and the man had more experience being abused than sharing intimacies. They were the sunblind leading the sandblind.

Temar smiled so that little lines gathered at the corners of his eyes. "We aren't doing bad." He shifted back, leaving the bed altogether before he moved to the side and sat down. Shan scooted back so he was all the way on the bed, and in the process, he managed to wiggle out of his pants—more by accident than by intent. Temar watched, his gaze focusing on Shan's hard cock. "We aren't doing bad at all," he repeated, his voice a distracted whisper. He reached over and traced the line of Shan's jaw with a single finger.

After tracing the line of Shan's jaw, Temar slipped his fingers behind Shan's neck and slowly pulled him close. Yielding to the gentle pressure, Shan leaned forward. Temar gently sucked on Shan's lip, dull teeth running along the edge, and Shan pushed closer, his cock demanding touch. Rocking his body against Temar, Shan gasped, which allowed Temar's tongue to slip inside, and suddenly Temar pushed Shan onto his back.

Shan squirmed and dug his heels into the mattress as he pushed up. Hands scrambled at his underwear, and Shan divided his attention between kissing the sensual mouth that was devouring him and raising his ass so Temar could get them off. Thank God he didn't wear shoes around the relay station, or they'd have a tangled mess.

Warm skin pressed down on him, and Shan shivered as he pulled a nude Temar closer. He wasn't sure when Temar had shed his pants, and he didn't care. Shan opened his mouth more, and the kiss grew more frantic. Now Temar was groaning in need as he thrust down into Shan's body. Fabric tangled around Shan's legs, and he struggled to kick his shorts free. Temar shifted, and Shan was suddenly frozen by the realization that Temar's hard cock was pressed up against his. He had one second of panicked indecision before Temar wrapped his hand around both their cocks and started thrusting against Shan. Shan knew this. This was familiar. This was good.

Arching his back, Shan surged up so their bodies rubbed against each other, their cocks trapped in the heat and sweat that gathered between them. Shan cried out softly with each movement until he finally felt his balls tighten. He pulled Temar close and bucked up wildly as need erased anything other than the movement of body against body. Temar thrust down equally hard, and Shan yelled out as he came.

His mouth hung open, and he bucked as he came with a flare of pleasure. Waves traveled his spine as little shivers stole his control, so that Shan arched and writhed mindlessly. With a few more thrusts, Temar came, his own back arched so sharply he was nearly bent backward, his hands braced on Shan's shoulders. He came and then dropped his weight down onto Shan.

Lethargy dragged Shan down as every muscle that had been tense for the past three months decided to relax at once. He was sand-shifting into a new shape, a new drift, and the old simply vanished. He was Temar's lover. That was the new shape. Shan panted, and he could hear the heavy gasps as Temar struggled to regain his own breath. Temar shifted so that their legs tangled, and his weight slipped off to the side of Shan, only one arm still draped over Shan's stomach.

They lay still and silent, and the fever-heat faded as Shan's body cooled. His cock itched, and Shan reached down to rub it; he came away with a sticky hand that he wiped off on his own hip.

"Very not bad," Temar muttered sleepily.

"Worth leaving the priesthood for," Shan agreed without opening his eyes. He never would have left for sex, but sex this good was a nice bonus. "No offense, God," he added with a quick gesture as he crossed himself.

"I promise to leave your brother out of our sex life, if you promise to leave God out," Temar said as he shifted so he could press closer to Shan's side. Shan followed the muscle on Temar's arms, tracing it back and forth with his fingertips.

"Deal," Shan agreed. They lay in silence, the wind whispering against the metal building as their bodies finally cooled enough that Shan started eyeing the covers at the foot of the bed.

chapter
three

THE SILENCE settled around them, and Shan gave up on the covers, burrowing into the warmth of his love lying next to him. At thirty-two, he'd finally found himself… a little later than most. Most people, by this age, were taking on their first apprentices and considering children. But this had been worth the wait. Temar shifted against him. He was a slight man, but he had sharp knees. Shan grunted as one caught him on the thigh.

"Sorry," Temar offered.

"Not a problem." Shan traced circles on Temar's skin. It had been so long he'd forgotten the simple pleasure of exploring another's shape, the texture of their skin and the warmth of it.

"You didn't actually leave the priesthood for me or sex or anything, did you?" Temar asked, unexpectedly breaking the quiet mood.

"Um…. No. We talked about this. I always was more interested in fixing the church's pews than its sinners. That's not a good combination for a priest." Shan opened one eye and considered Temar. For someone who was generally more open and communicative than most, Temar wasn't doing a lot of communicating lately. Shan studied Temar's tense shoulders and the way his gaze kept skittering off to the corners. "Why are you asking now?"

That got another sigh. Given that they'd just had really good sex, Shan was starting to develop a neurosis of his own. "Have you heard Wistia's latest ballad?" Temar finally asked in a near whisper.

"No. I mean, there's a lot of technical reading around here, and every day I find out that some other piece of maintenance has been ignored for twenty years. I've been too busy to come to town."

"'The Ballad of the Lonely Priest,'" Temar said softly.

Shan felt a wave of horror run through him. "Oh, please tell me that it's not about…."

"Yep. You get the starring role. I'm the sweet young man who makes you question your faith."

Shan closed his eyes and struggled to find some core of calm that would allow him to avoid the emotional explosion building in his chest. She had no right. Worse, her ballad was a lie, and considering that Livre's history was largely told through song, that was a sin in itself. "I'll hold Wistia down if you want to drop the sandrat on her stomach and let it chew through her," Shan finally offered. No wonder Temar was having trouble keeping his emotional balance. It worried Shan that Temar didn't react to his joking threat at all. He decided to take the ballad more seriously.

"Div must have objected. He must be telling people that she's wrong. I didn't leave the church because I chose you over God. God showed me that I needed to walk another path." Shan thought about the events leading up to his decision. "Actually, God showed me, I ignored him, and God sort of shoved me off into the dirt because I wasn't listening."

Temar nodded, but he stayed silent. Reaching up, Shan ran his fingers through Temar's hair. Sweat stained the blond strands darker where they stuck together.

"I care about you, Temar, but my choice to leave the church came from a realization that I didn't fit there."

Temar got an arm under him and propped himself up, one hand braced on Shan's chest. "I don't want to think that I took away something important. I mean, the church was important to you, and I thought maybe you weren't touching me because you weren't sure about leaving it."

Shan shook his head. "God is important to me. Well, the church is, too, but not as a priest. I haven't given up on God, I haven't given up the church, and I should have given up the priesthood a long time ago. I can love the first two and still love you."

"So, I'm not breaking any God rules here?" Temar asked. He hadn't been one for coming to church until he was a young man. His father had blamed God when Temar's mother died, so Shan doubted old Erqu Gazer would have taught Temar much of anything about the word.

"The Gospel does favor marriage before the sex," Shan started slowly, "but that's what forgiveness is for."

"Marriage." Temar swallowed, and Shan could have kicked himself for bringing that up so soon. They weren't even an hour past their first sexual act, and he was bringing up marriage. Truly he was a fool when it came to relationships.

Shan hurried to say, "We don't have to—"

"Do you think about marriage, about us and being married?" Temar gave Shan such an intense look that the easy answer that had had been resting on the tip of his tongue vanished. Temar didn't want an easy answer; he didn't want some apology for pressing forward too fast.

Swallowing all his fears, Shan braced himself to tell the truth. "I do. I suppose I hope, if this works out between us, that you'll be willing to give it a try even if neither one of us has a great role model." Both their mothers had died young, and both their fathers had been some variation on failure.

Temar's smile was slow and timid, but he gave a little nod. "Wistia is going to write a new ballad." That sounded a lot like a yes. Shan swallowed, emotions pressing up faster than he could really think them through or even feel them.

"As long as she gets her facts straight this time, that's fine." Temar settled back down onto the pillow, their legs still tangled, and Shan realized that, in the end, it didn't matter. When confused, Temar came to him and asked him outright if he was interested, and as long as they turned to each other in trouble, they'd be fine. Wistia, on the other hand, was going to face a council complaint as soon as Shan could get a copy of the words to her new song.

Right now, though, Shan only cared about this moment, about Temar's warm body pressed to his side, about his sated cock and his sated body and his bone-deep desire to curl up with his lover and sleep.

They lay, drifting in and out of sleep for a time, until Shan's bladder started insisting that he get up. Despite the fact that he desperately didn't want to move, Shan eventually had to admit it was visit the bathroom or wet the bed. He was a little old for the latter, and he doubted Temar would appreciate it much.

"Problem?"

"Yeah, a bladder that's too small," Shan answered as he climbed out of the warm bed. Livre was never truly cold, but there was a chill in the air that suggested night was falling. This inner room didn't have a window to check the time, but it felt right.

"I hope you'll stay rather than risk running the dunes this late," Shan said before he headed into the bathroom.

"So, I can either stay or break my neck and get eaten by sandrats. I think I'll stay," Temar said with some amusement.

"I didn't mean...." Shan sighed as he finally started peeing a stream. "I made that sound like a threat, didn't I?"

"A little. You made it sound like an offer to stay wouldn't be good enough without the threat of death. Trust me, it is." Temar's voice turned hollow as he went into the mechanical room. Sound echoed in there. Shan refused to even hum, because the notes reverberated oddly off the walls. Their ancestors had considered sterile, harsh places like this normal, and had, from what Shan had read of their stored records, considered Livre inhospitable and brutal.

Livre was dangerous—Shan knew that better than most, but he also knew the beauty of a sunrise after a good sandstorm, the air glowing gold and red as the sun lifted over the horizon. He knew the floating shadows of a double moon and the soft, sweeping shapes of a sand dune. The windwood trees taught of survival, the sandrats taught conservation, and the buteo and raptors that soared above the sands made a man think of freedom. And every time he stood out on the sands, he could feel God. He couldn't imagine the world the settlers had described—the horrors and stark desolation they saw in the landscape.

Shan finished and shook the last drops off before heading for the bedroom in search of clothing. "What are all these lights?" Temar called from the control room. His voice bounced around the metal walls when he spoke too loud, and Shan grabbed his pants and padded out there rather than risk more of those odd, disconcerting echoes.

"Systems. The family that ran the place kept the water systems in top form."

"Well, yeah, because they were stealing water," Temar pointed out.

"True. The other systems were all in some stage of disrepair or shut down."

"Huh." Temar let his hands flow over the control panel, thin fingers tracing the switches and the indicator lights, red, blue, and green—mostly red. "I thought the relay was supposed to listen for the inner worlds' signals."

"They were. I guess they figured that if they were going to steal water and a ship, it didn't matter if anyone was sending them messages about the inner worlds or their war."

"Which is stupid. If I'm going to fly an old ship into the middle of unknown space, I would want to know how the war is going."

Shan leaned back against the wall and considered Temar's form. He seemed taller now, although that had to be illusion. Shan calculated that Temar had to be twenty-two or twenty-three... old enough that he'd stopped growing. He had grown thinner in the days since Shan had really paid attention to his body... his ribs evident, and his muscles were hard lines of cord under the skin. It worried Shan that he seemed so thin. Not unhealthy, necessarily, but painfully thin.

"Did you even hear what I said?"

Shan blinked as he realized he'd tuned Temar out for a time. "Um... not exactly."

Instead of getting upset, Temar slowly smiled. "I suppose I should be complimented that my naked backside is that distracting."

Shan blushed. "It is. It's been a while." Shan stopped, painfully aware that Temar had been sexually active far more recently.

"Well, then, welcome back," Temar said, either not noticing or not commenting on Shan's discomfort. "I asked which of these monitors the inner worlds. Maybe we can find out something about their idiotic war."

"I don't know." Shan went over to one of the stations and turned the interface on. "I've been trying to get the mechanical systems up and running—battery recharging, mechanics, planetside communication. I think I can get Landing and Red Plain back in radio contact, although Blue Hope's tower was taken out by a storm thirty years ago, and Gambles never did have the right equipment. There's a lot of inventory here that no one knows about, so there's a chance I've got the right materials to get one or both added to the system, but I really thought getting local communications up should take priority."

Temar came over as Shan went through assorted menus. The old ship systems were getting easier to understand and navigate, but when he'd first started, he'd questioned the logic of the programmers more than once. Years of having to translate Latin had improved his patience, though, so he was slowly deciphering the logic behind various chains of commands.

"That's my Shan, always the practical one."

Shan laughed. "Tell my brother that."

"Oh, I don't think so. He seems to think he's the one with his feet on the ground. Actually," Temar said, his tone shifting, "I think he's really annoyed that you were right and he was wrong about the whole slavery issue."

Shan's fingers stumbled on the keyboard.

"You can talk about it, you know."

"I can, but when I do, I'm intensely uncomfortable," Shan pointed out. "Do you need to talk about it?" he added when it occurred to him that he was still putting what he wanted before what Temar wanted. He'd always considered himself as a thoughtful man, but that self-image was taking a few hits.

"No. But I don't want to walk around it, either." Temar rested his hands against Shan's shoulders and leaned into him. "My father was a drunk, your father was a rapist, Ben stole water and could have caused a whole lot of deaths. Evil happens." Temar didn't point out that he had been at the center of more than his share of that evil. Erqu Gazer had robbed his children of any sort of financial success with his drunken neglect. Ben had raped him. Ben's plot to fly a decommissioned ship off the planet, burning up a good deal of the colony's remaining water in the process, had put Temar on ground zero. Shan still remembered standing in the abandoned mining base with Ben's coconspirators holding them captive. He remembered the earnestness in Ben's face when he'd offered to "rescue" Temar and take him off planet. The bastard had had his own sick and twisted affection for Temar, and that was an evil Shan couldn't understand. He couldn't understand how men like Ben could confuse love and rape.

Shan's father had been a quieter sort of evil. Yes, Yan Polli had raped his oldest son in the name of family love, and in doing so, had turned Naite into an angry man who had never finished any sort of training. Despite that, Shan had only seen the quietly neglectful and drunken side of his father.

None of it made sense to Shan. When he'd been a priest, he'd been so sure God had some plan, but after all this, it was so hard to believe that. Shan still had faith in God, but he understood Him less than ever.

Shan considered his answer carefully, concerned that Temar's attitude couldn't be the full truth. "It shouldn't have. God—"

"No, not God," Temar interrupted. "What happened had very little to do with God. So, if you want to talk, we can talk about greed or stupidity or evil, but not God."

Shan took a deep breath and let it out as he tried to reorganize his thoughts. "Fair enough," he said slowly. "Ben was evil, and his greed led him to do things, and I want you to know you're safe to say whatever you want, and I will still see you as an incredibly strong, ethical man." Shan focused on the computer instead of turning around, trying to give Temar the privacy to really consider that offer.

For a long time, Temar stayed quiet. Shan worked through subroutines and cross-referenced repair manuals and programming specifications as he tried to figure out the inner world communication network. It had been one of the first to fail and go unrepaired.

"Do you want me to say I'm angry?"

"If you are. If you want to," Shan said, his fingers pausing.

"I am, you know." Temar retreated, and Shan missed the contact where Temar had been touching him. "I'm so angry that sometimes I feel like I'm going to crack, but Ben is gone, and almost everyone who conspired with him is gone, and the few that aren't are slaved out, and they'll never earn anyone's trust ever again. Who is left for me to be angry with?" Temar made a strangled noise and then left the room, his feet slapping against the bare floors.

Shan swung his chair around and sent up a quick prayer, asking for some guidance here. He'd counseled people through grief and anger, listened to their fears and talked them through loss. None of that mattered now, because he didn't know what to say to Temar. After waiting long enough to give Temar a little time to collect himself, Shan followed him back into his living quarters. The sitting room was empty, so Shan headed into the bedroom.

Temar sat on the edge of the bed with his pants on and his shirt in his hand. "I don't want to be angry." His voice sounded so pained, it tore at Shan's heart. The man had survived so much, but he had a few more wounds than he was ready to let most people see.

"Okay." Shan wasn't sure what else he could say to that.

Temar looked up, his eyes bright, but he rubbed the moisture away with the heel of his hand. "You have no idea what to say here, do you?"

Shan sighed, not sure he liked that Temar could read him so easily. "This is why I was a terrible priest. I really don't. I had a habit of parroting back Div's advice when people came to me. I rarely had inspiration from my own heart."

Temar took a deep, shaky breath. He wondered if they hadn't pushed too fast, no matter what Temar had said when he showed up. "What would Div say to this?" Temar asked.

"I have no idea. This situation never came up." Shan moved carefully closer, watching Temar. Choosing the chair, he sat down so he was level with Temar. "When you rang the bell, and I could see your shape through the glass without being able to see who you were, my first thought was about Ista and Ben." Shan's words made Temar's head snap up. "My second thought was that I am alone far too much if I'm expecting dead people to show up at my door."

"So, I'm not crazy when I wake up at night, certain that Ben is about to come back and get into bed with me?"

Shan rested his elbows on his knees and consciously tried to open himself to Temar, to let his lover see the truth of his words. "Only if I am for expecting him to ring my bell and ambush me."

"Maybe we're both crazy," Temar said with a rough laugh.

"Or maybe we're normal and getting through this," Shan countered. "Do you want to talk?"

"No, not really. I want to stop feeling so off balance." Temar shook his head. "Stop thinking you're to blame for this. I have enough issues without your guilt," Temar said as he stood.

"I didn't say anything," Shan protested.

"I can see your guilt all over your face. You helped." Temar lowered his voice. "This helped. I feel like I have a chance for something good—Ben didn't ruin that. So stop feeling guilty and show me the inner world communication network."

Shan didn't know when Temar had learned to read him so well, but if Temar said that their relationship helped him regain his happiness, Shan could only believe him and hope it was true in the long run. "One inner world communication network, coming right up," he promised as he stood. "Well, maybe not right up, because these systems are a mess, and every time I try to read a repair manual, I have to look up two dozen other systems in order to understand what I'm supposed to be fixing."

"That bad?" Temar asked.

Shan made a face. "It's almost enough to drive me back to the priesthood. But for you, I will face the disaster that is that computer system."

Feeling like a warrior of old about to go into battle—although his battle would involve computer relays and switches and corroded circuits that needed replacing—Shan held out a hand to invite Temar to join him. Temar's expression turned almost shy as he took Shan's hand, and they headed back into battle with the circuit demons.

chapter
four

SHAN'S HANDS worked the keyboard with a confidence that Temar envied. His own thoughts darted through his head faster than he could sort them. He hadn't touched another man since Ben, but Shan couldn't be more different. Where Ben always knew what he wanted, Shan hesitated. His hands moved slower; they ghosted over Temar's flesh instead of bruising it. Temar would never confuse them. However, when Shan wasn't touching him, the lingering traces of Ben haunted him. It was as if he was poorly heated glass, and the tiny particles still lingered in the clear melt.

Insisting on news of the war… that revealed an imperfection in the glass. Temar couldn't stop obsessing over what might have been. If Ben had escaped Livre in that old space ship he'd found hidden in an abandoned base, would he have walked into a war? Would he have been shot down?

Ben had insisted that he had a right to escape a dying planet, even if it meant stealing the very resources everyone else needed to survive. Would the people up there have seen Ben's plot as a clever man surviving and escaping a dying world or as a manipulative man condemning others to death? Would Ben have taken him? Looking back, Temar could almost see the twisted affection Ben had for him, this sick belief that he was favoring Temar every time he raped him. Naite insisted that his own father had been the same, but Temar's guts twisted at the idea that Ben would have dragged him out into the universe.

Of course, the alternative included being trapped in Ben's secret base, a forgotten launching station left over from the earliest Livre miners. Would Ben have left him to die of thirst and hunger in that hidden base?

When abandoned in the desert, Shan had walked out like some hero from a ballad, but Temar didn't have the physical strength to do that. Shan and Naite were both imposing men. When Shan had been a priest, Temar had never noticed it, but now, he could see Shan had a strength, a surety in his movements, a physical presence that Temar couldn't match. Not only was Shan six inches taller, but Temar had a beauty that tended to make people dismiss him, and fair skin that would be dangerously burnt within hours of being on the desert. So, would he have given up and died in that base? Would he have tried to walk out?

The thoughts circled, a sandrat in a pipe trap, always circling until the poison seeped in so much that the animal died. And Temar didn't know how to escape. The worst part was that he knew Shan would do anything he asked to relieve this pain... so would Naite and Tom and Hannal, and even Cyla had made a few awkward attempts to offer sympathy. It wasn't an emotion she did well, but he appreciated the effort.

Now Hannal knew how to do sympathy. Tom's wife had found excuses to be over at his farm several times a week, her children exploring every nook of it as she sat and shared lemonade with him. He didn't remember his mother, but he could imagine from the stories people told that she was a lot like Hannal, with her soft voice and her willingness to sit and stare out a window as she waited for whatever pieces Temar chose to share. All these people would shovel sand dunes one spadeful at a time if he could only tell them what he needed, and he didn't know.

Even Dee'eta Sun had offered him her apologies with tears in her eyes, up to the point where she'd left the room, too emotional to talk to him. All these people cared about him, and that should be enough. He should take all that support and turn it into an ability to move past this maelstrom that buffeted him. But he couldn't. He obsessed over the "might haves" and saw ghosts in the shadows.

"You want some dinner?" Shan asked, still poking away at the computer.

"I'm fine," Temar said. His stomach tightened at the thought of eating.

"Well, I'm not." Shan pushed himself back from the computer. "I'm going to have to replace circuits on the tower. I should start apologizing to God now for the cursing I'm about to do."

Temar's guilt knotted his stomach. "You don't have to do this. It was a stupid thought."

"Eventually, I have to get all this up and running, but you know me. I've been spending more time on the mechanical systems. I understand them better." Shan stood and stretched his back. "Right now, though, I need food. I have a potato stew going."

"That sounds good," Temar said, even though he really didn't want anything that heavy. He followed Shan into the living areas, leaning against a wall as he watched Shan gather bowls and fill them. "Why would they have let the communications systems fail? I mean, if I was planning on flying into a war zone, I would want to know if I was likely to get shot down."

Shan carried the bowls to the table and headed back for something else. Spoons, maybe. "I don't know," Shan admitted. "I know the inner planets have ways to monitor the systems, so maybe they were afraid that they'd get caught stealing water."

"Great. Some inner world would know that someone stole water. What difference would that make?" If the inner worlds couldn't be bothered with their contractual obligations to finish the terraforming, he couldn't see them showing up to arrest Ben and his coconspirators for theft.

Shan turned around, bread and silverware in hand. "I have no idea. I do know that they were obsessed with their secrets. You would have to be, to keep a secret that good for fifteen years."

Temar shrugged. "They knew what would happen if anyone found out. That's a lot of motivation to keep your mouth shut."

"True." Shan headed to the table, sitting down and giving Temar a concerned look. Temar supposed he should probably try to eat instead of standing against the wall, staring at the food.

"Looks good." Temar didn't sound convincing, even to himself, but Shan simply pulled off a chunk of bread and soaked it in the stew before eating it. "Do you think they knew they'd get exile?" Temar blurted.

Shan seemed to think for a long time. "Ben must have," he said slowly. But then Ben hadn't only stolen water, he'd committed rape. That wasn't a crime the councils had any patience for. "The others should have. If they'd succeeded, people would have eventually died."

"They may anyway," Temar pointed out. The extra water would give their farmers more time to develop drought-resistant crops, but in the end, Livre wasn't terraformed. It didn't have enough water to permanently sustain itself without help from the inner worlds. And the fact was the inner worlds were more concerned with war than a dying colony. Shan didn't answer that. Livre children learned the truth young and lived with it their whole lives, had been for three generations now. Eighty-two years. Eighty-two years, and the inner worlds hadn't shown up to fulfill the promise they'd made to the first settlers.

"Did you know Naite went out to watch?" Temar changed the topic.

"Watch what?"

"Ben."

Shan hesitated with his spoon halfway to his mouth, and Temar pulled off a bit of bread and focused on dunking it in the pale stew.

"He… he watched?"

Temar nodded.

Shan sighed and put his spoon back down. "I sometimes worry about my brother's soul."

"I'm glad someone saw him die," Temar disagreed. Part of him wished he'd been out there on a hauler watching Ben walk the dunes in bare feet. He wondered if Ben sat down or if he fought the whole way, struggling against the Livre desert. Naite refused to tell him.

"Part of me did wonder if he had some other plan, some way of saving himself," Shan said quietly. "I'm not sorry to have the proof, but to stand by and watch while a man dies…." Shan fell silent. His sense of morality had always seemed more developed than Temar's. Cold anger still dominated Temar's thoughts about Ben.

When Temar didn't answer, Shan turned to his meal. Temar tried eating what he could, not wanting to waste food, but the discussion of Ben had pretty much ruined his appetite. After getting out of Ben's house, Temar had been so proud of himself. He'd fought back, he'd demanded respect, he'd helped bring down a conspiracy against his world. He'd been okay. Now little parts of himself were unraveling. He'd left Dee'eta Sun's after the cooled punty had caused the piece to fall to the ground and shatter, but he hadn't finished the story when he'd talked to Shan.

After Dee'eta Sun had tried explaining how to recycle scraps, Temar had confronted her, demanded to know why she couldn't respect him enough as an apprentice to hold him accountable for his actions. That had been the general question, although the tone had been a good deal angrier. He'd stormed out of the tent, knocking over another piece of glass and leaving Dee'eta, two assistants, and another apprentice staring at him in shock. Temar had always wanted to work glass—he'd never had another dream in his whole life—but the very act of watching the glass grow and form on the end of a blowpipe, the sight of glass bending to Dee'eta's will, annoyed him. Angered him. It was the most illogical reaction Temar could imagine, and yet he couldn't escape it.

The stew settled poorly in his stomach, and Temar listlessly poked at the chunks of potato and pork.

chapter
five

"TRY NOW." Shan's voice came through the computer, and Temar could admit the technology made him a little uneasy. He flipped the switch Shan had showed him.

"Done," he answered. He looked at the open manual and tried to understand the explanation of subspace communications relays. It was beyond him, but at least it provided a good distraction.

"Did anything change colors?" Shan asked.

Temar looked at the line of lights. "The top row is all blue now. Is that good?"

An inventive string of curses came through the computer speaker. "Lord, forgive me, but even you would be frustrated by this machine," Shan added at the end. Temar smiled. Even if Shan managed to get the communication system up, Temar figured there was a good chance no one was on the other end, yet he was up there working to fix this only because Temar had asked. He'd never had anyone willing to put everything aside for him like this.

"The top lights turned green," Temar said loudly into the microphone. Micro. Small. Phone. Sound. He eyed the device and tried to figure out the logic of that name.

"Yes!" Shan called out triumphantly. "There has not been a machine built that I can't fix."

Temar doubted that. The first colonists came in huge ships with subspace drives, folded space generators, and fusion reactors, and those had little to do with life on Livre, but he did imagine Shan could fix anything on Livre.

"The line of lights below are all blinking blue and green," Temar said, hoping he wasn't destroying Shan's joy with some bit of news that meant the whole system was on the verge of blowing up.

"That's normal. The system is trying to connect with a subspace broadcast. Fair warning, it could be that no one is sending updates our direction anymore. This system has been off-line for years."

Temar ran his fingers across the little indicator lights. All this might be for nothing—it could be that no one out there cared enough to even watch one little colony on the edge of the universe, but still, Shan had spent all of twilight and a good deal of the night battling the equipment. That meant more than his awkward, aborted attempt to suggest that they get married. Married. That was such an odd thought, Temar had never entertained it. He had always been the shy kid who never fit in, so he'd resigned himself to being the same as an adult.

"Thank you for trying, either way," Temar said into the microphone.

"You're welcome. I'm coming back down. Can you turn on external lights?"

"Got it." Temar hit the switch for the outside lights. The speaker made a strange sort of clicking sound, and then the light above it faded from green to black as the system powered down. Temar wondered if they were draining the solar systems, running this many machines. If so, he would have to make it up to Shan. Coming over, Temar had been nervous about sex, but now that he'd felt Shan shudder and come under his hands, he was eager to try again. Leaving the control board and the confusing manual, he headed through the living space into Shan's sleeping area.

One side was taken up by a table covered with a thousand small parts that Temar didn't recognize, and the bed dominated the other side, the blanket on the floor at the foot of it and the sheets rumpled. Temar could see the starburst shaped wrinkles where Shan had fisted the fabric. Stepping forward, he let his fingers glide over the sheets as his body remembered the way it had felt to reach out for someone, to feel warm skin under his hand, and to feel safe in a bed. He could definitely repay Shan for his time and effort.

It took several minutes before he heard Shan call out, "Temar?"

"In here," Temar answered.

In a second, Shan appeared in the doorway, a long streak of dirt or oil down one cheek and his hair sticking up at odd angles. Temar smiled.

"Are you laughing at me?" Shan asked with a sort of mock indignation.

"Yes," Temar agreed, his smile growing even wider.

Shan reached up and ran his fingers through his hair, which only made the direction of the clumps change without fixing anything. "I had to hang over the edge of the platform to reach the burnt circuits."

"That explains the hair," Temar said, a laugh in his voice as he stepped closer. Shan immediately stilled, his eyes darkening. Despite the clear interest, he slowly lowered his arm and waited for Temar. Taking one more step, Temar stopped right in front of Shan and smoothed down his hair. Shan ran his thumb along Temar's jaw, his expression turning soft.

Temar caught his hand. "This time, I want to explore," he said. He brought Shan's hand up to his lips and kissed the knuckles. Shan yielded as Temar took a step backward and pulled Shan toward the bed.

"Making up for time we lost because I was acting like an idiot?" Shan asked.

"Yep."

Shan laughed. "That's fair. I should warn you that I can be an idiot on a fairly regular basis. I mean, I liked you from the time you started coming to church, and I wasted all that time."

"You did?" Temar was surprised. Back then, his father's drinking had been spiraling out of control, and he'd been showing signs of liver failure, and Cyla had been angry all the time. The church had been a refuge, and Shan had been a priest. Temar hadn't really thought of him as a man with hopes and lusts of his own.

"I was careful not to spend too much time around you, because you did tempt me," Shan admitted. "And every time someone else tried to catch your eye, I could feel a very unpriestly sort of jealousy."

Temar sat on the edge of the bed and pulled Shan down next to him. "Very few people ever tried to catch my eye."

"Oh, quite a few did. More than you noticed, clearly," Shan disagreed.

This wasn't the conversation Temar wanted to have. He didn't want to talk at all. He leaned closer and caught Shan by the back of his neck, pulling him close enough to kiss. He liked kissing Shan. Shan's lips parted, and Temar quested deeper with his tongue. Shan's hand came to rest against Temar's hip, his fingers pressing without bruising and his breathing growing more labored. Temar pulled back, and Shan looked utterly adorable with his eyes half closed and his mouth still slightly open. Temar had been so afraid that touching another would bring back the ghosts of Ben, yet those very fears and ghosts scattered every time he looked at Shan.

"Bed?" Temar suggested, scooting farther up the mattress.

"That works," Shan agreed. He got up and moved to the side of the bed, where he kicked off his shoes before getting in. He reached for Temar, but Temar intercepted his hand.

"You distracted me too much last time. This time I want to explore," he said.

Shan swallowed so that his Adam's apple bobbed as he settled his weight down onto his side. "Explore away." His voice was low and rough, and Temar realized he'd done that. He'd reduced Shan to this hard need that left his voice gravelly and his cock pressing up against his pants. Reaching down, Temar ran a finger over Shan's trapped cock, and Shan sucked in a fast breath, but he didn't protest. Temar shifted closer, pressing on Shan's shoulder to urge him to lie on his back. Once Shan had settled, Temar moved to straddle him. He looked down into warm, brown eyes that looked up at him with trust.

"I like making up for lost time," Shan said. He rested his hands against Temar's legs, sliding them up and down as he waited. Before, Temar had been driven to finish, to prove something, and to ease the growing lust that drove him out to the relay station. Funny how his anger with Dee'eta—with the world and even Shan—had turned into a lust that motivated him to confront Shan. But now that the anger had faded, he wanted something slower. He wanted to feel every second of this.

Temar rested his palms against Shan's waist, slipping his fingers up under his shirt and then sliding up to feel the warm skin. Shan's muscles tensed, his stomach growing firm as Temar stroked up the skin, feeling the texture of the chest hair under his fingers. The hem of Shan's shirt grew taut when Temar's questing fingers found Shan's nipples. He ran fingernails lightly over the pebbled skin. Shan arched his back and thrust up so hard that he pushed Temar a few inches into the air, but Temar rode it out, playing with the nipples and watching as Shan gasped for breath. He gave one a slightly harder pull, and Shan hissed loudly. When Temar finally stopped, Shan collapsed back onto the bed, his chest rising and falling with each loud gasp of air. Temar had done that to him.

"Good?" Temar asked.

Shan's eyes came open. "Very," he agreed. "I could show you."

"Another time," Temar said as he pulled on the bottom of Shan's shirt. Shan lifted himself to allow Temar to pull the shirt off, and then Temar could see the strong body under him. Shan's right forearm had a streak of blood, and Temar traced it back to a cut inside his elbow. He let his finger gently trace the new scab.

"I cut it on the access panel side," Shan explained before Temar could ask the question.

"I'll have to make that up to you."

Temar pulled his own shirt off, tossing it to the side before he started to lean in closer, but Shan's hand caught him on the shoulder, holding him off. "You don't have anything to make up to me," Shan said, his seriousness annoying Temar. He wanted this to be about hot lust and need, not about words. He'd never been good with words. Numbers he understood, glass he understood. He'd sat in his room doing equations to calculate water use for the whole valley, but it had been Cyla who tried to explain what he'd found, because he never had been comfortable with words. He truly wasn't comfortable with his lover's guilt looking him in the eye.

"I don't have to do anything," Temar agreed. "But I want to, and I really don't want to stop for conversation."

Shan's smile was slow but genuine. "I'm being an ass again, aren't I?" he asked, lowering his hand back to the bed.

"Yes," Temar answered, and then he leaned in and nipped at Shan's earlobe before moving down to kiss his neck. Shan shifted under him, making small, hungry noises. Temar moved down and tasted the skin at Shan's collarbone, tasting salt and musk. Pushing himself up, he blew across the damp skin, and Shan shivered, the hairs on his arms standing up.

"Oh God." Shan pressed his head back into the pillow. Temar ran his hands over Shan's shoulders, feeling the muscles strain as Shan pressed himself into the bed. Sliding down, Temar caught Shan's nipple in his mouth, sucking at him. Shan cried out and bucked up into the air. Temar had to hold on to Shan's arms to keep from getting pushed to the side.

When Shan collapsed back onto the bed, Temar looked at him. "Problem?" he teased.

Shan gave a breathy laugh. "A little."

Temar was tempted to make a "little" joke, but his mind skittered back to one that Ben had used against him once, and he shied away from the memory. Instead, he moved to the other nipple and sucked at it before giving it a gentle nip. Shan squirmed, but he didn't rise and buck this time. Temar was a little disappointed. Luckily, he had a good idea of what would drive Shan past control. Sitting up, Temar scooted back until he could reach Shan's pants.

After unzipping and then unbuttoning them, Temar took some time to trace the shape of Shan's cock through his underwear. Shan gasped for air, each breath coming with a half grunt that cut off in the middle. Temar could almost taste Shan's need to flip him over and rub their bodies together until he came. However, Shan lay under him, and that was about the sexiest thing Temar had ever seen. Stepping off the bed, he pulled Shan's pants off and dropped them on the floor. While he got his own pants off, Shan pushed his underwear off, dropping it beside the bed before lying back down.

Shan opened his mouth to say something, but Temar climbed on him, both their cocks now trapped between their bodies. Temar thrust down slowly and Shan's pupils widened. Once he was sure Shan was too worked up to try to start a conversation, Temar slid back, kissing the line of Shan's chest down over his stomach to his belly button.

When he sucked the skin just below Shan's belly button, Shan stopped breathing altogether, and his hands flew into the air, twitching for a second before he went back to clutching the sheets. Temar, when faced with Shan's cock, suddenly froze. His heartbeat sped up, and his mouth went dry. Shan's fingers stroked over his shoulder, a ghost touch that scattered demons, and Temar wanted this. He wanted to know what Shan tasted like.

He reached out, gathering one drop of precum on his finger. He slowly lifted the finger to his mouth and sucked it. From the way Shan sucked in a breath, Temar had surprised him.

Temar lowered his head and ran his tongue along the slit. Taking a deep breath, he slipped his mouth over the head and twirled his tongue around the end as he began sucking.

"Oh, God," Shan gasped, and his whole body writhed. Temar had to settle his weight onto Shan's legs and hold his hips to keep Shan from throwing him to the side. This was fun. Temar went back to work. He slid his mouth up and down the shaft, letting his tongue play with the vein that ran down the underside of Shan's cock and to his balls. He pulled back his head and worked his tongue against the slit. He slid down again until the head of Shan's cock brushed the back of his throat, and then he swallowed. Shan was crying out now, his words lost in the animalistic noises he was making. He'd pulled the sheets free of the bed, and one hand was tangled in them.

Letting go of Shan's hips, Temar closed his fist around the base of Shan's cock, holding it firmly as Shan bucked up into his mouth. Temar let Shan thrust while he worked his tongue around the cock in his mouth. With one final surge, Shan came, and Temar's mouth filled with the strong, familiar taste of semen.

"Oh, God," Shan said for about the ninth time. Temar had done that—he'd reduced Shan to exactly two words. For a time, Shan could only lie there, his mouth gaping open as he occasionally repeated those two words. After a few minutes, he seemed to pull himself back together, though. "Would you like a hand there?" Shan asked.

"Do you have one?" Temar asked playfully as he crawled up Shan's body to lie next to him. Shan's fingers wrapped gently around his cock and started sliding up and down, the foreskin moving to reveal the head of the cock and the slit, precum slicking the skin. Arching his back, Temar caught Shan's arm, holding on as Shan slowly stroked him until Temar's body grew tight. He dug his fingers into Shan's arm, his breath coming in hungry gasps as he almost ached with a need to come.

The need built until Temar couldn't control his body, and he rammed into Shan's fist. Shan stilled and Temar thrust harder, finding the pattern that made his orgasm inch closer, but as much as the lust increased, the ache increased, making his balls feel heavy and pushing him away from that edge where he could let go. The distant pain was like the rising sun that began to fill the horizon with light, and Temar cried out, desperate to finish before he could have this moment stolen. He needed this.

Shan's other hand came up to brush across his shoulder, and Temar lashed out, pushing Shan away and rolling to his other side so he could grab his own cock. This was comfortable. He stroked himself until he came with a shout.

He finished, but the shivers of pleasure from coming transformed into a trembling that Temar couldn't control. He didn't want to face Shan. God, how pathetic was he that he would turn his back on a willing lover?

"Temar?" Shan asked, his voice soft. "Can I touch you?"

Temar's breath came in little hiccups, and he nodded without answering. Shan's arms wrapped around him, one sliding in under his body. And then Shan was pulling him close so that he lay against Shan's chest, sharing Shan's warmth. "Shhh," Shan murmured, and that comforting was all it took to push Temar into the grief that had been stalking him so long. He cried, and Shan hugged him tighter. "It's okay," Shan whispered over and over. "You're safe."

Temar didn't know why that made him cry harder, but it did. He cried himself to sleep, Shan's arms around him to chase away the ghosts.

chapter
S I X

WHEN TEMAR woke, his face itched. Reaching up to scratch it, he found the tears had dried, leaving his skin feeling rough and stiff. "Damn." Pushing himself up, he rubbed his hand across his eyes. "Nothing like a little humiliation in the morning," he whispered to himself.

"There's nothing to feel humiliated about."

Temar almost jumped out of his skin when Shan appeared in the doorway.

"I brought tea," Shan offered, holding out the mug. Temar took it and wrapped his fingers around the dark glass mug. For a time, he focused on the drink, avoiding eye contact. "Do you want to talk?" Shan asked.

Temar cringed. "I'm really sorry."

"Hey." Shan sat down on the bed next to him. "You don't have to apologize."

"I really think I do." Temar had meant to repay Shan for all his work, and instead he'd ended up acting like a child and ruining the night. He couldn't believe he'd cried. He didn't even understand *why* he'd cried.

"Do you know why I hated slavery?" Shan asked quietly.

"Because Naite liked it?"

Shan laughed. "Okay, that might have been a little part of it."

He fell silent for a time, and Temar sipped the tea and wondered if he should walk out. He could come back later when he was less likely to break down over nothing. Before he could come to any decision, Shan started talking again. "I would listen to confessions, and I could see the pain it caused when people lost control over their own lives. I saw how much people struggled and how much they suffered."

Temar looked over. "Did anyone…." He stopped and swallowed.

"I can't violate their privacy. I can't tell you what I heard, but I can say that humans aren't designed for slavery. Give yourself time to recover."

"I've had months." Temar clamped his mouth shut before he could start spewing his anger and frustration.

"It took Naite years. Forgive me for being a judgmental ass, but most days I still think he hasn't healed."

Temar turned the mug in his hands. "Is that going to be me? Never recovering?"

"No," Shan said with far more confidence than Temar felt. "Give yourself some time. You've come a long way."

Temar had to laugh at that. "No, I haven't. I'm getting worse, Shan." Feelings he'd once been able to shove away would ambush him at the oddest time, and rages would wash through and leave him shaking with emotions that didn't feel like they were his.

"I don't believe that," Shan said firmly.

Temar looked at Shan in disbelief. Three months ago, he could ride into battle with Shan and throw himself into a fight. Now he cried. That didn't feel very strong.

"I don't believe that," Shan repeated. "You're a strong man, and I'm going to keep saying that until you believe me."

"You may have a very long wait." Temar stood before heading for the living area. He could go home, but if he did, he'd have to face Naite, and that man seemed able to see into his soul, which was more than a little uncomfortable. Besides, if he went home, he was going to have to deal with Cyla, the farm, and the crops. And Hannal would come over and offer tea. In the end, if he was going to be miserable with someone, he'd rather be miserable with Shan. That didn't exactly make him a great lover.

"If you—"

"Could we not talk about it right now?" Temar turned to Shan. "Please?" Temar could see the worry in Shan, but he didn't have any words of reassurance.

Shan looked away for a moment. "Take some time to get yourself together. We can talk later," Shan promised. It wasn't exactly the vow Temar had wanted, but at least he'd earned a respite from talking right now.

"Meanwhile," Shan said in a brighter tone, "you have a lot of reading to catch up on. It turns out that your idea about getting the subspace communication repaired paid off."

"You heard something?" Temar's mouth nearly fell open. In the morning light, it seemed such a silly request he had trouble believing it had worked.

"A lot of something," Shan agreed. "It just so happens that the war ended about twenty years ago and turned into a nasty, long-term scuffle with pirates and looting and accusations of government support for insurrectionists on either side."

Temar grabbed for the edge of the door to steady himself as his whole world rocked. "Wait. The war ended?"

Shan nodded.

The ground seemed to roll as Temar's brain made sense of the words. "Twenty years ago?" he asked, his voice weak and thready. All of Livre lived in hope of the war ending and the inner planets coming back to finish the terraforming. They battled the desert, had children, tended dew catchers, maintained irrigation systems, and generally fought with every breath to survive until the war ended. However, the war had ended when he was one or two years old.

Shan nodded again. "The older systems kept the name Planetary Alliance, but, about twelve planets pulled out. They call themselves the Alliance of Free Planets."

"They… but…."

"Are you as angry as I was two hours ago when I read the news?" Shan asked, and he almost sounded… amused… or maybe simply fascinated. He didn't sound angry.

Temar had to think about that, because his feelings were so tangled, he couldn't get a good grip on how he felt. "Furious," Temar finally answered. "The war is over?" It didn't feel real. Words shouldn't be able to redefine his reality.

"The Alliance of Free Planets has sent decades of info bursts about the other side stealing ships and financially raping planets. The Planetary Alliance has sent just as many warnings about the other side raiding and protecting pirates and condoning murder. Apparently, both sides pretty much gave up a while back when they didn't get an answer."

Temar turned and headed into the living area, desperate to get to a chair before he fell on his face. "We weren't answering," he said weakly. They weren't answering because Ben's buddies, who were in charge of the relay, had sabotaged the equipment. They hadn't answered because no one knew either alliance had called.

"Ironic, huh?" Shan asked. He stopped next to Temar for a second, his hand resting on Temar's shoulder before he went to the couch and sat down. "Ben thought he had to steal the rocket because the inner planets had forgotten us, but the inner planets gave up on us because Ben had the equipment turned off. He didn't even live long enough to see that he was a fool."

Temar agreed, but his brain was still trying to wrap around the idea that the inner planets had finished their war. Sort of. They'd split into parts, but the war, the armies fighting each other, was over.

"Are they going to come back?" Temar asked. He looked up, but Shan could only look back with a hopeless expression. They stared at each other until the silence grew uncomfortable.

"I don't know," he admitted.

Temar closed his eyes. If the war was over, and they'd decided to let Livre slowly die, who would stop them? "Twenty years." The words came out as a curse.

They sat in silence for a time, and Temar tried to reconcile his whole life to this new fact. Ben's betrayal, the general desperation of the whole planet, his father's farm slowly drying out and dying. All of that had happened after their war had ended. It didn't feel real.

"I have to go tell the council," Shan said.

They had to know that all their waiting was for nothing. The war had ended, and the inner planets hadn't come back to finish the terraforming. Again, the room fell silent except for the sound of a lazy wind across the top of the station.

Shan stood. Maybe he was leaving, maybe he was getting soup; whatever, Temar had to see these reports. He believed Shan without reservation, but he had to see the reports to make any of it real.

"I want to see it," Temar said. "I really hate how easily you're accepting all this, and I want to see the actual reports."

"I had the morning to get the shock out of the way, Temar," Shan said softly. "I had an entire morning of reading data burst after data burst as the two sides tried to figure out who we would align ourselves with."

"Align ourselves?" For a second, Temar was confused, but then the reality of it struck him. If the planets had broken into two alliances, each side would want to know if Livre was friend or enemy. Should they bomb the planet, or use it as a camp for enemy prisoners of war? Could they count on Livre to provide glass sands or attack landing ships? In a very few minutes, the world had become far more complicated and dangerous than it had been when he went to bed. Actually, the world was the same, but his awareness of it had changed. Awareness sucked. Becoming aware that he was a very small part of a very large universe sucked even worse.

"And if you hadn't asked for that relay to take priority on the repairs and been here to help, we still wouldn't know any of this," Shan pointed out.

"I didn't help," Temar protested halfheartedly, since it really didn't matter.

"Yes, you did. If you weren't here, I would have had to climb down the ladder every time I worked a circuit to see if the system came online. Trust me, I would have made it up that ladder twice before I would have given up and gone to work on getting a water tap repaired. And there aren't a lot of people clamoring to come out here to the middle of nowhere to help get the station running. Although," Shan said with a slow and thoughtful voice, "that may change now. A lot of things may change now."

Temar understood that. Suddenly his personal dramas and his stupid crying seemed twice as stupid.

"Come on, I'll show you the reports. You can look through them while I check over a sand bike so we can head back to Landing." Shan headed into the control room without even offering breakfast—not that Temar's stomach could face food right now.

chapter
s e v e n

TEMAR THUMBED the controls to roll the screen to a new page. He skipped the technical data at the front and moved to the narrative section—one more demand that Livre declare allegiance with the Alliance of Free Planets or face the consequences. Obviously they hadn't suffered any consequences, but Temar wondered how the councils would have reacted if they'd received any of the messages.

The bursts from the Planetary Alliance were more nicely worded, but Temar could still feel the threat in each one. When the war was over, those planets who had failed to maintain membership in the alliance had forfeited their rights. That came down to, "Help us or we won't finish terraforming." Well, they'd followed through with that threat, but looking at a map of which alliance owned which planets, Temar wasn't sure they would have kept terraforming either way. The Alliance of Free Planets held most of the local territory, with the Planetary Alliance sort of controlling a sickle-shaped wedge of space that reached out toward Livre and included their closest neighbor, a planet called Minga.

Temar jumped when Shan's hand landed on his shoulder. "Sorry," Shan quickly offered, and Temar felt a twinge of guilt at making Shan feel like he had to apologize for doing something so normal. "I brought you a sandwich." Shan held it out and Temar took it, more because he didn't want to make Shan feel worse than because of any hunger. He honestly wasn't hungry.

"Have you read all these?" Temar asked.

Shan settled into the second chair with a sandwich of his own. "I gave up after I decided that it sounded like the universe was being run by fifteen-year-olds throwing insults on the playground."

"Huh." Temar looked at the report. "I'm still at the part where they sound like thirteen-year-olds making threats."

"Oh, it gets better," Shan said sarcastically before taking a big bite of sandwich.

Temar was deep into a report with one side blaming the other for terrorist attacks when the board started to whine. It was a high-pitched sound that made Temar cringe. "I didn't touch anything," he cried out, putting his hands up as if that would prove he hadn't broken the machine.

"Crap," Shan muttered before he crammed his sandwich in his mouth and dropped to the floor, pulling the lower panel off the computer. He pressed against Temar's legs, and Temar slid out of the chair to give him more room.

"What is it?" Temar asked. The whine rose and fell, the sound cutting through his head and making his ever-present headache throb in time with the noise.

"I don't know." Shan's voice was muffled. "Get my gray tool kit, the small one by the door to my bedroom." Temar turned and ran from the room, grabbed up the bag, and came back. Shan knelt on the floor, his large hands moving as though tracing some wire, but the machine was such a mass of wires, glass circuits, and control boards that Temar couldn't understand any of it. He slid the bag in next to Shan and bit his lip.

Shan grabbed several tools and went to work. Three indicator lights went to red and then black, and Temar opened his mouth to warn Shan, but he didn't want to break the intense concentration he could sense, so he waited.

"You little sandrat. That's where you are," Shan muttered, and then the whine vanished, replaced with a persistent beeping noise that was less painful, even if it was equally annoying. "That's really not much better." Shan pushed himself up to his knees and peered at the panel. Inching closer, Temar watched the pattern of flashing blue, green, and violet lights. Violet was new.

"Is it broken?"

Shan gave an exaggerated shrug. "I don't think so."

"So it's supposed to flash like that?"

"Clearly under some circumstances, it is. I'll look it up." Shan got up before heading for the other computer and pulling up what looked like more of the repair and use manuals.

"It's the left-hand indicators blinking violet," Temar offered. Shan made a small grunting noise as he read through the material, and Temar watched Shan's eyebrows come down as he frowned at the text. It was funny—everything had seemed to come easy for Ben. He'd laughed easily, talked to people easily, stolen water easily, and raped Temar easily. But Shan had this intensity, like he had to really concentrate on whatever he was doing. He was that way when he tried to talk to Temar about something important, and he seemed to throw everything into concentrating on his screen now. Temar studied the curve of Shan's shoulder, the finger that ran down the screen as though trying to keep track of his place in the reading.

Temar stood behind him and rested his hand on Shan's shoulder. Shan looked up, offering a quick smile before he went back to reading the manual. "It's definitely the communication system. Nothing else seems to connect to that workstation," Shan said, his voice distant as his finger ran down the screen before he scrolled it down and started his finger at the top of the screen again.

"Okay, that alarm either means we have a new incoming stream or...."

"Or?"

"Or the system is going to blow up," Shan said, but from his tone, he was joking.

"I'll make sure to stand behind you, then," Temar teased right back. "So, who's sending us a new set of complaints?"

"Who knows?" Shan said. "These people do seem very capable of complaining."

"I have to admit that I'm a little surprised at how talented they are at that."

"Same here. I always thought of the inner planets as these powerful people with incredible technology that allowed them to control entire planets."

"I think they are all that," Temar said. "They're also petty and vindictive and really obsessed with making threats." Temar stepped back to allow Shan to change seats.

"Yeah, I think I'm glad that they're up there and we're down here." Shan hesitated for a second, his hands pausing over the control board, and Temar knew exactly what he was thinking. If the inner planets had come back earlier, Ben might not have hurt Temar.

"Me too," Temar said as he stepped close enough to put his hand back on Shan's shoulder. What had happened to him wasn't on the same level as interplanetary war. Sometimes he had to remind himself of that, but it wasn't. He was here and safe, and Ben was nothing more than bone fragments in a sandrat nest. "So, what do we have?"

Shan touched a number of controls, sorting through menus that came up on the computer screen until a face appeared. A few of the messages were actual vid recordings, but most had been text. Temar figured the texts were easier to transmit, because the man in the picture had the edges of his face pixilating in and out of existence.

"That's new," Temar said as he looked at the fancy uniform. Most of the messages that had come from vid had been from some woman or man in a plain uniform sitting in the middle of a room crowded with electronics. This man had gray hair, but he still had the sort of stiff posture and wide shoulders that reminded Temar of vids of soldiers.

"Greetings from the Alliance of Free Planets. I'm Commander Peter Stovall. I have to say, gentlemen, you have surprised us all. Welcome back, Libre."

Temar closed his mouth, his teeth clicking together. Standing behind Shan, he couldn't see the expression on Shan's face, but he had to be shocked. Actually, shock didn't even describe the feeling that ran through Temar right now, bleeding into every cell of his body. Commander Stovall was a real man... this was someone from another planet staring at them. This was too inconceivable for his brain to comprehend.

"Um, greetings," Shan said, his voice weak. "We've had some technical issues down here." It was several seconds before Commander Stovall answered, but that was still much faster than Temar expected. In school, they'd learned that subspace wasn't really space or beneath anything, but rather one of many contiguous dimensions with rules of physics that allowed signals to travel faster than light, but the relays and stations required for subspace communications meant that it took minutes or even hours for signals to get from point A to point B. Temar studied Shan to see if he was surprised. After all, Shan understood the technical end of space far better than Temar... or almost anyone else on Livre at this point.

"That's some technical issue. You've been missing in action for a quarter of a century. I don't mind telling you that we thought the planet had died."

"We... uh... the mechanic in charge of the unit recently... passed away." Shan cleared his throat. "So we recently had someone new look at it."

After the few seconds it took for Shan's words to cross space and reach him, Commander Stovall smiled. "Well, we're glad to have you back. We had a mission planned for Libre in a few years, but we honestly didn't expect to find survivors."

"Livre," Shan corrected the man.

"Excuse me? I didn't read that." Commander Stovall leaned forward and did something to his controls.

"Livre, with a V. The planet is Livre," Shan said.

Commander Stovall leaned back. "Copy that. The prewar records have some holes in them. Old-world agents blew a couple of our document storages, so we'll get that updated. Livre it is. And we are glad to see you. The old saying goes that survivors survive, and colony people have a habit of surviving in unlikely situations. We're glad to see you surviving."

"We are," Shan answered, but he didn't sound like himself. His voice was strained, and when he glanced over his shoulder at Temar, his eyes were wide with shock.

For several seconds, silence reigned.

Commander Stovall tilted his head to the side, as though Shan was doing something particularly confusing, and acid rose up in Temar's throat. "We don't have any diplomats on hand for negotiations," Commander Stovall said, his voice softer than before, "but I assume you've received our invitations to join the AFP."

"AFP," Shan echoed. Temar wished he could contribute something, to share the weight of the conversation with Shan, but he couldn't think of one single thing to say to this man. More than that, he felt more than a little guilt that he'd asked to poke this particular hornets' nest, and he didn't know how to fix that mistake.

"Alliance of Free Planets," Commander Stovall explained. "I'm sure it will take a while to get up to speed. We've separated from the inner planets and their over-taxation and manipulation. We have stable borders, and with the exception of some state-sponsored terrorism from the old worlds, we are safer than we ever were under the old government."

"That's... that's good." Shan cleared his throat and seemed to find his voice. "We honestly didn't expect anyone to be sitting on the other end, waiting for a call from us."

Commander Stovall nodded. "I can understand that. You're decades out of date on the technology, but subspace communication has improved significantly, and we have an entire network of microstations designed to carry signals in near-real time. It helps that I'm on a station only six light-years away, practically sitting on top of you," he offered with another bright smile. Temar didn't know if he was a particularly happy soldier or if he was trying to ease the tension. "We've had a lot of other advances—medicine, travel, communication, and laser technology are all having a renaissance of a sort."

"I imagine war would lead to that," Shan said.

"Yes, as horrific as war is, the advances and the freedoms are often worth the price."

Temar didn't believe that, but Commander Stovall clearly did.

"We haven't had a chance to even read the backlog of messages, so I'm afraid we're truly in the dark about the war, the advances, and even the state of politics out there in the universe. We're rather isolated," Shan said, and Temar could hear the caution in Shan's voice.

Commander Stovall nodded. "Understandable. Just to keep you informed, I did contact authorities at Capital, and they're sending out a negotiating team. You will receive full diplomatic status as a sovereign power. We don't want you to think this is business as usual, the way the old planets ran things. The negotiating team is offering to either come down to Livre or I've offered the station as a neutral ground for any talks."

"The station," Shan answered quickly, and Temar looked down at him, shocked at the answer. Temar couldn't imagine a half-dozen people on the entire planet who would want to leave to go and talk to people who thought war and killing were the solution for disagreements. The memory of Ben flashed through Temar's mind. Ben would have gone. Ben would have loved a chance to return to space. However, forty-three people from Landing alone had died because they wanted to go into space, and considering the rest of the people were still reeling over that, he doubted anyone else would rush to leave.

"You're welcome up here," Commander Stovall promised. "We've improved shuttle service quite a bit since your ancestors took drop ships down. We have a two-stage shuttle system the soldiers call a 'scoop and skip' that can get you up here in no time. A pilot will land a scoop shuttle that can only reach low orbit, load, take off from the planet, and then rendezvous with a skip shuttle that will dip down into low orbit, allow the scoop to dock, and then head into space. It's a brilliant system. It makes planetside visits much more economical." The commander looked like someone's uncle describing a favorite nephew.

"We don't have water to refuel here," Shan said cautiously.

"I have no doubt of that. You colonists have been incredibly frugal with your resources to make it this long, so the scoop will bring all its own supplies."

"So, how long will it take for the shuttle to arrive?"

Commander Stovall leaned over so that he disappeared from the screen in a pixilated streak. He came back into the picture a minute later. "Are you still using the same primary relay site?"

"Yes," Shan said.

"The shuttle can make a sand landing south of your position, but it will take a few adaptations on the shuttle itself. We estimate three days for reengineering the shuttle with five more days for travel. So, what do you say we estimate planetfall in eight standard days?"

"Eight days. That sounds good," Shan said, his voice weaker than ever.

With a smile, Commander Stovall gave a nod. "I am looking forward to meeting you, as is the negotiating team."

"We look forward to seeing you." Shan sounded like he was saying the words from rote.

Commander Stovall kept staring at them from the screen, and Temar wondered if they had an off switch. He and Shan couldn't exactly talk with the man watching, and Temar really wanted to ask why Shan had agreed to send a delegation into space. It seemed utterly unreasonable.

"I was wondering if I could give the negotiating team the name of our primary contact," Commander Stovall suggested.

Shan sat upright. "I apologize, Commander. I think you understand this has been a surprise. I'm Shan Polli, and this is Temar Gazer." Shan stood up to gesture toward Temar.

"Shan Polli and Temar Gazer, I am pleased to meet you, and on behalf of the AFP, welcome back to the universe, gentlemen." Commander Stovall bowed his head formally. "Unless you have other issues to discuss, I should sign off and handle some business on my end."

"Of course. We're very pleased to meet you, and we will be looking for the shuttle in eight days. Good day."

"Good day," Commander Stovall repeated. The screen flickered and then turned gray.

Once the man from the ship had vanished, Temar realized his knees felt too weak to hold his weight. Maybe Shan felt the same way because he dropped back down into his chair. For a long time, they both stared at each other, the silence clinging to them. For his part, Temar couldn't quite grasp the idea that he'd talked to a man from outer space. Actually, he'd watched Shan talk to a man from outer space, but there wasn't a lot of difference between the two concepts.

"Why go up there?" Temar finally asked.

Shan sat with his forearms resting against his knees, his whole body slumped forward. He looked up at the question. "Our ancestors hated this place," he said.

Temar walked carefully to the next chair, aware that his knees threatened to collapse with every step, but he managed to reach his destination before dropping down into the seat. "What? They chose to move here."

Shan shook his head. "They wanted to make money, a few hoped to earn enough to buy passage back off Livre before retiring. They hated the dryness, the desert, the sandrats, the chokeweed, and the pipe traps. They thought the world was harsh and ugly."

Temar frowned and tried to imagine anyone failing to see the beauty in the shifting lines of white sand that shimmered in the midday sun or the swooping flight of a bueto. Chokeweed wasn't particularly pretty, the gray-green leaves hiding burrs that could rip someone's feet to shreds, but he could see beauty in pipe plants and wisp grass, with their vivid green leaves against the white sand. True, their world was dry, but the double moons over the rocky mountains and the deep desert had inspired generations of artists. Dee'eta Sun had a series of drinking vessels that mimicked the shape of barchan dunes, with drinking lips on either side of the graceful curve of glass.

"They hated the world," Shan whispered. "They saw the sand as barren and dead. If those people come down here, that's what they'll see."

Temar frowned. He didn't like the idea of someone looking at Livre and failing to see the beauty, but that wouldn't have led him to agree to send a delegation into space. Landing was the largest of the towns, so their council would have a good deal of influence over who went. Temar figured Lilian Freeland would end up having to negotiate with these people, and Temar did not want to be the one to tell her she had to leave her farm and family to go up into space. The woman might be a diminutive, white-haired grandmother, but she had a tongue sharp enough to shred a man. "Why does that mean they can't be down here?"

Shan sighed and swung his chair around. "Would you believe me if I said that I acted on instinct? I simply didn't want some group of foreigners down here hating our world and our people."

"Okay." Temar said the word slowly, still not understanding the motive.

"You don't agree."

That required some thought. "I don't know," Temar finally answered. "I don't know them well enough to know whether I want them down here or whether I trust them enough to send Lilian Freeland up there."

Shan made a face. "If we send Lilian up, I'll be more concerned about them. That woman does not compromise."

"And she seems so nice when you first meet her," Temar agreed. The first time he and Cyla had tried to go to the council about the water theft, Lilian had listened to them so carefully, resting her chin on her hand and studying Cyla as though she was the most interesting person on the planet. And then she'd told them they didn't have any evidence and they should come back at season-end with something other than slanderous words. He felt as if he'd been running and put his foot into a sand trap. She'd shocked him. And then after he'd screwed up, Lilian had condemned him to slavery. Of course, she never would have allowed Ben to abuse him if she'd known about it. Hell, after she found out about the abuse, she had led the charge to compensate Temar for all his suffering… but still, she made him uncomfortable. She had so much power, and she wielded it so easily that his guts tightened when he saw her.

"Lilian seems nice until you realize you've traded away your firstborn and second-born and agreed to apprentice some grandchild you didn't know she had," Shan agreed. "She could negotiate a sandcat out of its nest."

"And you're going to tell her that she has to go up and talk these people out of the promised water," Temar pointed out. Shan cringed.

"She's going to kill me."

"Very possibly," Temar agreed.

chapter
eight

SHAN GUIDED the bike through the narrow walking gate, since the wind hadn't shifted yet and the blowers hadn't cleared the main gates. The bike's rear tire slipped, sending it fishtailing, and Temar pressed closer to him. God forgive him, but that felt good. And Shan should not be thinking that when Temar clearly needed more time to recover. Unfortunately, Shan's cock was not quite as ethical as he might like the traitorous beast to be. Temar's heat pressed against his back and his arms tight around Shan's waist. Shan's cock started to harden.

The path straightened out, and Temar shifted back so there was an inch of space between them. "I can't believe how fast you take those turns."

"I've been riding for a long time," Shan said over his shoulder as he geared the engine down and let the bike coast through the stone passage that led around the main gate. The engine echoed against the smooth walls until they approached the far end. Temar's farm was closest to the gate, and as they entered the main valley, Shan could see a number of workers walking the fields and sinking water rods into the ground every six or seven feet. Naite was walking the closest furrow, and he turned as they came down the path.

From a distance, he looked friendly enough. He stopped to talk to another worker, offering a slap on the shoulder before he handed them his water rod and stepped over a line of potato plants. However, something in his body language still set Shan on edge. Unless he missed his guess, Naite was not happy.

He strode across the bare ground and waited as Shan negotiated the narrow trail that led down to the valley floor. Shan had stopped, but he hadn't yet turned off the engine when Naite started.

"Temar, you deal with that sister of yours or I'm going to seriously consider dropping her on her head four or five times," Naite said in place of a greeting, and from the look on his face, he wasn't joking.

"Hello to you too," Shan muttered, but Temar was already getting off the bike.

"What happened?" he asked.

"She tried ordering a whole farm's worth of cotton seed. You put that much cotton in and you aren't going to have any workers to pick it. That shit is miserable work, and facing a whole farm of it would make any worker worth his salt move to another farm."

"Oh shit. Did she—"

"I told Young that if he even tried to fill that order that I would make it my personal mission to make sure you never paid a cent for any of it. He had no business trying to negotiate with Cyla. She doesn't own this farm." Naite's hands were clenched into fists, and Shan figured that conversation had come with one or two tacit threats of a more direct variety. Naite might be a council member and one of the best workers on the planet, but his control of his temper sometimes got a little frayed.

"But she was willing to talk to him, like she did have the authority," Temar said wearily. Shan wished he could carry some of this burden for him, but it was Temar's farm and Temar's sister. Shan certainly didn't know anything about the running of a farm. Of course, from the sounds of it, neither did Cyla.

Naite poked a thick finger toward Temar. "Both of them need attitude adjustment. Mind you, it's too late to change George Young's greed, but if someone doesn't set Cyla straight, she's going to end up just as bad. And every time I talk to her, I get it thrown back at me that I'm a slave here."

Temar flinched. Naite didn't seem too bothered by Cyla's word choice, but then he didn't have the same associations with slavery that Temar did. "She didn't," Temar said in the sort of weary tone that suggested he fully believed she had.

"Talk to her before I drop her in the recycler," Naite said, and then he turned his back and strode away. A knot of workers had gathered in the potato field, but when Naite turned around, they all hurried back to their rows and started the ground probes again.

"I can't believe she'd do this," Temar said with a sigh. "Oh wait, yes I can. If the plan looks good on paper, then she's going to believe that instead of listening to Naite. I can't believe she threw it back at him that he's slaved to the farm—like that means anything. He's the one who knows how to run a farm." Temar ripped off his sand veil, his voice rising with every word.

Shan didn't normally see Temar angry, but he understood better than most how much a sibling could get under your skin.

"It's not like we don't have bigger problems on the horizon, but no, she has to go and do this." Without another word, Temar started for the house, his entire body tight with anger.

Even if Temar had inherited Ben's land to compensate him for the abuse, he hadn't inherited Ben's ability to work the land. Shan followed him, noticing that all the workers, including Naite, had stopped to watch them pass. More than once Temar had visited him with stories from the farm. Workers were uncomfortable around Temar. All Ben's workers had found jobs in other valleys to avoid even looking at the man they had all failed to help. Shan could understand the guilt, even though he couldn't forgive them for leaving Temar short of employees. Other workers avoided the place because Ben had been less than charitable toward children, and many of the families wanted to wait, to see if conditions improved, before committing to the farm. And then Cyla's conflicts with Naite had driven off another group of workers who didn't want to deal with the open hostility.

Temar slammed the front door open and vanished into the house. Shan didn't come out here often, so for a moment he stood on the porch as cobweb memories clung to him. Temar had stood on this same porch, tied and bruised. The image of that night superimposed itself over reality, and Shan's guts knotted as he remembered. A shout brought him back to reality, and he hurried into the house.

"I don't care what you—" Temar started to say, but Cyla cut him off. She looked so much like Temar that no one would ever miss that they were related, but where Temar was normally reserved, angry seemed a default emotion for her, and she was angry now, her beautiful face twisted in rage and frustration.

"You aren't even here. You don't see what goes on every day. We can make this farm successful!" She was an inch or two shorter than Temar, but she got close and poked her finger in his chest.

"Not if you drive off all the workers!"

"There aren't so many jobs around here that they can afford to quit when we're paying good wages."

"Yes, they can. If you ask them to pick and process a farm full of cotton, they will."

"It's the most profitable of—"

This time Temar cut her off. "Because it's the worst one to grow. No one produces a lot of cotton because it's a miserable crop, and you're asking people to pick a whole farm full."

"Just for a year or two."

"We won't have any workers after a week or two."

Shan stood back and watched them, not sure he could do anything to help, so he plastered himself to a wall and waited.

"This is just like you, always assuming that something can't be done. Well, I can do it." She spun on her heels and started to walk away, but Temar grabbed her arm, forcing her back around. When she came around, her fists were up, and Shan took a step forward. Sibling hatred was normal, but he wouldn't stand by and let it turn into a fistfight.

"No, you can't." Temar stared at her, his own anger clear in every taut muscle and the stiff line of his shoulders.

"Don't you even—"

"It's my farm!" Temar shouted, and Shan could see those words hit Cyla. Her mouth was open, ready to shout back, but she froze. "The council erased the slave term for both of us, but the farm is mine," Temar said again, though this time his voice was quieter. The council had reason for that. Only Temar had been raped, so they had decided to give the land to Temar alone.

"Just because I was wrong about George Young," Cyla said, but now her words were slow and careful. Oh, the anger was still there, but she was hiding it. When someone mentioned Ben or Temar's abuse, Cyla's reaction could be a little unpredictable, and Shan inched closer. He understood how guilt could spur on the darker emotions, but Cyla needed to stop before she really hurt someone with this anger and this aggression.

Temar backed away and sat on the couch. "This isn't about you being wrong. We were both wrong about George and about Ben."

"Then why won't you trust my judgment in this?" Cyla's anger started rising again, and her cheeks turned deep pink. "Two years of cotton would—"

"Ruin the damn farm!" Temar snapped.

Cyla physically pulled back, and Temar dropped his head for a moment, looking as weary as Shan had ever seen him. He wanted to go sit next to Temar, but he instinctively knew that if Cyla thought they were ganging up on her, two against one, it would feed her anger more, so he waited.

"Cyla, I love you, but the cotton is a mistake, and we can't afford to waste the money on seed."

Cyla didn't answer, but from the way she set her jaw, she didn't agree. If Cyla and Naite ever decided to get together and have children, Shan figured he'd have to find another planet to live on. Any child of theirs would terrorize universes. It was probably a good thing they hated each other. The worst part was that Cyla was such a small woman, with light hair and fair skin that pinked every time she got angry. A person expected a man of Naite's size to have some rage, but tiny little Cyla seemed to have twice as much. It was frightening to watch her go off on someone.

"So," she said slowly, "you're taking away my allowance?" The words were nasty and sarcastic enough that Temar flinched away from them.

For long seconds, Temar was silent. As the more reasonable end of his own sibling rivalry, Shan understood how frustrating idiot brothers and sisters could be. That didn't mean he knew how to help.

"I know how much you want this farm to be a success." Temar had a tight rein on his emotions, so that when he looked up at her, Shan couldn't tell what he was thinking.

"And it can be. I can—"

"No." Temar stood. "No, let me talk." Cyla rolled her eyes, but she fell silent. Maybe she understood that she didn't have the power here.

"I love you, and I know how much it would kill you to ruin this farm."

Her mouth came open, and Temar held up a hand to stop her from interrupting.

"And if you keep fighting Naite, you *will* ruin the farm. He knows what it takes to make one profitable, and he's the one I picked to manage the farm. So, either you will start treating him like the farm manager, a man who has the right to say what happens—"

"But—" Cyla said, and Temar raised his voice without losing the reasonable tone.

"Or I will hire you an apprenticeship somewhere far, far away and ban you from this land."

Cyla lost all color from her face in one heartbeat's time. "You wouldn't," she said softly, but she sounded scared now. Temar flinched from the pain, but Shan had to give the man credit for pressing forward.

"I would. I would rather have you angry with me forever than watch you destroy this farm and then live with the guilt and shame of that. Our family doesn't deal with grief well, and you don't deal with failure well," Temar said firmly. He drew himself up straight and looked at her. "One more example of you disrespecting Naite or trying to make decisions for the farm, and you will be out. You will not be allowed back here until you're trained as a skilled worker." Without waiting for agreement, Temar turned and hurried out of the house.

Shan was left alone, Cyla staring at him as if he'd had some part in this. She might be a hellcat, but right now her pain was so close to the surface Shan could see it. If he were still a priest, he knew how he'd start the conversation. As Temar's lover, he wasn't sure what to say. He wasn't a neutral party in all this, and part of him wanted to take this moment when her defenses were down to yell at her for making Temar's life more difficult. Rather than do that, he turned and followed Temar back out into the midday sun.

It took him a second to find Temar where he stood in the shade of the barn, watching the fields. The workers had vanished. At noon, even the screens that covered the valley and caught the dew offered only minimal protection, so they were probably doing indoor chores. Either that, or they'd all decided to give Temar some privacy for that fight. Of course, on a farm, privacy was relative. Most of them had probably stayed close enough to hear at least part of the fight. They'd want to know if Temar planned to back down from Cyla. If he had, they probably would have gone out looking for other jobs.

Shan covered the distance between them, pulling off his sand veil and wiping the sweat from his neck. "You handled that well," he offered.

"I think I'm going to throw up." Temar leaned against the bleached white wood of the barn, his eyes closed and sweat gathering along his nose.

"You gave her a choice, and you did it without being cruel." That last part wasn't entirely true, but Temar had gone out of his way to avoid being intentionally cruel, and Shan was impressed. He'd never handled his brother that well, that was for sure. Considering how he and Naite had treated each other when they'd been on the council together, Shan was surprised the other council members hadn't killed them both.

"I don't want to send her away," Temar whispered. He was a ghastly shade of white.

"Will you?"

Temar opened his eyes and looked at Shan, misery etched into his face. "Yes."

Shan nodded and looked around at the farm with its neat rows of potato plants and solid buildings. "Good, because you're right that she's going to hate herself if she ruins all this."

"Well, hopefully she'll see that eventually, because right now, she hates me."

"At least she'll have something new to obsess about for a while." Shan waited until Temar looked at him with a confused frown. "She can try to come up with ways to make money off the crazy people from space." Shan pointed up toward the sky.

"Oh God." Temar thunked his head back against the barn and closed his eyes. "Can you believe I forgot that for a few minutes?"

"Yeah, I can." The barn door opened and Naite stood there. He looked pretty damn self-satisfied, which meant he'd probably eavesdropped on the whole conversation. Shan bit down on an urge to say something very cutting about Naite's morals. The problem was, Naite wouldn't give a damn what Shan thought, so it wasn't worth saying.

"Are you two going to stand out in the heat like idiots?" he asked.

Temar looked at Naite wearily. "I was thinking about it. I was also thinking of vomiting."

Naite snorted. "Get your asses in here. Idiots." He disappeared inside, the barn door slamming shut behind him.

"Naite will have the fans going in there," Shan offered. It was miserably hot, and the heat wouldn't start breaking for a couple of hours. Of course, on the open desert, it wouldn't really break until sundown, but at least the ride to Landing was a short one from here.

"Fine. I guess I can throw up in there as well as out here," Temar said. He pushed away from the barn, and his hand came up and caught Shan's shoulder as he steadied himself.

"You okay?"

"Not really. I'm not even sure I'm joking about throwing up."

"But you followed through and did the right thing," Shan pointed out. "So if you have to throw up, remember that."

"Great," Temar said dryly before he headed for the barn door. Shan followed, his hand coming down to rest on Temar's back. Temar smiled at him.

"So," Shan said as he pushed the door open. The fans moved the air quickly enough to give an illusion of cool, but Shan could still feel the sweat gathering along his spine. "Guess who we talked to today?" he said to Naite.

Temar lost his balance and stumbled a bit as he gave a rough laugh that sounded almost like he was choking. Shan got a hand under Temar's arm to make sure he didn't fall.

"What the hell is wrong with you two?" Naite demanded.

"Oh, you're not even going to believe this one," Shan said. This was going to be one hell of a story, and as a council member, Naite was going to get a chance to call Shan all kinds of an idiot for stepping in this pipe trap. "It all started when Temar asked about the war." He started the story, wondering how many times he was going to have to tell it.

chapter
nine

LILIAN SAT with her hands steepled in front of her, but Shan had never seen her look so shocked. Kevin and Bari had both pushed back their chairs, their faces utterly devoid of emotion, and Dee'eta Sun clutched the edge of the table as though she needed to hang on to something. Shan had expected Div to represent the church, but the new priest who'd trained at White Hills sat in Div's place, her mouth hanging open. She was a heavy woman with a large belly and more years than a newly trained apprentice usually had. Shan had heard rumors that she came to the priesthood after losing her two children to a cave-in in one of the local caverns, where they'd been playing. The kids over at White Hills had deep, cool caves to explore, and it wasn't all that unusual a story for the town.

"Twenty years," she asked, her voice squeaking, and Shan wished he could remember her name.

"So many years of rationing and fights over water, and they've been finished with their war for twenty years." Kevin slammed his hand down on the table so hard that the sound echoed off the metal walls of the council room. After lurching up out of his chair, he turned his back on the group and stood looking out the same window Shan had once looked out, when the group had debated enslaving Temar. It felt like another lifetime.

"Lilian, you should go," Shan offered. "I'll use the communications station to introduce you to the commander." If anyone could handle recalcitrant alliances, Lilian could. However, she shook her head before Shan even finished.

"No, I won't go," she said firmly.

"You would be the best choice," Bari pointed out. "All the towns and valleys respect how much you've done to help negotiate peaceful solutions in some tricky cases."

"No, Bari. I'm too old to even properly run a farm," she said with a wave of her hand. "If my children have to take over my farm chores, I'm certainly not strong enough to go running off to space. We need to send someone, but it won't be me."

"You're no older than I am," Kevin disagreed, turning around to pin Lilian with a hard look.

"And you're old," she snapped right back. "Stars above, Kevin, our grandchildren are old enough to have children. I would have retired from the council a long time ago, but I enjoy intimidating the local idiots." She sighed and rubbed her eyes, a gesture Shan had never seen the woman use.

"Which is why you're the best choice," Kevin insisted.

Lilian shook her head. "Ten years ago, maybe. But I don't know that I'd survive the pressures of the travel, and if I go up there, they'll have leverage to hold over me."

"Leverage?" Bari jumped on the word.

Lilian looked around the room, and Shan leaned forward, not sure what was wrong, but something was. Of all the people in the room, only the new priest didn't look worried, but then she hadn't known Lilian as long as the rest of them. She wouldn't recognize that this was the sort of verbal tap dancing Lilian did before dropping some metaphorical bomb into their midst.

"Leverage," Lilian said firmly. "Frankle says I have a few months to live, but there are hard growths inside me. I'm dying, and I won't go up there and have them hold out some miracle if only I make a bad trade for my world."

Shan stopped breathing. For one instant, it felt like the world had stopped spinning for Lilian. He'd been so sure she would go up there and she'd fix all of this, force someone to finish the terraforming contract. Dying. Lilian Freeland was dying.

"Oh, stop looking at me like I'm going to drop dead in the next two minutes," she barked at all of them. "I have months, maybe a year, and given the mess up there in the universe, it sounds like I've had a longer and better life here than I would have if I'd been born to those idiots up there." She gave a dramatic roll of her eyes. "But that means we need to send someone else to negotiate for us, and I vote to send Shan."

For the second time, the world seemed to pause as Shan blinked in shock.

Naite didn't hide his skepticism. "Shan?"

Lilian pinned Naite with a sharp gaze. "He's not strongly tied to any group: landowners, skilled workers, unskilled workers, child raisers, artists. He's not even aligned with the church anymore, so that will minimize the accusations that he negotiated for one group over another," Lilian said firmly, and even if she was dying, her tone made it clear she still intended on insisting that the council do what she wanted. She had a force of personality that had always made others look to her, and Shan couldn't compete with that. Without her to negotiate, his view of the future had dimmed considerably.

"Lilian," he said, gathering his words carefully, "you yourself once commented that you wished there was another representative from the church to take my place on the council. I'm not a negotiator or a statesman, so I don't think I'm the best choice for sending up there." Shan didn't add that he wasn't sure he wanted to go.

"Because you lose all logic when you're within six feet of your brother," Lilian said with another sharp look over in Naite's direction.

"Don't blame me. He's always illogical," Naite said. Considering this was the man Shan had trusted with his life, with Temar's life, their relationship clearly hadn't improved all that much.

"Only when he's around you," Lilian said wearily. "Bari, what do you think?"

Bari blinked at Lilian for a second, clearly not willing to jump into the debate this quickly, but he swallowed and gave a short nod before answering. "I think he has as good a chance as any of us. I don't expect anyone up there has a whole lot of respect for us, so winning any sort of negotiations won't be easy."

Dee'eta spoke up. "They colonized this planet because they needed high-quality glass. I'll get samples together, both the best glasswork and the purest. If they want circuit-quality glass, they have to know that we have it. We have so much of it that we make drinking glasses out of it."

"But we don't," Temar said. Shan didn't know enough about glassblowing to understand the conversation, so he looked to Temar with a questioning expression. "Glass that pure takes sustained heat that is very hard to maintain. No one makes a simple drinking glass after putting in that much effort."

"I will," Dee'eta said. "If they want to know what we have to trade, they're going to find out. But if you can negotiate for a high capacity and regulated solar smelter, it would make any future circuit quality glass a lot easier to produce."

"Shan knows the computer systems better than anyone," Kevin added. "Face it, if any of us go up there, we're likely to make ourselves look like idiots because we don't know how to open a door or use their slosh stalls. You've had months at the relay to get used to the tech."

Shan wanted to point out that he hadn't really been trying to get used to the tech. Most of the time he'd been fixing machines. However, the logic fit together in a way that made him unwilling to refuse. He wanted to say that he wasn't old enough or experienced enough to handle this, but he was in his thirties and had over a decade of work as a priest behind him, which was as close as Livre came to having a diplomat. What's more, they were right that he had certain skills the rest of them didn't. He hated that they were right, but he couldn't find a counterargument that made sense.

"So you're sending Shan up and hoping he doesn't make a fool of himself." Naite sighed. "Well, there are worse people on the planet you could send."

Shan glared at his brother. "Thank you for that endorsement." He might poke at Naite, but he was feeling the same way. He knew the tech, but he'd left the church because of his inability to handle people. Earlier, Temar had said that his fight with Cyla left him physically sick, and that described how Shan felt right now. He'd finally listened to God. He'd finally stopped trying to make himself into Div and accepted that his talent lay with his hands, with fixing things. This felt like a step backward into a life he'd never truly fit into.

Lilian laughed softly. "From Naite, I think that's as much of an endorsement as you're getting. So can we agree to vote on Shan as the representative?" Lilian looked around the room, and the council members all inclined their heads in agreement. "Good. By acclamation, Shan Polli is now the chosen negotiator for Livre. Now we have to go out to the other towns and make sure they vote the same way."

"Should you be…." Kevin let his voice trail off.

"Kevin Starwalker," Lilian said in a dark tone, "if you even suggest that I'm too old or sick to manipulate a few Blue Hope council members, I'm going to take offense, and you know I'm not nice when I take offense at something."

"Who, me?" Kevin asked with exaggerated innocence. "I would never suggest anything of the sort. I was simply going to offer you a ride."

Lilian gave a little huff, but she didn't turn him down.

"I'll go on one condition," Shan said. The entire council looked at him. "I don't know glass, and that's the one thing they want from us. I need Temar to come with me."

"Me?" Temar sounded shocked.

Surprisingly, Naite spoke up. "Temar's got a cooler head than Shan, and he's a watcher. He observes a situation until he's sure what side to take. I'd be more comfortable with him going along to keep Shan from offending the universe with his almighty morals."

Shan gritted his teeth. "I don't go around offending people."

"You'd be surprised," Naite shot back.

Kevin returned to the table and sat down. "Temar, would you want to go? You have a farm to tend and an apprenticeship you just started."

Both were true. Temar had a lot of reasons to stay here, and not a lot of reasons to go with him. Temar looked around the room for a second. "I have Naite to run the farm, and I think Dee'eta can tell you that I don't really have the patience for glass right now. Maybe I don't have the temperament for it at all."

"That's not true," Dee'eta spoke up. "Glass is a living creature, sensitive to your moods, and you need time to find the calm that will allow you to work a piece. You will be a great glassblower, one day."

"But not any day soon," Temar said, and Dee'eta didn't disagree.

"So you'll go?" Lilian asked.

"As long as I make this clear," Temar added, and Shan waited for some sort of condition or maybe a salary demand. In hindsight, a salary wasn't unreasonable, at least if they managed to pull this off. "I told Cyla that if she tried ignoring any more of Naite's advice that she'd be banned from my land and I would pay for her to apprentice anywhere that wasn't near the farm. I need the council to enforce that if Naite comes with a complaint."

Lilian leaned on her hand and studied Temar until he started shifting nervously. Shan could understand because as much as he respected Lilian, he wasn't exactly comfortable around her. Slowly, she smiled. "I have underestimated you, and I'm not used to reading people wrong," she finally offered. "You have my word that if Cyla gets out of hand I'll take her off the farm myself."

"I can handle her fine now that Temar's made it clear that I'm in charge," Naite said. Clearly he didn't like the idea of Lilian running to his rescue.

"Then I'll back you up," Lilian said without taking offense. "So, we all have work to do. I know it's too late to go back to the relay today. You can stay in town if you like."

Shan looked over to Temar to see what he wanted to do.

"We can get out to my place," Temar said, and there was only a trace of trepidation in the smile he gave Lilian. Going back out to Ben's old place meant facing Cyla. Sometimes Shan wondered if siblings were the Lord's way of testing a person's patience.

"Okay, then you're free to leave. The rest of us have to decide how to approach the other councils." With that, Lilian dismissed them. Temar stood up to leave, but Shan hesitated.

"Don't you want to discuss what you want out of negotiations, what we're willing to offer?"

Lilian looked at him and smiled, and for the first time Shan was truly aware of her age. Her face was heavily lined and her hair thinning. She looked more insubstantial than she had just months ago. "You know what we need, Shan, and you know what we have to offer. Do the best you can to negotiate with sandrats that abandoned our grandparents. That's all we ask."

"Some new copper piping might be nice," Naite added.

"And computer pads," Bari added.

"I really could use that high-capacity smelter," Dee'eta offered.

"You people," Lilian interrupted with a disgusted voice. "Why don't you write a shopping list, like he's your spouse heading to market? You two," she said, pointing at Shan and Temar, "get out. This is council work now."

"Yes, ma'am," Shan said, standing up and following Temar out of the council room. The Lord might move in mysterious ways, but Shan never had expected those ways to lead him into space. As they headed outside, Shan squinted at the blue sky. It had a pink tinge to it as the sun sank toward the horizon, so there was a sandstorm out there somewhere, throwing up grains of sand to glow as the sun reflected off it.

Temar stopped so close to him that their shoulders brushed. For a time they stood silently. When Shan finally looked down, his eyes stinging from the light, he could see people gathering in the street. An unannounced full council meeting in the middle of the week was sure to catch people's attention. He wondered how long it would be before rumors started to spread. Wistia leaned against the side of a carpet-maker's stall, watching. Her dark hair blew in the breeze, and her harp was strapped to her back.

"Well, crap," Shan muttered.

"What's wrong?"

Shan nodded toward the woman. "I forgot to file a complaint."

Temar looked over, studying the street until he spotted Wistia, and then he laughed. Frowning at him, Shan demanded, "What?"

Lowering his voice, Temar leaned closer. "We're about to try to talk evil alien worlds into water to keep our planet alive, and you're worried about a song."

"It's the principle of the matter," Shan said in his own defense.

"Uh-huh," Temar said as he went to Naite's hauler and climbed up into the back. They'd figured Naite would have to stay for a council meeting, so they'd loaded the sand bike into the back. Temar started pulling off the straps that held it in place.

"It is," Shan said as he got up into the hauler and started helping.

"It doesn't matter."

"It did yesterday."

Temar stopped and leaned against the bike as he carefully studied Shan. Shan wasn't sure what Temar meant by the gesture, and he shifted uncomfortably. "What?" he asked again.

"Yesterday it mattered, today it doesn't," Temar said with a shrug. Shan couldn't argue with logic like that, since it wasn't logical, so he helped Temar unload the bike. It'd be close to dark before they got back to the farm. That meant they had seven days until the shuttle showed up.

"Do you think they're calling us right now?" Shan asked as he muscled the bike off the truck and let it bounce on its tires as it hit the ground.

"I don't know."

Shan thought about that. "They're used to living in metal boxes and having communication devices within a few feet of them all the time. They don't understand the idea of being busy or out of communication. They're calling us."

"So, what do they think we're doing? Ignoring them?"

Shan looked out at the windwood trees bending in the evening wind. "I have no idea," he admitted.

"Well, this is going to be interesting." That was all Temar offered before he fastened his sand veil over his face. "Coming?"

"Yeah," Shan agreed, throwing his leg over the sand bike and starting the engine.

chapter
t e n

NIGHT HAD fallen and the large moon was a half crescent in the sky before he pulled the bike up to Temar's farm. Three older kids sat playing cards under a dim lamp, but Shan supposed even that was an improvement over the days when Ben managed to alienate most of the parents with his attitude toward having children on the farm. How had none of them noticed that he was such an arrogant, self-involved jerk? Even now, Shan felt deep guilt over that. No wonder the workers who had hired on under Ben had all left. They'd lived on the same farm with the man, worked next to him, watched him rest his hands on Temar's shoulders, and they'd never known. A few people whispered that some of them must have noticed something, but Shan didn't believe that. He remembered when he'd visited and Sua had talked about Temar's temper and how patient Ben had been. They'd believed that.

"You're thinking awfully loud," Temar said, and Shan pulled himself out of that memory. "Worried?"

"If we screw this up, a lot of people will suffer."

"That was true last time too," Temar pointed out as he got off the bike. Shan hadn't really thought about that. Actually, he hadn't had time to think or worry at the time. They'd figured out that Ben was stealing the last of Livre's water to get an old, abandoned rocket off-planet, and from that time until the end of their adventure when Naite had come riding to their rescue, they'd been reacting, not acting. And afterward, he had been too busy defending himself from Naite's recriminations.

"When did you get so wise?" Shan teased.

Temar stopped and looked at him, his face serious. "I had a lot of time to sit still and really think. I guess it did change me."

Shan stared at Temar, not sure what to say. It wasn't right to imply that the abuse had helped Temar. It felt too close to what Ben believed, that he had been teaching Temar. It was too close to Shan's father's drunken rambling about how he was going to make his sons strong. That was something Shan didn't want to look at too closely.

A number of workers started toward them. "What's going on?" Facia Clark asked, pulling Shan away from his thoughts. She hurried over, straightening her shirt, even though one braid had hair sticking out at all angles, which made it clear what she'd been doing. Her husband, Robert Clark, was two steps behind her.

"The council has some work tonight. Naite may be out late," Shan said. Temar pulled off his sand veil and headed for the house. Shan figured he had been elected to explain this.

"Why?" Robert demanded. Even in the dim glow from the crescent moon and the few lamps, he looked worried. Everyone had suffered from Ben's schemes, and Shan couldn't give them answers, not yet.

"This is council business, and I'm not council anymore. I can't tell you."

Cyla came out on the porch. She stayed up there, not coming down into the yard as more workers came out of the barn. Shan wished he could tell them, but the Landing council needed to talk to the other councils first. If information leaked to the wrong people at the wrong time, there could be panic and fighting. They didn't need that—not now, when the planet had to present a united face.

"Are there more people, more conspirators?" a thin man Shan didn't know asked.

"No. That's over," Shan said, his voice slipping into that tone he'd used to comfort people when he'd been a priest. "That was a horrible time, but it's over."

"Then what's going on?" Facia demanded. The children had abandoned their card game and watched with worried faces.

"I truly can't say," he apologized. "I can only say that if this goes well, it's good news."

"And if it goes poorly?" Robert demanded.

Shan considered the man. These people had a right to the truth, but that didn't mean telling them would do any good. Shan only hoped the councils chose to call town meetings quickly. "We're desert people,

Robert. Do you ask the desert what would happen if things went poorly?"

Shan kept his voice soft even if the words were harsh. These people lived with death, knew it intimately. The children with their cards were old enough to know the planet was dying, the towns were dying. They'd probably seen some animal ripped apart on the desert. Going up to the rocks and searching the sand for the long, threaded trails that meant sandrats were tunneling under the sand was a childhood tradition. And when you had sandrats, you had hawks trying to grab a meal and rats trying to use sheer numbers to pull down hawks. Life wasn't easy, and if things went poorly, something died. Every child older than six understood that.

Facia turned and caught Robert's arm, and the others shifted uncomfortably; however, Shan didn't want them afraid. This could be the answer to their prayers. It could be the return of water to Livre and the finishing of the terraforming. The desert would always rule most of the planet, but with enough water, enough resources, and enough valleys, they could run a sustaining ecosystem.

"The better question is what will happen if it goes well," Shan said. Reaching out, he rested his hand on Facia's shoulder. "Truly, this is something only the council can share, but this could be good news."

"Had Ben hidden more water?" Targ Villanova called from near the back of the crowd.

"I can't say," Shan said. "I am truly sorry, but I cannot tell anyone council business. I have to head back to the relay early, so I should head to bed, but as soon as the council shares, I will answer any questions I can. I promise." Shan didn't tell them that he doubted he would be on the planet when the news broke. "Good night." Making sure the bike was settled on its stand, Shan headed for the house. Cyla was still there, leaning on a post as she watched him.

Shan climbed the stairs up to the porch. "Evening," he offered politely. If he and Temar did marry, Cyla would be his sister, so it seemed wise to keep the peace.

"Temar knows, doesn't he?" Cyla asked quietly while she watched the others as they broke up into little knots of conversation.

"Yes," Shan said, "he does."

Cyla looked at him. "And you're not going to tell me, are you?"

Shan sighed. He didn't want to add to her pain, but he couldn't give her answers, either. "No, I'm not." He walked quickly into the house. His guts were already in knots; he didn't need to add more conflict to the mess. The bedrooms were upstairs, but Shan realized he didn't know which Temar used.

"Temar?" he called at the top of the stairs.

"You can have the slosh stall after me," Temar yelled back, his voice muffled through the closed door of the bathroom. At the third door, Shan found the room with the unmistakable signs of Temar. The bed covering was a complex swirl of blues and grays with a white thread edging, and a series of vivid green copper-glass bowls sat on a shelf. Going over to the shelf, he ran a finger along an edge. These were nice, but a beginner had made them. The lip thinned and widened randomly. Shan wondered if Temar had made these. School gave everyone a chance to try each of the trades, but Shan's own week of glassblowing had produced nothing more than a colorful collection of broken shards and bulbous shapes that had no actual purpose. He'd been useless.

Shan picked the largest bowl up. It felt balanced in his hands, but tiny air bubbles traveled under the surface. If this was Temar's work, he'd learned glass faster than anyone Shan had seen. Despite the flaws, the work was balanced and beautiful. Shan had visited the Gazer home after Erqu Gazer died, and he couldn't remember any of this displayed there.

"I made it."

Shan turned around and Temar stood there, his skin still pink from having been scrubbed clean, and a pair of sleep pants hanging low around his waist.

"I figured you had. In school?"

Temar nodded.

"You're good."

Temar came over and took the bowl out of Shan's hands. "It's flawed. Anyone who sold it would be lucky to get the cost of the materials out of it."

"That's not true," Shan said. Temar looked over in disbelief. "Okay, it is flawed," Shan amended himself, "but it's still a beautiful and well-balanced piece, and it would bring a fair price. I'm impressed you could do something so difficult in a school class. I never made anything good enough to hold water long enough to get it from a faucet to a mouth."

Temar smiled, but he kept clutching the bowl, and Shan knew there was something there under the surface, something Temar wasn't sharing. It made his heart hurt to know Temar wasn't comfortable sharing.

"The slosh stall is open. I left a pair of sleep pants for you. They're my largest, but they may come up a little short on the leg." Temar put the bowl back on the shelf and turned to the window. Shan reached out, wanting to touch Temar's shoulder, but something stopped him. He remembered the way Temar had pushed him away, the tears and the raw pain that had poured out when he'd offered comfort. Pulling his hand back, he turned and headed into the bathroom.

After pouring a measure of water into the bucket, Shan took the cup and poured it over his shoulders before smoothing the cleaning sands over his skin. The fact was he didn't want to go up into space. Now that he'd had more time to think on it, he really had no business taking Temar up. The man had strength that Shan couldn't even imagine. However, he wasn't indestructible. Yet he'd rushed right ahead and volunteered.

Most of the time, Shan couldn't understand the people who had first settled Livre. He didn't understand their need for metal walls or their disgust at the sight of a hawk feeding or even their obsessive need to always talk to each other. In those first generations, every single one of them had carried communications devices, and Shan had never understood that. Did they ever accomplish anything with their constant need to talk about everything? Right now, he knew one thing though… he'd give a lot to be able to pick up one of those personal communicators and call Div and ask him for his advice.

Shan used the cup to pour the lukewarm water over himself, rinsing off the soap before he used his hands to brush off the excess water, so it would go down the drain and get back into the cycle system. With the sun down, the planet cooled quickly, and the chill started to settle into the house. Shan was shivering before he had swept enough of the water clear of his body to open the sealed door of the slosh stall. He grabbed the sleep pants and then pulled them on, the last traces of moisture making the fabric cling to his legs. Their ancestors used towels. Shan had read about that in one of the journals he'd found. They'd used fabric to dry themselves and then let the dry air leech the moisture out of the fabric.

It was such a small difference, but the horror Shan felt at the idea of wasting that much water left him nauseous. How were they supposed to talk to people when their cultures had slipped away from each other in so many ways? And how was he supposed to take Temar into space when a touch could pull all the pain out of him so easily?

Shan's brain circled the pipe trap, unable to find any good answers. Maybe there weren't any.

He certainly wasn't going to find any tonight. Shan headed back into Temar's bedroom. Temar stood at the window, looking out. "They're all still talking, trying to figure out what's going on with the council," he said. The window faced the rock wall, but Temar leaned out so he could watch a sliver of the yard.

"They'll never guess," Shan said as he moved closer. He stopped a foot away, not sure what to do. He'd gone from waiting, to being Temar's lover, to making Temar cry. He felt a little awkward.

Temar looked at him and frowned. "Shan?" he asked, holding out a hand to invite Shan to step closer. Shan did. He took Temar's hand in his and moved until he brushed against Temar's arm, close enough to touch without crowding.

"Temar, I don't want to hurt you," Shan said as awkwardly as some teenager trying to hold someone else's newborn baby, like one wrong touch would do irreparable harm.

Temar tightened his fingers around Shan's hand. "You don't hurt me. You've never hurt me."

Given how their last encounter had ended, Shan might have debated that. "I can wait," he promised. "I honestly don't mind."

"I do," Temar said, showing more of that firm resolve that Shan admired. The problem was that he wasn't sure how deep the resolve went and when he might trigger that raw pain that hid inside Temar. If Ben wasn't already dead, Shan would have considered going out in the hauler with Naite to watch the son of a bitch die in the desert.

Temar sighed. Maybe he could read the doubt in Shan's face. "When you touch me, it chases away the ghosts. Promise."

"But…." Shan stopped. He didn't want to push Temar to talk about last night, but he didn't want to ignore the problem. Feeling Temar pushing him away and then crying… it had ripped at Shan's heart.

Temar angled his body so he faced Shan and raised his hand to rest against Shan's chest.

"I lost control of the feelings for a second—that doesn't mean I don't want you." Temar's voice was so soft Shan could barely hear it.

"I know that. I've never doubted that," Shan said. "Sometimes I wonder what you see in me, but I've grown used to the idea that you have flawed judgment."

Temar gave a snort of laughter as the mood in the room shifted, and Shan smiled at having offered that small comfort. Shan waited as Temar gathered his thoughts. Sometimes silence was a better counselor than words.

"You trust me at your back," Temar said, his voice not quite a question, but not quite sure, either.

"Always," Shan agreed. "You had every right to give up, and you kept fighting. I trust you as much as I trust that idiot brother of mine, and I like you a whole lot more."

Temar's smile grew sad. "You trust me more than I trust myself."

Shan sucked in a breath, shocked at that confession, and this did feel like a confession to him. He just wasn't sure if Temar wanted his absolution or God's. As far as Shan was concerned, Temar had no sins to confess in this. "You did more than I would have in the situation. You survived better," Shan promised, and it was true. He had his own scars, and he hadn't dealt with nearly as much pain as Temar had.

"Did I?" Temar turned back to the window. "I don't want to remember his touch, but—"

Shan stood still, afraid one move could unbalance something he couldn't understand. After a second, Temar's muscles rippled, like a goat shivering off an unwanted touch, and Shan pulled back. However, Temar turned again, and caught Shan's hand and pressed it up against his own bare chest. "I love the feel of you. I love that we can touch."

"But sometimes the memories push in?" Shan guessed. Temar dropped his gaze to the floor, but he kept holding Shan's hand to his chest.

When his answer came, it was so soft Shan wasn't sure he heard right. "I don't know how to push them away."

Shan wished he had some wisdom, but he didn't. He suspected Naite would have an answer, but he doubted it would be a good one, seeing as how his brother never had handled relationships well. "Give yourself some time."

Temar gave a half sob and moved closer until he leaned into Shan, his arms going around Shan. "I've had three months, which is longer than I was with Ben."

"And if you need three more years, that's okay," Shan promised, returning the hug gently. He slowly tightened his arms, ordering himself not to treat Temar like some breakable object. That had caused their problem in the first place.

"I'm tired of being alone."

"I didn't say you had to be alone while you waited. I'll wait with you. And if my touch chases away ghosts, then it sounds like that's the place to start. We can just touch."

Temar leaned back a little so he could look Shan in the face. "Either you're the most patient man in the world or you're not all that interested in sleeping with me, because if someone told me I had to wait three years between the touching and the sex, I'd be unhappy."

Shan laughed. "Yes, but you weren't a priest. Priests are highly skilled and well practiced with waiting. My right hand and I have a long, deeply committed relationship that I'm happy to continue until you're back on the market."

Temar's smile finally reached his eyes, the corners crinkling.

"You're insane."

"Yes, but don't tell anyone. Oh, and don't tell them about the hand thing, because people are entirely too willing to believe a priest somehow isn't human and doesn't have a need for some sort of sexual relationship, even if it's with a hand."

Temar tilted his head as though he had to study Shan to come up with an answer for that. "Deal," Temar finally promised.

"So, bed?" Shan asked.

"Bed."

Urging Temar toward the bed, Shan turned to get the light. Bedsprings creaked as Temar climbed in, and Shan followed once the lights were off. Without hesitation, Temar moved in, his arm resting across Shan's chest as he placed a kiss on Shan's jaw.

"Good night," Temar whispered, and then he shifted a bit, settling in next to Shan.

"Good night," Shan answered. His cock gave an experimental little twinge, but a quick thought of Ben settled it down as Shan closed his eyes to sleep.

chapter
eleven

SHAN WOKE to a hand trailing down his chest. He brought his hand up and braced it on Temar's forearm, blinking to chase the sleep from his eyes.

"Temar, are you—"

"Shhh," Temar said, his hand running over Shan's stomach to tease at the waist of his sleep pants, and every word in Shan's brain skittered away like sandrats when a hawk appears in the sky. Temar shifted closer, his lips pressing against Shan's as he kissed him, gently at first and then with more passion. Shan parted his lips, and Temar sucked on Shan's lower lip, running teeth along it. Forgetting his fears, Shan kissed back, hungrily, fiercely. His cock ached already, and Temar's hardness pressed against his thigh.

Shan made a strangled noise as Temar cupped his cock, pressing hard enough to make Shan's whole body tremble.

Temar turned to Shan's neck, tasting the skin before running his teeth over it. "Oh God," Shan gasped as Temar's hand moved back up his body, stroking his sweat-damp skin. Shan wasn't sure when he'd started sweating, but he radiated heat, and his muscles tightened as his still half-asleep body shifted immediately into the heat of desire.

"Is that a good 'Oh God'?" Temar asked before sucking at Shan's earlobe.

"Yes," Shan said. He tried to clear his brain enough to reciprocate. He ran his hand over Temar's shoulders. The weight Temar had lost recently emphasized the wiry muscles under the skin, and Shan traced one, soaking up the warmth Temar was shedding.

Temar kissed his way down to Shan's collarbone, his fingers running over Shan's shoulders as he squirmed. His thigh pressed into Shan's cock, and Shan moaned, determined not to come in his sleep pants like a teenager. When Shan tilted his head back down to look at Temar, Temar had a feral smile.

"With age comes control, but not that much control," Shan warned, his breath coming in hungry gasps. Warm hands returned to Shan's chest, stroking up his sides before Temar focused on Shan's nipples, pulling at them gently.

Shan lost control and thrust up into Temar's body, his need overcoming his pride. He didn't care if he came prematurely at this point. Temar lowered himself so he was lying on Shan, pressing him down into the bed. "Meaning?" Temar asked in a breathy voice.

"Meaning I'm going to come in my pants," Shan warned. If this was teasing, if Temar planned to go no further, he needed to stop now so Shan could finish himself off. Otherwise, his balls were going to fall off. Then Temar looked down at him with such hunger that Shan realized something had changed overnight. He reached behind Temar's neck and pulled him close for another kiss. For a few seconds, Temar yielded. Then Temar's hands were on his shoulders, pressing, and Shan let go, allowing Temar to escape even though he desperately wanted more. He wanted more, and his body was quickly getting to a point that he couldn't remember why he wasn't supposed to demand more.

"God, you're beautiful," Temar said as he sat up, and pulled on Shan's sleep pants.

"No, I'm really not," Shan said. His nose was too curved and his features too sharp for beauty. However, he didn't care about any of that. His hard cock stuck up, the head already pressing forward out of the foreskin. Temar had lost his own pants at some point, and now he grabbed both cocks, one in each hand. Shan's heart pounded so hard it echoed in his ears as he waited for Temar to finish this, but Temar moved painfully slow, his hand moving up and down on each cock with the sort of agonizing deliberateness Shan could never inflict on himself. With a gasp, Shan caught Temar's shoulder.

Letting go, Temar dropped down onto Shan; despite his recent weight loss, he still weighed more than he looked like he would. The pressure on Shan's cock was too much for him to resist, and he arched up into Temar. He felt a flash of guilt at using Temar, but that passed when Temar thrust down into him just as enthusiastically.

With his body already tight from the approaching orgasm, Shan grabbed both Temar's shoulders and angled his hips to buck upwards. Both their bodies were slicked with sweat now, and his hand slipped off

Temar's shoulder, throwing Shan's balance off. Then Temar shifted, and their cocks pressed against each other, both trapped between their overheated bodies.

Temar shuddered, his whole body jerking and his face twisting into an expression of absolute ecstasy. Twice more, Temar gave abortive thrusts, his muscles tensing as he came. Shan's cock slid even more easily now, and he dug his heels into the mattress and thrust up so hard that he lifted Temar from the bed. His balls drew up, and then he was sliding into his own orgasm, his muscles tensing as his body rushed out of control.

He collapsed, Temar's weight still on him. They both gasped for air, their ragged breathing filling the room. Shan was overstretched rubber, unable to find its true shape again, and he didn't care. He was happy being overstretched and well used, and if Temar woke him up like this too often, he was going to need to eat more protein.

"Not quite what I had planned, but I lost control there at the end."

"Loss of control can be good," Shan said, his heart still pounding fast enough to feel the pulse of it. It might not have been the most elegant sexual encounter, but it was going down as the best Shan had ever experienced. "So, what was that?" After last night, Shan thought they'd agreed to wait until Temar was ready. Either Temar had recovered in record time, or the plan had changed.

"I decided I get in trouble when I think too much. I know what feels good, and I trust you, so I need not to overthink this."

Shan opened one eye and reached over to trace small circles on Temar's shoulder with his thumb. "You think too much?"

"Less thinking and more doing feels… safer."

"So I should expect more ambush sex?" Shan asked. The moment he did, he could see the doubt and hesitation in Temar's expression. Shan reached up and ran a thumb along Temar's lower lip. "You're going to spoil me, and one of these days you aren't going to bother jumping me, and I'm going to be heartbroken. I can see it coming now, so I guess I'd better enjoy it while I get it, huh?"

"I'll never get tired of jumping you," Temar said, the smile back on his face. Leaning forward, he gave Shan a quick kiss. "And I'm going to steal all the good pears for breakfast if you don't get up fast enough to stop me." Before Shan could object, Temar rolled over and bounded out of bed. Dancing on one foot, he pulled his pants on before grabbing a shirt and heading out the door. It was just as well, because

Shan was so exhausted he couldn't get up to save his soul. He was old enough to need a little time to get his systems restarted after sex that good. Most times he didn't really feel the ten-year difference between them, but right now Shan felt like his muscles had all been taken out and given a good shaking, so that they were limp. He could just lie here all day and be perfectly happy to do nothing, the universe and its politics forgotten. At least, he would if he wasn't such a sweaty, cum-stained mess.

With a grunt, he sat up and pushed his sleep pants off, grabbing them and wiping his stomach. He could learn to like ambush sex.

chapter

twelve

DESPITE TEMAR'S warning, there were pears, apples, and very flat, dry pancakes waiting for breakfast. "Cyla made them," Temar offered, pointing at the cakes with his fork. Shan grabbed a plate and took several. The edges crumbled, but it had been a long time since he'd eaten anyone's cooking but his own, and they smelled great. "It's her way of apologizing," Temar explained as he poured more mashed apple and butter sauce over his own. He passed the sauce to Shan.

"As apologies go, it's not bad," Shan pointed out. The sauce was a little lumpy and the cakes crumbled when he took his fork to them, but it all tasted wonderful. Shan pulled a strip of apple peel out from between his teeth and chewed on it.

"I really hope she can learn to work with Naite."

Shan snorted. "It's not like Naite is a saint. I'm sure he's done his share of aggravating Cyla." He looked at Temar. When the two were young, Cyla had been the more aggressive Gazer, and Temar had pretty much followed in her shadow, even when he didn't agree with her. Shan figured that, from her point of view, the world had changed faster than she'd had time to adapt. "She's not used to having people argue with her, and Naite is a champion arguer."

Temar paused, putting his fork back down on his plate. "You'd think slavery would have taught her better."

"My owner barely talked to me." Shan looked up to see Cyla standing in the doorway. "She was a little like you've been since we moved here."

Shan's stomach soured. It was too early in the morning for this argument.

"Cyla," Temar said softly.

"I hear a lot of rumors. I hear people whisper that it was my fault that my little brother got...." Cyla's voice broke, and she didn't finish the sentence. She drew in a rough breath, and the raw pain was a reflection of Temar's face. Shan put his fork down and studied the table. "I hear people call me all sorts of names," she edited herself. "And I hear people point out that I'm not any good for you. I get in your face and everyone thinks you need to be patted on the head and told how wonderful you are."

"I don't want that," Temar said, his voice firm even though he had turned a pasty color.

"Maybe," Cyla said. "But then you throw fits in the middle of Dee'eta Sun's place and you lock yourself in your room, and you aren't exactly the image of okay with that kind of behavior."

Shan looked at Temar with concern. While Temar had admitted he and Dee'eta had disagreed, Shan certainly hadn't heard any stories that would fit Cyla's description of Temar throwing a fit.

Pressing his lips together, Temar slammed his fork down on the table. "I'm sorry if I'm not acting well enough to meet your standards. I'll try to change." The sarcasm from Temar made Shan flinch. Siblings truly were God's revenge on humanity. "What do you want me to do?"

"I don't know," Cyla nearly shouted, and then she stopped, her breathing coming hard and fast. She chewed on her lower lip for long seconds, and Shan could hear the faint voices of workers outside. Inside, the silence seemed to crowd out every sound. "I don't know how to treat you because you won't even talk to me. Ista with her morning orders followed by a day of obstinate silence was more communicative than you. I don't know which rumors are true and which aren't. I don't know you." The last part came out as a near wail, and now Shan could see the fear and hurt rising up from under all those layers of anger.

"Cyla," Temar said softly.

"Tell me something important," Cyla almost begged. "I'm not going to go spreading rumors, but tell me one thing that's important." She looked from Temar to Shan, including him in the request.

Shan looked to Temar; he was clenching his fork like it was a lifeline in a sandstorm. From the way he chewed his lip, he didn't know what to say. Then again, when it was your own sibling, there was so much history, so many hurts and obligations, that it was hard to see past all that. Shan could see Cyla's vivid need to know she was still family, but he didn't know what Temar saw when he looked at her. Did he see the young woman who had led him into trouble on George Young's farm or the girl who had been with him as they survived their father's drunkenness? Based on his own tangled feelings for Naite, he figured Temar might not even know his own mind.

"We fixed the communications equipment and found that the war up there is over," Shan said quickly before he could change his mind.

For a second, both siblings stared at him with open mouths, but Cyla recovered faster. "The war? The war between the planets? Really?" Cyla stepped into the room, the anger falling away in an instant.

"Shhhh," Shan hushed her with a desperate look toward the windows. Telling Cyla was one thing; telling the whole farm would get him censured by the council, and Naite would skip the censure and jump right to killing him.

With a sigh and one last frown in Shan's direction, Temar nodded. "Really," Temar confirmed. "We weren't supposed to tell anyone because the council is going to go out to all the other towns and talk to them about what we should do." Temar looked right at Shan.

"The planets." Cyla breathed the words. "Earth and Loralei and Minga and Alpha-C and all of them? They're done fighting?"

"Cyla always loved the history of the planets in school. She used to play this game where we imagined what we would do if a new wave of colonists came down here after the war ended," Temar said, his voice growing softer.

Shan smiled at both Gazers. "I don't know if people are going to want to live in a world this barren, but who knows? The worlds up there may be ripped apart by war. Maybe some people will be moving down here."

Cyla sat in the chair opposite Shan, her mouth still open.

"That's why we have to get back to the relay, Cyla," Temar said. "Shan has to be there for the messages."

"And you?" Cyla asked sharply as she looked from one of them to the other.

"I don't want him out there alone. He shouldn't have to deal with this by himself." Temar took Cyla's hand. "But I can't worry about you making some mistake back here. That's why I was so hard on you yesterday."

"You were an ass," Cyla said softly.

"Well, I learned from the best." Temar didn't say it meanly, but he made it clear he didn't regret his words. "I told the council to back Naite if he brought a complaint against you, so please don't do anything stupid. Lilian has promised to get involved, and no one wants Lilian involved in this, especially not Naite."

Cyla tilted her head to one side. "Wait… why would you have to tell the council to side with Naite? If you lost your temper with me, why wouldn't you go to the council then?"

Shan stopped breathing as Cyla went right to the heart of the issue. She might be angry and hurting and more abrasive than Lilian and Naite combined, but she wasn't stupid. Usually. When she'd played detective on the George Young farm, leading to all the damage that had led to both of them getting sentenced to slavery… that had been spectacularly stupid, even in hindsight. Even Shan, who had a real lack of talent with making plans, could see that.

"I… um…." Temar winced and looked to Shan for help. The silence grew heavy as Cyla turned to him, waiting for the answer.

"The two of us are possible candidates for having to negotiate with this new alliance that's formed," Shan said. It was stretching the truth but not entirely breaking it, since Lilian and the others hadn't technically gotten approval from the other councils. One of the other councils might have their own team that they would propose as an alternative. And water might fall as rain out of the sky. No one went up against Lilian unless they had a very good reason. Shan mentally promised the Lord two prayers of contrition for the sin.

"You two?" Cyla didn't even hide her surprise.

"Yes, us. You don't have to sound surprised that someone might think we can negotiate," Temar said, the aggravation back in his voice.

"You can't even remember to eat without me nagging you," Cyla countered. "Why aren't they sending Lilian Freeland or Kevin Starwalker or even Bari Ruiz? Why you two?"

"They all have families, Cyla," Shan pointed out. "We don't."

"So?"

She still looked confused, but then it occurred to Shan that she probably assumed they would negotiate over the communicator, or maybe she thought this new alliance was coming to Livre. In hindsight, Shan should have suggested both those alternatives before committing someone to going to space. He'd been an idiot.

However, after reading how much those early settlers loathed the same world that made Shan feel so close to God, he'd almost felt like outsiders would corrupt his world. They certainly were going to look down on the people of Livre if they realized how poor they all were. The early settlers had complained bitterly about being limited to four hundred pounds of personal belongings, but Shan knew very few people who owned more than they could carry on their backs. He didn't want these people to see that. He felt no shame in poverty. Christ had lived in poverty and had made it abundantly clear that any person who wouldn't walk away from their possessions had no place in the kingdom of heaven. He simply didn't need to see these strangers dismiss them for the way they lived their lives.

"The negotiators will be traveling to a station six light-years away to discuss the terms of a trade," Shan explained.

Cyla lost every bit of color in her face. "But…. You can't…. Really?" The last word came out as a whisper.

"Really," Temar said. "So, I won't be here to try to get you and Naite to be nice to each other. Naite's the farm manager. You need to learn to be nice to him without me being there to distract him." Temar reached over and caught Cyla's hand.

Cyla gritted her teeth so hard the muscle on the side of her jaw stood out, but she didn't comment. Maybe she understood that Temar had changed… he wouldn't follow her blindly anymore. Shan picked up his fork and started eating again. He seriously hoped he wasn't leading Temar into another disaster by agreeing to leave the planet. They'd be trapped up there, relying on these people's need for optic-quality glass to earn them a treaty and a ride back home when they finished.

"Great pancakes," Shan offered when the silence continued a little too long. Temar pulled his hand away from his sister and nodded his agreement as he started eating his own. He muttered something that might have been, "Really good," but it was hard to tell with his mouth full.

"I just wanted to make sure you ate something," Cyla said, looking at Temar. Before either of them could answer, she got up from the table and headed for the other room. "You should get some seed. George Young would pay through the nose for some new genetic lines of wheat or corn to play with," she called out. Temar almost choked.

"Cyla, a little quieter, please," he begged as he left his plate and chased after her. Considering they were on a farm surrounded by workers, she really was talking a little too loud. She and Temar had grown up on their land without workers, but it was a different world here. There might be privacy on the upper levels, but not on the first floor, with workers wandering by the windows.

Low, insistent voices drifted in from the front room, but the actual words were lost in the general murmur of unhappy tones. A door slammed, and there was a dull thump as something hit the floor, but it didn't sound like a body, and as long as they weren't throwing fists, Shan figured he needed to stay out of their fight. Shan kept eating, watching the doorway until Temar returned, his shoulders angled as though carrying a weight heavy enough to take him down.

"She tells me I should stop trying to run her life," Temar said. He sat down and stared at his pancakes before pushing them away.

"You should eat."

"If I were hungry, I would," Temar answered sharply.

Shan put his fork down and watched Temar.

Slowly, Temar became aware of the scrutiny and he shifted in his chair, looking around before he finally demanded, "What?"

"If you aren't hungry after this morning's sex, I'm clearly too old to do it right," Shan said as he scooped up his last bite of pancakes and eyed the last one on the serving plate.

"You are not old."

"I'm older than you by a good ten or eleven years, and I'm feeling older than that if I can't even make you work up an appetite."

Temar frowned at Shan for a good minute. "You're trying to manipulate me into eating."

"Yep," Shan agreed with a smile. His plan worked, because Temar gave Shan an indulgent smile.

"Fine, I'll eat."

"Good, because you need to keep up your energy for ambush attacks," Shan said as he stabbed the last pancake and tried to pull it over to his plate. It disintegrated into a pile of pieces and crumbs that he had to scoop off the platter.

"She acts like she knows everything... like I'm being unreasonable and she's indulging me."

"So, she's acting like Naite?" Shan summed it up.

Temar snorted. "Yeah, but I like Naite better. At least he calls you an idiot and then does what he can to help. She calls me an idiot and then stands around to repeat it until I agree." Temar shoved a large bite of pancake into his mouth.

"She'll grow up," Shan said. Temar gave him a quizzical look. "Some people take longer than others. Until I was thirty-one, I was hiding in the church because I didn't want to deal with relationships and feelings and fears that I couldn't understand."

Temar swallowed, coughed, and grabbed for a glass of water. "Hiding?" he asked. "You were a great priest. People loved you."

"I was hiding as a priest. I couldn't remember Biblical passages, I fixed the church roof more often than I went out of my way to counsel members of that church, and I was generally confused. And if people loved me it was because I never told them the hard truths I should have. Maybe if I had talked more about hell and the need for confession and forgiveness, Ben wouldn't have gotten out of hand."

"You think... do you really blame yourself for that?" Temar leaned forward, his bright blue eyes focused intensely on Shan.

"Most days, no," he admitted. He stopped, swallowing as an old memory caught him.

"Shan?" Temar's hand rested on his arm.

Part of Shan wanted to push his memory away, but that felt disrespectful, both of the lover who wanted to be part of his life and the mother who had loved him. "Have I told you about my mother?"

Temar shook his head.

As a child, Shan would sit on the step after Naite had gone to school and watch her in the fields with his father and the one worker they could afford to hire. "She was really something. She used to get out there and have furrow races with the hired worker and my father to see who could plant a row without missing a spot or ruining a seedling. She had this laugh... like she couldn't stop until she was out of breath and grabbing for something to keep her upright. She lived so big." Shan stopped, his emotions threatening to escape their reins.

"Did she die in childbirth?" Temar asked. It was a logical question, since so many did, either because of the lack of water, the lack of the right nutrients, or the lack of any real medical help, but Shan shook his head.

"No, she got hurt on the farm, and an infection set in."

Temar's fingers tightened on Shan's arm. "I'm sorry."

When Shan breathed in, the sound stuttered for a moment as he tried to focus on what he wanted to say. This wasn't about him throwing himself a pity party. "When she was alive, my father would sometimes get... not angry, exactly. It was more like he wanted revenge on anyone who hurt him, even when it was only one of his sons making a stupid mistake. But Mom would step in and read him the riot act. She'd pull him to one side and rip into him in this soft voice." Shan tried to figure out how to explain what he was feeling.

Temar watched intently. "What would she say?"

"I honestly don't know. I'd catch a few words of it. She'd talk about his father, talk about the future. Sometimes I'd hear her talk about God or Div, who was the priest even back then. But she'd have this intensity, and Dad's anger would turn into this embarrassment that would make him avoid the house until it was so late that Naite and I had gone to bed." Shan pushed his plate away. "She reminded him that he needed to be good. She never raised her voice, but she would tear into him with this intense tone that would make him stop and really think about what he was doing. Sometimes Div would do that when people came to see him for counseling. But Temar, I never did. I never tried to warn people away from doing evil, so I can't pretend that I didn't have some part in the evil that grew in Landing."

Temar reared back. "You can't blame yourself for the fact that other people chose to be evil."

"I was a council member. I was the priest. Who else is supposed to stop evil?"

"I don't know, maybe the people who are being evil?" Temar had this expression of utter confusion on his face.

Shan scratched his chin. He hadn't shaved yet, and he itched. "But I certainly didn't have any inspiration from God when it came to Ben and his schemes."

"And neither did anyone else. I was happy when he bought my contract," Temar pointed out. "Shan, you're not responsible for anyone else."

"Am I my brother's keeper?" Shan whispered. Taking refuge in Cain's excuse didn't seem like a particularly good idea, but then again, Cain had committed murder. Chronic naïveté seemed like Shan's worst sin. He hadn't understood himself or his calling or Ben.

"No, you aren't," Temar said firmly. "You didn't see Ben's evil, and you thought my father was evil when he was really just weak, and I thought you were some stuffy priest who didn't have a life beyond reading the Bible all week so he could preach on Sunday. Clearly we all have some version of sandblindness that only affects how well we see other people."

Shan lowered his voice until it was little more than a whisper. "So, the planet is relying on two idiots to negotiate a treaty?"

Temar made an expression of exaggerated horror. "We're all doomed."

Shan laughed, the negative emotions slipping back into the shadows of his mind. "If we don't live up to Lilian's expectations, we will be."

"Then we'd better start doing a little research."

"Research? On what?" Shan asked.

Temar stared at Shan in surprise. After a second, he leaned in closer and whispered in an earnest voice, "Which chemicals did they want to export? Where are the mineral deposits? What did they need other than optic-quality glass? How much optic-quality glass did they hope to export every year? How much water did we get shorted in the terraforming? How have the prices of raw materials changed in the last eighty years?"

Shan leaned back in his chair, shocked at how much of an idiot he'd been. He knew all about the colonists' machines, and he'd read their diaries and their journals. He knew how they saw Livre, and how much they'd hated it. He knew a lot of things, but listening to Temar's quick list, he didn't know anything important.

"Clearly, I'm a moron."

"What? No, you aren't," Temar quickly disagreed.

"No, really I am." Shan shook his head at his own foolishness. "Well, it sounds like we have some researching to do in the next week. I'm sure we can find the answers either in the relay station computers or in one of the downloads." Shan broke off as he heard the door slam. He was on his feet, his heart pounding for no good reason, as Naite walked in the door.

chapter
thirteen

TEMAR COULD see the way Shan relaxed once only Naite appeared in the doorway. They were both as jumpy as sandrats. The council would have been better off choosing negotiators who didn't start at shadows, but Temar suspected it was too late to change plans now, and he wasn't going to allow Shan to go off world alone. Naite sat down at the table, shadows under his eyes. Grabbing an apple, he looked at the serving platter. "I don't suppose you saved any food?"

"We would have if we'd known you were coming back this morning," Shan answered, and he already had an edge to his voice.

This time Naite didn't rise to the bait. He gave a grunt and started eating the apple. "I'm heading out to Blue Hope this morning, so load your bike and let's get moving."

Temar exchanged a concerned look with Shan. Naite didn't look awake enough to drive anywhere, much less a full day across the deepest part of the desert.

"Did you get any sleep last night?" Shan asked carefully. He still earned a nasty glare from Naite.

"I'm fine," Naite snapped.

"But did you sleep?" Temar asked. It was a valid question, one that Naite wasn't answering.

Naite gave a huge sigh and considered Temar for a long time. They had an unusual relationship. In a lot of ways, Temar turned to Naite for advice. He'd run a farm and he'd learned to live with nightmares so vivid they could make a man break out in a cold sweat and wake up screaming. On the other hand, technically, Temar owned Naite and would for another two years. Naite had certain beliefs about slavery and what it meant, even if Temar never enforced any rules with Naite. With another sigh, Naite finally answered. "No, we debated until after dark, and then I spent the night waking people up and gathering supplies."

"If the council is trying to keep things quiet, waking people up to gather supplies isn't the best way to do that," Shan said, disgust in his voice.

"I'll make sure the council knows you disapprove of their methods," Naite answered dryly.

"What supplies?" Temar asked before Shan and Naite could get into it.

Naite got up and headed over to the sink for a glass of water. "Dee'eta sent quite a bit of glass." Normally Naite's voice boomed loud enough to be heard across fields, but he kept it soft. "She said she has more to send later in the week, optic-quality, but she sent along supplies of various forms and colors of glass she produces. Bari pulled together a database of family names. He figures there will be folks who want to know where their distant cousins got to."

Temar cringed. They would have cousins out there in space, cousins who might not appreciate the fact that the council had condemned more than a hundred and fifty people to death—forty-three from Landing alone.

"Kevin sent along some finer pieces of woodworking, and Lilian is coordinating the council, gathering up all damaged tech to send up with you. I think she's hoping you two can talk them into fixing a few hundred datapads, communicators, computers, optic lines, motherboard chips, and random crap." Naite finished and then drank his water in huge gulps.

"Can we take that much up?" Temar asked, turning to Shan.

Shan shrugged. "Probably we can. These systems are usually designed for carrying raw materials, so if you don't have a big enough lift payload, it isn't worth the fuel it takes to break away from gravity."

"Yeah, well I'm not going to hold my breath on you getting the shit fixed, but most of it is trash if we can't get it repaired, so no loss there." Naite put his glass back on the counter. "Bylla is outside with the hauler, and we're scheduled to be in Blue Hope before the end of the day, so move like you have sandcats on your ass."

"Bylla?" Shan asked.

Temar looked at Shan, surprised he didn't recognize the name of the new priest. "Bylla Sullivan, the priest," he said softly.

Shan cringed. "Oh." He didn't hide his embarrassment at not knowing the woman's name.

Naite snorted.

"And has she had any sleep?" Shan demanded.

Sometimes Shan's emotions changed so fast that Temar couldn't keep up, and his anxiety rose as Shan's soft shame at his own ignorance turned to a sharp verbal jab.

"We can all sleep after we're sure they aren't going to blow us all up," Naite snapped back.

Temar stepped between the brothers. "Why don't you and Bylla grab pillows and throws and set up beds in back. You two can sleep during the drive out to the relay station." Naite's mouth came open, but Temar talked faster, before he could be interrupted. Sometimes it was an advantage owning Naite, because he tended to limit how rude he'd get with Temar. "Shan will even promise to drive slower and more carefully than he normally does. No extending the sails and letting the hauler head straight down the side of a dune." Temar frowned at Shan.

After a second, Shan gave a small nod. "I can do that," he agreed. "Naite, why is the council risking this getting out? There may not be many communicators, but a few of the rescue teams have them, and you know that a dozen kids have trained hawks to carry messages. This is going to fuel rumors."

"It's going to get out that something big is going on, but a little panic will convince the others to act quickly. With the shuttle coming in a week, Lilian thinks the biggest danger is people wanting to debate this to death. So, we're putting the planet on notice that something big is happening, and by the time it comes out that the inner planets are coming back, hopefully they'll all be willing to back us since we're already in place."

Temar could understand the logic. Lilian might be manipulative, but she was right that they didn't have time to debate when the inner worlds were ready to show up on their doorstep. None of them even knew what the worlds wanted out of them. "It makes a twisted sort of sense."

"Lilian's plans usually do," Naite said. "I'll grab some pillows and tell Bylla we're bunking in back, but"—Naite poked a finger in Shan's direction—"so much as one suicide slide down a dune, and I'm throwing you under the hauler."

Shan rolled his eyes as Naite stalked out of the kitchen. The second Naite left, the tension level in the room dropped, and Temar took a deep breath.

"Please tell me that I don't act that bad when Cyla's in the room," Temar asked.

Shan looked over. "Are we that bad?"

"Yes." Temar grabbed the plates from the table and stacked them on the counter. "So, what are we taking with us?"

"All my belongings are at the station." Shan frowned, a furrow between his eyes. Temar hoped Shan wasn't about to call him on his fight with Dee'eta. Putting the leftover food in the cooling unit, Temar silently cursed Cyla for bringing that up. However, Temar finished with the food, and Shan still had the same frown.

Temar went to Shan's side and rested his hand on Shan's arm. "What's wrong?"

Shan shook his head and the frown vanished, replaced with a more thoughtful expression. "They're going to think we're ignorant, poor people. I don't know how we're going to get them to take us seriously."

"Poor?" Temar sometimes had trouble believing it, but he was one of the richest people on Livre, right up with George Young and Lilian herself. If the rumors were right that she planned to divide her farm between three of her children, Temar would be one of the two richest people on Livre after her death.

"Every single one of them owned hundreds of pounds of possessions. They would change clothing every day and sometimes during the day because they didn't like how sand felt against their skin."

Temar's mouth fell open. They didn't like how sand felt? This was Livre. There was sand in the clothing, the food, the sheep's wool when they sheared them, and the goat's hooves. Sand came in through windows every time a sandstorm raged over the valley walls. In town, things were even worse. There, the sand could drift up to turn the center road into an obstacle course. Parents would hang nets over cribs to keep the dust off young children when they slept. "They'd change clothes to get rid of sand?" Temar asked, not sure he could wrap his mind around the concept.

Shan nodded. "They did. I've read their journals, and they seem almost offended that their children would come in with so much dust clinging to their clothes that they'd track sand throughout the house."

"Why immigrate to Livre if you don't like sand?" Sand was a way of life, even if you weren't on one of the rescue teams that would go out after lost travelers or some craftsman who would head out into deep desert for salts or arsenic for glassmaking. Those people loved the desert, but even the town-born craftsman who never set foot on deep desert accepted sand as part of life.

With a sigh, Shan shrugged at his own ignorance. "For the money, I guess. Some wanted to make a fortune and go home. A few of the early settlers did leave when they lifted the exports off-planet."

Temar looked around at his neat home, with the metal struts that had been stripped straight off a drop ship. "Did any of them come here planning on building homes and families?" He felt a little like a child who had just learned that Saint Nicholas didn't live at the top of the White Mountains. He wanted to think their ancestors had come here to build a new world, a better one. He didn't want to think they were as selfish and greedy as the inner planets who had abandoned them.

"Some did." Shan sighed. "I haven't read all the journals. I know one man came here seeking God."

Temar tried hard to resist an urge to roll his eyes. He loved Shan and he respected the man's faith in God, but the church had been a pleasant place for Temar to escape from life—not a house of God. And if there was a God, he hadn't shown much interest in Temar's life. "So, these were materialistic people? Is that what's bothering you?"

"No, it's…." Shan took a deep breath and started over. "If they don't respect us, are they going to treat us fairly? They're going to assume we're dirty if we don't change our clothes every day. If they know that most of us don't own much more than would fit on the back of a sand cycle, will they assume we'll trade away our world for a bag of toys?" Shan ran a hand over his face. "I'm probably overreacting."

Temar walked over and rested his hand against Shan's shoulder as he leaned into him. "The night you found me here—" Temar stopped. For a moment, he could feel the rope around his wrists, a ghost impression that made him scratch the skin.

"You don't have to talk about it," Shan said.

Temar took a step back and shook his head. "I was going to the bathroom down here when I saw a figure out in the field."

Shan frowned, obviously not following the conversation.

"There's a toilet on the second floor," Temar pointed out, looking up toward the second story. "I came down here because I had this ridiculous idea that if there was a little more space between me and Ben, it mattered. It didn't. I mean, my hands were tied, and it didn't matter what bathroom I used, but I came down here because I wanted a few more yards between me and the man who...." Temar swallowed and then forced the words past the lump in his throat. "Who raped me."

"I wish I could do something to erase all that." Shan looked absolutely miserable, and that hadn't been Temar's point.

Shaking his head, Temar walked to the door where he'd first seen Shan out in the field. "I wasn't logical. People aren't logical," Temar said, struggling to explain what he was feeling. "We can't expect logic from human beings no matter what planet they're from, so I think you're right that they're going look down on us."

Shan blew out a breath and closed his eyes. The expression on his face made Temar suspect that Shan had hoped he would dismiss the idea as paranoid. However, Shan was right. "So, what? We take a lot of changes of clothing?" Shan asked. He blinked several times and got a more thoughtful look on his face. "Actually, that might not be a bad idea."

"We could find out about fashion. Do the men wear jewelry? Is there some material that implies wealth?"

"So, we con them?" Shan smiled.

"I wouldn't call it conning them as much as finding our inner Lilian Freeland and embracing the power of manipulation," Temar said. He remembered how Ben would come on strong, his wide smile distracting everyone from the corruption inside. Manipulation worked better than most people wanted to admit. And if it took a little manipulating to protect his home, he could do that.

"Our inner Lilian, huh?" Shan smiled. "If we can do that, they'll never know what hit them."

Temar was still looking out the door, so when Shan patted him on the shoulder, Temar jerked and gave a little gasp. Immediately, Shan pulled his hand back, his smile fading. Hating his own weakness, Temar caught Shan's hand and pulled him closer until Temar could lean back into Shan's strength. Without a word, Shan carefully wrapped his arms around Temar. "We'll win," Temar said softly. "I don't know what we'll win, but we'll win." Shan's arms tightened a little more, and Temar let his head fall back against Shan's shoulder. They would. Neither of them would accept anything less.

chapter
fourteen

TEMAR LOOKED at the cramped storage room in amazement. The relay station rooms were obscenely large, large enough for several families to live in comfortably. However, after one week of unloading broken machines, trade goods, and raw materials, Temar was fairly sure they couldn't fit another thing into the station. Shan was only sleeping two or three hours a night as he tried to sort the machines he could fix from those that truly needed the attention of the inner planets, and Temar had a bone-deep weariness that grew deeper with the coming trip.

"It's good to see this world rejoin the universe before I go," Lilian said as she leaned against the doorway.

"You aren't going anywhere," Temar said.

Lilian gave a soft laugh. "I might be known for getting my way, but if you talk to Shan, he'll tell you that not even my powers will convince God to change the rules of mortality."

"I try to avoid the topic of God," Temar said, the words slipping out before he could edit himself. Lilian looked at him curiously, but she remained silent. The quiet dragged out into minutes, and Temar shifted uncomfortably. A tiny, old woman shouldn't make him so uncomfortable.

"He has his beliefs, and I'm fine with that. I just don't share them," Temar explained when it became clear that Lilian wasn't planning to move on until her curiosity was sated. She gave a single nod, and Temar felt like he had failed some test. He might respect Lilian, but he was supremely glad she wasn't his mother. He wouldn't have survived her tacit disappointment.

The silence continued, but Lilian didn't seem to mind. Again, Temar shifted uncomfortably. When Temar had appeared in front of the council, Lilian had voted in favor of his slavery, just as Naite, Dee'eta, and Kevin had done. All these people insisted they owed him because they'd sentenced him to years of service to a man who had abused him. Temar figured Ben carried the blame for that, and maybe he carried a little of the blame himself because he'd screwed up and ended up in front of the council in the first place. However, these people he'd grown up admiring all blamed themselves for not checking on him or protecting him. He never knew how to feel around most of them. Naite made it a little easier by snapping at him about how the farm was run and distracting him from any discomfort, but Lilian was harder to understand. She'd paid an outrageous fine to him in the form of a herd of goats, nearly forty meat cavies, crop seed, and an extra allotment of water, but she'd never said one word about his enslavement. By the time Lilian cleared her throat, Temar was on the edge of a panic. "His beliefs often lead him to make the right choice when others make easy choices," she said quietly.

"I know that." Temar frowned, wondering where that had come from. He knew better than anyone just how good a heart Shan had.

Lilian looked at him. "His choices are sometimes better than his execution."

Temar studied a stack of broken datapads. He didn't have an answer for that. Sure, it was true. Naite had pointed that out loudly and colorfully more than once. On the other hand, Shan was his lover, and Temar trusted the man... trusted him absolutely. He didn't want to have a conversation with Lilian Freeland about his lover's faults.

Lilian fell silent again, and Temar started mentally casting around for any safe topic to discuss. "I found the original economic and manufacturing charter."

"Shan said you were interested in finding what these people might want. An excellent plan." The compliment surprised Temar.

"Thank you. Shan is so busy trying to figure out where to have them land the shuttle and how to sort the equipment that I don't think he has time to really think about the people we're meeting."

"And I imagine that you're a little more cautious about what people might want."

Temar sucked in a breath. He hadn't thought about why he was researching, but in that one line, Lilian had implied that Ben had taught him a caution... a paranoia... that Temar didn't want to see in himself. He wanted to be the same person who had followed his sister, trusting her to understand the world better than he did. He wanted to think that, even though he knew that he would never follow her into George's fields now. Looking back, he could hardly believe he'd been so naïve. Instead of spending too much time thinking about what Lilian had said, Temar focused on the facts he'd found.

"They actually wanted a number of materials from Livre. Antimony trioxide is used by ships to put out fires, zirconium for weapons, lanthanum oxide for displays, and tantalum for medical and scientific equipment. Livre is sitting on enough rare elements that they'd pay a fortune to have all the sand of our deserts up in their ship."

"Which means they'll be willing to fight for it," Lilian mused.

Temar didn't answer, but he figured she was right.

"I'm too old to have this conversation standing up," Lilian said softly before she turned around and headed into the living areas. Shan was using the living room for sorting equipment, so she had to weave her way around piles to reach the couch. Sitting down, she rested a finger against her lips. Temar followed her, staying close to the exit. He considered leaving her, but dozens of workers were outside, placing markers the shuttle or airship would need to land. Shan had explained the scoop and skip two-ship system for off-planet flights, but Temar honestly didn't understand it. He was used to glass that moved slowly, sluggishly. When you applied too much heat, the molten mass would start to run, the heavy drops bending toward gravity, but Temar honestly couldn't wrap his mind around ships that flew fast enough to leave a planet. Physics had never been his favorite science.

Shan came into the room, wiping his hands on his pants before he went to clasp her hands in greeting. "Lilian? When did you get here?"

"I thought I would see how many people were helping. I see that you're almost buried in assistance," she said with some amusement.

Temar watched them as Shan sat next to Lilian on the couch. He was much bigger than her, but he still sat far enough away that it was as if her personal space was much larger than her body.

Shan smiled at her before turning his smile toward Temar. "We're taking off tomorrow. I think everyone wants to have some part in this."

Lilian added, "And many have donated goods to send up."

Shan laughed. "Yes, but I'm not sure it counts as a donation when you hope to get fair market value for it on the other end."

"True." Lilian gave a small laugh of her own, her eyes scanning the room until they found Temar. She watched him, her forefinger brushing over her lip. "People have a lot of hopes resting on this flight."

"Is that supposed to motivate us or terrify us?" Shan asked. Temar could see the dark shadows under his eyes. He had worked long, hard hours, with Naite being the only one to work harder. Hannal had come, setting up a kitchen to feed the workers, with most of the farms in Landing, Hope Valley, and Zhang all sending what food they could, along with workers. Long rows of radio markers lined the sands north of the relay, where a low set of rocky hills created a rough break where the larger barchan dunes rarely drifted; the people from space insisted that their craft could land on sand as long as the sand didn't then bury the ship. Even Cyla had taken to running regular hauler loads between the three valleys and the relay. Temar wasn't sure why that surprised him, because Cyla always had been a hard worker, but he still felt some shock at her willingness to drive long, hard hours for people who were too tired to offer much thanks. It was as if the entire planet had been turned on its side in the course of a week.

"I am simply offering up my view of reality," Lilian said.

"Uh-huh." Shan didn't sound particularly convinced.

"You're growing suspicious in your old age, Shan."

"I'm not old."

"But you are growing suspicious," Lilian pointed out. "I think I'm grateful for a little suspicion in this mess." She leaned back and shook her head. "Then again, you were the only one suspicious of slavery, so perhaps the emotion is more a part of you than I've given you credit for."

"You're worried," Temar said from the doorway. He came closer, stopping on the far side of a number of broken vacuum seals.

"I am," Lilian agreed. "We have much that they want. I came here hoping that one of you would make me feel better about sending you up there like this without any help."

"You think we're in danger," Temar said, his guts knotting. He knew what helplessness felt like, and he hated the idea of heading back into a situation where he might face it again.

"Do you think it's that bad?" Shan wiped his hands against his pants over and over. "I know it's going to be a hard negotiation, but do you think it's actually dangerous?" Shan looked over toward Temar, and Temar worked hard to keep his face neutral.

For a time, Lilian sat with her wrinkled finger tapping against her cheek, her expression thoughtful. "I think if it is that bad, we're all in a difficult situation. What they want is down here, so if they're desperate, I don't know where one would find safety."

Temar's knotted stomach tightened until he nearly threw up the lunch Hannal had fixed. "You think they'll attack?"

Lilian pursed her lips and shook her head. "I doubt they'd be that crass. I would expect a politician to find a much neater way of getting what he wants without having to resort to crude means, at least not in the open where anyone might see him."

Shan leaned back. "So you think they'll try to manipulate us?"

"I would," Lilian answered. "If you had what I desperately needed, I would smile and manipulate and convince you to think of me as your best friend and savior."

"And you're afraid we're going to fall for that?" Temar asked, not sure whether he should be offended or angry. Maybe both. He wasn't some child who couldn't see past a slick way with words, and neither was Shan. He stepped farther into the room, crossing his arms over his chest. Oddly, Lilian smiled at him, tilting her head in a way that might look coy on a younger woman.

"I'm afraid you two are working yourselves to death. I'm afraid you're going to make errors in judgment because you're so busy preparing things that you aren't preparing yourselves," Lilian said in a matter-of-fact tone.

Temar didn't think that was true of himself. He'd sat at a console, poking buttons and searching for information—he hadn't been physically laboring. However, he did know it was true of Shan. The man looked exhausted, and in one week, his muscles had bulked up considerably as he worked long hours hauling rope through the sands to mark out landing areas and sorting equipment.

"We're fine," Shan said with a roll of his eyes. "Neither of us needs mothering, Lilian."

"That is not how I hear Hannal describe it," Lilian said dryly. "Now, Hannal is likely to exaggerate some. Despite her sharp tongue, she has an exceptionally soft heart, and when Naite comments that you look worn to nothing, I take note."

"Naite?" Shan almost growled the name, but Lilian didn't seem impressed.

"He's right," Temar said, quick to take advantage of the situation. Shan needed rest, both sleep and a chance to stop thinking about how many people were relying on them. "We need to take a break. They'll be here tomorrow, and we're in no shape to meet anyone. They won't be impressed with either of us if we have bags under our eyes." Temar included himself in that to try to ease the insult, but now that Temar was really paying attention, Shan looked like he'd passed exhaustion two seasons back.

"Once we get on the airship, it'll take a good hour or two to run checks for the takeoff. Then we hold low orbit while the shuttle comes in for the scoop, and after that we have to stay in the airship while the shuttle maneuvers in-system. We'll be stuck in our seats for a good six to ten hours before we hit subspace and the ship opens internal ports. I can sleep then."

Lilian raised a white eyebrow. "After you've already ruined your chance to make a notable first impression? I've seen the jewelry Nual made for you two. If you dishonor his calcite and malachite jewelry by looking so disreputable that it fails to make an impression, that man will not forgive you. Nor should he."

"Shan," Temar said softly, but he could see by the set of Shan's jaw that he had his back up. Lilian shouldn't have mentioned Naite. That tactical error could cost her. "We're both exhausted. The goal here is to impress the inner planets, not to sort equipment or even track the daily price of arsenic salts." Shan was still frowning, but his jaw muscle had eased some. Temar moved closer, intentionally uncrossing his arms even if Lilian did leave him disquieted. "We need to keep the goal in mind, so let someone else sort the rest and if we leave a few datapads behind or don't have the most up-to-date commodity prices, that's not going to be the end of the world."

"I'm more concerned about taking up equipment that could be easily fixed and having them think we're incompetent," Shan pointed out.

"If I look as worn out as you do, they're going to think that anyway."

Lilian leaned back and steepled her fingers as she watched with poorly hidden amusement.

"I think I look worse," Shan admitted after a few minutes. "If Naite is worried about me, I must look like shit."

"You do," Temar agreed.

Shan gave him a disgusted look, and Temar held up his hands in a placating gesture. "I love you and I will always think you handsome, but you look like shit," he repeated.

"You two are ganging up on me," Shan complained wearily.

Temar knew one offer that Shan wouldn't turn down. "If you take the rest of the day and tonight off, I'll have Hannal send over an entire feast."

Sitting forward on the couch, Shan studied him carefully. "Yes, but will you eat it?"

"As much as I can," Temar offered.

Ironically, he was eating more now. He'd sit at the computer and absentmindedly work his way through the cheeses or breads Hannal would send in. He'd even started gaining a little weight. The irony was that Shan nagged twice as much as Cyla had. Even with Temar's improved eating habits, he acted like Temar wanted to starve himself. He didn't. He just didn't often get hungry, and sometimes waves of weariness or nausea would roll through. He'd smell the sweat of some worker coming through carrying boxes, and it was as if Ben was there, his sweat-stink filling Temar's nose. The memory would return so vividly that any food Temar had eaten recently would end up in the toilet. Sometimes he wondered if he would ever recover completely.

"I'll sleep if you'll eat," Shan finally agreed as he stood up. Then he turned to Lilian. "But only if you agree to stop nagging."

"Nagging? Me?" She smiled sweetly. "I manipulate, connive, beguile, control, and finesse. I do not nag." She gave Shan a haughty expression, but as she stood, she gasped and grabbed the arm of the couch. Shan sprang forward and caught her, one hand around her waist, but immediately, she started batting at him. "I'm fine. Good Lord, you fuss. You and Kevin are both enough to drive an old woman to drink," she complained, pushing at Shan until he retreated, all offers to help her withdrawn. "So, go sleep before you fall down, and you." She pointed a thin finger toward Temar. He expected her to order him to get something to eat, but she surprised him. "Make sure he's not sneaking out in the middle of the night to sort broken bits."

"Yes, ma'am," Temar answered.

Lilian gave him a little wink before she headed for the door. "And I'm telling Hannal that you wanted a celebratory feast, just the two of you. You'll have Wistia writing new ballads about your grand, romantic gestures." Lilian snorted to make her opinion on the matter of romantic gestures clear. With that, she left, although Temar suspected she wasn't through yet.

Shan sighed as the door closed behind her. "Does she scare you as much as me?"

"Yes," Temar agreed emphatically.

Shan sank back down onto the couch. "Half of me wonders if she wouldn't be better for this job, even as sick as she is."

"One of us could develop some pain or something," Temar said weakly. He doubted anyone would truly believe either of them succumbing to a convenient attack of inexplicable pain, but no one would force them to go up either. "She'd go if there wasn't anyone else to take the job." He didn't like the idea, but if Shan really thought Lilian was their best choice, he wouldn't argue, either.

Shan looked at him, his mouth open in shock. "You want to try to manipulate Lilian Freeland?"

"Don't you think it would work?"

Closing his mouth with an audible click of his teeth, Shan shrugged. "It might, it might not. I just want to take a second to appreciate the audacity of anyone with the balls to try to manipulate Lilian. If she guts you, I'll go to your funeral."

Temar rolled his eyes as he crossed the room to sit next to Shan. "Are you serious about wanting her to go up?"

That seemed to require some thought. Finally Shan shook his head. "No, but I am going to secretly curse the universe for not having this happen ten years ago. Lilian would have terrified them into handing over entire planets."

Temar nodded without answering, but he wasn't so convinced. Ever since Shan had brought up the need to hide their poverty, Temar kept having the strangest ideas. Watching people slowly bend to Lilian the way hot glass yielded to gravity and fire, he wondered whether she would have the same power on a station. On Livre, her herds and fields were wealth. Her position on the largest council on Livre was power. But would people from another planet see that? Would her fire and gravity be too weak to make them bend the way she maneuvered the people of Livre?

"So, I should clean up, or the sheets are going to be disgusting in the morning," Shan said, and he suddenly sounded twice as weary. Shan used the arm of the sofa to push himself up. Lilian was right—he needed rest.

"I'll check on the food and power down the computer," Temar said. Shan didn't answer as he moved slowly into the bedroom.

chapter
fifteen

STANDING IN the bathroom, Temar watched as Shan rolled to his other side and pulled viciously at the pillow. Hannal had taken the leftovers from their dinner, and Temar was uncomfortably full. Shan seemed uncomfortable as well, turning again.

"I promise to stop rolling around if you'll just come to bed, Temar," Shan called. Sitting up, he scooted toward the top of the bed and wrapped his arms around his knees. He had such strong shoulders, but Temar didn't normally notice. Most of the time, he preferred to watch Shan's hands.

"I'm really not tired," Temar said as he came into the room. He hid a small vial in his hands. He didn't know if Shan had left it for him in the bathroom or if one of their well-intentioned guests had, but it had juice from a gakka plant. They were a relative of the wisp grass that grew in the deepest valleys of the dunes, only a thick, succulent trunk-like stalk that rose out of the center and deep roots that could tap into the only source of native water on Livre, an unconfined aquifer that shifted as often as the sands, making wells pointless. Gatherers would sometimes go out and split open a stalk and take some of the thick, sap-like juice before carefully tying the stalk back together so the plant could heal; however, doing that meant risking your ankles, if not your life. Sandrats and sandcats always congregated around the gakka.

"You're not going to go back to that computer, are you?" Shan asked. Temar shook his head. "Good, because I think you're as exhausted as I am." With a sigh, Shan threw himself down on his side and pulled at his pillow. "And despite the fact I'm exhausted, I'm never going to get to sleep. I should have taken Hannal up on her offer of a sedative tea." Shan turned over to face the wall.

The light was low, the red of the setting sun leaking in around the sole window's covering. It created soft shadows all over the room as Temar sat on his side of the bed. His side. A week they'd both slept here, but other than claiming sides of the bed, nothing had happened. Other than the one night when Shan had rolled over in his sleep, an arm draping over Temar's chest possessively so that Temar had woken in a cold sweat. But Shan hadn't tried to push. Then again, Shan hadn't been sleeping for more than three hours a night, and he'd been too distracted with broken computers and machines to notice Temar.

Temar slipped under the light sheet and inched closer, lust and need and fear all wrapped around his spine so tight he felt like he might break. He was scared of this, but he wanted it. He needed to stop thinking too much and start acting—start taking back his life. Temar leaned forward and kissed Shan's shoulder.

Shan started to turn, and Temar caught a glimpse of a smile, but he pushed against Shan's shoulder, pressing him down onto his stomach before Temar straddled his waist. "Is this an ambush?" Shan asked as he yielded.

"Yes," Temar said, his voice sounding more firm than he really felt, but watching Shan's strong back lying under him, Temar's cock definitely wanted this. "I found this in the bathroom." Temar put the vial next to Shan, on the pillow, as he rested his hands against Shan's shoulders, giving him the illusion that he'd pinned Shan to the bed. Shan certainly didn't protest as Temar started rubbing small circles against his neck.

"Someone likes us," Shan said with a low chuckle. "Maybe Wistia's ballads aren't completely worthless."

There really was only one activity people used raw gakka juice for. Leaning close, Temar whispered in Shan's ear, "Do you want to?"

"Oh yes. I want it, but it's been a long time, Temar. You probably need to move slow."

"So, a slow ambush? I can do that." Smiling, Temar reached down for the bottle and pulled the glass stopper. The unmistakable spice of gakka drifted through the room.

"Do you want—"

"Shhh," Temar said. "Just let me ambush you here."

Shan chuckled again and tucked his hands under his pillow. "Feel free."

Temar let his weight rest on Shan's back as he pushed the sheet away, revealing Shan's well-curved ass, barely hidden by thin sleep pants. Temar took a moment to run his hand over the warm flesh, enjoying the feel of Shan shivering below him. Leaning down, he kissed Shan's shoulder, nipping at the skin before he peppered a line of kisses down Shan's body, feeling his back muscles twitch as Temar finally reached the small of Shan's back, just above the waistband. Sucking on the skin, he could taste the salt.

Arching his back, Shan let out a long, hissing breath as Temar teased the warm skin for a moment before scooting down the bed and sliding his hand under the fabric of the sleep pants, exploring the curve of Shan's butt and brushing teasingly over his hole. Making a sound between a gasp and a grunt, Shan spread his legs in invitation, but Temar pulled away and considered the body laid out in front of him, waiting for him. Taking the bottle in hand, Temar let a small amount of thick, white juice run out onto his fingers, the gakka warming them slightly.

Temar slipped his hand back under the waistband and ran his slicked fingers down the crevice to the entrance of Shan's hole, stroking the sensitive skin and then farther up to the perineum and to the bulge where the scrotum started. Letting his slicked fingers glide back and forth, Temar gave the gakka time to warm the skin. His finger started to tingle about the same time Shan started squirming, his hips thrusting down into the bed as he made hungry little noises.

Retrieving the glass stopper and pressing it firmly into place, Temar set the vial to one side and started pulling Shan's sleep pants down over the round of his ass and then to his thighs. That allowed him to blow over the gakka-stained skin. Shan arched up off the bed, gasping loudly. "God, yes." Shan's voice was a raspy cry.

Temar pressed himself against Shan's back, reaching around to tweak Shan's nipples while the man was bracing himself on his arms. Bearing down on Shan's back, made Shan's arms tremble, but Temar continued to rest on Shan's back as he pulled at Shan's nipples.

"Temar," Shan gasped out, and Temar pulled his hands out of the way just as Shan collapsed onto the bed, panting heavily. The vial bounced and started to roll for the edge before Temar grabbed for it, saving it at the last second. "Oh God," Shan gasped, thrusting down into the mattress again. His back was fever-hot now, sweat gathering along his spine.

Licking his lips, Temar considered his next move. Shan writhed on the bed, the gakka doing its work. Moving to the foot of the bed, Temar pushed Shan's sleep pants off, and immediately Shan threw his legs open wide, his hips slowing, although he still made little thrusts down into the mattress. Temar ran his teeth over Shan's backside, his right hand over the small of Shan's back before trailing fingers down the crack to his entrance. Shan started moaning softly, pressing his face into the pillow.

Temar ghosted his finger over Shan's entrance before slowly pressing one finger against the ring. The muscle yielded easily, and Temar slipped his finger inside that warmth. Shan allowed him in, opened to him, and Temar pressed deep into that heat as he pressed kisses against Shan's back.

"Please, Temar," Shan moaned. "Please. Please." Every breath turned into a plea, a mantra Shan murmured continuously as Temar pressed deep inside, letting the gakka warm the skin, relaxing it so Shan would open easily. Temar had felt the rushed pain of a hurried coupling and the incredible pleasure of a slow one, and he knew what he wanted for Shan. The moment he nudged the prostate, Shan's pleas grew in volume, and he arched his back, his shoulders coming up off the mattress again. The hairs at the back of his neck curled and stuck to the skin as the sweat soaked into them.

"Ready?" Temar asked.

Shan groaned louder. "I want you in me."

Retrieving the vial, Temar poured another dollop out onto his fingers and then put the rest on the side table, knocking a datapad off in the process. Temar figured Shan was truly lost in his own need when he didn't even react to the sound of the datapad clattering against the tile floor.

Gently pushing two fingers back into the hot hole, Temar probed deeper, twisting as the heat made the gakka start tingling faster. Shan's cry muted into little mewls that matched each thrust of Temar's fingers deeper into his body. Carefully scissoring his fingers, Temar used his free hand to stroke Shan's side and ass, to feel the muscles straining. Once again, Temar found the prostate, and this time Shan rounded his back, his face pressed to the mattress and a bead of sweat rolling over his dark skin. Reaching down, Temar ran two fingers from the back of Shan's scrotum to his hole, one on either side of the center tendon. Shan's whole body started to shake, and Temar pulled his fingers out, rubbing the remaining slick over his own cock.

He had been ignoring his own body, but now that he stroked his hand up the hard shaft, Temar's balls tightened, and he leaned forward, struggling against his need to come. He wanted this. He needed to feel Shan around him, but his body almost slipped out of his control. It took some panting and some time before he could move without being in danger of coming all over the back of Shan's thighs, and by that time, Shan had sunk back down to the bed, panting so heavily that his shoulders heaved with each breath. Spreading Shan's legs more, Temar pressed in slowly, the tingling and the heat and the tight passage forcing him to control every movement as he fought his own body for control. He wanted to wildly thrust, to claim, to come. However, he pushed deliberately and steadily, his cock vanishing into Shan's body.

Their bodies joined, Shan stretching to take him in. Shan started making an atonal hum that replaced the cries and moans and pleas. His hands clung to the edge of the mattress, and he pressed his forehead against his pillow. Temar slid forward until his thighs pressed up against Shan's backside, and then he stopped, panting, as need threatened to overwhelm him. Shan's movements, like his cries, were almost muted now, a twitch of his shoulder, a tightening of his fingers into the edge of the bed, a fast rise and fall of his back as he gasped for breath. It was as if the desire had reached a point where he couldn't cry out anymore, and Temar rested his hands against Shan's hips as he squirmed. The sheets were too slick and he didn't have a good angle for thrusting, but he pulled out a little, pushing back in immediately. Shan shivered, the motion traveling down his back, and his legs spreading more. Temar grunted as he realized he might have to pull out to reposition himself, and he didn't want to.

"Please," Shan whispered, his voice rough.

Temar bent forward until most of his weight rested on Shan's back, his cock still deep inside his lover. "I need you on your knees," Temar whispered. He placed a kiss on the back of Shan's neck, smelling the sweat-musk that had gathered. When Temar started to sit up so he could pull out to reposition, he found himself lifted into the air as Shan shoved with his arm, pushing them both backward and lifting himself to his knees. Then he allowed his shoulders to collapse back to the bed, so his ass was pushed neatly up into the air.

The angle was right, and Temar pulled out before pressing back in, slowly at first and then faster, their skin slapping as he sunk himself into Shan's body. The gakka and their own heat gathered, the tingling growing until Temar teetered on the brink of orgasm. Reaching around, he fisted Shan's cock, and Shan gave one good thrust before he came, his muscles tightening around Temar's cock as he cried out. Temar gave his own strangled cry as he finally came, his pleasure rushing through him until he got light-headed.

Collapsing forward, Temar was vaguely aware that they were falling, Shan not able to hold them up as they collapsed back to the bed, Temar still inside Shan. His softening cock slipped free as they landed. However, Temar only had the energy to lie against Shan's back, his breath coming in hungry gulps as he tried to recover. He'd had sex. He'd actually had more sex than he cared to think about some days. But he'd never had sex like that.

Below him, Shan moaned softly, the sort of sound someone makes when eating a truly good piece of chocolate.

"I should move," Temar said blearily, aware he was heavy enough to make an uncomfortable blanket.

"Don't. You're fine where you are," Shan answered. Temar kissed the shoulder under his cheek and then let his eyes drift closed. Shan wasn't as comfortable to lie on as the bed, but still… Temar didn't want to move.

chapter
s i x t e e n

WAKING IN a tangle of sheets, Temar cracked open one eye. The light was spilling in from the bathroom and not the window. Dawn hadn't come, but the bed was empty. Pushing himself onto his side, Temar reached down and scratched his crotch, the dried gakka making his skin feel tight. Curious where Shan had gone to, Temar swung his legs off the side and sat up, for a moment lacking the energy to get any farther. He sat squinting at the clock, but the light wasn't bright enough to illuminate the long hands.

After pushing himself up, Temar shuffled to the bathroom door and pushed it open. Shan was in the sealed slosh stall and the bubbled glass showed his silhouette as he brushed the water off his body toward the drain. "Shan?" Temar called. He'd tried to be careful last night, but he was painfully aware that it had been years, possibly over a decade, since Shan had let anyone top him, and when muscles hadn't been stretched in that long, accidents could happen.

"Temar?" Shan's silhouette paused. "I'm sorry. I didn't mean to wake you." He went back to brushing the water off his skin.

"Are you okay?"

"I'm fine." Shan paused again. "I'm better than fine. I'm wondering how much privacy we're going to have up there, because I really don't want to wait long to do that again."

"So, you aren't hurt?"

Again, Shan paused, his silhouette frozen. "No. I'm fine, Temar."

Letting out a breath he didn't realize he'd been holding, Temar sank down onto the closed toilet. "Happy stars," he muttered to himself.

"Are you okay?" Shan called out.

Temar opened his mouth, ready to say he was fine, but he wouldn't get an honest answer out of Shan without offering up a little honesty himself. "I woke up and found you gone, and I was afraid I'd gone too fast and hurt you," he admitted.

"If you'd gone any slower, I would have a permanent crick in my cock," Shan said with some amusement.

Temar smiled, but then something else occurred to him. "So, why are you up?"

Shan pulled a forced air nozzle from the side of the wall and moved it down his body. Apparently, the first settlers to find themselves cut off from terraforming water had considered installing the air system on all slosh stalls to minimize the water loss, but they'd run out of supplies. The longer Temar was here at relay, the more keenly he was aware of how short they were on so many supplies. The air machine whirred as Shan finished, and he let the hose retract before he opened the sealed door and stepped out. "I kept hearing motors. A lot of motors."

"Really?" Temar turned and headed out into the bedroom to look out the window, but it was still pitch black, the stars bright points against the night sky. Both moons were down, and a man could break his neck in a pipe trap before he ever saw it. However, when he listened, he could hear the distant whine of motors.

"What's going on?"

"I don't know, but I'm suspecting Lilian," Shan said as he came out of the bathroom with a shirt and socks on but no pants. Temar cleared his throat to keep from chuckling at the odd sight. He was fairly sure that laughing at a half-naked lover broke some unwritten rule.

"Lilian's running a machine?"

Shan pulled clean workpants off a shelf. "There are too many engine noises, too many different kinds of engine noises. Sun will be up in a few minutes, and I plan to be at the top of the tower where I can see whatever she has set up." Shan stopped with one leg in his pants and one lifted into the air as he looked at Temar. "You weren't keeping me busy for her, were you?"

"Me? No. God, Shan, the woman makes me uncomfortable when I'm in the same room with her. I'm not going to conspire against my lover for her."

Shan smiled when Temar said "lover" and slipped his second leg into his pants, but the smile quickly vanished. "She makes you uncomfortable?" Shan sounded surprised.

That was a topic Temar hadn't wanted to get into, but he'd stepped in it now. "I don't know how to act around her."

"Why?"

"Because she's the one person on the council who really decided to sell me into slavery. Naite would have followed her lead, and I know you argued against slavery, and Dee'eta isn't really one to poke sandrat nests, so I'm pretty sure it was mostly Lilian."

Shan stopped right in the middle of taking a step. After a space of a dozen heartbeats, he turned toward Temar. "I'm sorry."

"You're the one who argued against slavery." Temar made a face. "Actually, I was in favor of slavery too, since I thought the other option was exile. That makes it seem a little hypocritical to be uncomfortable around Lilian."

"Is that why you had trouble working with Dee'eta?" Shan asked gently, apparently forgetting his self-imposed mission. "Because she didn't argue?"

Temar shrugged. The fact was he didn't know what had happened in that council room, but now that he knew so many of the people, he could take some guesses. He didn't know how Kevin and Bari had voted, but he suspected Dee'eta hadn't said one word either way, and he'd bet an entire season's harvest that she'd voted with Lilian without thinking twice. Was that the only reason he'd been unable to work with her? "I honestly don't know," he admitted. "Part of it, maybe. Part of it was frustration because every time I tried to work the glass, I made a mistake. I screwed up things I shouldn't have."

"And she didn't trust you enough to tell you to get your act together, the way Naite did," Shan finished for him when Temar fell silent.

Again, Temar could only shrug. "If I ever get my own feelings sorted, you'll be the first to know."

Shan took one step closer before he stopped. The only light spilled out from the bathroom, creating a long shadow behind Shan. "You don't owe me answers, Temar. I have problems sorting my own emotions—so does Cyla, so does Naite, so does Tom. I'm starting to think that confusion and emotional flailing is the natural human condition and people like Div are just... weird."

"Div's weird?" A laugh slipped out of Temar, because of all the things he had expected Shan to say, that was about the single most surprising thing Temar could imagine.

"Oh, Div's very weird. You just don't know him well enough to notice," Shan agreed. "So, are you going to get dressed and head up to the tower with me, maybe see what mischief Lilian's up to before we get surprised?"

"Give me a second." Temar grabbed clothes from the floor and quickly pulled them on. The new outfits made for their trip were so beautiful that Temar didn't want to put them on without washing first. He wasn't sure that people from water-wealthy planets would appreciate the finely woven cottons, but he did. He'd change later. Shan headed out of the bedroom as Temar pulled on his second shoe, and he hurried to follow.

As a tall man with long legs, Shan had a stride that Temar had to trot to keep up with. And the closer they came to the access ladder up to the tower, the faster Shan walked. If Lilian was playing games with this landing, Shan was going to be furious. Temar wasn't sure, though, whether Shan would do anything about any schemes. It occurred to Temar that Lilian's illness was another force, like gravity and fire, that allowed her to bend the glass.

Shan climbed the ladder faster than Temar could. He followed, finally climbing up into the observation deck, where thick glass separated them from the desert. The tower rose far above the protective cliffs on either side of the station, so that the first stain of sunrise made the dunes seem to stretch out, their long shadows reaching across the white sand hiding the valleys and the lines of rope Naite's team had lined up to Shan's specifications. The wooden spires marking the beginning and end of the landing zone were little more than black streaks against the land.

"Can you see anything?" Temar whispered, even though the height and tower gave them privacy.

Shan leaned against one of the metal rails that lined the platform. "Not yet."

Closing the distance between them, Temar rested his hand on Shan's arm. After a quick smile over his shoulder, Shan returned to watching the north, and Temar leaned in, his cheek resting against Shan's shoulder as they stood watch together. The desert always cooled at night, and the morning sun brought a brisk wind that stirred up dust devils and started moving the large barchan dunes farther east. Normally the sand was an unbroken sheet of white, the dunes looking like long wrinkles where some hand had failed to smooth the fabric, but Temar could see rough crags covering the north plain.

"What is that?" Temar lifted his head from Shan's shoulder and moved closer to the glass.

"I have no idea."

The sun crept up over the horizon, casting long, stark shadows, and Temar frowned, still not understanding what he was seeing. The spots were south of the west landing area, a long trail that thinned and thickened as it led between the far edge of the landing zone and the edge of the valley. "It looks like rocks," Temar said, even though that was impossible. The Zhang mountains were the only source of sizable boulders in the area, and no one could haul rocks that far. No one sane, anyway.

"They aren't. They're vehicles," Shan said. "It's several hundred vehicles all parked out there."

As Shan said it, the shapes seemed to suddenly sharpen so that Temar could see the haulers, bikes, and sleds, the sand cars and the wide profiles of sand hunters, designed for shooters to stand on either side, and the rescue sleds, with their oversized engines that could power through the worst sandstorm and had heavy canopies to protect the crew.

"It's thousands of vehicles," Shan corrected himself in an awed whisper.

Temar understood the emotion. He put his hand out to touch the glass, as if the vision might vanish as the sun rose. "I didn't know there were that many vehicles on the entire planet."

"There aren't," Shan answered. Temar gave him a questioning look, and Shan shrugged. "At least there aren't that many vehicles that run. Some of those must have been towed out here. God above, why would people tow broken loaders out here? Does Lilian think I can shove one airship full of broken haulers the way I would broken datapads?"

Temar tilted his head. From this high up, he imagined the ship pilot who landed would see something like this, a scattering of vehicles randomly parked across the sand. With no rows or order, it looked like thousands and thousands of people had driven to the station and randomly parked wherever they wanted. Thousands and thousands and thousands of people. Hell, even if Shan was right that drivers had towed many of the vehicles out here, it must have taken hundreds of people to coordinate something like this.

"It's Lilian's plan," Temar said softly as he thought about the shuttle pilot seeing a culture with so many vehicles, so many people, so much spare time that they could drop everything to come watch a ship land. It was smoke and mirrors—an illusion that wouldn't stand up to a good poke with a stick.

"What plan?" Shan demanded.

"To make them think we're strong. She's trying to make them see that we're strong enough to fight them if they try to take our world."

Shan remained quiet for so long that Temar suspected he disagreed. Blindly reaching out, Shan groped for the rail, seeming to find it by rapping his knuckles against it hard enough to make a dull ringing. "If they want to fight for this planet, we aren't strong enough to hold off a combat cruiser, much less an alliance."

"Well, then, we need to make sure they don't try," Temar said. "At least Lilian is giving us a good first impression."

With a sigh, Shan turned toward the ladder. "Some days I think God blessed us by giving us Lilian Freeland. Other days, I do wish that woman had the good manners to explain what she was doing before she did it." Pausing at the top of the ladder, Shan looked back toward that north-facing window. "Do you think it'll work? Do you think the pilot will report back that he sees a significant force?"

Temar let his gaze go out to the gathering. "I don't know. What can their scanners see?" Temar asked.

Shan sucked air through his front teeth. "I have no idea," he finally admitted. "A military IMINT system would see metal husks with the engines ripped out and nonfunctional tracts and broken windshields and probably more than one cracked body. However, I don't know if they have a military IMINT system or that they want to risk equipment that expensive on a ship that's dropping into atmosphere." Shan took a deep breath. "I'd say there's at least a fifty-fifty chance that they're going to believe we could rally that many vehicles if it came down to a fight."

"And there's a fifty-fifty chance that they're going to start this negotiation believing that we're weak liars who can't even lie well," Temar said. The odds weren't ones he liked.

Putting his foot on the ladder, Shan started climbing down. "That's about it. If we get back in one piece, I'm killing Lilian myself."

"Not if I get there first," Temar muttered to himself. Either she'd given them a fighting chance or she'd set them up for complete, unmitigated disaster. It wasn't unlike going back into slavery. With that depressing thought, Temar headed down the ladder. He might not like the situation, but he wasn't going to let Shan go into it alone.

chapter
s e v e n t e e n

"PEOPLE HAVE a right to witness history," Lilian said, not a trace of apology in her voice as she sat on the back of a heavy hauler. Kevin and Dee'eta had come with her, and Naite stood off to the side. Shan slowly turned red, but he didn't seem to have an answer for that. It'd taken them two hours to find Lilian, and Temar suspected that wasn't an accident. Already a bright star shone in the blue sky—the skip shuttle coming low enough to release the airship that would land. Or maybe it already had released the airship, and in minutes a winged monster would follow the long line of green rope pegged across the sand.

"They're in danger, and this plan... you don't know what they can see from their ships." Shan's voice had the shrill edge of someone about to truly explode. Dee'eta Sun looked around as though desperate to avoid watching the fight, but Kevin didn't hide his amusement as he looked from one of them to the other.

"Council business, go secure the tarps over that tall load," Naite ordered someone who wandered too near, and Temar noticed that a number of people edged away. No one wanted to volunteer for another of Naite's jobs.

"Our people have survived worse," Lilian said as she looked around at the crowds gathered between the vehicles. A few younger children were running circles around their mothers, but for the most part, the crowd was full of adult men and women with knives strapped to their waistbands and guns in hand. Temar didn't recognize his own people.

"A military IMINT system will see that these are old junked pieces of equipment." Shan gestured toward the field of vehicles.

"If they have a military IMINT system," she said calmly.

"Lilian Freeland." Shan's voice was a rough growl, and Naite stepped closer, his gaze locked on his brother.

Lilian finally stopped scanning the landing site and really focused on Shan. "What sort of people would go to all the trouble to drag broken machines across such a deep desert? Those must be some very determined and rather unreasonable people, yes?"

Temar frowned as he considered that. If nothing else, that sort of behavior would make anyone question their sanity.

"Who the hell cares about their ships? Do you have any idea how much this is going to cost us at harvest?" Naite asked.

"Yes," Lilian said with a smile. The look Naite gave her came frighteningly close to the look he usually gave Shan.

"How long do you plan to ask people to stay out here?" Naite asked.

"Do you really think you could get anyone to leave?" Lilian asked quietly.

Naite crossed his arms. "After you asked them to come? No."

"They want to see the ship, Naite. This is history." Lilian gestured at the world, her newly forged jewelry shining in the sun. Even though she had half Naite's height and a third his mass, for that one moment, she was unimaginably large. Then she cringed and pressed her fingers to her side.

"Lilian," Kevin said softly.

"Stop mothering. I sent my two sons away, and I'll send you away too," she warned, poking her sharp finger in his direction.

"I wouldn't go. Unlike your sons, I'm not terrified of you, Lilian," Kevin pointed out. "But Lilian's right, Naite. This is a time to look at the sky, not the fields. We'll all work twice as hard to make up for lost time, but the world is changing and the people of this world have a right to watch it."

Naite harrumphed. "This is a sandcat of a pilot who is here to take Shan and Temar up there to meet more sandcats who don't give a shit about us," Naite said, summing it up. Sadly, it was probably pretty accurate.

"Now, Naite, you don't always have to be so pessimistic. If the world were as dark as you seemed to think, Ben would be up there telling them all sorts of tales, and we'd all be starving to death because we didn't tend the crops well enough. Give the boys and God some room to work here," Lilian ordered.

"It's not God I'm worried about," Naite grumbled as he gave Temar a look devoid of any sort of emotion. "And I'm not going to be there to ride to their rescue if they do something particularly stupid."

"You're assuming there's going to be trouble," Kevin said, coming to Shan and Temar's defense.

Temar suspected that Naite might be right. The AFP people liked to bash the Planetary Alliance and they'd made a few references to security and Planetary Alliance terrorists, so he knew they had security issues. Temar's stomach had been in knots for the past week, and unlike the previous months, he couldn't dismiss it as some stupid, lingering effect from Ben. He wasn't afraid of ghosts from his past—he was afraid of these people coming down out of the sky.

"Even if there *is* trouble, Shan and Temar can take care of themselves," Lilian said. Temar tried not to take it personally when no one else added their vote of confidence to that.

"We'll be keeping the communications relay open," Kevin said after the silence grew awkward. "Jim Hu and his wife, Yheta, are going to move out here and the rescue teams are ready to move if we have unauthorized landings. You can count on us to enforce whatever conditions you set for them." Kevin hopped down from the end of the hauler and slapped Shan on the shoulder.

After that, no one really seemed to want to talk as eyes turned toward the sky. All the movement had attracted a number of buteo that circled above them, looking for prey. Temar stood next to the hauler, too nervous to sit down, and Shan came to stand behind him, slowly slipping his arm around Temar's waist.

"There!" a voice called out from far down the line of vehicles, but soon more followed, and Temar could see hands going up into the air, all pointing to the north.

"Is that...." Temar stopped when a flash appeared in the blue sky. It looked like a small bird soaring over the sand, but as he watched, the spot doubled in size and then doubled again until he could see the silver clearly.

"It's the airship." Shan pressed closer and went so still, Temar suspected he wasn't breathing.

It was like watching a vid in slow motion, the way the ship slowly got bigger and bigger. The rush of words from the gathered crowd slowly stilled as the wings and the main body of the ship grew distinct, so by the time the engine roar rumbled through the air, every person watching was utterly silent. The children had moved closer to their parents, and Temar wrapped his hands around Shan's arms and held on tight as the ship turned slightly, so that the length of it lined up with the runway.

By the time the plane started to drop, the wind rose, creating strange, curled wisps that rose straight into the air, and people scrambled to get in their vehicles.

"Hurry up," Kevin called as he started unfurling the cover. Naite helped Dee'eta up into the empty bed with Lilian, and Temar scrambled to follow. Shan gave him a helping shove and then climbed up while Naite and Kevin rolled the heavy tarp down and the back of the truck went dark.

"I guess we're not going to see that landing after all," Lilian commented wryly.

"If you want a good case of sandblindness, I can open the cover," Kevin offered. Temar could hear her hit at him even over the sand scratching against the cover and the engine rumble. The ship's engine got louder until the entire truck vibrated, and Temar grabbed an arm—hopefully Shan's.

"They aren't landing on top of us, are they?" Dee'eta yelled over the sound. Sand hit the cover, forcing its way through a thousand cracks until the air was thick. Temar pulled his shirt up around his nose and mouth, tucking his arms close to his body. When the sound had grown so loud that Temar cringed from the noise, it suddenly changed, like a hauler shifting gears, the sound tapering off to a faint growl. The sand hitting the tarp eased and went silent, although the air was still full of dust. They couldn't have ships land near the cities, that was for sure.

"I think we have guests," Kevin said. Temar could hear the click of the tarp lock opening, and then he pulled back a corner so they could see the gray sky stained with dust.

"Noisy guests," Naite said as he unhooked the other cover and helped Kevin push it back. Temar looked around, horrified to see all their best clothes covered by a layer of fine dust. Lilian's white hair didn't show the sand, but everyone else looked as if they'd gone gray in an instant, and the bright colors of Dee'eta's loose blouse had all been muted by the dirt. Only Naite looked the same in his dusty work clothes and scuffed boots.

"We're going to make quite a first impression," Lilian said with a smile as she brushed off her shirt. "Well, when you kick dirt in someone's face, you have to expect them to get dirty."

Naite snorted, and from the expression on Shan's face, he would have done the same if Naite hadn't done it first.

"Let's get out there and meet them," Shan said as he let down the end of the loader bed and jumped down.

"This is it," Temar whispered as he looked at the shadow of a ship through a cloud of slowly settling sand. Shan's arm slipped around his waist, and Temar offered a weak smile. Even better, he avoided throwing up all over Shan's legs, which was a real possibility, given how his stomach felt.

"Hurry up, people," Lilian called as she strode toward the ship. It was a huge silver beast, taller than three men standing on each other's shoulders, with wings that seemed to go on for miles. Two enormous engines with gaping mouths pointed toward the rear sat on top of the machine, and though Temar had assumed they were all well back from the landing strip, a few of the vehicles were dangerously close to the path of the wing.

"Lilian, don't get too close. It's going to be hot," Shan said as he hurried after her, and Temar was left with Kevin and Dee'eta to bring up the rear. Surprisingly, Naite stayed behind, leaning against the hauler with a long gun now in his hand. Bylla started walking toward them from another direction. Unlike the rest of them, she had on a plain outfit, a dark gray that had to be hot in the sun and now was mottled with dust.

Temar had chosen an outfit with swirled lavender and blue, a ring with a blue quartz on one hand, and an intricate piece of coiled glass hanging from a heavy chain around his neck. The pieces felt awkward, but at least he'd talked Cyla out of the jeweled nose ring she'd tried to press on him. Temar sneezed and pinched his nose for a second to keep from doing it again. Yeah, a nose ring on a desert planet didn't make much sense, but then, Cyla's plans often didn't.

An electronic whine made most of the gathered crowd flinch back, and then a voice with a slightly electronic tone filled the air. "Hi, folks. The ship is still pretty hot. If you want to keep about twenty feet back, I'm going to hit it with a supercooled charge of air." Shan caught Lilian's arm and pulled her to a stop.

"Is that the pilot?" Kevin asked.

"I think so," Temar said. Shan would know better. He angled around a trio of men still wearing their sand veils to move closer to Shan and Lilian. Another cluster of people was moving toward them, threading their way through the crowd. "Who's that?" Temar asked Shan and Lilian as he stopped at Shan's side.

Lilian glanced over. "It's the council from Blue Hope. The Red Plain council is at the back of the crowd, ready to handle trouble on-site, and the White Hills council is on notice."

Temar blinked, shocked that Lilian would have gone to that length. It implied that she thought there might be military action. Looking at Shan, he tried to decide if Shan had known about this, but he seemed equally shocked.

"Here it comes, folks," the voice over the loudspeaker announced, and then the ship gave an enormous sigh and the sand scattered, creating a bubble of blue around the ship. One second later, a rush of cool air that smelled of medicine swept over them, and the muttering crowd went silent again. "Landing procedures are complete, but the ship may have hot or cold spots for several hours, so avoid getting too close. I'm coming out now." The voice ended with a loud click, and Temar's mouth went dry and he stared at the ship, waiting for his first sign of a door. It took several minutes before a line appeared in the side of the ship and a section of the metal slowly lowered until it formed a ramp down to the sand, and a man with brown hair and a dark brown uniform stood with the light from the ship behind him.

Lilian found her voice first. "Welcome to Livre," she called out loudly as she walked forward. By the time Shan reached for her arm, she had already moved out of reach. Giving Temar an unreadable look, Shan followed after her. "You took your precious time getting down here again, young man, although I suppose your officers carry more of that blame," Lilian said, her tone going from warm to a grandmotherly sort of chastisement in an instant. The man blinked at her.

"Um, I am sorry about that, ma'am."

"Your officers and elected officials should be sorry, not you. You weren't even born when this mess started," she said, and that wasn't the tone Temar had expected her to take. The man looked around as though searching for someone to save him from Lilian, who had not even introduced herself yet.

"Welcome to the planet. I'm Shan Polli," Shan said, holding out a hand. The stranger looked at it for a brief second, long enough to suggest he hadn't expected to shake hands, but then he came down the rest of the ramp and took it, shaking solemnly.

"It's a pleasure to meet you. I'm Corporal William Kester with the Alliance of Free Planets."

"Welcome," Shan repeated. "This is Temar Gazer," he said with a gesture toward Temar, "and Kevin Starwalker and Bylla Sullivan."

"Starwalker?" Corporal William Kester asked with a strangled laugh. When no one laughed with him, he quickly cleared his throat, all signs of a smile gone. "It's a pleasure to meet you folks. I'm actually only the taxi driver here, so I have orders to load whatever you would like to take up and ferry you to the *Brazica*. If you point me to what needs loading and maybe one or two people to help...." He let his voice trail off as he looked around at the thousands of people gathered, most leaning on vehicles, and nearly all of them showing their weapons openly. He swallowed. "Your people are well-armed for farmers," he said, his voice considerably shakier.

"A man or woman who can't shoot a sandcat from a hundred yards is likely to end up as food for one," Lilian lied airily. "Ambassadors Polli and Gazer and I need to get cleaned up after your landing. I'm sure someone can help you." Lilian turned her back on him and started walking away. "Naite!" she called out into the crowd. Kevin had pulled Bylla back somewhat.

"Ma'am," Naite said, striding through the vehicles with a gun nearly as large as he was braced on one hip. Temar knew Naite could have a glare on him under the best of situations, but when Naite stopped, that gun propped up on one hip, and gave the corporal the sort of glare he normally saved for Shan, Temar almost felt sorry for the man. The corporal took a step backward up the ramp.

"Help him get this sorted," she suggested before walking away.

"Yes, ma'am," Naite agreed. Clearly they'd planned this, but Temar wasn't sure what message the AFP was supposed to get, other than the people of Livre weren't the friendliest bunch in the universe.

The corporal nodded. "If you point to what needs shifting, I'll show you how we secure loads."

Naite gave him a long, cold look before he turned and held his weapon out for another worker to take. "Fine. But I'm not carrying shit unless you are too. I'm not your fucking workhorse," he snapped.

"Hey, I'm just a corporal," the man hurried to say. "I'm the one who gets ordered to lift shit. Do you want to start grabbing the cargo or do you want to see the equipment first?"

Naite answered by striding up the ramp and passing the corporal to go into the ship without warning. The corporal looked around at the rest of them before giving a half bow and hurrying after Naite.

"Come on, let's get inside," Kevin urged them. He and Bylla headed that way, but Temar really wanted to stay and watch these strange interactions. Naite could certainly be that sharp, but he normally didn't act like that until someone had pissed him off. If a worker ruined seedlings or dropped valuable equipment, he would verbally shred them. This corporal hadn't done anything, and he'd gotten Naite's nastiest attitude.

"What is going on?" Temar whispered, not sure if the ship had microphones.

"I have no idea, but I think Lilian does," Shan said. "Let Naite handle loading the ship, Ambassador Gazer."

Temar snorted. He'd noticed that bit of obfuscation. That he could understand, though. The man had introduced himself with his title first, so these people clearly cared a whole lot about titles. Lilian was probably right to give them titles. Now the rudeness, that seemed a little less logical.

But that was probably the point. History was full of illogical people who had committed terrible acts of violence in the name of their beliefs. Maybe Lilian wanted these people to wonder if this wasn't a planet of crazy, violent people—which still didn't make sense, because if that was true, they should go home and leave Livre to die. Temar realized Shan was heading for the station, and he ran to catch up.

The council from Blue Hope stood off to one side, whispering among themselves, and Temar wondered how far these plans had gone. He suspected the council wouldn't have stood back and let Lilian treat their guest like that unless it'd been preplanned. Lilian might frighten most of the planet, but that didn't mean they'd stand back and let her act crazy. No, she'd convinced them ahead of time that this was the most logical course.

By the time Temar got down the ladder and headed into the living room, the conversation was already going.

Kevin sounded frustrated. "… wait until we knew for sure."

"How much more evidence do you need, Kevin?" Lilian demanded.

"*Some* evidence would be nice." Shan threw his hands up into the air in exasperation as Temar came around the corner. Most of the boxes had been moved out during the night, so the living room looked like a living room again. Shan was pacing near the food preparation station, his arms going while Lilian sat on the couch, brushing dust from her shirt. Bylla had retreated to a corner, where she watched. "He laughed. Maybe Kevin's name means something different up there, but that wasn't him being rude."

"Sit down, Shan," Lilian said.

Shan stopped pacing, but he crossed his arms and glared at her, making it perfectly clear that he wouldn't sit. With a sigh, Kevin sat down next to Lilian. Dee'eta had vanished altogether. Maybe she was overseeing the loading of the glass. Temar wished he could get away with going to help her rather than getting in the middle of the brewing fight.

"They were rude for sending that boy in the first place," Lilian said.

"I was surprised the pilot was alone," Kevin mused. "I expected some sort of official or officer or something."

"Exactly," Lilian said, holding a finger up in the air.

Shan dropped his arms to his side. "I understand that. Yes, it was thoughtless to send someone that young to deal with this."

Temar didn't comment on the fact that the corporal was about the same age he was.

Taking a step forward, Shan rested his hands on the back of the chair. "But to treat him like that isn't going to win us any points."

"It won't win us points to accept rude behavior." Lilian stopped brushing at her outfit long enough to glare at Shan.

Shan's voice was thick with carefully controlled anger. "They were probably afraid of what the ship would find. The way you have people out there armed, I can't even claim it's an unjustified fear. But if there's trouble, they don't want an ambassador or officer down here on a planet with a bunch of clearly unstable farmers."

"As opposed to our two ambassadors going up there with clearly unstable politicians who would declare war on each other?" Lilian asked, and the room went uncomfortably silent. Kevin dropped his gaze to the floor, Bylla studied her hands, and Temar watched Lilian and

Shan stare at each other. Shan's mouth was open, but Lilian's lips were pressed together in a tight line.

Lilian yielded first. "Your instincts were right. If they come down here, they're going to learn too much about us, and that's going to lead them to wonder if our planet wouldn't fall faster than one of the worlds they've been at war with. So, I am not questioning your judgment, Shan. However, you have to keep them off guard. You have to make it clear that they will respect us or we will not play nice with them. You make sure they know that people who try to mine the planet on their own will have to deal with not only us but sandcats, pipe traps, raptors, sand lice, infections, sandblindness, sandstorms, and barchan dunes that can swallow entire towns if you're foolish enough to put them in the wrong place. You make sure they know we are the only way to get what they want. We all know how many of the first-generation settlers died, so you make sure they know." Most of the time, Lilian was one to silently watch as others debated, coming in only to settle the matter with her final ruling. Temar had never heard her argue so passionately, but he swallowed as he heard what she wasn't saying. She expected violence.

"If they won't listen to us?" Temar asked as he walked farther into the room.

She gave him a small smile. "My dear, you convinced Ben that you would play nice with him until you brought destruction down on his head. I know you can do this." She turned back toward Shan. "And Shan, you survived that sandrat of a father of yours and have reinvented yourself a half-dozen times. Put away Priest Shan and Mechanic Shan and Apprentice Shan and even that Angry Shan I knew when you were sixteen years old. No one else in the world can reinvent himself like you can, so if they're starting this with disrespect and suspicion, you make them regret that."

"Lilian," Shan said wearily.

"No, no excuses, Shan. You are one of the only men I know who gets stronger every time the wind blows. The wind is blowing, so you get strong enough to survive it. They don't respect us. That's where we're starting. You show them that they have to." Lilian stood, and Kevin was at her side. Temar blinked, suddenly realizing that Kevin always stood a little closer to her than anyone else. He was her lover. How had Temar missed that? "These two need time to talk and clean up. We have a certain image. Kevin, you said there's another bathroom in this place?"

"This way," Kevin said, gesturing toward the door to the control room, which led to the other half of the station. He kept his hand under her elbow as they headed out of the room. Shan sank into a chair, looking twenty years older.

Bylla took a step toward the door. "Div has faith in you, and he trusts that you have faith enough in God and your people to do this job. He would have come to council himself and argued against this trip if he thought you couldn't succeed," she said softly.

"I know. He's not exactly one to stay quiet when he thinks something's wrong," Shan said.

"I don't know you two well, but from what I hear, that's true of you too. The people out there trust you to make the right choices. I'm sorry that Lilian's plan.... She should have told you about her plans. When I moved here, they warned me about her, but I have to admit that I assumed they were exaggerating."

Shan laughed. "No, no exaggeration. She didn't used to be quite this bad, but she's dying. She doesn't have to worry about aggravating people."

"But she does have to make sure the world is safe for her grandchildren. I understand that. Before I lost my children, I would have done anything to protect them, and if anything had included throwing you two to the wolves up there in space, I would have done that too. But she wouldn't send you up if she didn't think you could protect her grandchildren." Having said that, Bylla headed for the door. She left, and the door closed behind her.

Temar came forward and sat carefully on the table next to Shan's chair, reaching out to rest his hand on Shan's shoulder. Shan's eyes came open briefly before he closed them again. "Am I the only one feeling a need to throw up?"

"No, I am too," Temar confirmed.

"Do they really disrespect us that much?"

The young corporal had backed away from Naite and laughed at Kevin's name. He didn't have any training in working with people, and that's who they'd sent down. "Yeah, they do," Temar agreed.

"Great," Shan said sarcastically. "I guess we should get cleaned up."

Temar wished he had some way to make Shan feel better, but right now, if he didn't throw up, he'd call this a successful day. He would never tell Shan, but he was grateful Lilian hadn't talked about these plans and fears of hers. If Temar had been this stressed for an entire week, his heart would have given out and he would have been dead long before their idiot corporal showed up.

chapter
eighteen

SHAN CLENCHED his teeth as he looked around the crowded loading bay. Every piece of equipment and glass was loaded, and there wasn't another reason to delay. Glancing over, he saw Temar had that same flat expression on his face that he'd had at Ben's farm. That made his stomach knot even more.

"I've done my best with the glass, but some of those pieces are so delicate that I'm not sure the foam will have the right density to protect them. Are you sure you don't want to leave some of the pieces here, Ambassador Polli?" Corporal Kester asked for about the third time.

"If it breaks, it breaks. However, try to avoid doing anything that would make it more likely to break," Shan said, dismissing the concern. Most of the pieces had been made for this trip, and Dee'eta Sun wouldn't have sent anything too valuable to replace. Temar moved to one of the metal crates and ran his long fingers along the edge. Shan wanted to grab Temar and run for the distant dunes and never come back. It would be a romantic image, except for the part where they'd die of thirst and get eaten by sandrats.

"Yes, sir," Corporal Kester answered, even though he sounded very unhappy about the answer.

Naite stuck his head into the cargo hold. "We have a report of a sandcat pack attack out by Hope Valley. I was going to head over there, if it's okay with you," he said, raising his gun. It was a staged performance, but Corporal Kester's eyes went large exactly as planned.

Shan nodded. "Take off. Ride safe, okay?" He hated leaving Naite behind. Now that he faced going into space, he had to admit he wished his brother would be close enough to ride to the rescue if they needed it. Instead, they were on their own.

"You too, Shan," Naite said, that roughness dropping away, and for one second, Shan could see the worry and love on his brother's face. Oh, he always knew it was there, but Naite rarely let it show. After that flash of honest emotion, Naite turned and left the ship. He and a dozen other armed hunters would take a sand hunter and head for Hope Valley at full speed, showing their guests that the people of Livre knew how to take care of business.

"Sandcats?" Corporal Kester asked in an unsteady voice. He looked ready to slam the door closed and run for it.

Shan grunted and gave a quick nod. "Local predators. Usually they're more solitary, but they can take down a man easily. A pack can take down three or four full-grown and armed men in minutes." It was true, but a pack almost never formed. Sandcats turned on each other the second food was scarce. The only reports of sandcat packs came from the early days of colonization when the settlers and their animals had been easy prey. But that worked to their advantage too. These people probably had those early reports, when Livre managed to kill at least half the people who landed on her. These days, few people died from predator attacks, and the ones who did were like Ben—exiled—or like Shan's father—drunk and stupid enough to lie on the sand to watch sunrise instead of the rock he normally chose for his naps.

"Oh geez," the corporal whispered. Shan looked over to find Temar watching with that blank expression.

"Are we taking off now?" Shan demanded more harshly than he needed to. He hated the wall that had come down around Temar, hiding the emotions that normally flitted across his expressive face.

"Yes, sir." Corporal Kester went to the ramp and hit the close button to lift the ramp. Shan watched the sequence of buttons carefully. "I have your luggage in the front passenger area, and I'll show you and Ambassador Gazer to your seats."

Corporal Kester headed toward a narrow door that led into a tight passage that led up to the front pilot area. Temar stood to one side, waiting for Shan to follow the corporal before he did. Two hours ago, Shan had thought he understood Temar, but now he looked at the blank expression and bile rose in Shan's throat. Temar was closed down so tightly Shan couldn't even judge whether he was panicking. He should be staying home, and Shan tried to find one good excuse to leave Temar behind, where he'd be safe. The problem was that Shan wasn't sure Livre was all that safe right now. If Lilian was right, they were all in danger, and as much as Shan hated Lilian right now, he trusted the woman to understand politics.

"Ambassador Polli," the corporal said, offering a seat in a huge chair with deep cushions, with electronics going up either side. "Pull the net restraint down over you with this bar when we're ready to take off." He demonstrated with a handle at the top of the chair, showing how to lock it in near the seat. Shan fisted his hands, not wanting Temar to have that sort of restraint on him. "Release it with this," Corporal Kester said, showing a recessed button.

"Temar, did you see that?" Shan asked. He wouldn't have Temar feeling trapped for even one second.

"Ambassador Polli?" Temar asked in an utterly neutral voice.

"Show him the controls," Shan ordered. Corporal Kester backed up some to show Temar the mechanics on the chair next to Shan. There were six chairs behind the two pilot seats, and Shan and Temar had the two right behind the pilot. They wouldn't have a lot of privacy.

"Thank you, Corporal," Temar said before he sat and tested the bar by pulling it down so the net caught him across the chest and pushed him into the padded seat, and then he released it, letting the net retract into the top of the chair.

"Yes, sir."

"How long until we lift off and how long until the skip shuttle picks us up?" Shan asked as the corporal settled into the pilot's chair.

"Preflight check is about ten minutes, but we should wait until people get clear of the area."

"Why?" Temar asked, worry flashing across his face before that same neutral mask slipped back in place.

The corporal turned around, his whole seat swiveling, to look at them. "This puppy is going to throw up a lot of sand. People could get caught in that."

"My people are used to sandstorms that could bury this ship under fifty feet of Livre dune," Shan pointed out. "They'll be fine. Take off as soon as you're ready."

"Yes, sir," Corporal Kester agreed, swiveling his seat to face front. "The skip shuttle will take about two or three hours for maneuvering before it enters subspace and we can move ships. Our final destination is the cruiser *Brazica*. We should reach it in about sixteen hours."

Sixteen hours. Shan frowned as he realized the rest of the universe was closer than he had ever thought. Why wouldn't someone come and investigate Livre?

Shan looked over at Temar, reaching out to brush his fingers across the back of his hand. Temar pulled his hand away, but then he glanced over and gave Shan a small smile. Respecting the fact that Temar needed a little space, Shan turned to the front and watched as much of the pilot's actions as he could. Shan could tell one panel was fuel consumption, but most of the controls had nothing familiar that Shan could use to start trying to decipher them. That made sense, since the schematics in the relay computer had been for rockets. This was different technology, but Shan noticed the AFP hadn't sent them any technical specifications on flying one of these—just the cargo capacity. Then again, Shan hadn't asked.

Corporal Kester turned a switch. "Shuttle Beta-Two-Beta, this is Airship Two-Beta-Nine preparing for preflight sequence. I have two guests, Ambassadors Polli and Gazer, and am massing at 72 percent cargo mass. Confirm." He turned a number of other switches, and machines started to whine under them.

"Confirm for preflight, Airship Two-Beta-Nine," a voice from space said over the radio. Minutes sped by as the pilot's hands moved across more controls than Shan could track. He'd identified the communications systems and what might be internal sensors, as well as fuel, but that still left a lot of mystery switches.

The pilot reached over his head and pulled down his own net restraint. "We're getting ready for lift. You need to strap in, sirs."

Shan looked over to see if Temar was okay. Given Temar's history with restraints, this made Shan uncomfortable, but Temar pulled the net down and locked it into place without showing any emotion. That would have reassured Shan more if Temar hadn't been pretty much emotionless since they'd walked up to the corporal.

Corporal Kester touched a communication switch again. "Three minutes to burn. Shuttle Beta-Two-Beta, be advised, I have priceless artwork on board. We would all appreciate a soft skip here."

Shan frowned at the description of priceless artwork, and when he looked over, Temar looked equally confused.

"Come again, Airship?" the man on the other end of the radio asked.

"Artwork. Priceless glass artwork. A hard skip is going to destroy millions of credits here, so a little patience would be appreciated," Corporal Kester repeated.

They were talking about Dee'eta's work. He certainly appreciated her work. She'd made the complex knot of blue and clear glass Temar was wearing like a pendant, and Shan couldn't imagine how she could get glass to bend in such fantastic ways. However, if he was flying a ship into space, he would be far more concerned about people than glass. It wasn't as if glass itself were rare. It wasn't. Only the exceptionally high-quality glass required to encase computer chips without interfering with optical properties had a lot of value. The optic-quality glass was made in neat rods to show off the utter clarity, but Temar had told him optic-quality glass didn't have the right properties for the sort of manipulation and artistry Dee'eta was famous for.

"They're bringing artwork?" the shuttle asked. Clearly they were doubting someone's sanity.

"Yes, sir, they are. A lot of artwork. I was sweating with fear as I packed it, so please give us the softest skip in history."

There was a long pause where the radio was unnaturally silent. "Understood, Airship. We will be coming in at 6.95 miles per second. Command advises you to increase to 4.5 miles per second before contact."

Kester touched a number of controls, and numbers flashed by the screens on the fuel unit. "Understood. 4.5 miles per second confirmed, Shuttle," he finally agreed. "I just hope you grab us on the first skip because at that rate of burn I have two minutes of fuel on board."

"Two minutes, confirmed," the shuttle promised.

The pilot reached over and turned off a switch. "And hopefully we won't shake ourselves to death." Angling his chair so he could look back at them, Kester gave them a wry look. "Next time they have a diplomatic mission, make sure they're sending a diplomatic airship and not a ground-pounder bus before you bring the good glass, okay?"

Shan didn't answer since he didn't really know what to say, and Temar had gone frighteningly silent. After a second, Kester turned his seat back around and tended his controls. The computer made a loud ticking sound that reminded Shan of a cooling engine, and then they started rolling.

"We're going to roll clear of the crowd before full burn," Kester offered.

Shan watched the sand of his home roll past the window. The gathered crowds were on the far side of the shuttle, but Shan silently said his good-byes and sent a prayer up to God as the ground started rushing by faster.

"Brace for full burn. Lean all the way back in the seats to avoid sore necks, sirs. In five, four, three, two, one…."

Shan felt like someone had punched him in the stomach as the ship lurched forward, slamming him back into the seat, and then the white sand vanished as they climbed up into the sky. They were leaving Livre.

chapter
n i n e t e e n

AFTER THE airship, where they'd been trapped in the chairs, and the shuttle, where they'd had a small room with couches facing each other and a tiny window the size of a man's hand, the *Brazica* looked enormous, even though Shan hadn't seen anything other than the landing hangar so far. Straight metal beams rose several stories above them, making this a tall, narrow space, and Shan felt like he was buried alive inside metal walls with no windows and no sunlight. Instead, strips of light shined from the walls and bright lights high overhead created a yellow glow that was giving him a headache.

"Welcome to the *Brazica*, Ambassador Polli, Ambassador Gazer," a tall woman greeted them with a smile, crossing the metal floor with long strides. She walked beside an older man, with a dozen others following behind in a clump that reminded Shan of sheep pushing together. The woman had long brown hair that hung around her shoulders and a white outfit cut exactly the same as most of the people that circled the ships in this landing bay; only the others, like Kester, had brown uniforms. The older man walking beside her was the odd man out in his formal suit.

"I'm Protocol Officer Natalie Aral," the woman said when she came close. "This is Ambassador Richard Melton. Ambassador Melton, may I present Ambassador Shan Polli and Ambassador Temar Gazer of Livre?" Natalie's name sounded vaguely familiar, and Shan suspected she had talked to them on the communicator. He'd paid more attention to the message than the messenger, though, so he couldn't be sure.

Ambassador Melton was an older man with gray hair and a pinched expression. Either that or all his features were simply too close to the center of his face. Shan held out his hand. "Ambassador Melton," he offered. At least these people had bothered to have an ambassador come to the landing bay.

Protocol Officer Aral took a step backward. "Gentlemen, if you will excuse me, I am going to see how the cargo survived. I do hope we were able to avoid any damage. I'll designate a storage area and arrange for a breakage report." Smiling at all of them, she backed away, leaving Shan and Temar with Ambassador Melton and a lot of people whose names they hadn't been given.

Melton studied them so closely that Shan was on the verge of taking offense when the man started talking. "I must apologize, Ambassador Polli. We are short of shuttles in this area or we would have sent a more modern ship. We had no idea you would be bringing fragile merchandise, though, and time seemed more important than the shuttle specifications. I'm afraid that we may have some misinformation regarding Livre."

"Really?" Shan asked as he studied the enormous bay with shuttles tucked into nooks on either side of a short landing area. The sheer volume of the ship staggered him, and he noted that most of the spaces for shuttles were empty, so he believed the ship was short on shuttles.

"Indeed. I'm afraid I had an initial briefing that suggested Livre would have little in the way of wealth and would likely be a source of refugees rather than resources."

Shan looked at the ambassador, wondering if he'd misheard or if the man really had just admitted that they had never come to Livre because they would rather leave refugees to starve to death. "My people are more resilient that you might think," Shan said, struggling to keep a pleasant smile on his face.

"So it would seem. Officer Aral says that you still have much of the original equipment working. With that sort of talent, I'm wondering if the admiral shouldn't send some of our mechanics down to train with your people."

"We've learned not to be wasteful," Shan said, his skin starting to crawl. The friendliness reminded him entirely too much of Ben. Then again, he'd liked Ben, so maybe the ambassador wasn't all that similar after all. Shan desperately wanted to look at Temar, to see if this was affecting him, but Shan feared seeing panic in those blue eyes when there was very little he could do at this point. He'd put them both in this situation, and now they had to muddle through.

Ambassador Melton pursed his lips. "That's an admirable trait for any people, but I have to admit it's particularly important for those of us who are in the borderlands. The core alliance," he said, spitting out the name, "can rape other planets to feed their need for resources, but we must always rely on ourselves. I'm sure you will find that Livre's beliefs fit well within the AFP." He nodded and looked toward the ship. "Officer Aral will return shortly."

Shan looked over at the shuttle that had brought them up. "I didn't realize we were waiting for her."

"She's quite the expert on Livre. She's studied all the precolonization and early reports and the transmissions you've sent since reestablishing communication."

Shan really didn't have much to say about that, and he went back to looking around while trying to keep a surreptitious eye on Temar, who had retreated several steps and stood watching the assembled group, his fingers tracing the glass knot at his neck.

"So, the merchandise you've brought… are these trade goods?" the ambassador asked.

"Some trade goods, some equipment beyond our ability to fix that we had hoped to trade for repairs, some sample goods."

"And I hear you've brought artwork."

"We brought glass and carved wood," Shan said.

"We had expected samples of optic-quality glass if you had it, and I can promise you that the AFP will pay well."

"I'm sure you will." Shan cleared his throat as he realized who the ambassador really reminded him of. George Young. It wasn't a compliment.

Shan remembered when he'd had to mediate a conflict because one of the workers had agreed to seven credits per day and Young had tried to deduct one credit because, as a large man, the worker had eaten more food than any other worker. Sadly, Young honestly thought he had a case. Shan had tried to mediate and get Young to see that he was being petty, and that his pettiness was the main reason why he was already paying seven credits a day instead of six like most landowners. When Tom had hard times, he'd dropped his pay to five, and Shan didn't know of a single worker who had left because of it. However, Young was entirely convinced of his arguments, and had ignored Shan before going on to lose in council.

The worst part was that Young still insisted to anyone who would listen that the council had ruled against him only because he was personally unpopular. Shan wondered if Ambassador Melton would measure how much food a man ate. Probably. Maybe the ambassador recognized Shan's discomfort, because he fell silent.

Officer Aral came down out of the ship, a smile still on her face. "I've made the arrangements. I only had a chance to open one crate, but it looked like the pieces came through. That is beautiful work, clearly not out of a mold. Glass art will find a significant following, especially such intricate and unique pieces. So, gentlemen, let's find a place where we can all sit and learn a little about each other."

Melton frowned. "I have a very tight schedule, and I'm sure Ambassadors Polli and Gazer do as well." He turned to Shan. "If you have an inventory, we could begin discussing the current trade before talking about treaties."

Officer Aral's smile faltered.

Shan looked over at Temar, but he continued to watch silently. Shan could feel that little seed of panic over Temar's state of mind begin to sprout. Moving closer to Temar, Shan lowered his voice. "Would you like to see the ship first?" he asked quietly. He wanted to see how technology had shifted in the last eighty years, but he didn't want to drag Temar around the ship if he was close to an emotional edge, and Shan couldn't read his expression well enough to judge.

Temar gave a small nod. "It'd be interesting." They were the first words he'd spoken since they'd left Livre, and the fear in Shan's gut untangled at the normal tone. He'd heard that tone from Temar back before the slavery, when he'd visited the church. Shan associated it with Temar trying very hard to stay out of the way, but he didn't have to. Shan wanted him involved.

Slipping a hand behind Temar's back, he urged the man forward to join the rest of them. "Then perhaps we could have a tour," Shan suggested, not missing the surprise on the ambassador's face. Maybe these people preferred to rush from place to place, but Shan didn't. Even on his bike, he was seeing the world, feeling the motor between his legs and judging the slide of sand as he sailed down the face of a dune. Sitting still for hours on end had left him jittery and uncomfortable. Either that, or the feeling that he was buried alive in a giant piece of metal had him on edge—both were possible.

"A tour is an excellent idea. So often we rush to some business before getting to know each other," Officer Aral said enthusiastically. "I have a list of ship facilities. Perhaps I can show you around while Ambassador Melton reviews the materials you've brought."

From the frown on Melton's face, he wasn't used to having an officer tell him what to do, but Aral's plan sounded much better than Melton's. Shan didn't want to go to a small room and argue over trade.

"We would love a chance to look around," Shan answered, even though Temar seemed to have returned to looking around the room, this time at a group of workers gathering around the shuttle that had brought them in.

"Excellent—does anything on this list interest you?" Officer Aral moved closer to show him a datapad. "Observation deck" and "Gardens" and "Recreational facilities" were followed by the phrase, "Don't let them see you two are together."

Shan blinked, shocked, but when he looked again, Aral had touched the screen and her cryptic message had vanished, replaced by "Food preparation areas" and "Crew quarters."

"Ambassador Polli?" she asked him with wide-eyed innocence. Shan looked over at Temar, and from the way he only casually glanced toward the datapad, Shan guessed that he hadn't seen her message.

"The gardens would be interesting," Temar said before offering her a smile.

"The gardens are beautiful," she said with a wide smile. "Being from a desert world, you will appreciate the open streams. The advantage of having a sealed ecosystem within a ship is that all water is eventually reclaimed by the air circulation system, so we can have open water sources."

"Like lakes?" Temar asked, suddenly showing interest. Shan thought about the historical vids he'd seen of lakes, and he had to admit some curiosity.

"Yes, we do have a lake, of sorts." With a touch on Shan's arm, Officer Aral gestured them toward the far side of the landing hangar. "Ambassador Melton, would you care to join us, or review the materials list?" She held out the old datapad that Shan had secured to the top of one of the crates. Compared to the datapads from the ship, the Livre version looked thick and dirty, and the screen was blurred.

Shan noticed that the ambassador still looked aggravated, but he took the old datapad. "I believe I will review the goods."

"Of course, Ambassador." She turned to Shan and Temar. "Sirs, if you would follow me, I will give you a tour."

Shan almost reached for Temar's arm, but he forced himself to keep his hand at his side. Up until now Temar had been largely silent and his emotions had stayed hidden behind a neutral mask, but now he gave Shan a quick frown. Caught between wanting to reach out to his lover and fear over Officer Aral's warning, Shan waited too long and Temar headed toward the exit, leaving Shan to follow. Aral fell in next to Shan, and another woman in a brown uniform moved closer to Temar. The hair on Shan's neck stood up as he watched the woman. She moved with a loose-limbed gait that Shan had only seen in vids, the sort of fluid movement of a warrior.

"Rula Lish is my… assistant," Officer Aral offered with just enough of a pause to make it clear that she had lied.

"Ah." Shan wasn't sure what else he could say, so he closed his mouth and worried as they headed out the hangar doors into a corridor. A man in another brown uniform rushed by them, and Rula moved close to Temar to let him pass. Shan's whole body tightened in alarm. Rula leaned closer and said something, and Temar answered, his head tilting to the side.

Officer Aral wasn't offering any conversation, and Shan certainly couldn't come up with any small talk as they followed Rula and Temar down the corridor. The slow curve of the ship and the way corridors met at odd angles meant Shan quickly found himself completely disoriented.

Technically that didn't matter, since they were trapped on the ship even if they could find the shuttle again, but as they walked, Shan developed a sinking feeling that continued to grow worse. Rula Lish and Temar stopped in front of a door large enough to ride a loader through.

"These are the gardens… well, the public recreation part," Officer Aral explained. "The hydroponics generate most of the ship's oxygen, but the smell in there is enough to make you pass out, and watching algae slowly float from one level to another isn't very interesting," she said as she pressed her thumb to a black square. The doors made a thunking sound that reminded Shan of a heavy lock before they slowly opened. The security measures made the sinking feeling in his gut worse, but when he saw inside, all that was momentarily forgotten.

Shan blinked, his brain in shock at the green that filled every corner of the enormous room he was looking into. Shelves with lights on the underside were covered in greenery that spread out wide, dark green leaves to soak up the energy. Shan took a step closer, and Temar moved to his side.

"Stars above," Temar breathed as he stepped in, his hand going up to trace a heart-shaped leaf. Shan followed, aware of the heavy door closing once the two women had come inside.

"They're plants—don't you have those?" Rula Lish asked. She was a thick woman; her gracefulness when moving vanished when she stopped and put her hands on her waist. Her dark red hair was pulled back into a tight ponytail that had a black cord wrapped around it to keep stray hairs from escaping.

"We do," Temar said, "but most have leaves that try to avoid the sun. Well, except the crop plants, of course, but even those are never this dark green."

"No doubt the sunlight on Livre would burn these plants in hours," Officer Aral said. "If you'd like to follow me, the pathways are farther in." She started forward, but Shan waited until Temar was ready, walking next to him, which left Rula behind them. Shan's gut churned.

Growing up in his father's house, he'd often felt trapped. After his mother died, everyone kept telling him to give his father time to recover. They kept talking about what a hard life old Yan Polli had suffered, and Shan had learned to stop complaining. He'd stopped complaining about the fact that his father only paid attention to Naite, praising him for every little success, while Shan failed to even get his father's attention. Then Naite had started acting out—damaging neighbors' fields and getting sentences, first to days of work and then years. Shan only suspected the truth after Naite had left and his father had started finally paying attention to him. Disinterest turned to soft touches against Shan's cheek and moments when his father stood close enough to press their bodies together. After he'd started to suspect his father had been abusing Naite in that house, he'd felt nauseous… trapped. His bike had been his only escape.

He'd come home after a day apprenticing with Holmes, and his father would watch him with this intensity that Shan had learned to hate. He would endure the feeling of being enmeshed in his father's desire as long as he could, and then he'd encourage his father to have a little pipe juice to make himself feel better. Just a little. And once the old man drank too much, Shan would flee on his bike. He'd ride the sands in the middle of the night, and if a sandcat or a dune had killed him, he wouldn't have cared.

Enmeshed. That described the feeling about as well as anything else Shan could come up with. And unfortunately, that's exactly what he felt now. He and Temar were tangled up with politics he couldn't possibly understand, and that old nauseous feeling caught him off guard, and he had no way to escape out to the dunes with his bike. The feeling made it hard to appreciate the tall trees with their thick, straight trunks and the grasses that swayed slowly as some hidden fan stirred the air. Shan could hear a roar in the distance, and in his current state of stress and paranoia, he searched for the source, but the path bent and twisted through tall foliage that didn't allow him to see very far.

"Ambassador Gazer, that is a stunning necklace," Officer Aral said.

Temar's hand went up to the glass knot. "Thank you, but please call me Temar."

She ducked her head, a gesture Shan had seen the other ambassador use as well. "Thank you," she said. "In that case, you should call me Natalie. Are there many artists with that kind of talent on Livre?" She gestured toward the necklace.

Temar looked down at the glass. "Dee'eta is amazing, but there are four or five glass workers who could come close to her skill, perhaps even match it. Of course, I'm biased since I know Dee'eta."

"That is an amazing piece." Natalie moved closer. "May I?" she asked, looking at the pendant.

Temar nodded, and Natalie reached up to finger the delicate curves. "When the war broke out, very few artists remained with the AFP. The inner planets have more money and resources, and they can afford to give grants so people have time to develop artistically. It became a point of patriotic pride to get rid of artwork from the inner planets, which has left us a little lacking."

Shan wasn't sure he bought that explanation. Livre was as poor as a planet could be, yet every unskilled worker had an appreciation for beauty. The planet certainly had a number of artists. "We brought carved wood art pieces as well," Shan said, watching Natalie.

She looked over at him with wide eyes. "I thought Livre didn't have trees."

"We have windwood trees… very thin flexible trunks that bend with the wind. A good artist can twist the wood pieces together to make some beautiful art. I believe Kevin sent along one of his carved birds."

"I would love to see that, Ambassador Polli."

"Shan."

Both her eyebrows went up, and she traded a surprised look with Rula. "Shan," she repeated carefully. "I look forward to seeing the piece, even if you decide against trading it."

"I'll make sure you have a chance to," Shan said carefully, not sure where this conversation was going. "So, the war with the inner planets... it doesn't sound as though it's as finished as we thought."

Temar had been crouching on the path, his fingers exploring a plant with long sprays of tiny yellow flowers, but he looked up at that.

"We certainly have some lingering issues." Natalie's gaze slid upward, and Shan followed it, not sure what he was looking at. There were the same metal walls and lines of lights he'd seen in the landing hangar. "War leaves hard feelings, and there are people on either side who resent the peace agreements the alliances have reached." Her voice had a stiffness to it, and she turned her back on him before starting down the path. "There is a waterfall that you truly must see."

Shan paused, looking over at Temar for a second, but he looked only mildly confused. With no real understanding of the situation, Shan followed Natalie. They left the racks of plants behind, and the path opened up into a field of sorts, with plants crowded together in narrow tiers that rose up to near shoulder level. Bright red and orange flowers interrupted the vivid green leaves that spilled over metal planting beds. The path curved through the rounded planting beds, and the roar grew so loud that it seemed to pound in Shan's head.

Feeling like he had sand tickling his face, Shan raised his hand to wipe it, only to find his skin damp. Blinking, he turned to look at Temar, but he'd stopped to sit on the edge of a planter and explore an enormous pod-like structure hanging under yellow fruit. The pink pod had loose petals lined in dark red. It was a stunning structure framed with enormous leaves. From the look on Temar's face, the plant interested him far more than the idea of water in the air.

Shan turned back to talk to Natalie, but she was forty feet down the path. Caught between wanting to understand her and wanting to stay with Temar, Shan hesitated. "Temar?" he asked, turning his back on Natalie. Rula sat on the edge of the planter near Temar, and that made Shan nervous too.

"Yes?" Temar looked up, a distant expression in his face.

"Do you want me to…." Shan let his voice trail off as he looked over his shoulder at Natalie.

"I'm fine," Temar said, smiling, and Shan could see he was at ease. Wishing he had a little of that calm, Shan nodded before he forced himself to back up.

"If you're sure," he offered, silently hoping Temar would invite him to stay. Shan didn't want to hover. Temar was a man who could take care of himself, but right now, Shan wouldn't mind a little clinging.

"I'm fine. These are stunning." Temar ran his finger down one of the enormous petals. "I wonder if you could create this in glass." His voice softened, and Shan realized Temar was paying more attention to the flower than Shan or even their situation.

With a sigh, Shan turned toward Natalie and headed down the path. The floor here was a textured metal grate, and Shan could see drops of water gathering on the path and the leaves that arched over it. When Shan followed the twisted path around another turn, he stopped dead.

Far above, water fell out of a tall tower and crashed down over two terraces before falling into an enormous basin. Shan's brain whited-out for a second. He'd seen vids of waterfalls, but they hadn't prepared him for this. The roar of the water rushing down, the pounding thunder of water hitting the terraces hard enough to turn it white before it fell over the edge and landed in the lake. The sense of weight and movement. And the smell. Shan couldn't describe the warm scents that rose up from the water.

Inching closer, tiny drops struck his skin, some clinging and others dripping down. Shan looked at his arms; water droplets stuck to his arm hair, highlighting them oddly. "It's beautiful," Shan whispered, awe robbing his voice of any strength. He never expected to see water like this. Intellectually, he knew it was only water, but the majesty of it made him feel like he was sitting at God's feet. And this wasn't even a real waterfall or a real lake. Shan closed his eyes and tried to imagine what it would mean to have this much water openly flowing across the face of a planet. Despite his fourth-year science class, he couldn't really envision it.

"I thought you would appreciate it." Natalie had to shout to make herself heard.

"I truly do," Shan agreed. He wished Temar were here to see this. Turning, he glanced back down the path. When Natalie appeared right at his elbow, Shan sucked in a surprised breath.

"Microphones have trouble picking up voices here because of the water and noise. The AFP church says that homosexuality is a sin. They'll use it as an excuse to arrest you and extort glass and minerals out of your planet." Natalie smiled at him. Her mildly pleasant expression and her fingers resting against her upper lip in a casual expression of interest didn't match the words that left Shan blinking at her, his brain unable to process the message. Before he could pull himself out of his shock, Natalie was heading down the path in the direction of Temar and Rula.

Shan followed, the words sinking slowly into his awareness. The church certainly had its dark history. The two periods of sexualized priesthood bookended a dark Paulian phase when the church had lost touch with Christ and worshipped Paul, but Shan couldn't figure out what would drive the church he loved to return to that belief system. Paulians focused on limiting others—persecution of women and homosexuals and even women who wore short hair and men who wore theirs long. Shan swallowed as he hurried his steps. Natalie was talking to Temar, and for the first time, Shan noted that Natalie and Rula both had long hair, despite the fact that, as a fighter, Rula clearly would have been more comfortable with short hair.

"Is it true?" Temar asked with a bright smile, and Shan opened his mouth, not able to form words when his brain kept recycling every conversation he'd had since contacting the AFP. "Shan?" Temar left his oversized flower and closed the distance between them. Shan flinched back when Temar tried to touch him, and the shock on Temar's face made guilt crawl into Shan's stomach.

"The waterfall is amazing," Shan said weakly. "Absolutely amazing."

Temar frowned, one hand raised as though he still wanted to touch Shan, but Shan's brain whirled with thoughts of a hundred atrocities encouraged by the sort of discrimination Paulians represented. They took Christ's commandment to love others and turn the other cheek and twisted it into some belief where torturing someone else was justified as long as you tortured them in an attempt to bring them around to "correct" thinking. Div had forced him to learn the entire history of the church, insisted that every priest had to know the dangers. Right now, Shan would give anything to scrub certain memories out of his head. He looked around, almost expecting to see guards appear to arrest them for being abominations of nature. Nature. Yes, and Paul called it an abomination of nature for a man to have long hair, as well.

"Shan, you don't look well." Temar slowly lowered his hand and took a small step back.

Closing his eyes, Shan struggled to get a firm grip on his fears. "Ever since we got off the shuttle, I keep feeling like the ground is still moving," he lied. He *had* felt that strange sense of trying to walk on shifting sand for a minute or two after getting off the shuttle, but the sensation had passed quickly. He must have lied well, because Natalie's growing alarm turned to sympathy, and Rula quickly moved to his side, her hand resting lightly against his arm.

"It's common," Rula promised in a soft voice that didn't match her appearance. "We should find someplace for you to sit down until it passes. It's not unusual for someone to fall down, and that can lead to serious injury."

"Why didn't you say something?" Temar asked with a hint of anger in his voice, but he kept his distance, clearly taking his hint from Shan's unwillingness to touch earlier. Even though Shan understood that Temar was following his lead, it still hurt to watch Temar physically retreat.

"I didn't want to interrupt the tour."

Natalie moved in on his other side. "The rest of the tour can wait until you're feeling better, Ambassador Polli."

"Shan," he corrected her as he realized he really did feel sick.

chapter

SHAN SAT at the table in his quarters, his head pounding in time with his heartbeat.

"Are you feeling any better?" Natalie asked, sliding a cup in front of him. Shan wrapped his hands around the cup, surprised to find it cold.

"A little," he said. He glanced toward the door that led into Temar's rooms.

"Well, the noise of the waterfall can be a bit much. It's nice and quiet in here." Natalie gave him a hard look that Shan would have to be an idiot to miss the significance of. It was quiet in here, meaning microphones could record them.

"Quiet is good," he said weakly, but he gave her a firm nod to tell her he'd received her message. If he believed these cryptic warnings, he couldn't trust anyone on this ship, and he couldn't even tell Temar what was going on. He really wished she had decided to tell Temar instead, but she hadn't and he figured asking her to take Temar to the waterfall would probably seem strange to anyone who'd been assigned to watch them.

"Ship sickness is an inner-ear disturbance, so it's not surprising that the noise of the waterfall would aggravate it." Natalie had turned all sympathy and smiles now that Shan seemed to be going along with the plan. Shan eyed her, wondering exactly what she had planned in all this. Ambassador Melton had called her an expert on Livre. How much did she know?

Shan rested his chin in his hand and slowly rotated the chilled cup as he tried to figure out how much they'd shared with the Free Planets. He knew no one had discussed sexuality. That simply wasn't done in public. Sex was a private affair, and even asking who someone was partnered with had a bit of a taboo attached. Shan always felt some ironic amusement at that fact, because the men and women of Livre tended to have sex quite a lot. Div remained silent on the matter as long as it didn't wander into the territory of adultery or coveting or people using the Lord's name in vain as they cursed each other out over some lover's quarrel. Short of that, Div encouraged people to take vows without condemning the sort of casual sex so many people engaged in.

And for most people, experimenting with sex started out with homosexuality. You certainly didn't want to risk a pregnancy when a woman was too young to carry it easily, and no man wanted to have his wages diverted to a child who didn't live in his home, so sex with the opposite gender waited until you met someone you wanted to start a life with. However, Shan knew very few people so inflexible that they'd chosen to wait rather than playing with people of the same gender.

One of the women he'd counseled as a priest, Marium, had been that way. She'd thought something was wrong with her because other women could never interest her, and she'd resorted to faking orgasms to avoid leaving partners feeling inadequate. Shan suggested that she just wait until she found a man she liked well enough to marry, but he knew she still felt awkward, like there was something wrong with her. When he'd been a young man, he'd avoided full anal sex out of fear, sticking with rubbing and mouths on the rare occasions when he'd been sexually active, and a lot of young men did that. The first time Shan had seen a fully erect cock, he hadn't believed anyone could physically make it fit up an ass.

Shan grimaced and wondered how these people from this alliance of supposedly "Free" Planets would appreciate his world. He suspected that if they were all Paulians, they wouldn't be amused.

"Do you need a pain reliever?" Natalie asked softly.

Shaking his head, Shan lifted his cup and drank. It was an iced drink that tasted of sweet balm. "Good," he said, raising his glass.

"It's lemonade. Livre didn't have cultivars for citrus, so I imagine it's a new flavor."

"We have a hot drink called sweet balm that's similar." Shan looked down at his cup. How was he supposed to negotiate with these people when he couldn't talk to them without having to weigh every word?

Natalie reached over and rested her hand on Shan's arm, and he looked up at her in surprise.

"Your planet is very resourceful. I shouldn't be surprised you found a way to make lemonade, even without lemons."

Shifting aside the larger concerns for now, Shan focused on Natalie. "I imagine you're fairly resourceful yourself. A protocol officer sounds like a rather high position."

"For a woman, you mean?" Natalie asked him with a smile. A stone settled in Shan's stomach at the evidence that the social corruption was so deep. Women tended Christ, watched his body, announced his return, and yet the Paulians would exclude them from any authority. Why hadn't Shan seen any signs of this when they'd talked over the communicator? Shan sighed as he wondered if he had been really listening or if he'd been so busy making his own plans that he'd missed the big, flashing warning signs.

"For anyone," Shan corrected her gently.

She smiled at him and tightened her fingers before pulling her hand away. "My parents died in an attack on Loralei and I ended up on a refugee ship to Minga, so I had to figure out how to make myself useful at a very young age. I had a talent for explaining things."

"Minga. Isn't that in the Planetary Alliance?"

"Now. Back then it was a battlefront. I found a group of AFP soldiers hiding during a Planetary Alliance sweep, and I helped them."

So, she'd done what she had to in order to survive and found herself on the wrong side of the war. Maybe. Shan was seeing the AFP's flaws, but he didn't know whether the Planetary Alliance was worse. More and more, Shan wished he could go back in time and break the communication equipment until no one could fix it. If the Lord had a plan in mind, He hadn't yet shared it with Shan. "And Rula?"

Natalie's eyes narrowed. "What about Rula?" Based on the suspicion in her voice, Shan suspected he wasn't the only one trying to hide a lover.

"Is it normal for women to become soldiers?" If Livre had fought in the war, the women would have gone up with the men. Women like Sua Smith and Aila Freewind could swing an ax or a gun just as well as Naite.

"Most people don't realize she's a soldier. How did you?"

"She moves like one."

"She has the mouth of one," Natalie said with an amused huff, and Shan waited for some sort of explanation. Natalie drew her lips up in an odd expression. "She can be overly blunt, which is why she has orders to avoid talking to the senior ambassador. I think Ambassador

Melton is afraid she'll say something to make negotiations more difficult."

That was ironic. Natalie had already made things nearly as difficult as they could get. "Why do you have a soldier as an assistant?" Shan asked. "Do you really think Temar or I would pose any sort of danger?"

All expression left Natalie's face as she blinked at him. Her eyes flickered up toward the ceiling, and her mouth opened once, closed, and then she pressed her lips together tightly. The entire display worried Shan more than any words.

"Assigning a security detail is a matter of protocol," she finally said in a voice so sweet it could turn olives to candy.

"So you don't expect Temar to pull a knife and try to hijack the ship?"

Natalie laughed. "No, no, I really don't. We honestly never even thought you would spot Rula as a soldier at all. Most people think she's my assistant."

That hadn't been Shan's first assumption, but he wasn't going to discuss that here. "As long as we haven't given you the impression that you have to put guards on us."

"You did put on quite a show for the airship pilot."

"Show?" Shan frowned.

Natalie leaned close. "Do you really have local predators that could take out a man?"

Shan leaned back and wondered whether she'd been sent to ask this exact question. If so, he wasn't sure she was on their side. "My father, Yan Polli, died in a sandrat attack," Shan said quietly. Natalie lost most of the color out of her face. "They're pack predators. They'll use razor teeth to rip the feet out from under larger prey and then pull them to the ground, where they eat them alive. The larger sandcats are the same species, but while they can and have formed exceptionally dangerous packs, they more often hunt alone. Last year, Landing alone lost forty-three people to predator attacks in the desert." Shan stood, uncomfortable with using the memory of those exiled people this way. Moving across the room, he focused on a vidscreen showing a field of stars. "There isn't a person on Livre who doesn't know someone who's died on that desert."

"Ambassador Polli, I apologize," Natalie offered.

"Shan," he corrected her for the third or fourth time.

"Shan," she echoed. "I certainly didn't mean to bring up bad memories. I was simply surprised. The early reports had very little to say about the local fauna."

"And then humans came down and they found a new food source." Shan turned to face her. "I love Livre. I love the orange and green streaks in the sky after a sandstorm. I love the wide spaces and the feel of a bike flying down a duneface. However, *I've* nearly died on that desert. I've known dozens of people who have died out there, so I love it without ever underestimating its power."

"I understand."

"Do you?" The words slipped out even though Shan knew they were rude.

Natalie stood and moved closer to him, her hands tucked behind her back in a pose that Shan found suggestive of military training. Rula might not be the only soldier. "I do know, Shan. I understand you can love something dangerous. And I apologize for doubting the veracity of your claims. I absolutely believe you're being honest." Her eyes flicked up toward the ceiling again, and Shan frowned. "I absolutely believe you," she repeated, and she turned her head to look toward the couch. It took Shan a second to spot the small tan disk planted inside her ear, but when he did, he still wasn't sure what to make of it.

"Apology accepted."

Natalie gave him a bright smile. "I am glad. You're not at all what I expected. Very few ambassadors ride bikes or risk their lives on the desert. I would hate to offend you."

"You haven't. Trust me, it takes a good deal more than that to offend me."

"I'm glad. I had hoped to invite you to dinner. My degree in sociology suggests that people from rural areas give more weight to socializing and getting to know individuals rather than the details of the financial trade. So, did my professors get that right?"

"They did. I'll get Temar," Shan said, turning toward the door. He hated that Temar was alone with Rula, so he appreciated the excuse to get him.

Natalie caught his arm, stopping him. "Do you need him to come along?" From her expression, she definitely wanted him to say "no."

"I should talk to him," Shan said, unsure what he should do or which side Natalie served.

"Rula is good company. She can play a ruthless game of cards. They'll be fine."

Natalie still had that intense expression, but Shan pulled his arm away from her and headed for the door. Pushing it open, Shan found himself in a bedroom/sitting room combination, which surprised him, because the joint sitting room connected their two personal quarters. Exactly how much sitting were two men supposed to do? Rula and Temar sat in front of a vid screen, images of artwork in tiny squares until Rula clicked one and it filled the small screen.

"Temar?" Shan asked.

Temar leaned back in his chair. The wide smile suggested that he'd been enjoying his tour of art, and Shan felt a flare of jealousy that he couldn't share that joy—not without making these people suspicious.

"Natalie invited us out for dinner."

"Oh?" Temar swiveled his chair around, and Natalie pressed close to Shan from behind.

"You're welcome to join us or stay here and review the art pieces you're enjoying. Rula rarely gets a dinner partner who shares her interest in art. We can have some food sent down from the officers' hall." Natalie's voice sounded pleasant enough, but Shan could see the stiffening in Temar's body, and he looked from Shan to Natalie with a frown that projected his confusion.

"I could show you the crap that passes for paintings on Vitalis Three," Rula offered, and Shan could see the words pulling Temar closer toward Natalie's plan. Temar looked to Shan, clearly wanting some sort of hint about whether he should stay or go with them, but Shan didn't know what to advise, and if Natalie had told him the truth about people listening, he couldn't have that conversation with Temar. He hated this.

"Honestly, I'd rather stay here than try to deal with a lot of strangers," Temar said almost apologetically.

"That's fine." Shan hid his disappointment. "I'm sure you'll enjoy talking art with someone, and I know I'm not always the best person for that conversation."

"What, just because you compliment glass spun by a sixth-year student? Why would I question your good taste?" Temar teased, easing the tension in the room.

Shan grinned at him. "If you'd seen the crap I spun when I tried that in *my* sixth year, you'd show a little more appreciation for your own talent." Shan basked in Temar's smile until Natalie moved closer, wrapping her hands around Shan's arm. Shan froze, and the smile faded from Temar's face.

"We should go. The food gets less predictable as the night gets later. There are rumors that the chef does a little imbibing of the cooking sherry," Natalie said brightly. Shan opened his mouth to say something to reassure Temar or order Natalie away, but she pulled at him, and before he could gather his thoughts, they were back in the sitting room heading for the door.

"I'm not sure—"

"They'll be fine," Natalie said, but she clenched her jaw and her fingernails dug into the soft meat on the inside of Shan's elbow. Confused and worried, Shan closed his mouth and let her pull him out to dinner, when he suspected he'd enjoy himself more if he stayed with Temar and looked at art.

chapter
twenty-one

BY THE time Shan got back to the quarters he shared with Temar, he didn't know what to believe. Natalie had charmed him—some might say flirted with him, but it'd been a long time since he had any experience with flirting, so he wasn't sure. He wasn't sure about a whole lot, since the wine she'd offered him at dinner was stronger than he'd thought.

Shan let himself into the quarters, nodding to the soldier who had been escorting him ever since he left dinner with Natalie. The main sitting room was quiet, and Shan headed toward the door to Temar's room. He hated that Temar had a separate room, but after a night full of veiled hints about religion and violence, Shan wasn't about to seduce his lover as long as they were on this ship. He was also going to start avoiding wine.

Letting himself into Temar's room, Shan saw that he was asleep, his leg tangled in a white sheet with his arm thrown over his eyes. His gray sleep pants rode so low that Shan could see the trail of barely visible blond hair that led from his belly button down, to disappear under the waistband.

Shan wasn't sure how long he stood there before Temar shifted, his arm lifting as he blinked. "Shan?" he asked, and Shan realized that, with the light from the sitting room spilling in behind him, Temar couldn't see him.

"Yeah, it's me."

Temar sat up, shifting around in the bed. "How was your night?"

Shan paused, not sure how to answer with their potential audience listening in. "I'm not sure."

"What?" Temar squinted at Shan. "What happened?"

"We just got to know each other."

"Uh-huh."

Shan squirmed, truly uncomfortable now.

"Is she nice?"

"Yeah. She has a degree in sociology, even though she lost her entire family in the war. I'm pretty sure she was in the service before she started doing this protocol thing. They have wine. It's a little like drinking the world's weakest pipe juice flavored with grapes and wood."

Temar pushed the sheet off, swung his legs off the bed, and got up. "Okay, that sounds disgusting."

"It was actually kind of good. Better than pipe juice. Were you and Rula okay?"

"Yeah, we were fine." Temar moved to Shan's side, and Shan flinched back from his touch. If he let Temar touch him, that was going to lead to something, and Shan couldn't have anything happen. Temar let his hands drop to his side. "Shan, are you sure you're okay?"

There were a lot of things wrong with him, but Shan was almost sure Temar meant physically. "Do you know how I was after I nearly died on the desert?"

"Are you that sick?"

"No, no, I'm not. I'm sort of in that fuzzy state where things are mostly fitting together in reality but not quite."

Temar took a step backward. "So, no hallucinations?"

"Not even one. I am, however, feeling a little uneasy."

"Like you might throw up?"

"No. It's weird. I don't have any of the side effects of pipe juice. I don't feel like passing out or throwing up, but I am a little fuzzy around the edges." Turning around, Shan headed for his room. "I'm really glad that we don't have wine on Livre, or we would have a lot more drunks."

"That's one thing we won't ask for, then." Temar followed him, pulling his sleep pants up.

"They'll like that."

"Who?"

Shan headed into his room and dropped onto the bed without taking any of his clothes off. They had more clothes. "The AFP," Shan answered. "They're very religious."

"You should like that," Temar said in a tone that made Shan look at him. "What does that have to do with wine?"

Shan let his head fall back to the bed. "Drunkenness. Drunkenness is not religious. They wouldn't appreciate it if we traded away our glass and raw materials for too much wine."

"If that's the case, you must have made a great impression on them. Seriously, Shan, what is going on?"

"I think the wine is more like pipe juice than I thought."

"Obviously." Temar came and sat on the side of the bed, and Shan looked at him, wanting him but really not wanting him enough to get them both killed by bigots.

"I don't think I'll be drinking anymore."

"Good idea," Temar agreed.

"I don't want to tell them the truth." Shan closed his eyes, and immediately sleep started pulling at him.

"Oh, what truth are we avoiding?"

Shan grunted. He didn't want to talk about this. He wanted to sleep. "We have to avoid it."

"Avoid what?"

"Ask Natalie," Shan muttered.

"Natalie?" Temar's voice went up, and Shan opened one eye to look at him. "Exactly what am I asking Natalie about?" Temar asked.

"Um…." Shan's mind whited-out as he tried to figure out what he could say without putting them all at risk. Natalie's obscure references to bloodshed had him a little unsure about just how crazy these people were. Shan knew from church history that religious violence was the worst.

When Shan couldn't come up with an explanation, Temar stood and patted him on the leg. "Get some sleep, Shan. We can talk about it tomorrow, okay?"

That wasn't okay. Nothing was okay. However, Shan blinked and Temar was gone, leaving Shan alone with his tangled thoughts. "Well, shit," he muttered as he closed his eyes. That hadn't gone well.

chapter
twenty-two

ONE AWKWARD morning with curious looks from Temar and one very awkward day with Ambassador Melton and Shan's headache had grown to epic proportions. Melton had tried to link any sales to Livre joining the AFP, and he didn't seem to understand why Shan might have doubts about that. Worse, he kept giving Natalie little looks, clearly encouraging her to try to convince him to go along with the program. The more Natalie talked, the more Shan started to wonder if she hadn't manipulated him so he would trust her judgment.

Every time she urged him to consider the advantages of being a member planet, a sandrat started eating Shan's brain just behind his right eye. It didn't help that Temar kept watching, his chin resting on his hand as he kept looking around with this wide-eyed confusion that made Shan feel two inches high.

He ate the food they brought during one break without tasting it, turning down the wine that appeared.

"I am not comfortable committing my planet to an alliance," Shan said for about the hundredth time. Naite would have been a better ambassador. He would have ended the interminable debates with one well-placed fist, and then they could have all moved on.

"The border planets need to present a strong front. I know your people missed the war, but I understand that Officer Aral explained the horror of it to you last night." Melton looked toward Natalie for confirmation.

"It was a horrible time," Natalie agreed.

"I understand that." Shan looked over to Temar for some sort of support.

"I think Ambassador Polli believes that we simply don't know anyone well enough to make permanent friendships," Temar said softly. Ambassador Melton gave him only a quick glance before turning back to Shan.

"We have the military strength to protect you from the Inner Alliance. They have control of Minga, right on your border, and they'd do a lot to get control of these sorts of resources. Their rules, their taxes, their intrusive beliefs are impossible to live under, and that's what you're risking."

Shan took a deep breath. "Ambassador," he said, "the people of Livre aren't likely to support any alliance made quickly, and I can tell you this about my people… they don't put up with anyone telling them what to do. If, as you suggest, the Planetary Alliance came to Livre and tried to tax the people, they'd find that no one on the planet owned more than one shirt and glass would vanish under the sands. We can be a rather disagreeable people when we're pushed."

Shan imagined someone from either alliance trying to tell Lilian what to do. Considering that the woman's sons couldn't handle her and her two daughters had both moved off the farm, telling people they loved their mother but they would murder her in cold blood if they had to live with her any longer, it wouldn't end well. And Naite wouldn't even bother being polite while he suggested both sides shove their rules right up their backsides, only he'd use much more colorful language.

Ambassador Melton laughed. "I think I like your people. That is why we should be allies."

"Ambassador Melton," Natalie said in that ingratiating voice Shan mistrusted, "perhaps we need to move slowly. We could have a presence on the planet. Perhaps I could act as a local liaison, and perhaps Livre could appoint a permanent ambassador to the AFP."

Shan stared at the woman. Right now, all he wanted was to get off the ship without having to ever talk to these people again.

"If we established a trading office in Landing, we could start building the sort of relationship that would help Livre to come into the alliance." Natalie turned and smiled at Shan before reaching over to brush her fingers over his arm. Shan blinked. Either she was seriously flirting with him or she was trying to buy a ticket out of the AFP, and at this point, Shan didn't trust himself to know which was more likely. Looking over at Temar, he could see Temar watching Natalie's hand with a small frown, and Shan yanked his arm away.

"I understand the need to move slow, but this is a major investment of water and resources. Ambassador Polli, you can see why we would want a long-term relationship. in return for this kind of investment."

"At this point, I'm not sure it's fair to call this an investment as much as a trade. We have merchandise. We'll trade for water, technology, and animals." Shan tried to keep his face neutral, but it wasn't easy with Natalie rolling her chair closer and Temar on the other side of the table watching with an intensity that suddenly looked more like Lilian Freeland than Shan wanted to think about. It was probably because they had the same fair skin and blue eyes, but Shan was starting to get that same uneasy feeling as when Lilian was unhappy with him.

Melton leaned back. "We can certainly deal with this as if it was a one-time trade, but that means you're asking us to divert an ice-mining ship and a drop system for water when this might be a one-time deal. That's an expensive proposition."

Shan frowned. "Why would this be one time?"

Melton's mouth hung open several seconds before he spoke. "I keep trying to offer you a long-term arrangement, and you continually turn it down."

Shan shook his head. "No, you're offering to have us in your alliance, which would limit us to working with you."

"Would you rather work with the Inner Alliance?" he demanded, puffing up like George Young.

Shan didn't have an answer, and he had the feeling he'd badly misspoken. "No, I'm sure we wouldn't," Shan said in his most soothing voice. The longer he spent talking to these people, the more he liked machines better than people.

"Ambassador Melton," Temar said softly, "our people have a saying. They say that the truth is finer than sand."

Melton frowned, looking from Shan to Temar in confusion as Temar seemed to gather his thoughts.

"If someone's story doesn't make sense, we'll say that it doesn't even hold stones, much less sand, and of course if truth is finer than sand, it runs through a much finer mesh. We aren't saying we want to trade with someone else or even that we don't want an alliance with you."

Shan figured Temar could say that honestly, since he didn't have all the information, but Shan didn't interrupt as Temar seemed to talk their way out of the mess Shan had made. Melton was leaning back in his chair, his fingers steepled in front of him as he concentrated on Temar.

"We are suggesting," Temar continued, "that we carry this bag for a while and see if it holds the truth. We're a cautious people, and if we have to pay a little extra because of our caution, you can understand that, yes?"

Melton still looked concerned, but it was Natalie who spoke up.

"Coming from a world where local predators attack from under the sand without warning and where humans can be prey, this sort of caution is predictable. I like your saying, Ambassador Gazer. Truth is finer than sand." She smiled at Temar, and the sandrat gnawing on Shan's brain chewed a little harder.

"Ambassador Polli?" Melton asked.

"Temar is right. I never meant to offend you, but my people are much too stubborn to accept any alliance quickly or easily. As Ambassador Gazer points out, they'll want proof that the mesh is woven tightly enough to hold both sand and truth."

Melton frowned as he glanced back down at the datapad with their latest numbers.

The current trade represented more wealth than Shan had seen in his life. The water wouldn't be enough to finish terraforming the planet, but it was enough to make the current farms run for another seventy or eighty years. And this was one deal. Shan tried hard not to show any emotion. After all, he'd listened to confession while people talked about adultery and fighting and cursing, and he'd gotten pretty good at keeping a straight face through it. He'd even gotten to the point where he could meet people on the street and not twitch as he remembered what they'd told him during their previous confession.

"The deal includes the optic glass samples?" he asked.

Shan looked over at Temar to see if he had any opinion on whether to try to push for more. He gazed back at Shan, his eyes flicking to Natalie, and Shan quickly looked away. "Those are samples. If you want to buy them, another thirty-three thousand gallons per sample would work."

"Deal," Melton said, far too quickly. The people of Livre would consider it a good trade, even if Melton would have paid a lot more, and from his tone, it seemed like he would. "We can stay here until the water ships have confirmed their first delivery, if you'd like, Ambassador Polli."

Shan would much rather saw off his own leg than stay with these people longer than necessary, but he pasted on a smile. "We should start this with trust and assume the mesh will hold the truth. You can distribute our goods, and we are happy to return to Livre, announce the deal, and wait for the deliveries."

Melton smiled so wide his whole face seemed to stretch in new directions. "We are going to be allies. Those of us out here on the border know the value of a handshake and a word. And I'm offering you mine. You'll get the trade goods." Standing up, he offered his hand, and Shan rose, shaking it solemnly. "Ambassador Gazer," he said, offering his hand to Temar. Temar shook it, but that emotionless mask allowed only for a small, insincere smile. Shan had to talk to him, explain a few things before the trust between them eroded too much.

"Ambassador Melton, yesterday I was ill, forcing our tour to be cut short before Temar could see the waterfall. I simply have to allow him to see it, since it's unlikely that either of us will have the chance again."

"Of course, of course." Melton was still all smiles, but his attention had turned to a datapad where he furiously typed—probably orders to send out the Livre goods. Then he looked up. "Ambassadors, you will have to join me some time on Loralei. The tropical jungles are magnificent, and I have a house built into the side of a cliff that overlooks the most magnificent waterfall. It plummets almost nine hundred meters to the lake below."

That surprised Shan, since he'd gotten the feeling from Natalie that the border worlds had issues with poverty that meant ships sometimes went unrepaired. "It sounds lovely," he said. Right now, there was only one waterfall he cared about, and as amazing as it was to see water flow that way, it wasn't the water he was interested in, per se.

"I can show them the way," Natalie said. She stood, and now they were all standing, so Shan inched backward toward the door.

"Of course. Thank you." Melton had returned to his datapad, and Shan gave a quick nod and then turned and headed for the door. Temar was already there, watching with those sharp blue eyes, and Shan wondered how fast he was going to have to talk to explain this whole mess.

"This way," Natalie said with a smile as she gestured toward the door. Shan headed out, unsurprised to see Rula waiting. "I do hope you don't mind that I invited myself to your planet. Livre sounds beautiful, and I know that we can learn so much from each other." Rula looked over her shoulder at Natalie before striding down the hall.

Shan had to assume she knew they wanted to visit the waterfall, and he followed. "No, I don't mind at all, as long as you understand that Livre doesn't have a lot of the… things you're used to," Shan warned. Either that, or he was promising she wouldn't encounter the same homophobia.

"I grew up in a war zone. Trust me, I know how to do without. I really should bring Rula, though. I'll need an assistant, and as much as I trust your people, your world sounds rather dangerous. She's rather good at taking care of herself."

"I suspect you're not bad at doing that for yourself," Shan muttered. "You're welcome to bring Rula. I assume it will just be the two of you? No offense, but I don't think most Livre residents want an invasion of immigrants who don't know how to walk the dunes without getting buried under them. It will take some teaching to keep you out of trouble."

"I think the two of us can manage quite nicely," Natalie said as she moved closer, walking so that their shoulders brushed against each other. Shan might not know much about flirting, but he did recognize the look she gave him as she ducked her head and watched through her lashes. He recognized it, but he really had no idea how to handle it. He stared ahead at Rula's and Temar's backs.

"Here we are," Rula announced as they stopped in front of the double doors that led to the gardens.

"Great." Shan moved forward so fast he brushed past Temar, only to turn and offer an apologetic look. Temar's eyebrow went up, but he didn't say anything as Rula opened the doors. The scent of flowers and wet earth rolled out of the room like a slow sandstorm that sluggishly moved the lazy sands. However, the desert never smelled anything like this. Now that Shan knew what the plants hid, he could pick out the rumble of the waterfall even from the door. He wondered what purpose they had in dropping water over those terraces, but he suspected it had more to do with water purification or maybe the life cycle of some species than having an attraction people could enjoy. These people didn't strike Shan as the sort that cared all that much about others' enjoyment, not unless the people in question were high-ranking ambassadors.

Immediately, Shan started down the path, stopping when Temar paused to finger a delicate flower. "Temar?" Shan asked. Maybe it was his tone of voice, because Temar dropped his hand to his side and headed after Shan.

"Coming," he offered cheerfully. Shan headed down the path, Temar and Natalie in tow. Now he needed to get rid of Natalie.

When they reached the section where the path turned from textured metal to the textured grate that allowed the falling water drops to escape through it, Shan turned and rested his hand on Natalie's arm. "Could you check on the shipment, make sure that everything is loaded safely?" he shouted over the waterfall's roar. They still had to follow another turn in the path to see it, so Shan wasn't sure if this part of the path could be recorded or not.

"I'm sure they'll be careful," she shouted back, tiny drops of water gathering on her thick lashes. Her brown hair darkened with the moisture, and she gave him a look that made it clear she did not want to leave his side.

"Please?" he asked, raising his voice. "I trust you to make sure that everything is done right. After they sent an old shuttle down to pick us up, I'm not sure I trust everyone here to understand how fragile glass can be."

Natalie gave him a searching look. "I'll leave a guide at the door to lead you to your quarters or to the dining hall when you're done. Just let him know where you want to go." She turned and gave Temar a nod before heading back the way they'd come. Shan wondered whether she needed Rula or if she didn't trust them to keep her lover safe. Of course, from the way Natalie acted toward him, he was starting to question himself about whether those two were truly lovers. Right now, though, he cared more about his own lover.

chapter
twenty-three

"THE WATERFALL'S this way," Shan said, which was obvious enough, but Temar smiled and started down the path. The second time around, the waterfall was equally impressive. Shan slowed as it came in sight, appreciating the sheer power of such a simple thing as water. "Running water," Shan said reverently. Seeing it on vids could not match seeing it in reality.

Temar leaned close. "I've seen water run. Remember?"

Shan looked down, and Temar had an amused look on his face, even though the one time he'd seen running water had not been an amusing incident.

"I haven't." Shan leaned close so he wouldn't have to shout. The water roared over the artificial rocks, and the cool wind flowing past them carried drops of water. "I'm still awed by it."

"It really is awe-inspiring," Temar agreed. He leaned closer, and Shan looked across the open water to the walkway, where a man in a uniform watched them.

"I want to get a closer look. This water is amazing. I never thought I'd see open water like this." Shan let his hand fall away, even though he wanted that contract. When Temar let him walk away without comment, Shan's guts tightened. He walked to the edge of the water, where he could stand behind a plant larger than him. He was used to wisp grass and pipe traps and chokeweed. They were gray plants with tiny leaves that hid in the sands. Even growing up in the valley, the crops had thin leaves and small flowers. This thing had leaves larger than his head—fat, arrow-shaped dark green leaves.

"It's beautiful," Temar offered as he came up behind Shan, but instead of touching Shan, he reached out to run his fingers along the edge of the plant's leaf.

"I can explain," Shan whispered. Hopefully the roar of the water would hide his words, because if Natalie was right, they were on dangerous territory.

"Explain what?" Temar whispered back.

"I'm not interested in Natalie, not like… not sexually," Shan said, desperate to say that before someone could interrupt them. He couldn't lose Temar over this. He couldn't.

Temar frowned at him for a second. "I know that," he finally said.

Shan opened his mouth, fully prepared to defend himself, and then it sank in that Temar wasn't asking him to defend his actions. Temar said he believed him, and from the expression on his face, he didn't have a shadow of doubt on that front. Shan was temporarily stunned into stillness.

"What I don't know is why you're acting like this," Temar added.

"You don't think… I mean… not that I'm interested in having sex with her, because I'm not, but you never thought I was?"

The best description of Temar's face was amused, and Shan didn't have any idea how to take that. Leaning closer, Temar whispered, "You believed me when I told you something impossible, chased my hallucination across a desert, rescued me from a madman, rode into a fight with me as your only backup, left the priesthood to find out if we could make it together, and came with me into space. Do you think I'd forget all that to assume you'd sleep with a woman you just met?" Temar's eyebrows arched up, one higher than the other. "Do you really think that some very odd behavior on your part is going to make me doubt that you kind of adore me?" Temar's amusement grew. "You're odd."

"Obviously, I can be," Shan said weakly. He'd tortured himself with the fear that Temar might not understand why Shan had acted so strangely, and it turned out that Temar wasn't worried at all. Shan's fear vanished like a dust devil settling back to the ground when the wind that carried it failed. He also felt like an idiot, an idiot who didn't have a headache.

Temar stretched and feigned an interest in a bright red flower. "What is going on?"

Shan dropped his voice, leaning in until he could whisper in Temar's ear, and even then paranoia wrapped around his spine. "Natalie slipped me a note. These people are not fond of same-sex couples. It's called Paulism… the worship of the teacher Paul instead of Christ," Shan whispered. "And there have been some very violent and bloody periods of time associated with Paulists."

Temar glanced toward him before shifting his gaze to the "guide" who watched from the walkway. The guide felt a whole lot more like a guard than anything else, but Shan wasn't sure what to do about it. They couldn't exactly jump on a sand bike and go home, but if these people had any idea that Livre considered homosexuality normal, they were not going to be amused.

"Violent?" Temar turned a subtle shade of white.

Shan nodded, his mind supplying historical images that turned his stomach, but Temar didn't need the details. "Very violent, and Natalie keeps dropping hints about violence and crime and the need for guards."

"Shit." Temar sat down and rubbed a hand over his face. He pulled his hand back to look at it in confusion, and Shan realized that he'd been surprised to find himself wet. Shan sat down next to him, close enough to press their thighs together. He'd make whatever excuses he had to later—right now, his lover needed him.

"And they want us as allies," Shan pointed out. That was ironic. That also would not end well.

Standing up, Temar stepped away from Shan. "Shan, can you imagine people at home seeing this or these people seeing what life is like back on Livre?" Temar asked, shouting over the waterfall. He kept his face toward the guard. The moment he did that, Shan realized that whispering behind a plant probably wasn't the most subtle thing to do.

"They'd have heart attacks and then bomb someone," Shan muttered. They might too. Nearly half the marriages Shan had performed as a priest were of two people of the same sex, and these Paulists were likely to start talking about Sodom and Gomorrah and fiery swords.

"You really like Natalie, don't you?" Temar asked brightly. Shan blinked, not quite understanding where the conversation was going. Temar's eyes widened, and he leaned closer to Shan, his eyes flickering over toward the guard when Shan didn't respond.

"Oh." Shan stood and made sure he faced that distant watcher, assuming the man was watching, as opposed to being some random soldier standing there watching the waterfall and thinking about how he'd just broken up with his girlfriend. On this ship, it was hard to tell.

"Yes, she's intelligent, beautiful, and she has this inner strength that anyone would find sexy," Shan said as he looked Temar up and down, making it clear who he was really describing. Temar started turning pink, and Shan forced himself to pay more attention to the water.

"Shan?"

"Yes?"

"Are you interested in inviting Natalie to the planet permanently? I know this is fast...."

"Very fast," Shan said, and while he thought he'd been understanding Temar's logic, now he was back to being confused.

"Sometimes love happens that way... fast." Temar smiled at him, and Shan's whole body warmed. It wasn't the hard lust he'd felt as a youngster or even the frustration he'd sometimes endured as a priest when he could never reach out and touch what he really wanted. This was a bone-deep realization that, even if he had to wait, he would have his lover, now and forever. Shan smiled back, and for a moment, they stood in silence, tiny drops of water sliding down Shan's face and catching in Temar's hair so that the light sparkled as though through glass.

"Maybe you should ask her to move her belongings down to Livre—not just as a culture liaison, but forever."

"And if it doesn't work?"

Temar ducked his head and leaned a little closer. "When it's right, it's right, and you know it. She can leave again if she wants, but...."

Shan thought about it for a second. "But if she comes down only as a temporary liaison, they could order her back up here at any time."

"I know you, Shan Polli. You may not fall in love easily, but you can go to some ridiculous lengths once you give your heart away."

"I really can," Shan agreed. "But I don't want her to be alone down there. I wonder if Rula would be interested in moving or if she has some friend she could bring down."

"Rula?" Temar frowned, and Shan realized he'd missed that part of the conversation.

Leaning forward, Shan angled his body to hopefully make it harder for anyone to catch his words. "I think Rula and Natalie are as close as you and I."

"Like sisters, then?" Temar asked, but he had a twinkle in his eye that didn't suggest siblings.

"Exactly like that," Shan agreed.

"She wouldn't want to be dropped down on a planet that's 65 percent male by herself," Temar said firmly.

So Temar had grasped that relationship. "Probably not," Shan agreed. "Besides, I can see Rula and Naite getting along well."

Temar's eyebrows went up. "Rula and Naite?"

"They're both very physical, very…." Shan paused. Okay, he was making this up, and he couldn't come up with one reason why they would like each other.

Temar patted Shan on the arm. "Rula might be nearly as muscled as Naite, but she likes talking about art and laughing at silly puns, at least when she's not on duty being all serious. Trust me, they might respect each other, but Naite is not going to want a woman to discuss art with him."

"Probably not," Shan agreed.

"Someone will court her," Temar said with a shrug before he started back down the path toward the exit. Shan agreed—they were probably pushing their luck with how long they could hide from the microphones, and even here, he wasn't too sure they were safely hidden.

"And maybe I will have a chance to properly court someone," Shan pointed out. Just about the time he'd figured out Temar was ready for a relationship, all this drama with the inner planets had interfered. Shan still hated himself for dropping marriage into the conversation so casually, but he did want a chance to court Temar, to charm him and convince him to stand in front of an altar and make a life commitment to each other.

Temar looked over and gave Shan a mischievous smile. "You do like your formal courting, don't you? I've heard certain people complain that you're even a little slow-moving when it comes to courting."

Shan narrowed his eyes. "Unlike some people, I think courting *should* go slowly. Now, it's not that I don't enjoy being caught off guard by a romantic ambush… or two or three…." Shan smiled as the tops of Temar's ears turned a nice shade of pink. "But I want to court someone, to make sure that they know I want them in my life forever."

They had reached the spot with that giant, pink pod-like flower, and Temar reached out to run a finger along the surface as he gave Shan a searching look. "So, if you're courting, you wouldn't have sex unless it was a forever thing?"

"Well," Shan said slowly, "I certainly wouldn't sleep with someone unless I'd had thoughts about forever."

"Really?" Temar feigned surprise.

"Definitely," Shan said firmly. "When I court someone, it's because I care for them. If I sleep with someone, it's because I love them. You know how I feel about God, and I would not have a relationship that I couldn't proclaim in front of God and the whole community. I never have." Shan frowned. "Well, except when I was sixteen, but at sixteen young humans are idiots, and God understands that." Shan frowned, wondering exactly how they'd gotten into a conversation this serious, given the awkward situation. He wished they were back home, sitting on the crest of a dune with the sunset in front of them and the bike waiting to take them home.

"So, sex for you doesn't come without at least passing thoughts of marriage," Temar summarized.

Shan moved closer, willing Temar to understand just how serious he was. Maybe the lingering traces of fear that he'd hurt Temar were making him too bold, but he had to say this. "If I keep sleeping with someone, I'm probably making plans for a wedding and wondering how long I had to wait to ask them without risking getting turned down." Shan saw the look of utter shock on Temar's face, and he cleared his throat. Clearly that was not the tack to take. "Or I might consider the marriage without actually making formal plans, because sometimes I push too hard, and I'm okay with someone telling me to back off," he added, trying to undo the damage. Temar still looked shocked.

Temar finally cleared his throat, his expression turning more neutral. "You said you like getting caught off guard by a romantic ambush, but it sounds like you do some ambushing of your own."

Shan sighed. "Not intentionally. I do, however, say things without fully thinking them through, sometimes. I do things without thinking them through too. You should ask Naite. He'll be very happy to regale you with stories of how very stupid I am."

Temar laughed. "I've heard one or two variations on that."

"Yeah, well, many of them are probably true." Shan started back toward the formal path. Their moment of privacy was over, but he felt better now that he knew Temar understood. "Of course, I think my brother is an idiot, so we're even."

"I understand sibling rivalry. My sister isn't an idiot, but she can be very annoying... and thoughtless and rude and pushy," Temar said as they stepped onto the path. They continued with the pointless conversation, discussing things they both understood quite well. At the door, a guide joined them.

"Did you enjoy yourself?" he asked politely. Temar ducked his head and turned to study a tree with wide, pointed leaves while Shan answered for them.

"Coming from a desert, having open water like this is amazing."

"The ship systems recapture all moisture, no matter how it's used inside the facility," the man offered. "There are a number of moons with similar planetside bases, so you could have gardens and waterfalls on Livre."

Shan looked around and wondered what people on Livre would think of this. Lilian would snort, declare the whole thing a waste of water, and go back to her farm. Naite would too. Some people, like Dee'eta Sun, would probably appreciate the beauty of the place, but Shan doubted anyone would vote to spend precious resources on a water-drenched park. "It is very beautiful," he said without mentioning how little interest they had in it.

The guide smiled at them. "I'm glad that you enjoyed yourself. Would you like to see other parts of the ship? The manufacturing sector, perhaps? Few people get to see it, so it's quite an honor to let you inside the security zone."

"Manufacturing?" Shan perked up. That sounded interesting. He turned to look at Temar, who rolled his eyes.

"You're not subtle," Temar informed him.

"When it comes to machines, I don't have to be," Shan pointed out. He didn't say that he liked machines better than many people for that very reason, but he was fairly sure Temar understood.

"Manufacturing it is, then," Temar said, with a smile for Shan.

Shan realized the sandrat that had been eating his brain had vanished at some point. They'd made a good trade, Temar understood his feelings, and Shan was 90 percent sure they were rescuing two innocent women from Paulists. Life was good.

chapter
twenty-four

TEMAR WATCHED Shan's face light with pleasure as he stuck his head in another machine while a mechanic explained how it worked. Temar never thought he'd be jealous of a big hunk of metal, but he was. Natalie had certainly never earned that rapt expression from Shan. However, Temar figured that if Shan didn't keep his attention on something or someone else, he would give away the game. Every time Shan had looked to Temar, Ambassador Melton had seemed a little more concerned and confused.

At the time, Temar hadn't understood the dynamics in the room, and he'd held back as he'd watched Natalie try to charm Shan, and Shan try to keep his temper, and Melton get more brusque. The ambassador knew he was missing something. Now that Temar knew the AFP was antihomosexuality, he suspected Melton had seen some of the looks that passed between Shan and Temar and had questioned them. Maybe Natalie's flirting was nothing more than a distraction to keep them out of trouble. Or maybe she really did see Livre as a way to get her and her lover out of a dangerous situation.

Temar didn't see any signs of love between the two women, but if they were together, they had a lot more experience hiding than anyone Temar knew. On Livre, you only hid relationships when you knew the other person's parents were going to hate you on sight. Temar had done that a few times. He'd also gotten caught every time. Shan was right about one thing—teenagers were idiots.

Shan pulled out of the machine and turned to Temar. "Isn't this amazing?" His eyes were bright with curiosity, and he turned to the mechanic. "What's the RPM rate and fatigue strength in the arms?"

The mechanic answered in a series of incomprehensible phrases that left Shan nodding in rapt attention while Temar looked around.

Overhead, an enormous bladder of air seemed to twist, puffs escaping from seams that ran the length of the piece.

Temar had no idea what it was, but his hands itched with a need to try to twist glass to match the sinuous form. For months, every time Temar looked at glass, he'd only seen glass… flat, plain glass. For the first time in entirely too long, he looked around the world and he wanted a blowpipe and time to try to twist glass to his will. The banana flower, with its light-pink hanging pod that opened to reveal vivid red petals, would be fairly easy to replicate. Well, not easy, but Temar could envision the techniques now.

He'd have to join an opaque white glass with a vivid burgundy, so that the color was hidden until someone explored the piece. Tin, gold, maybe some manganese salts should duplicate the color. He let his mind wander as Shan and his mechanic friend followed a huge rod of metal farther back into the ship. Temar followed without really listening. He was more interested in studying the shapes of the strange machines.

These weren't the drive engines, but they clearly ran something important, given the number of men and women hovering just outside the small bubble that Shan and Temar seemed to form everywhere they went on the ship. A woman with her hair bound into a bun actually hopped over a low cluster of pipes to avoid passing too near them. Without Natalie and Rula, the bubble seemed to have shrunk some, and workers watched curiously as long as they had a piece of machinery to stand behind. It worried Temar that these people had given them a wider berth with the two women escorting them. It made him wonder what everyone else knew.

Temar glanced toward Shan. Clearly he trusted Natalie and believed she was trying to honestly warn them of the danger. However, Temar couldn't help but think of the way Ben had shown so much concern for Temar as they drove to the farm that first day.

The worst part was that Temar couldn't separate paranoia from reasonable suspicion. He looked at everyone and had that kernel of doubt, that suspicion that clung to him. Well, almost everyone. He trusted Shan and Naite and…. Actually, Shan and Naite were about it. Trust was a limited commodity when it came to anyone else.

When Natalie came walking down the aisle, Temar watched her. The flirting she'd done in the meeting somehow didn't match her long stride, the way her boots clipped against the gray metal corridors, or her long hair that hung in soft waves. Having a sister, Temar knew how much work it took to get hair to look like that. Cyla used to tie her hair up with strips of cloth that made her look like a lumpy pincushion, but she never did get her hair to do the perfectly even wave. Temar couldn't easily explain Natalie, and that made him twitchy.

"Shan, Temar," she called out happily, and Shan pulled his head out of the machinery.

"Natalie, hi."

"Ambassador Melton sent me out to find you."

Temar could see the flash of worry dart across Shan's face, but he covered it with a smile. "Oh? I thought we had finished negotiations."

"I'm sure everything's satisfactory." Natalie moved closer, edging her way past Temar with only a glance. That was fine—Temar really didn't want to catch anyone's attention. "I think the ambassador wants to discuss the future and some opportunities to bring our worlds closer together."

Shan glanced over, but Temar didn't have any answers.

"This soon?"

Natalie smiled. "I suspect he just finished calling the vice president and has authorization to make some new offers. After all, you have shown that you're willing to let us carry the bag and test the strength of it to hold the truth. I think they were expecting you to be either more desperate or more argumentative."

"Oh, I can argue, when I think there's something to argue about," Shan said, his hand resting against Natalie's back, and he started heading back the way they came. As they passed, Shan looked at Temar, silently telegraphing his willingness to drop the whole act if Temar wanted him to. It gave Temar an odd warmth to realize Shan loved him so much he would anger an entire planetary alliance before crossing Temar. Temar gave Shan a small smile, and the tension in Shan's shoulders visibly eased.

When Shan had mentioned marriage, shock had robbed Temar of the ability to really consider it. Growing up, Temar had always seen himself as the loner. He'd had a few sexual experiments and a couple of lovers, but they'd never lasted, and Temar hadn't wanted them to last. They'd been a distraction from his father's drinking or from Cyla's increasingly sharp temper. They'd been a way to spend an hour not thinking about the farmland ruined with pipe traps or the apprenticeship

Temar would never be able to afford. While he'd liked them, he hadn't ever yearned for them—he had yearned to get away from his life.

Watching Shan walk ahead with his hand on Natalie's back, Temar could feel the hot need to be with his lover. He missed Shan. The sex was tender and slow. Temar appreciated that, but it wasn't simply the sex. He missed the way Shan would let his hand rest on Temar's knee as they sat next to each other or the way Shan would walk with his hand on Temar's back. He missed leaning into Shan's body and feeling those strong arms wrap around his stomach. He wanted to wake up with Shan's warmth pressed up against his back, the soft snoring marking time in lazy seconds. He could see himself waking up to that every morning for the rest of his life. These people wouldn't appreciate that, though. Temar had difficulty understanding that hatred, but the longer they were on the ship, the more he realized he didn't understand much at all when it came to the Alliance of Free Planets.

"You look like you're thinking too hard," Rula teased in a near whisper as she fell in place next to him.

Temar blinked at her. "Do I?"

"Yes. I thought negotiations went well, but that is a worried expression."

Considering they would have given twice as many goods for half the water, Temar had to agree both sides had come out winners. "They did go well."

"So why do you look so worried?"

"Why are we going back to meet with Ambassador Melton?"

Rula gave a little puff of laughter. "Do you really think I would know the answer to that? I'm a little low on the totem pole to get that kind of information."

"Natalie didn't tell you?"

Rula gave him an odd look. "Protocol Officer Aral only advises me on her schedule when it affects my ability to provide assistance. She doesn't brief me on the contents of any meetings."

Temar had crossed a fairly large line. If the women were together, they couldn't be seen acting like a couple, not in this government. He focused on following Natalie and Shan without saying anything else stupid. They passed a long window that wasn't more than six inches high but ran for seven or eight feet along the length of the hall and gave them a view out into the blackness, blue and yellow glimmers from distant suns the only indication of life outside the ship. At the very edge of the field of vision, Temar could see the square, gray end of one of the *Brazica*'s other "arms" poking out into space.

The ship was a cylindrical center hub crossed by four large arms that jutted out at stark angles, and as near as Temar could tell, they'd spent most of their visit in one arm, with their most recent visit to the mechanical room being their first trip to the central hub. Shan had explained that a good third of the ship would be the giant jump engines, but no one had offered to take them any farther than that. On Livre, landowners would happily show anyone their territory. A visitor from Blue Hope could expect to have a full tour of every row, every pipe, every building, and every plant on his host's land.

Temar wondered if these people had changed that much in a century or if the people of Livre had. He worried that, in the end, it might not matter. The entire situation made Temar feel vaguely on guard and disquieted. Maybe the best solution would be to trade and otherwise avoid each other whenever possible.

By the time they got back to the negotiating suite, a series of nested offices that opened up one into another, fear was crawling up Temar's spine.

"Ambassador Polli, you should go in," Natalie said, giving Shan a flirty smile.

"You're not coming?" Shan frowned.

"The ambassador requested that I not attend. I am hoping that means hc is planning to discuss the possibility that I might transfer to Livre." Natalie opened the door for Shan and gestured.

"I hope so," Shan said, and for one moment, Temar could see the naked honesty in that. Shan wanted to help her so much that his eagerness shone through all the worry. Natalie graced him with a brilliant smile, and then Shan headed into the meeting room.

Temar tried to follow, but Natalie closed the door. "Ambassador Melton wants to have a private discussion with Shan," she offered apologetically.

Temar jerked back in alarm. "Why?"

Natalie exchanged a look with Rula, but both women seemed more confused than hostile or aggressive. "He feels that some information is sensitive enough to present to a senior diplomat first," Natalie said carefully. "He certainly meant no offense to you, Ambassador Gazer."

"Senior?" Temar asked. He certainly knew the word, but generally it referred to someone more trained, and neither he nor Shan had enough training at diplomacy to be senior. They were one step up from utterly clueless. "You mean as in older, or as in more influential, or more trained?"

"I think all three," Natalie said with a sort of kind smile that she probably meant to soften the blow.

"So, he's assuming I'm not as important as Shan without even asking?" Temar crossed his arms as aggravation made his palms itch with sweat. He didn't like being pushed aside, and he didn't like that Shan hadn't come back out looking for him.

"Perhaps he spoke to Ambassador Polli." Natalie traded more worried looks with Rula.

"No, I know that's not true. Shan would never say I was less important." Temar figured that, given their respective histories and Shan's unfounded guilt after failing to convince the council to denounce slavery, Shan would cut off his own arm before saying anything of the sort. However, Natalie looked more confused.

"He wouldn't?"

"No, he definitely wouldn't."

Natalie frowned. "Ambassador Gazer, I certainly don't mean to offend, but I really need to clarify this point. Is Ambassador Polli the senior official?"

Now he was aggravated. "Only if by senior you mean older."

"Oh dear." Natalie visibly flinched before reaching out for the door to the inner office. "I do apologize. I certainly understand the importance of rank, and I should not have assumed that age defined the ranking structure." She pulled on the door, but it didn't open. With a quick and awkward smile in Temar's general direction, she knocked on the door. "Ambassador Melton, we have a miscommunication that needs immediate attention," she called out. Silence answered her. She and Rula traded glances, and Rula reached up to touch her ear. Natalie knocked again, "Ambassador Melton?"

"Officer Aral," Rula said as she moved in fast, pulling Natalie away from the door and stepping in front. She beat on the door, the sound echoing around the room, pounding at Temar's head as something that felt a lot like panic wormed its way up his throat. "Ambassador Melton, this is Security Officer Lish. Open the door, or I will initiate an emergency override."

Still, silence answered.

"Get back. Move," Rula ordered, and before Temar could get sound out of his open mouth, her hands were on him, shoving him back toward the door to the outer office. "Move."

Natalie already had the door open, and Rula hurled him toward it before Temar could object. He stopped in the outer office, whirling around to confront someone, but Natalie had a handheld computer out, and Rula was on the interface set into the wall.

"Captain, we have a nonresponsive office. Red-seven-seven-four, requesting security override and open."

"Security, who is compromised?" a male voice on the other end demanded with the sort of terse tone that never boded well.

"Ambassadors Melton and Polli. Assistant Lieutenant Chardon. Assistant Technicians Pentalia, Leon, and Kossel. Security Officer Daedali." Finally Temar had names to put with the nameless men and women who seemed to hover around Ambassador Melton. That didn't reassure him, especially not with people throwing around words like "compromised."

The voice came back after no more than a half-second. "Officer Lish, be advised that security override has failed. We have mechanical interference."

"Fuck on a pogo stick," Rula snarled, and then the world upended itself. Temar flew backward and slammed into the wall so hard his legs couldn't hold his weight and he crumpled to the floor, which was his first sign that something was horrendously wrong.

chapter
twenty-five

"SHAN? SHAN!" Temar struggled to his feet, and then the whole world rocked again, the metal floor heaving up and then dropping so fast that Temar's feet lost contact with it.

"Ambassador, stay down." Rula dove toward him, grabbing Temar's arm and yanking him to the cold floor as the metal shuddered violently.

Temar got an arm under himself and tried to push up. "Shan's in there!"

"Rescue teams will be coming out. We have to clear the area."

Temar silently struggled, but Rula was too strong. Her hands wrapped around his arms, and he flashed on the feel of Ben's hands holding him, trapping him. Panic—panic for Shan, panic for himself—merged until his chest ached with the force of his beating heart. Another explosion made the world jerk, and then gravity failed. Twisting his body around, Temar tried to flail, but Rula pulled him closer, centering his world as papers and datapads floated up, all of them drifting toward one wall.

"We have to get Shan," Temar begged.

"We have to stay out of the way so we don't distract the rescue crew. They need to focus on Shan, and that means we can't be out there to get in their way," Rula told him, but her eyes focused on Natalie. Unlike Temar, whose first reactions included panicking and flailing, she had positioned herself under the table, her back against one leg, while she braced her boot against the nearest table strut.

"You okay?" Rula asked.

Natalie looked over and gave a smile. "Not half as bad as that time in the Inster Docks."

Rula snorted. "If it was, I'd be a good deal more worried."

Temar yanked one arm free and twisted so he could glare at Rula. "We have to get to Shan."

"Temar, that's a missile-resistant metal door embedded in structural beams," Natalie said. "I understand that you want to get to him, but if that door doesn't come open on its own, we don't have any way to get through it."

"And if it does come open, we need to be clear of this area," Rula added.

Temar's stomach lurched. He wouldn't leave Shan. "He could be hurt. We have to—" He had a whole host of arguments, but Rula cut him off.

"Temar, the fire systems haven't activated, and we still have pressure. Whatever is going on, the ship is in one piece. It will be okay," Rula promised him, but her words didn't scratch the panic that crawled through his belly.

"No." Temar wasn't even sure what he was saying no to. Reality, maybe. He wanted to deny that any of this was happening, but Rula manhandled him toward the exit. No matter how Temar threw his elbows and twisted, she kept him moving, and the lack of gravity meant Temar couldn't do much except flail. He hit the door to the corridor face-first, and he wanted to push off, to fly toward Shan and beat on the door and beg until someone opened it, but Rula braced her body behind his and grabbed an embedded handhold, pinning him to the door. Natalie seemingly flew out from under the table, her body stretched out toward the controls.

"We'll get him back, Ambassador," she promised, hitting the button to trigger the door so that Temar helplessly slipped out into the hall.

Men in white uniforms were there, black weapons larger than a cow's thighbone held at the ready. Temar arched his back and tried to retreat from the armed force, but without gravity, he floated helplessly right into their midst. One reached out and caught him, a strong arm jerking Temar close and then wrapping around his neck, so that Temar was effectively helpless.

"He's on our side," Natalie said as she pulled herself around the edge of the door, carefully holding on to the handles set into the wall. Temar had thought the intermittent curves of metal set into the wall were decorative. They weren't. Temar didn't want to think what it implied that they built handholds into their corridors.

"Hostages?" one of the white-uniformed men asked.

"Potentially," Natalie agreed.

The man who'd grabbed Temar loosened his hold and gave Temar a small nudge toward the wall, and Temar drifted that way without control. By grabbing one of the handles, he stopped his flight, watching as the men marched forward, their boots artificially heavy against the metal flooring, the lack of gravity not seeming to apply to them.

"Why can they move around?" Temar demanded of Natalie as she moved closer.

"Magnetic boots. They're a quick-response team, some of our best."

"Quick response." Temar couldn't catch his breath as reality slammed him in the face. Quick response. That meant that they often needed to respond quickly. They'd said the war was over, that it was safe to rejoin the universe. A soft touch distracted him, and Temar jerked his hand away from Natalie's worthless attempt to offer comfort.

"Who?" Temar demanded.

Natalie and Rula exchanged a long look, but no one answered him.

"I don't care about your rules. They have Shan, and I want to know who."

It took a long time before Natalie answered. "It's probably one of the religious separatist groups. It could be a personal rights extremist."

Temar looked from one woman to the other, struggling to get his mind around the fact that more than one group wanted to blow them up. He couldn't breathe… it was like he was in the middle of a huge sandstorm and he didn't have a veil to keep him from choking to death on reality.

Natalie sighed. "Temar, this war isn't between two alliances anymore—it's between two alliances and about a half-dozen terrorist groups that are all trying to blackmail one planet or another into changing sides or breaking away. The two alliances have declared a sort of awkward truce and hands-off policy. The insurrectionists and rebels and terrorists have not."

"And now they have Shan." Temar struggled to think this through. They would want goods or maybe leverage over Livre. Whatever they wanted, it wasn't worth Shan's life. Temar had to make that clear.

"The team will get them back," Rula promised from the other side of the corridor. The ship shivered again, a low wailing filling the air.

"Gravity's coming back. Get your feet under you," Natalie advised him. Temar barely had time to do that before the whole ship jerked and heaved and then gravity returned, pulling him down so fast that Temar had to clench his teeth to stop from vomiting all over the deck.

"We need to clear the area." Rula crossed the hall and got a hand under Temar's arm, urging him down the hallway, but Temar braced himself.

"No. I'm staying here until they get Shan back safely."

Rula gave him a withering glare.

"I don't care," he told her. "I'm staying."

"If they have explosions in the area, they'll need to move medical teams through here, and we'll be in the way. That isn't helping Shan. And it won't help to make ourselves attractive secondary targets."

Medical teams. Temar closed his eyes for a moment as panic rolled through him. "I want to see the captain," he said as calmly as he could. Natalie and Rula couldn't tell him what was going on. Based on the number of looks they'd already traded, he suspected they were skirting the rules by giving him as much information as they had. However, Temar wouldn't entrust Shan's safety to people he didn't know and couldn't trust.

Natalie answered first. "Temar, you don't understand. We're junior officers. We aren't welcome on the bridge."

"Because you're junior officers?" Temar stared at Natalie. He couldn't understand that. Anyone could go to a council. Even when he'd been young and untrained and ghosting through the shadows of glassblower tents trying to convince someone to let him apprentice— even then he'd had the right to go to the council.

"The captain is busy, Temar—too busy to worry about us. But he'll move heaven and hell to get Ambassadors Melton and Polli back." She reached as though to touch him, but she pulled her hand back after Temar glared at it.

"Because they're not junior officers?" Temar demanded, emphasizing the word "junior."

"Temar, understand that we are a people very used to combat. You have to focus, secure the high-value targets, and minimize the distractions."

"Like me."

From the dramatic sigh, Temar could guess that Natalie did not want to have this conversation. Normally, Temar would back away from that kind of open dislike, but it would take more than some discomfort to make him give up on Shan. Pressing his lips together, he glared at her.

"Like all three of us," she eventually offered. "Temar, rank is a good thing. The captain will do anything to get the ambassadors back. Ambassador Melton is the ranking officer on this ship. Other than matters of mechanical soundness, his decisions supersede the captain, and his safety is the paramount concern. Ambassador Polli is not far behind him in importance, and since he's in the same room with Ambassador Melton, they will be rescued together. I promise that, Temar. You simply need to have faith in us. I know this is hard, but this is not the first terrorist attack we've seen."

Temar clenched his teeth. Part of him wanted to let other people handle this. But every time he'd done that, it hadn't ended well. He'd trusted Cyla and her stupid plan to prove that Young had stolen water. And he hadn't. He'd trusted Shan to go chasing off across a desert, and if Naite hadn't followed them, they'd be so very dead. And now Natalie wanted him to follow, and as much as Temar wanted to—and he desperately wanted someone else to be responsible—he couldn't do it. He didn't trust these people as far as he could throw them.

"I'm going to find the captain, so you can either show me where he is or I can wander around this ship poking random controls," Temar announced.

"Temar," Rula said in an almost disappointed voice as she stepped in front of him. Physically, she had the power. She could force him to go back to their quarters, but physical power wasn't everything. Temar drew himself up and turned to Natalie, the real authority in this partnership.

"You're wrong about me, so if you're really interested in having an alliance with Livre, I want to see the captain now."

"That isn't a good idea."

Temar swallowed. These people weren't offering power, so he had to take some. Well, he'd certainly been around enough people who had modeled that for him. He smiled at Natalie. "I don't care. Your preferences and requests are not my first, second, or third concern, and I will see the captain now. Yes, Shan was on the governing council, and he is a well-respected man on Livre. The truth is, I'm more well-known, and I'm the second or third wealthiest man on that planet. I personally know every man and woman that sent trade goods up with us." He was technically telling the truth, even if it was a shade of the truth that wouldn't hold up to the full sun. Maybe he had some talent for lying, because Natalie was staring at him, her eyebrows drawn.

"You're that senior?"

Then again, maybe he didn't have talent, because she didn't sound convinced. "We don't think of rank the way you do. Shan and I would make any decisions together. He has more experience than I do. However, he would cut off his own arm before making a decision without me." Temar wasn't shading the truth on that statement.

Natalie traded a confused look with Rula. She might talk about how rank determined worth, but she seemed willing to ignore rank easily enough when it came to Rula. For the first time, Temar could see what had made Shan assume they were lovers.

"Luck of the stars," he cursed softly. "I had to get stuck up here with people who can't see that other cultures don't have the same rules." He channeled Naite's glare as he considered Natalie. Sure enough, she blushed all the way up to the tops of her ears. With her long brown hair pulled back, Temar could see the way they pinked up.

"Temar, I understand that you're worried about Shan," Natalie said in that tone he'd often heard parents use when their children's lying was particularly transparent. A hard bubble of hysteria grew in Temar's stomach as he thought about how much Ben would have appreciated being challenged. In another universe, if circumstances had been a little bit different, that's who Natalie would have dealt with.

"Believe what you want," Temar told her. "I'm going to find the captain. If you touch me, I will consider that an act of violence." Temar didn't add that he was close enough to a panic attack that he also might scream, flail, and huddle in the corner with his arms around his knees. He wanted to do that. He really did. Instead he strode forward, forcing Rula to back away to the side of the hall as she tried to avoid touching him.

"Temar, you'll never find the captain," Natalie called after him.

Temar turned around. "Maybe not, but I'm going to enjoy causing a lot of trouble while I try. I don't like having my demands questioned by"—he looked Natalie up and down, feeling slimy as he mimicked Ben's old gesture—"junior officers," he finished, making it clear that he considered her beneath him.

Natalie stepped forward, her voice a desperate whisper. "Ambassador Gazer, you don't want to do this."

He looked her in the eye. "No, I don't. I also don't want to lose my partner and I don't want to put up with being manipulated and I would rather not walk around the ship verbally attacking every person I meet as I press random buttons hoping to break something really vital. I don't want any of that, but some things are more likely than others." Temar raised his eyebrows and waited for her response. Natalie pressed her lips together so tightly that they turned white.

"Fine," she finally answered, "I will give you an invitation to meet the captain, but one word from him, and Rula will physically drag you off the bridge and throw you into a cell until we can straighten this out. We have laws against refusing orders during an attack and against making threats."

"I can't say I care what your laws say," Temar responded.

"And I thought you were the nice one," Natalie said with a sigh.

Temar didn't believe that. Natalie had assumed that he was the unimportant one. She'd focused so much on Shan that he doubted she'd given him two seconds of consideration, and normally, he'd be fine with that. Getting her full attention this way made him feel like his stomach had twisted inside out and his ribs were shrinking so that everything in his chest didn't fit. He'd rather be in the background, but he wouldn't stand back and let these people handle anything.

Natalie started down the hall, her long legs carrying her faster than Temar could follow without breaking into a trot. Even though she was only a couple of inches taller, she made good use of it. Rula stayed at his side, her hand resting on her belt, and Temar suspected she had some sort of weapon in there. This time when they hit the main cylindrical section, people rushed by in either direction. No one ran, but the sense of urgency came from the silent dodging of bodies around each other and the variety of uniforms. Temar had seen the brown uniform that most of them wore, but there were an alarming number of white uniformed men with large weapons and green uniformed men and women with strange equipment, some so large that two of them were carrying it.

Pausing for a second to allow a tight group of four men to pass, Natalie headed right, detouring around a man with blood covering him, supported by people on either side. The sharp stink of blood made Temar swallow down the bile that threatened to rise. The man was walking, so he probably wouldn't die, and Temar had seen death in his life, but he couldn't help but imagine Shan being injured.

When Ben had threatened Cyla, Temar had felt utterly trapped. The threat had held him more securely than any rope, and he could feel it tightening around him again. He wouldn't do it. He wouldn't lie down and let some terrorist group rape him, literally or metaphorically.

"Here." Natalie opened a door to show a tiny space behind it. It took Temar's brain a half second to supply the word "elevator." By that time Rula had already gotten in, and Natalie was looking at him with a frown. Temar followed Rula and caught hold of one of the curved handles. When Natalie got in, she manipulated the controls, and Temar's body jerked so hard to the right that he physically crashed into Rula. He'd expected up and down, but this was a side-to-side elevator. Rula gave him a sympathetic look as Temar struggled for balance.

"Last chance to stop, Temar. We can handle this." Natalie didn't add that Temar would screw everything up, but Temar thought that was implied.

"This is my partner and my fight," Temar said with far more confidence than he felt.

Natalie turned her back on him and stood with her nose to the wall door until the elevator jerked to a stop so sharply that Temar wrenched his shoulder trying not to fall down. The door opened, and Temar looked at the bridge and into the barrels of guns from two white-uniformed men who had drawn weapons on them.

chapter
twenty-six

NATALIE HELD both hands up, and Temar hurried to do the same. "Protocol Officer Natalie Aral, reporting to the bridge on the orders of Ambassador Temar Gazer," she said. One of the men tilted his head to the side and did something with his ear without lowering his weapon. Taking his cues from Natalie and Rula, Temar stood in place, his hands up.

The first man said something to his partner, and they both dropped their weapons so that they pointed to the ground. "You don't have authorization for bridge access."

"Ambassador Gazer demanded access."

The man searched Temar with a cold gaze, and Temar stepped forward. "Where's the captain?"

"Unavailable."

"Then he better find a way to make himself available, or I will invalidate all trades and demand the return of all Livre trade goods." Temar narrowed his eyes and silently prayed no one pointed out that he had no way to enforce that rule. Naite got away with ordering a whole lot of people around, not because he had any authority, as an unskilled worker, but because no one really wanted to cross him. Temar worried that he might not be able to pull it off without another foot of growth and a good hundred pounds, but after a second of looking at Temar, the guard nodded to his partner and turned to head across the bridge.

Temar had expected something grand, but the reality of the bridge was less than impressive. A dozen tiny, boxlike stations were lined up in the middle of the room, each with a man or woman inside the low walls, typing away on a computer. There weren't any windows out into space. One wall was covered with huge screens, and three people sat at a long, narrow table facing the scrolling displays, vid feeds, and images of space. Temar tried to find some image of Shan, but the elevator was on the side of the room, and the angle was wrong for him to see any details in the pictures.

Eyeing the remaining guard, Temar wondered if he should risk trying to walk past the man to find some vid feed from the negotiations room. He didn't like the idea of getting shot, though. The guard's partner stopped at the skinny table, talking to the man in the middle. So that was the captain.

The man stood and turned to face Temar. His body was angled oddly, and it took Temar a second to realize one of his legs was damaged. The man headed over toward them, the soldier following. With every step, he swung his right leg out wide, and his right hand had burn-slick skin across the backs of the fingers.

"Ambassador," he said wearily, "go to your quarters, or I will have to order you there."

Temar might have said something inappropriate, except Natalie stepped forward. "Captain, we have a problem."

"We have a lot of them, Officer," the captain retorted with a dry sort of humor. "Unless you have a report, clear the bridge."

"I want to know what you're doing to find out if Shan Polli is safe," Temar demanded.

The captain gave him a look while he blew out a long breath. "Look, I understand that you're worried, but right now, you're in the way. Clear the bridge, Ambassador."

"No."

The captain's expression darkened. "Excuse me?"

"Would you ask Ambassador Polli to leave the bridge?" Temar demanded. From the momentary blankness on the captain's face, the answer was clear. "I'm certainly wealthier and better known than Ambassador Polli. My vote carries as much weight, and if he finds out that you shut me out of decision-making, you're unlikely to get either of our votes for any sort of deal." Temar wanted to go on, to beg, to plead, to give all the reasons why they should let him stay. However, begging didn't project strength, so he clamped his mouth shut and swallowed all the arguments and fears and anger until he was afraid he might throw it all up again.

Eventually, the captain sighed. "Officer Aral, would you like to provide some introductions?"

"Yes, sir. Ambassador, this is Captain Miles Helgen. Captain, this is Ambassador Temar Gazer."

The captain started right in. "Ambassador, you are a guest, not part of our rank structure. As a guest, I will include you in any discussions regarding your colleague, but in the end, the decision will be mine as to how we proceed. Understood?"

Despite the fact that his first instinct was to agree, Temar pursed his lips and considered the captain for some time. "I understand that you would prefer that, yes," he finally offered.

The sour look on the captain's face suggested that this wouldn't be a happy friendship. "Ambassador, we had a major explosion in the jump engine. We ejected the combustible material before the fire could breach security, which is why the detonation didn't rip through half my ship. We have catastrophic failures on sixteen decks, with damage isolated to areas on the opposite end of the ship from diplomatic quarters." The captain turned his back and strode across the room of narrow aisles and cramped workers in their little spaces until he got back to his table overlooking the displays. Temar followed, searching the images for any sign of Shan. He'd only understood about 60 percent of the captain's speech, but none of it had sounded particularly good.

"Life support?" Rula asked.

"Security Officer Lish, this is not a tactical debriefing," the captain snapped, and Rula stiffened as she stood at Natalie's side.

"Are we in danger?" Temar asked.

The captain spared an unhappy look toward Rula before answering. "Ambassador, if there were significant threat to your life, I would order you evacuated, and quite frankly, I wouldn't care if you threw your weight around."

"Then you'd better get Ambassador Polli back in one piece, because if you do that before securing him, you will not have a treaty with Livre."

"Not my first concern, Ambassador."

Natalie had moved closer to the screens, and she was focused on one, her head tilted as she looked at it. Temar frowned. "Is that the conference room?"

The captain looked over at the screen. "It's the footage right before the attack. One of the techs is running a loop to identify enemies and technology."

"It's Pentalia. He's out of position and blocking Ambassador Polli from returning to the outer office," Natalie commented.

"We think he's the point man. He waited until he had the two ambassadors in the room with as few additional personnel as possible before somehow triggering a coordinated attack. We're tracking down his history and accounting for all personnel."

Natalie turned around. "Officer Lish and I were in the outer office with no access to sensitive equipment."

"I know." Captain Helgen sat down in his chair, and Temar could see a single screen display inset in the table light up. "I checked you two first."

Temar would have been offended, but Natalie simply nodded, as if it were normal for her own people to investigate her. Temar seriously hated this alliance. "Do you know anything about Ambassador Polli?" he asked, focusing on his need to save Shan and not his general disgust for the entire situation.

The captain tapped his screen and one of the images grew larger, pushing the others to the side. It gave Temar a headache to look at a wall with so many images—readouts and text and vid and diagrams with squiggle lines all flashing at once. However, he focused on the center image. In it, Shan was clearly angry, although without sound, Temar couldn't tell what he was angry about. He moved toward the door, and a tall man with no hair stepped between him and the exit, leaving Shan to stumble back.

"Pentalia," Natalie said softly.

Shan got his finger up in the man's face, and Ambassador Melton was on his feet now, his normal entourage of assistants looking either alarmed or confused. Shan turned his back on Pentalia, and then the whole screen shook. Shan hit the table and then rolled off to the floor, but that might have been for the best, because Pentalia had a gun, and he shot two men and a woman, their bodies flying back and slamming into the ground. Without sound, it was a surreal image, seemingly less tangible than the vids Temar had watched in school—except that was his lover with his arm thrown over his head. The ambassador and one man were left. The man threw his hands up, moving behind Ambassador Melton, who stared with an open mouth.

Shan reached up for the edge of the table, and the expression on his face would have made Naite take a step back. He was furious. Pentalia pointed the gun in Shan's direction, but Shan was saying something, his mouth moving and his hand flying up in a wild gesture. The second shock must have hit, because Shan stumbled to the side and

Ambassador Melton sat in his chair, grabbing the edge of the table. The third explosion came close on the heels of the second. By this time, Temar had been in the third office with Rula holding him down as he pointlessly struggled to get to Shan.

Sure enough, the silent figures in the silent image floated up into the air as gravity failed. Two of the bodies trailed little dotted lines of blood drops that followed them as they drifted up and to the right. One didn't. His skull was half-gone, and larger red globs escaped at less regular intervals.

"One confirmed kill, two seriously injured, assumed dead. Three hostages," the captain said, and then Pentalia turned to the camera, smiling into it before raising his weapon. The screen turned to static. "That's the entire stream." With a click, the captain made the images shrink down again as they restarted with Shan walking into the room, that hopeful smile on his face.

Temar turned away, not willing to watch that horror twice. Shan was alive. Shan wasn't hurt. He had to hold on to that, because if he didn't, his sanity was going to slip out from under him like loose sand. Either that or it would explode like glass cooled too quickly, and everyone in the room would be showered with hot shrapnel. Temar wasn't sure how he was going to react. He only knew the anger growing in his chest was too much for him to carry. He wanted to reach through that vid screen, take Pentalia by the neck, and squeeze the life out of him. His feelings for Ben had been a poor, sun-bleached imitation of hatred compared to how he felt about Pentalia.

A new explosion rocked the bridge, and Temar might have fallen except Rula grabbed him and hauled him close. It was hard to fall down when someone that muscled had hold of your arms.

"Report!"

"Epsilon seven through eleven, catastrophic failure. Epsilon twelve through fourteen, critical damage. Epsilon six, fifteen, nineteen suffered serious damage. Trivial damage shipwide." With all the technicians all in their little boxes, Temar couldn't tell who had called out the report, but everyone's expression turned somber.

"Rula?" he whispered.

"Shuttle bays," Rula whispered back. She let go of his arms, and Temar rubbed them, the flesh already bruised from her harsh hold.

"All teams, I want sections cleared. Nonessential personal to emergency areas. Possible ship fragmentation imminent," Captain

Helgen snapped out, and a good half of the screens on the big wall suddenly shifted to new figures and new images.

Temar inched closer to Rula, waiting until she leaned close to whisper an explanation. "Last stage emergency in case of sabotage—all sections seal themselves off with emergency rations. Internal, controlled explosions blow the sections apart, turning the *Brazica* into sixty-five separate life pods. Each one can support two hundred people for three days."

"But Shan?" Temar looked at the screen, but whoever had been looping the image of the negotiation room had turned to other work. Temar's breath caught in his chest. He had an irrational need to see Shan, even if it was a recorded image.

"Sir, incoming message—one-point-one-three Hertz."

Captain Helgen touched his ear and nodded. Radios. They had radio communicators in their ears. Temar had noticed the tiny disks, but the idea of making a communicator smaller than a fingernail made no sense. How did they control it? Why would they even bother with technology like that?

"Targeting, report all active weapons, visual only, display seven-three-alpha," he barked.

"Captain." Temar stepped forward, ignoring the way Rula had tried to catch his arm to stop him. "What's going on?"

"Not now, Ambassador."

"Yes, now. You're getting messages. Are they from Pentalia?"

"Ambassador, I would dislike the amount of paper I would have to fill out if I ordered Officer Lish to tie you up and throw you in a closet. Don't assume I won't do it anyway," Captain Helgen warned.

"I don't assume that. I do assume that you would intentionally leave me ignorant because you don't think I have the rank or you don't want to listen to my opinion."

"I really don't want to listen to your opinion," Helgen agreed, "but I know you have rank. Melton didn't see it, but I've been watching these screens since you came onboard. Ambassador Polli never made a final decision without looking to you for confirmation, and one unhappy look would send him trying to change the deal. I had hoped you would keep up the ruse so that I could order you off my bridge, so no, I don't have a problem seeing you as the commanding officer, Ambassador Gazer. I won't, however, let you command my ship. Stay out of this."

"Is it Pentalia?" Temar demanded, ignoring the rest of the argument and even his shock at the thought that someone watching them could come to that kind of conclusion about his relationship with Shan.

"No." Helgen was passing aggravated and moving into being angry, but Temar didn't trust him. He didn't trust any of these people, and having them not mention the terrorism problem hadn't helped.

"Who is it?" Temar asked as calmly as he could, but his face flushed and his heart pounded faster as his control over his overheated temper weakened.

Reaching over, Helgen flipped a control switch so a voice came over the speaker. "AFP Cruiser *Brazica*, do you need assistance?" the voice asked.

Helgen pinned Temar with a smug look. "It's the Planetary Alliance, Ambassador Gazer."

Temar's mouth fell open as the other side of this war appeared on one of the screens, a sleek ship with a blunt nose and short wings. "Perhaps you should allow me to handle this," Helgen suggested.

Temar had been rather successfully channeling Lilian and Naite and even Ben in order to bully everyone on the ship, but he suspected that not a one of them would have any idea how to react to this. He sure as hell didn't.

"Get me that weapons report," Helgen shouted to his men, and Temar took a step backward, too confused to have an opinion on the whole mess.

chapter
twenty-seven

"UNIDENTIFIED PA ship, pull out of AFP space or we will open fire," Captain Helgen ordered. Temar frowned. If someone offered help, that wouldn't be his first reaction.

"With what, captain?" the voice asked. "This is PA Ship *Phrike* offering assistance. I have no interest in getting into a battle, but you look like you've taken significant damage, Captain."

"So you decided to drop by and offer yourself up less than an hour after a terrorist attack?" Captain Helgen demanded. "The timing is more than suspicious."

Surprisingly, the pilot didn't even seem surprised to be accused of terrorism. "I've been monitoring Minga space for some time. Your ship was near enough to catch my interest, and when the explosion registered on my sensors, I immediately came to offer assistance, nothing more."

"And what sort of assistance are you offering? I don't think you'd want us to commandeer your ship, and I doubt I could fit my whole crew on a scout ship."

"That wouldn't be my first offer." The pilot had some humor in his voice, which Temar found odd… as if he'd been dropped into another universe where their ship hadn't been blown up. People should not be able to find humor under these circumstances. The pilot continued. "If you have a clear landing bay, I can bring the ship in and load the worst of the injured for treatment at the nearest PA facility. If not, I can tether. I have medical facilities for fifteen, twenty if your people really like each other. If you have damaged communication, I can relay a message to the nearest AFP ship."

"It's not exactly survivors we need help with," Temar blurted. "We have attackers still on board, and they're holding people." Temar wasn't even sure if his outburst would transmit, but Captain Helgen whirled around, fury etched on his face, and the voice from the other ship answered.

"I have monitoring equipment and limited weaponry. I can help any way possible until tactical ships are on-site," the nameless man in the PA ship offered.

"Not necessary. Withdraw from AFP space," Helgen ordered.

"Contested space, Captain, not AFP."

"Withdraw, or when those tactical ships we sent for show up, you will be fired on."

"How long will the tactical ships take to get here?" Temar asked, his mind spinning as he studied the various information feeds on the wall of vids, all of them devoid of any images of Shan. "Can the PA ship monitor inside the room where Shan is?"

Helgen's spine stiffened. "Ambassador, leave the bridge."

Temar shook his head. "I'll take any advantage I can if it helps us save Ambassador Polli."

"The Planetary Alliance probably sent Pentalia. We can't trust them."

"I didn't say that we should give this pilot the keys to the sand bike," Temar snapped. "If he can give us information, I want it. And I really doubt the Planetary Alliance sent someone to attack us. I think there are plenty of groups, religious and otherwise, who would do that on their own."

The captain punched a control even as he sucked in a fast breath. He was surprised. Slowly, the man turned to consider Temar. "You seem to know more than I would expect." Helgen sounded suspicious now, but Temar didn't have time to worry about himself, not with Shan stuck in a room with a murderer.

"I like to listen," Temar said with a shrug. "Now, I want to find out what that ship can do to help us. Unless you have the same ability to scan inside the diplomatic rooms, you need to get him back on the radio."

Temar crossed his arms. The captain wasn't intimidated, that was for sure. He glared daggers at Temar, but if he thought that would deter Temar, he had another thought coming. Temar knew how to survive a whole lot worse, so he remained silent as the captain finally reached over and pressed a control. Temar nodded to the captain before speaking to the pilot. "PA Ship *Phrike*, can you get us an image inside a room if we give you the right directions to the room?" Temar asked.

"Directions?" The pilot sounded briefly confused, but then he kept going. "My name is Verly Black, Ambassador. If you want eyes inside, I'm a scout ship. I can get you that."

From the way Helgen's jaw bulged, Temar figured he was pretty close to ordering someone to stuff Temar in a closet. Temar moved closer and whispered, "Just take his data—don't trust him."

The pilot answered him with that same oddly amused voice. "I don't ask for trust, but if you have people in trouble, I'll help. Consider it my contribution to universal peace."

Temar cringed, not realizing that the microphone would work so well. Maybe the root words in "microphone" did make sense after all. Helgen was giving Temar a disgusted look as he hit the control button again.

"Ambassador Gazer," the captain said in the carefully controlled tones of a man about to explode, "you are a guest on this ship. You do not decide tactics, strategy, or policy. You certainly don't get to tell me how to handle myself on my ship, clear?"

Knowing he'd pushed a little too hard, Temar nodded. "I understand, Captain. I really do. I understand that you don't trust him. Personally, I don't trust much of anyone. When I first met Shan, I certainly didn't trust him, and he had to nearly kill himself before I could." Temar stopped, fighting to find a way to heat this argument in a way that would shape it in his favor. "Captain. I communicated that poorly, but I was simply trying to say that I wouldn't ask you to trust this man, especially not when you have a history here. However, I'm certainly not going to give up on a source of information."

Helgen didn't answer, but his jaw did slowly unclench until he swung his chair around to face Temar. "How much tactical experience do you have, Ambassador?"

"Tactical?"

"Warfare, tactics, strategy. How much war is there on your planet?"

Temar would like to say that his planet didn't have war, but what had happened with Ben looked a lot like a war. Two sides had tried killing each other over resources. It wasn't the sort of war Temar had grown up learning about in school, but it felt the same. Locked in the hidden base knowing Ben had won... it felt a lot like the current disaster, only this time, Naite wouldn't be riding in to the rescue. "I don't know that you would say we have had a traditional war," he said slowly.

Helgen gave a weary laugh. "Which means you've seen the nastier side of war. At least you aren't a complete novice. Hiding your rank turned out to be wiser than I expected. If we take his data, you have to recognize that he might be feeding us false information."

"To help Pentalia," Temar said softly.

With a nod, Helgen stood. "You're right that the PA doesn't directly hire these terrorists, but there are connections."

Temar studied the man, wondering how many terrorist organizations his own government sponsored. If Natalie could be believed, not only did her government persecute people, but she was putting herself in a lot of danger to try to find a way out. He didn't know who to trust at this point… other than Shan.

"For all I know, he's part of Pentalia's plan," Temar admitted, "but if he is, I'd rather keep an eye on him."

Captain Helgen looked at Temar for a long time. Behind him, Temar could hear the bridge workers typing on computers and the hushed whisper of dozens of people trying to be quiet. Then the captain nodded and turned back to the controls set into the table, turning on the communicator. "Well, Verly Black, we will provide coordinates and consider any data that you might relay as a favor to Ambassador Gazer. However, if your ship lands one grapple hook in my hull, if you threaten one crew member, or if you step one foot outside the lines of good manners, I will have our ships shoot you, assuming I can't find one working missile to jam down your throat."

One screen enlarged, flickering with static for a second before a man's face appeared on screen. His light brown hair was cut so short it almost looked like a shadow against his pale skin, and his dark blue uniform and square jaw gave him a stark appearance… until he smiled. He had a crooked smile, even when being threatened. "I never expected any less," he said. Behind him, Temar could see a room filled with far more gadgets than the *Brazica* had.

"Officer Pacet, send the coordinates of the diplomatic quarters." Helgen stood, faced off against Black, and said in a voice as rough as a sandstorm, "Give me one excuse, and I'll shoot you myself." The hostility went beyond the simple political hatred Temar had heard in Helgen's voice seconds earlier. Something had shifted. Temar felt a flash of anger that he found himself on the outside trying to understand... again.

"And if you give that order and I decide that you acted hastily, I will make sure your entire alliance pays," Temar warned. The murderous look in the captain's eyes warned Temar that the situation was sliding off balance. Too much heat on one side.

Turning to face Verly Black's image on the screen, he ignored a voice in his head that advised he should be polite to a stranger who had the decency to offer help. When manipulating glass, fire wasn't polite. Here, he might be manipulating people instead of blown glass, but Temar could feel the same stress fractures as the piece threatened to crack without a little more evening out of the fire. "And if you are part of this, if you do anything to contribute to Ambassador Polli's death, I won't be merciful enough to allow him to shoot you," Temar warned Black. "I will request an escort back to Livre and personally watch as the sandcats strip the flesh from your screaming body." That might have been a little too much fire, because the pilot turned a stark shade of white.

"Yes, sir," he answered crisply. "Sir, I truly did just come to offer aid, even before I knew the situation was so interesting. I give you my word that I am not involved with this attack in any way." He wasn't smiling anymore.

"The word of the Planetary Alliance," Captain Helgen said in a disgusted voice.

"No, *my* word," Black corrected him. "If you have people being held by terrorists, I will help in any rescue mission I can." Volunteering to help with the rescue part of the mission was not the same as volunteering to capture or kill the terrorists, and Temar wondered if Captain Helgen had caught that. Probably. These people lived intimately with war in a way Temar couldn't imagine.

"Where is the image you promised?" Temar demanded.

"Calibrating now, sir." Black turned his attention to his controls. While most of his attention did focus on the technology, he kept glancing up. Temar didn't know what he found so interesting. Backing away from the captain, Temar took his place near Natalie and Rula. He didn't trust the women, but they were more familiar, and Shan trusted them.

"Picture coming now," Black said. One of the screens enlarged, and Temar had a view of something that looked like spilled paint, red and blue and dark gray. He blinked, and it took him a moment to realize that there were four distinct blobs with red centers and bluish arms as legs, as though their limbs were approaching white-hot. It was an odd view.

"Four life signs." Black announced, and the picture changed. Now the figures were light gray against dark gray with sharp lines surrounding them. It shifted again to a solid blue that faded to white at the bottom of the screen and then again to a greenish hue, with gray people walking through the space. Now Temar could see that one of the four was on the ground, one sat on a chair, and two were standing. Temar stopped breathing as he realized being able to see Shan didn't mean he could do anything to help his lover. He'd never felt more helpless in his entire life.

chapter
twenty-eight

THE CAPTAIN'S conference room was a long, narrow room with a matching table made up of vid screens set under glass or clear plastic. The table would normally seat a good thirty people on each side, but the far side of the room was loaded with boxes, a shelf crammed into one corner with electronic bits that reminded Temar of Shan's workroom. It meant they couldn't get around to the far side of the table at all.

Captain Helgen sat at the head of the table, and Temar sat on his left, watching the streaming image from Black's ship. Temar let his fingers rest against the image, the ache in his chest physically painful. "What do they want?" Temar asked softly. Pentalia hadn't asked for anything, and demands seemed like a logical part of this process. If Pentalia demanded something, then they could move, they could act, he could demand that the AFP fill the demand. However, the silence left Temar helpless and increasingly angry.

"Terrorists generally want to frighten the civilian population into doing something. If Pentalia were a criminal, he would have asked for money by now." Helgen made a face. "But most criminals would be smarter than to go with this plan. Pentalia knows he'll never get out of that room alive."

"Then what's his plan? What does he want?"

Helgen scratched his scarred hand and watched the feed for a second. Then he hit a control button. "Black, are you reading me?"

"I'm here, Captain."

"Do you have any transmissions?"

There was a silence for several minutes, and Helgen switched to rubbing his scars.

"I have one time-stamped standard current minus ninety-eight minutes, automatic recording on gigahertz twenty-seven point seven-one."

"Shit," Helgen said, the word almost a sigh.

"Captain?" Temar looked over to Rula and Natalie, but both women had their lips pressed together. Natalie had her eyes closed and her head tilted in a pose that screamed her grief. "What does that mean?" Temar demanded, panic rolling through his guts.

The man on the radio answered. "That frequency couldn't travel far. We have a snooper in local space."

"Meaning?" Temar could hear the sharp edge to his own voice.

The captain answered. "It means that they are using this to create vid. Pentalia is transmitting to someone local, and they'll take the images back for general distribution."

"Why?" This still didn't make any sense to Temar. Why wouldn't they ask for something? Temar would pay any price to get Shan back, but he couldn't make that clear if they weren't talking to the captain.

"To terrorize people. He's creating a vid that will terrorize people in the hopes that our government officials and citizens will be so frightened that they'll run to the Planetary Alliance for protection. Isn't that right, Black?" The captain glared at the table with the display, since Black wasn't in the room.

Black didn't answer.

"Send the message over," the captain ordered, his voice clipped. "Ambassador, you may not want to watch this."

Clamping his teeth together to avoid getting sick, Temar ignored the captain and kept his eyes on the screen.

"Captain," Black said, and then he paused. "I am sorry, but regulations forbid the transmitting of communications to an AFP vessel."

"You're already sending us vid," Temar argued when the others were silent too long.

"I'm skirting the edge of insubordination, but there's no actual rule against providing AFP with images when they request them. There is a rule against transmitting intelligence to an AFP ship. Ambassador, I am sorry, and I will send an immediate request for permission to share this, but...." He let his voice trail off, making it clear that either he didn't expect to get permission or he didn't expect it to come in time to do any good.

"*Brazica* out." With that curt statement, the captain flipped the communications off and stood. "Ambassador, I am sorry, but I can largely tell you the contents of the message. We've seen them before." Helgen stared off at the wall, his back oddly stiff. "Pentalia will make a number of political statements while pointing weapons at the ambassadors. He will likely force them to make statements in favor of a particular position, or perhaps force them to apologize for atrocities that the terrorists imagine our government commits. Then he will kill them and promise that his organization will do the same to any that oppose them before he shoots himself in the head. He may or may not have additional bombs placed on the *Brazica*, and if he does, rather than shooting himself, he will trigger that bomb and blow us all up as his final act." For the first time since starting his speech, Captain Helgen looked down at Temar with eyes that looked ancient and pained.

"Ambassador, I am sorry, but at this point, I'm going to have to take care of my ship and my people. We need all hands focusing on clearing the ship of dangers, now that we know we have a snooper collecting vid. I will not die in a commercial for terrorists and their ridiculous claims." The captain gave Temar a nod, and without waiting for Temar to marshal any arguments or make a last final demand for Shan's life, the man left.

Temar stared at the captain's chair, his brain unable to comprehend what he'd said.

"Temar?" Natalie asked, her voice soft. Temar looked over at her, unable to form words.

"I'm sorry. He was a good man. He was a truly good man." Her eyes shone, and she sucked in a fast breath as the tears threatened.

"He's not dead," Temar said. He wouldn't count Shan out, not now. Not ever.

Rula stood and came several steps closer before stopping. "We've all lost people to this war. I'm sorry that you're losing Shan when you aren't part of the fight, but war is messy. Natalie and I should help clear the ship. If there's a bomb, we can't let these people take anyone else."

"But you'll let them take Shan?" Temar demanded. Fury rose in his throat until he wanted to tear and rip at Rula, to take that sympathetic expression and turn it into pain and horror.

"Let them, no. They took him because we weren't good enough to protect him. I am sorry." Rula backed up a step. "Officer Aral?"

Natalie looked from Rula to Temar. "I do understand," she offered.

Temar exploded out of his chair, and Natalie stumbled backward, away from him. "No, no you don't. Rula is here and safe. Don't tell me that."

Once the shock passed, Natalie's face lost all emotion. "At eleven years old, I hid under a pile of trash while soldiers raped my mother and slit my father's stomach open so that he would live long enough to see her suffer. I lay there helpless while that happened, Ambassador Gazer." Her face turned hard. "I *do* understand. But I couldn't do anything then, and I can't do anything now." She looked at the ceiling for a second.

"We should help clear the decks," Rula said softly, but all of her sympathy had vanished as she glared at Temar. Natalie nodded, and she turned and strode out of the room without a backward glance.

Temar felt the tears hot in his eyes, but he refused to cry. Crying would mean giving up on Shan, and he wouldn't do that. Shan had walked off the desert. He'd survived Ben and old Yan Polli and Ben's minions who sent people after him to shoot him. Shan had put it all at the feet of God, laughing as he passed it off as God taking care of fools. But Temar had to believe it was Shan. Shan was too tough to die. He wouldn't give up, not ever, and Temar had to be the same.

Temar's eyes landed on the captain's controls at the head of the table. The pain and fear turned cold as a plan formed. Wiping at his eyes, he went to the captain's chair and paused to take enough breaths to make sure he could get words out past the fear lumped in his throat. Then he reached for the controls.

"Verly Black?"

"I'm here, Captain." The vid blinked on to show Black's face. "Oh, Ambassador, I apologize. What can I do for you?"

Right now Temar needed information. "If I transfer to your ship, could I see those feeds?" Temar asked.

Black blinked quickly—shock, probably. "Are you an official of the AFP?"

"No, I'm here trading goods for Livre."

"Livre?" Black did more blinking. "Do you have a standing alliance with the AFP or are you a member planet now?"

Temar shook his head. "No. Ambassador Polli and I turned down an offer of alliance. We're here to trade and to look around long enough to understand the universe."

Black's voice turned sympathetic. "And you got more of an understanding than you expected. If you are a free agent, there are no regulations against me transporting you or sharing communications. You're welcome on board, Ambassador. However, I would ask that you leave guards behind. I would prefer not to be outnumbered or outgunned on my own ship."

"I don't have guards."

"You don't? Ambassador, you are succeeding in shocking me when I thought I'd seen everything."

"My people generally try to avoid killing each other. If I do come over, will you allow me to come back here for transport back to Livre?"

Black took a second to think about that. "Yes, sir. I will warn you that if PA gunships get here first, the ranking officer will likely demand a meeting, but they cannot hold an official of a nonaligned planet for any extended time."

"Just a short time, then," Temar interpreted that. Black certainly didn't correct him. The entire universe had questionable sanity. "I want to transfer over. How do I do that?"

"Will the captain let me dock? That'd be easiest."

"I'll talk to him." The fear started to slip back to manageable levels as he had a definite task in front of him. "I'll call you back." Temar turned off the communications while Black still had his mouth open to respond.

Heading out onto the bridge, Temar immediately spotted the captain back in his chair. None of the screens on the wall showed the unreal images from Shan's room, but that didn't matter now. "Captain," Temar said calmly, walking up to the side of the captain's table. One of the two officers flanking the captain looked up, but Helgen kept his eyes on his work.

"I don't have time for debate, Ambassador."

"No debate, Captain. You have to take care of your people."

Helgen looked up, clearly surprised.

"Clear a place for Black to dock. I'm transferring to his ship."

Bolting out of his chair, Helgen moved into Temar's face, stopping only when they were scant inches apart, but Temar refused to back down. "The Planetary Alliance will get their hands on you and force your planet to join. You're volunteering to be a hostage against all your people. Are you willing to do that?"

Temar shrugged. "My planet is a lot more pragmatic than you think. They'd let Ambassador Polli and me both die before being forced to do anything. And if the PA tried to take over the planet, their bodies would feed the sandrats and the sandstorms would bury their ships in minutes. They're welcome to try."

"And they will. My grandfather worked for those soul-sucking bastards. They'll do anything to get their way."

"So will I," Temar pointed out. Helgen pulled back, studying Temar. "My first goal is to secure Ambassador Polli's safety. After that, the Planetary Alliance may find us as difficult to negotiate with as you do. Consider it passing along your headache."

That made Helgen smile. "Are you sure you're diplomatic? You sound more like a tactician."

"On Livre, we all learn to take care of ourselves when young."

The captain turned to look at the two officers who sat on either side of his chair before returning his attention to Temar. "Why all this effort for one man?" he asked with solemnity.

While the easy answer was that Temar loved Shan, Temar would take this risk for anyone, even some stranger from Blue Hope. He struggled to find a way to explain that to someone who clearly didn't have the same values. "It's who we are as a people," Temar said as he tried to explain the real difference. "We'll give up things easily enough. The desert teaches you to live without a lot. However, if one person on Livre is at risk, we'll all fight. We'll kill any enemy that even threatens our world, our citizens, or our water. We're not a very reasonable people."

The captain pursed his lips and studied Temar for a long time. "Arden, did you get a truth reading on that?"

"Yes, sir. He's completely truthful," one of the two flanking officers offered.

Captain Helgen took a long breath before he turned to his controls and starting pressing buttons. "Lieutenant Commander Black, you have clearance to dock on beta strut, emergency dock nine-two-nine. Confirm that you are reading the beacon."

"Affirmative. I have a lock on the beacon and am moving into position for an emergency dock."

"Remain on course for docking, and Black… I wouldn't suggest you try to meet us at the door."

"I wouldn't dream of it," Black immediately answered. Temar didn't understand the reference, but he suspected both sides were compromising as much as they could, given their clear hatred for each other. Helgen turned off the communications before turning to face Temar.

"Corpsman Reicks will walk you down to the dock. I really hope you know what you're doing, Ambassador."

"So do I," Temar admitted. "Thank you for your help."

"I hope our people will still work together in the future." The captain gave Temar an intense look, but then, if Temar had invited new friends over to his house only to have them blown up, he'd worry about the friendship too.

"I hope so too. We could both benefit from trade. I expect I'll hear from your alliance about having Officer Aral stationed to a diplomatic post planetside."

Helgen smiled. "I'll relay the request, Ambassador. Just make sure you're down there to meet her."

Temar nodded. At this point, he couldn't make promises. He didn't know what the PA would do, but he did know that if he had to risk his own life to save Shan, he'd do it in a second. He only hoped he'd have the chance.

A short man who looked younger than Hannal's oldest stepped forward. "Ambassador, if you'll follow me, I'll show you dock beta nine-two-nine." Temar took a deep breath and followed the escort.

chapter
twenty-nine

TEMAR WAITED in the air lock as the door to the *Brazica* sealed with a series of clicks and thumps. The door into the *Phrike* stayed sealed, the ship's name displayed in blocky letters above the door that would open to allow him into it. Despite the fact that he really didn't know what he was doing, doing something felt better than sitting and waiting.

The door behind him finally fell silent, and the *Phrike* door gave two good thunks before it swung open. Inside, Black stood waiting. He was a large man, larger than Temar had expected after seeing him on the screen. He stepped forward and offered his hand. "Lieutenant Commander Verly Black."

Temar took his hand and shook it. "Ambassador Temar Gazer of Livre."

Black wasn't quite as muscled as Naite, but his shoulders were wider than Shan's and he was taller than both brothers. Considering that Temar tended to use Naite as a measure of how large a person could get, Black was large.

"If you'll follow me, Ambassador, I'll set you up with the current feeds."

"Temar."

"Excuse me?"

Temar sighed and considered Black. They'd tried the quiet approach with the AFP and it hadn't gone well. Besides, Temar's nerves were frayed from too much verbal dancing and too little truth. "My people don't care about titles the way yours seem to. I'm Temar. If on any given day I'm an ambassador or a landowner or a glassblower, I'm still Temar."

"Yes, sir," Black offered. He gave Temar an odd look, but he headed into his ship and Temar followed. "I have the feeds tied into the copilot's chair. I can redirect them to private quarters if you prefer."

"I don't."

"I didn't figure you would," Black said with some amusement.

"Should I call you Lieutenant or Black or Verly?" Temar asked as Black started climbing a ladder. He looked down at Temar.

"I'd appreciate it if you didn't call me Lieutenant. That's a little more of a drop in rank than I'd prefer. If you want to call me by my rank, it's Lieutenant Commander. If there's more than one Lieutenant Commander around, you can add Black to the end of that. No one calls me Black, but if you want to call me Verly, it'd make me a little more comfortable about calling you Temar." With that, he started climbing.

Temar followed. This ship clearly wasn't designed for many people to share it, with narrow passages and ladders instead of elevators, but everything was clean and sleek. Verly headed down a narrow hall into a room that Temar immediately recognized. Dropping down into one seat, Verly gestured toward the second one. "Ambassador," he said, inviting Temar to sit.

"Have there been more signals?" Temar asked as he settled down into the chair. It had high sides, and even Temar's head was caught between two winglike structures that meant he could only look straight ahead without leaning forward. He shifted around until he got one leg under him and he could lean toward the control panel. One screen showed the greenish shadow forms that Temar had seen from the *Brazica*.

"No. But if there's a snooper in the area, they'll be transmitting on a tight beam, and the terrorists won't move to the next step until they have confirmation that the vid successfully reached its destination."

"Which is?"

Verly glanced over and then turned his whole chair to face Temar. "How much do you know about local politics?"

"Local as in who on Livre is most likely to file a council complaint about a neighbor's boar, a lot. Local as in all this?" Temar gestured toward the controls and vid screens. "Nothing. This is my first time up here."

Verly sighed and gave a nod. "Here's the short of it. The PA gets accused of being micromanaging warmongers who try to force everyone to follow their rules. The AFP is a repressive government that claims to offer freedom while anyone who disagrees with their definition of free disappears. There are at least four major terrorist groups—two are associated with trying to put pressure on the AFP in order to get planets to break away from them. One attacks the PA, pretty much to annoy us, since our allies aren't likely to change sides."

"And the fourth?"

Verly made a face. "They're sort of nuts. They think God has told them that humanity is a disease corrupting his perfect planets. And then you have any number of homegrown terrorists with less elaborate plots. This looks like an FFA operation, *Freedom for All*. They're the most vocal about condemning the AFP's sins, and they have a hit list of diplomats and officers they want to kill."

Temar closed his eyes and silently cursed the fact that he hadn't known any of this.

"I have the broadcast vid ready," Verly said after a moment.

Temar nodded. "Okay. Put it on."

Pentalia appeared on the screen. Shan knelt on the floor next to one of Ambassador Melton's aides, who had blood all over his shirt and face. Shan had his hands bound behind his back, while Melton sat in his chair with Pentalia's gun to the side of his head. Melton made a long confession to ordering the executions of workers who had disrupted the mining on some moon Temar didn't know. The ambassador was white-faced, with a bruised cheek that had a lazy trickle of blood sliding over it. The transmission ended with Pentalia making a grandiose claim that his group wouldn't stop until freedom meant free.

"Nothing more?" Temar asked.

Verly shook his head. "The snooper will wait for confirmation that the message made it through. Then he'll either torture Melton or simply execute him on vid."

"And Shan?"

"Have you done anything they might not like?"

"We've only been here two days."

"What did you trade to the AFP?"

Temar narrowed his eyes, wondering how much of this related to Shan and how much was Verly trying to get information for his own side. "A few pounds each of antimony trioxide, zirconium, and lanthanum oxide, samples of optic-quality glass, artwork, and a whole lot of broken computers we wanted fixed or replaced."

Verly grimaced. "Did that guy know the details of the deal?"

Temar nodded.

"Those are critical supplies. He'll probably force Shan to apologize and then he'll do the same thing—torture and/or execute him on screen."

A cold chill went through Temar. "That can't happen."

"Do you have rescue close enough to intervene?"

"We are the rescue," Temar said. Verly didn't look convinced of that. "We need to find a way to get in that room. Captain Helgen is focusing on his ship, so he isn't even trying to rescue the hostages."

"The FFA does like to blow themselves up with the ship." Verly sounded like he sympathized with the captain's position, but that wasn't what Temar wanted to hear.

"We have to find a way in there, either in person or through communication. Would Pentalia want to talk to you, since you're Planetary Alliance instead of AFP?"

"Unlikely," Verly said. "They know we condemn their actions, even if we sympathize with their position."

"And encourage it?" Temar asked, the words slipping out even though he knew it was stupid to antagonize the only person offering any help. Rushing on, Temar asked, "How many people do we have on this ship? Could we rush the corridor if we could get the door open?"

"The crew is you and I," Verly said. "This is a long-range scout, designed to monitor from the deep."

Temar looked around, as if some hero would miraculously appear from the air. That had happened before, when Naite had saved them from Ben's schemes. Right now, no one could follow any clues to them.

"Verly," Temar said, weighing every word before letting it escape, "I warned the AFP already that my people are stubborn. Your alliance left us to die of thirst, so we thrived, with farms and towns still running. The desert sends sandstorms to wipe us out, and we pull on sand veils and pull closer until it passes. If a terrorist group supporting your side murders Shan, it's not going to end well for your side."

"Meaning?" Verly asked.

Temar looked at him. "Meaning, I don't know. I don't know if the councils would vote to send tons of materials up on the condition it be used to hunt these terrorists down and deliver them to Livre or if my people would demand training and ships to track these people down themselves. On Livre, we expect justice."

"That's not how the universe works."

Temar nodded. He understood that. "Yes, but are you going to convince a planet full of people of that when their whole life has been about fixing whatever broke, even if it meant doing the impossible? If this is broken, I don't think anyone will like the consequences, so I'm telling you, you need to find a way to get me in that room. If Shan and I both die trying to fix this, that wouldn't go over nearly as bad as me going home and telling everyone that I watched two ships sit and do nothing while Shan was murdered in cold blood. You have no idea how badly that will go over."

"I don't have authorization to take action here," Verly said carefully.

"I don't care. Good people don't sit still while someone dies. Get me on that ship."

Verly fingered one of the controls on his panel. "You do know you're being unreasonable, correct?"

"Yes," Temar agreed.

"Just making sure you knew it." Verly turned his chair to face his control panel. "I'm not promising anything, but let me get a full set of scans before I tell you that you're going to have to accept that sometimes people die."

"Oh, I know people die, Verly. I've seen death. I won't sit here while Shan dies."

Verly didn't answer, and for some time Temar watched the green shadows on the vid. The angle was odd, as if they were several feet higher and looking in on the room. The two standing people had to be Shan and Pentalia, since the one on the floor was the injured assistant and Melton sat in the chair where Temar had last seen him. The two people who were standing slowly circled, and Temar imagined Shan trying to edge closer, talking about God and forgiveness and moral right. Normally Temar had a lot of faith in Shan's ability to talk. However, Shan had had his share of failures in that department, and Temar had to think that anyone who could blow up a ship of crewmates he'd lived with wouldn't care about Shan's God. Pentalia was more like Ben—convinced he was right while being utterly wrong.

"New message," Verly said before his fingers went back to their steady work on the control board. Pentalia appeared on the screen again. This time Shan was on his feet, standing to the side of the screen.

"Those who attack the people have to expect the people to attack back," Pentalia announced, his voice carrying a cold fury that frightened Temar.

"Gary, don't do this," Shan begged, taking a step forward. Melton was utterly white, and Pentalia pointed his weapon at Shan. Temar clutched the edge of the panel and leaned forward. *Shut up, Shan. Shut up. Don't get yourself killed,* he silently begged.

"And those that align themselves with evil can expect the same fate," Pentalia said. In a flash, he lowered the gun and pulled the trigger. Melton's head exploded, a spray of red spreading across the room. Shan flinched back, but Temar could see the red freckles of blood across the pale blue shirt Hannal had made especially for this trip. "People will die until freedom means free for everyone," Pentalia announced before the image vanished.

Temar stared at the blank screen, not realizing that he'd stopped breathing until the world wobbled uneasily. Sucking in air, Temar turned to Verly. "What now?"

"Now he tortures Shan until he can get an apology for supporting evil. He'll want that on a vid before…."

"Before he kills Shan," Temar finished when the silence continued too long. "Tell me you have a way into that ship. I don't care what kind of risk I have to take or what I have to promise him, but I want Shan back now."

"There is a plan. It's a bad one, but it's a plan," Verly offered carefully.

"Bad? How bad?"

"Compared to a bullet to the brain, it's a great plan. Compared to anything else, it's stupid, dangerous, and utterly unthinkable." Verly used the controls to bring up an image of the damaged ship. Temar could see where large chunks were missing, blown into space, leaving only ragged metal and floating garbage. "He's blockaded them here." A section of the undamaged ship glowed red. "Diplomatic quarters."

"There's only one way in there," Temar said. "It's a series of rooms that opens one into another."

"Security, which is great unless the terrorist is an inside man, and then all your security gets turned against you. The doors have manual locks from the inside that would require hours to cut through."

"By which time Shan would be dead," Temar's chest hurt.

"Exactly." Verly clicked the computer and the corridor connecting the sections the terrorists controlled glowed in red. "So, when you're cut off at the pass, go around." An animation of a stick figure floated into the picture. "I plant explosives here, and blow out the side of the chamber." The small stick figure touched the station and then floated away. Almost immediately, an explosion made little animated bits of station fly out. Tiny animated bodies flew out through the hole in the bulwark. "The sudden loss of pressure would pull them all out into space before they can detonate the explosives."

"But… that would kill him." Temar's chest grew too tight for his pounding heart.

"Not if we move fast. I would grab him, and then you would winch us both back into my ship." The animation image withdrew like a camera pulling back to show more of the picture, and now Temar could see a small, animated version of Verly's ship, and the small Verly stick figure and Shan were speeding toward it. "I could use the computer's scanner to identify which of the people in the hull is Shan, based on unique mineral compositions in your body created by living on Livre. Then I would detonate when Shan was closest to the blast point, minimizing the amount of time it would take me to get to him. The human body can last fifteen to twenty seconds before passing out, another thirty before suffering significant swelling, and up to two or three minutes before there's any dangerous damage."

"So, it's safe?" Temar asked. If this was Verly's definition of safe, Temar didn't trust the man as far as he could throw him.

"Not even. I could miss catching him, and any lengthy maneuvering to try to secure him could leave us outside the three-minute window. At that point, anything from brain damage to death is possible. The explosion could send debris into him, leading to any number of injuries. Pentalia could detonate any explosives the captain hasn't cleared from his decks, and Shan and I would both be killed."

Temar nodded, oddly reassured by the honesty. The plan was dangerous, but it was a plan, and the way Verly explained it, it might work. "What odds do you give it?" Temar asked, fighting to keep his voice even.

Verly turned off the animation and turned the chair around to look at Temar. "I need to tell you that I don't have the best reputation for plans. My plans… at least one of my plans… is rather infamous for going horribly wrong, leading to a lot of innocent deaths. This has less than a fifty-fifty chance. I'd put the odds at about 20 percent of us both getting out clean and 20 percent that we both die horrible deaths."

"And 60 percent chance of something in the middle," Temar finished, his voice weak. He didn't want to make this call, but Verly kept looking at him as if he expected an answer. How could Temar make this choice for Shan? What if he made the wrong choice? What if he did nothing and these people shot Shan in the head? Temar's stomach roiled with fear until he felt on the verge of throwing up on Verly's nice, clean floor. All these people had such clean floors. Staring at the metal seam that ran along the decking, Temar knew he had lost the train of logic somewhere, but his brain balked at the idea of considering anything more significant than space-people's obsession with clean floors.

"It's a hard decision. If you want me to make the call—"

"No." Temar looked up. "No, he's my… friend. If someone is going to make this call, it'll be me." Temar didn't add that if it turned out badly, he'd be the one living with the guilt, but from the sympathetic look on Verly's face, Temar was sure he knew it. Shan had told him once that it was horrible being the survivor, being the one who hadn't been hurt. Twice in his life, Shan had been the one who escaped a horrible fate unscathed, and Temar could admit he hadn't understood. He'd called Shan lucky. Maybe he hadn't said that to Shan's face, but he'd thought it. Shan hadn't been raped. He hadn't been tied up and abused. He hadn't died even when armed hunters had chased him through the desert. It was as if his God had shielded him and let everyone around Shan suffer. Naite, him, even Ben… how many victims did Shan know?

Now Temar knew how Shan felt. When someone hurt you, you knew you had to reach inside and survive. There was this stubborn determination to put one foot in front of the other and keep pushing through until something changed. But in some odd way, there was a power there. Temar had manipulated Ben on the good days. And when he came too close to relaxing into a life that was hell, he'd manipulated Ben into having bad days. When he could feel that rotting center in his soul start to feel good when Ben touched him gently, Temar would aggravate Ben into picking up a whip and laying into him. It reminded him to cling to hate. The power was sick and twisted—the rot in his soul sometimes stunk so bad that he wanted to gag, and other times the sweetness of that rot drowned out everything else. No matter how corrupt, there was a power there.

But now Temar didn't have any of that power. He couldn't make the choice to try to placate his captor or aggravate him into violence. Trapped on the outside, he could only sit and watch. The pain left him almost unable to think straight, and now... now Temar understood what Shan meant when he talked about how the ones who weren't hurt still suffered. Temar would give anything to be in there, to be at Shan's side, and he couldn't be. He could, however, make this choice.

"Do it," Temar whispered.

"I'll get the equipment ready. I'll be back in about twenty minutes to see if you want to still do this."

Temar nodded mutely.

Verly stood, but then he stopped. "You have good instincts, Ambassador Gazer. In the service, we always say there are watchers and flailers. Watchers stand back and gather intel until they understand a situation. Flailers go flying into a situation half blind. I've done my share of flailing, but you're a watcher through and through. So, if you pull the plug on this, I'll follow that order, and I won't question it." Verly turned toward the hatch.

"Lieutenant Commander?"

Verly turned around, and Temar took a deep breath as he tried to control the pain that ripped at him. "Can you think of any other plans?"

For several seconds, Verly looked at him, and then said firmly, "No."

Dropping his gaze, Temar stared at the seam in the floor. He wouldn't lose Shan. He wouldn't. "Do it. Tell me when you need me to come down, and I'll learn how to operate the winch, but I need a few minutes up here first."

"Yes, sir," Verly agreed before he headed off the bridge.

Sitting at the navigator seat, Temar stared out into the black. The ship was turned the wrong way for him to see the *Brazica* other than in the vid displays, but Verly's animation haunted him.

"God, you've protected him this long, please don't take him away from me," Temar prayed, the words little more than a rough whisper, but that was all he could force out through his painfully tight chest. "Please save him. Please don't take him, not yet. We need him here. Oh God, we need him here." Cold tracks from tears slid down his face, but his hands shook so badly he had to hang on to the arms of the chair to keep from breaking apart. "God, please. Please."

Temar kept whispering his plea as emotions rolled through him. He would have to pull himself together to play his part in the plan, but right now, he cried and prayed and hoped that Shan was right about someone listening.

chapter
thirty

"ARE YOU clear?" Verly asked. His voice sounded strange coming through the communicator built into his space suit, like he was standing in a very small cave with sounds bouncing around him.

Temar nodded, touching each control in turn. "Release, let more line out, retract the line, speed."

Verly nodded. "Repressurization?"

"Three dials." Temar gestured toward the wall.

"Emergency autopilot?"

Temar gave Verly a cold look.

"Right, you know. Try to avoid letting me die out there, okay?"

Temar nodded. "Wait," he blurted. "What about the other assistant?" Guilt rose as he realized he'd forgotten there was another person in that room they were about to blow up. Temar had no problem with Pentalia dying, but they hadn't talked about the other assistant.

Verly turned awkwardly in his bulky suit. "He's shot, Temar, probably dying if not dead already. And as soon as Pentalia is done, he'll be dead. You aren't changing his fate by trying to save Shan."

Temar clenched his teeth, but he couldn't disagree with the logic.

"Your call, Ambassador."

"Go," Temar said as firmly as he could. Verly nodded and walked toward the open door into the airlock, clicking the retractable line to his belt and pulling on it before he closed the heavy door. Temar could only wait now. He watched the screen while Verly floated out into space, his dark space suit almost invisible except for the pinpricks of light that appeared as tiny thrusters nudged him first one way and then the other. Slowly, he approached the giant *Brazica*; until Temar watched a human form approach the ship, he'd had no idea how truly massive the *Brazica* was. Everyone in Livre could probably fit inside without spending too much time stepping on each other's toes.

The pulley attached to the retractable line gave three long beeps. Verly had signaled.

Temar turned on the communicator. "This is Ambassador Gazer calling Captain Helgen."

It took several seconds before the captain's voice answered him. "Ambassador?"

"I'm getting Shan back, Captain." Temar turned off the communicator and gave the pulley's retract button one quick push to let Verly know he had warned Helgen. Verly had argued against that, claiming the terrorists were monitoring the communications. They probably were, but Temar didn't want to blow a hole in someone's ship without at least some warning. It seemed rude.

With his hand hovering over the pulley controls, Temar watched the screen as Verly's barely visible body slid closer to the main, cylindrical part of the *Brazica*. The explosion was silent, which seemed odd, but one second the flat wall of the ambassador's quarters were there, and the next, debris spilled out into space. Verly's suit flashed as he maneuvered closer to the field of rubble, reaching out. Temar held his breath, his fingertips tingling as fear rushed through every cell. Verly caught at something, and as it rotated, Temar could see the blue of a shirt. Temar gasped, desperate to hit the retract button, but if Verly hadn't secured Shan to his own body first, he might lose his grip. Instead, Temar watched the controls, his hand shaking now.

Three long beeps. Temar pressed the retract button so hard that for one second he had an irrational flash of panic that he'd break it and be forced to watch on screen as Shan died. He didn't. The cable pulled the two of them in much faster than Verly had gone out, but suddenly everything changed direction. Verly and Shan flew off the side of the screen and debris soared across the scene. Temar's mouth fell open as most of the arm that contained the ambassador's rooms disintegrated, chunks of metal radiating out into space and toward the *Brazica* and through the area where Verly had Shan in this ridiculous attempt at a rescue.

And Temar couldn't do anything.

Nothing.

He could only watch an empty screen with bits of floating trash and pray. Air refused to come all the way into his lungs as Temar divided his time between looking at the screen and staring through the thick viewport into the airlock.

Verly's back appeared first, the belt tight and his body bent from the force of the pull. It took Temar a half second too long to turn the pulley off, and the momentum and the artificial force of the ship's gravity combined to make Verly slam into the wall of the airlock, his body collapsing over Shan's. Temar hit the airlock doors, triggering the oxygen supply before the doors were even fully closed. He knew they had to depressurize slowly, but he turned the dial to the maximum setting Verly had shown him.

With a hand pressed up to the door and his nose on the viewport, Temar watched as Verly pulled his helmet off. That was the first time he noticed the blood.

Temar hit the switch on the door. "Verly, are you okay?"

"Shan caught shrapnel from the secondary blast. It's bad," Verly yelled. He moved, and Temar could see Shan's limp body, his pants red from blood and his face slack.

"Is he...."

"He's hurt. I can only control the bleeding. Get us out of here, Temar." Verly pulled off his gloves, throwing them to the side before ripping open Shan's shirt. Bits of his insides lay under the fabric, and Temar gagged once before turning and racing for the bridge.

The emergency autopilot was designed for a dying pilot to be able to hit one button and have the ship automatically find its way home. It worked just as well for someone who didn't know the first thing about ships. Temar flipped open the small cover and turned the switch. Engines rumbled below him, and Temar sat down in the copilot's seat and hit the communications controls. He was getting familiar with those.

"Ambassador Gazer to Captain Helgen."

This time, Temar got a visual on the captain. "Ambassador, do I take it that you blew another hole in my ship?" The captain did not look amused.

"We got Shan out," Temar said, refusing to apologize, even though he was seriously running out of backbone. He desperately wanted to curl up in a ball and let someone else handle things for a while. "Shan was seriously injured in that second explosion, though. We're heading to Lieutenant Commander Black's ship for medical help right now."

"The second… that large explosion wasn't you?"

Temar jerked back, shocked that Helgen would ever suspect him of putting everyone at risk like that. "No. That was whatever the terrorist had in the room with them. We blew a hole in the wall so we could grab Shan."

The captain blinked at him for a second. "You took him out through space? Without a suit? I'm rather inclined to believe you when you say your people are a little irrational."

"All people are, Captain. We just admit to it."

"Ambassador, come around and our medical teams will help."

Temar shook his head. "You have your own injured, and it will be at least twenty minutes before Verly and Shan are depressurized. Verly says that ships should already be heading this way from Minga because of his earlier messages, and we should meet them on the way. If Shan is going to survive, we need their medical equipment." Verly had been honest about most everything else, so Temar really hoped he'd been honest about his alliance's medical capabilities.

"The bastards are good with technology," Captain Helgen admitted unhappily. "Good luck handling them, Ambassador. I'll tell command that we have a deal, and that you've approved Officer Aral as a liaison."

"Thank you," Temar said. He had a lot to thank the captain for, first and foremost not shoving him in a closet.

"Travel safe, Ambassador," Helgen said, and then the screen went blank.

Temar sat in the chair, shaking so badly he wasn't sure he could keep his feet under him if he tried to climb the ladder down to the lower deck again, but that's where Shan was, and Temar intended to be there when the airlock repressurized. Shan had seen him bruised, tied, gagged, and humiliated. He could handle seeing Shan injured. Maybe. Temar's stomach rolled in warning, but he ignored that as he headed back down the narrow corridor to the lower deck.

chapter
thirty-one

TEMAR SHIFTED from foot to foot, unable to stand still as he watched the pressure gauge approach normal. As the number clicked over into the green, the doors slid open with a puff of air as the two sides finally equalized.

"Shan!" Temar ran to Shan's side, going to his knees next to him. Verly had hooked a machine up to his chest, a band going around his body. Another machine encased Shan's entire arm, displays showing numbers that made no sense, and his stomach was covered with a white bandage, the edges turning pink. Even his face was covered with a clear plastic mask that hissed air as regularly as Temar breathed. Temar grabbed Shan's free hand, twining their fingers together.

"I take it you're more than friends," Verly said. Temar ignored it. These people and their stupidity didn't matter to him… not now. "That must have gone over great with the AFP bigots." Verly touched some controls on the arm. "His blood pressure is barely holding, and the fluid replacements are keeping his heart and brain oxygenated."

"How long until we reach your people?"

"I couldn't tell from here. I'll go check the system for hails from PA ships." Verly stood, his white space suit streaked with blood, and hurried out of the room.

"Seriously, Shan," Temar whispered, "you have to stop this. First it's drinking pipe juice to get off the desert and now it's getting blown up in space. I should take you home to the farm and make you stay there until you learn not to do this. You're going to give me a heart attack." Shan's hand was limp in his, and Temar's face hurt from the effort not to bawl like a baby. Instead, he held Shan's hand tightly and whispered to him, promising all sorts of things if Shan would wake up: a bike ride out to Blue Hope, a lazy morning sleeping in and kissing until they fell asleep again, breakfast in bed. Temar would have kept promising things until he gave Shan the world, only Verly returned.

"I was right. A ship is coming out, eleven minutes to contact, thirteen to emergency docking. The captain wants to talk to you."

"Me?" Temar looked up.

Coming closer, Verly crouched down and looked over the display numbers on the machine around Shan's entire arm. "I told you I've made some bad calls and cost some people their lives. That happens in war. It also happens that when you do that, you aren't particularly popular, not even with your own side. They want to hear from you, Temar."

Temar frowned. "They think you screwed up."

Verly nodded. "They do."

"You saved Shan." Temar didn't leave any room for doubt in his statement. Shan would be okay. Temar wouldn't accept anything less.

"Thank you for the vote of confidence. Now go talk to the commander and the captain."

Temar stood and paused, hating that he still didn't understand these people. "Should I tell them this was my plan?" he asked, not wanting Verly to suffer after he'd saved Shan.

Verly gave him a crooked smile. "I appreciate the offer, Ambassador, but it would probably be better if you told them the truth. I came up with the plan and told you that it was not only stupid but that it came with about a 20 percent chance of working at all."

Temar nodded. He could shade the truth that way. "Thank you for the 20 percent chance," Temar said, hesitating at the door. "Call me if he wakes up or…."

"I'll call," Verly promised. "Go on." He gave Temar a smile that carried some emotion Temar couldn't quite understand. "I promise to take care of your Shan."

Temar headed into the control room to use the communications screen. He flipped the switch, and he could see a woman sitting in the center with a man standing close behind.

"Ambassador Gazer?" the woman asked. She sounded unsure.

Pulling himself together, Temar nodded. "Captain?"

"Yes, I'm Captain Flores of the *Athene*, this is my first officer, Commander Kennedy. We understand you have an injury on board, Ambassador Gazer."

Slightly annoyed by the woman's nonchalant tone, Temar struggled to focus. "Ambassador Polli of Livre was caught in the cross fire between a group of terrorists and the Alliance of Free Planets. He's badly wounded."

"After an attempted rescue?" The captain was fishing, and she wasn't particularly subtle about it.

"Yes," Temar said. "Captain Helgen of the *Brazica* refused to take any measures to save Ambassador Polli. I then asked Lieutenant Commander Black's help. As I explained to him, my people will go to extraordinary lengths to save our own, and I don't care if it's a sandstorm or a terrorist."

"Does blowing up a ship and risking war seem reasonable?"

"Yes." Temar stared at the woman, not flinching when she traded an unsubtle look with her second-in-command. Lilian would eat this woman alive and spit her bones out to bleach in the midday sun.

Captain Flores broke the silence first. "We're coming up on emergency docking procedures. Our doctors tell me they have secured the transmission from Ambassador Polli's emergency resuscitation, and while his wounds are critical, they believe he is holding strong for now."

"Not bad, considering that Black argued against it, offering only a 20 percent chance of success."

"Did he?" Flores was trying to sound nonchalant.

"He did. Of course, he also said there was a greater chance of his dying out there than of both of them getting back alive, and he doesn't have a scratch on him."

"And if he had been killed?" Captain Flores leaned forward. "That would have left you at the mercy of an AFP ship you had ordered him to bomb."

"If the lieutenant commander had been killed, I would have gone back to the *Brazica*." Temar smiled sweetly. "Captain Helgen was very understanding when we talked after the explosion. In fact, I confirmed our trade agreement just to make sure there weren't any misunderstandings."

Temar could see the reaction in the faces of both officers. Again, too much heat in one direction. "I would have preferred to postpone our meeting with the PA, since most of our trade goods and samples are either in transit to one of AFP stations or blown up on the ship. We don't have a single piece of optic glass to base a trade deal on."

"You would trade with us after trading with the AFP?" Flores spoke as though she couldn't understand her own words. The whole ship shivered as something bumped it, and Temar looked up. "We've caught you with a grapple, and we're pulling you in for an emergency docking," Flores explained. "Expect another jolt like that when the docking ports lock on."

"Understood." Temar looked at the captain for a second. Getting a formed piece off the rod was always the hardest part, and he struggled to find the right words to reach her. Right now, he was pretty sure she thought he was sun-maddened. "Captain," he said slowly, watching her reactions. She was easily read, but that didn't mean he understood which side to apply heat to or how far he could push her before she warped under the pressure. "My people have survived a lot, and part of that is because we've learned not to trust words. Both alliances have many words to describe the other. We have only seen both sides treat us fairly. Until that changes, Livre only has a grudge against the *Freedom for All* group. If any of them come to our world, they would, without a doubt, be sentenced to exile and death."

"Death?" Flores sat up straighter, and Temar could see the horror in her face.

"We don't impose death often, but like I said, my people believe in actions."

"The Alliance has a strict policy against capital punishment," Flores said as the whole ship shivered again as the docking finished.

"I suspect we do many things you have a policy against. I know we certainly broke more than a few of the AFP's policies." Temar shrugged as if it made no difference to him. "Once Ambassador Polli is awake and healthy, we can discuss trade and the many ways our two peoples won't like each other."

"Ambassador—"

"I hope to see you soon, Captain," Temar said, hitting the button to turn communications off as he spotted movement in the airlock. He didn't have the energy to play ambassador right now, and the stakes were too high if he said something wrong, so the captain would have to wait.

The airlock was crowded with men and women in light blue uniforms who swarmed over Shan. "Medical crew," Verly offered as he slid along the wall toward Shan, careful to keep out of the way. Temar got his first glimpse of a PA ship through the open door to the *Athene*, and it looked remarkably identical to the *Brazica*.

"Is he okay?" Temar trusted Verly's assessment more than the captain's.

"As far as I can see, he should recover. There was no interruption of oxygen to the brain. Of all the organs, the heart and brain are the only two organs that really can't be brought back to full recovery. Both are in perfect condition and the rest… it can be fixed. I've seen men with worse going out to get drunk with their buddies four months later."

Temar thought about Shan's insides lying outside the skin. "If you've seen worse, I wouldn't want to have your memories."

"War is never pretty."

Temar nodded.

"They're going to want to talk to you."

"Who?"

Verly looked around the room for a second before answering. "Either the diplomatic corps or the security corps, depending on what kind of impression you made in there."

That didn't sound promising, and exhaustion pulled at Temar so sharply that he wanted to sink down to the floor and never get up again. "Can I ask that you come along?" Temar asked. He might not know Verly well, but the man had offered help when no one else would.

"I'll be answering questions from the security corps," Verly said. Temar must have looked alarmed, because Verly shook his head. "It's standard operating procedure to share information after a mission. They need to know that you're crazy enough to walk into an AFP ship with your male lover and smart enough to walk out still on good terms with the bastards."

"Wait, you know?" Temar looked at Verly. He hadn't said Shan was a lover.

"It's not exactly hard to see."

The medical people lifted Shan, and the whole chaotic knot of humans rushed down the corridor. Temar was wrong. The PA ship wasn't identical to the *Brazica*. This ship had much larger corridors.

"Ambassador, it was good to work with you." Verly turned to him and offered a salute. Not sure what he should do, Temar stared. Verly dropped his hand to his side. "If all your people are as stubborn as you two, trying to talk a terrorist down at the point of a gun and authorizing a rescue by blowing a hole in an ally's ship, you should make this an interesting piece of space to patrol."

Temar gave a huff. "We're nothing. They wouldn't send Naite for fear he'd offend everyone, and we were afraid Lilian would try to take over the universe, and we didn't want to have to run it after she did." Temar was almost sure he was reaching that point of fatigue where hysteria made everything mildly amusing.

Verly smiled. "Good luck, Ambassador Gazer." Turning, he headed into the corridor.

More men in blue uniforms were coming down the now-empty hall, and Verly stopped to talk to them. They exchanged a few words that looked civil enough, and then Verly headed past them and the two men came to meet Temar. Pushing himself away from the safety of the wall that was holding him up, Temar met them at the door. Before either of them spoke, Temar started. "I am entirely too exhausted to handle negotiations right now. I need a place to get Shan's blood off me, updates from his doctors, fresh clothes, and a place to sit down before I fall on my face, because I'm pretty sure I have adrenaline poisoning after the last few hours of hell. It is hard to be the one watching instead of the one getting kidnapped for a change."

Sure enough, Temar's rush of words left the two blinking at him and looking at each other for some sort of reassurance. Temar might not trust words, but they were as useful as fire.

"The chair should probably come first, unless you want me to fall on my face," Temar prodded them.

"Of course, right this way, Ambassador," the shorter man offered, waving a hand toward the corridor. The taller man headed back the way they'd come, and Temar followed.

"Is there any word on Ambassador Polli yet?"

"No, sir. We're monitoring medical, but there's no reported change on his condition."

Temar nodded. He'd done everything he could, and he was back to waiting. No matter how exhausted he was, he suspected he wouldn't be getting any rest anytime soon.

chapter
thirty-two

TEMAR SHIFTED in the chair, his neck complaining as he found a new position. They'd offered him quarters, ones with computers set into the walls and a thick viewport that showed the stars. It had a huge bed and a bathtub and separate shower that made the AFP ship look barren by comparison. However, his quarters didn't have Shan, and until Shan could join him in their quarters with one giant bed for both of them, Temar would sleep in the chair.

"Ambassador Gazer?"

Temar opened his eyes a crack, glancing over at Shan before he focused on their visitor. Commander Green from the diplomatic corps had an expectant expression on his face as he waited for an invitation to come in. Shan had a private room with computers and shiny... things... everywhere. Temar was almost afraid to touch anything because it was like walking around inside a machine.

"Commander Green," Temar said with a nod. Green had gone out of his way to make sure that Temar and Shan were taken care of, although Temar suspected some of that was because of Verly's description. Temar hadn't seen the man again, but everyone on the ship kept a certain distance from Temar, as though not quite sure of his temper. Temar had seen that with Naite. Workers would tiptoe around him. Since Temar was five-foot-six on a good day and small, he'd never inspired fear in anyone, at least not before blowing up someone's ship. From the whispers Temar had overheard, they had him single-handedly blowing the *Brazica* into five evenly shaped pieces.

"How is he?" Green asked.

"The doctors say he'll wake any time now. His wounds are healing, and his brain function looks fine."

Green nodded. "I'm glad. These terrorists might think they're fighting for freedom, but they're hardening people's attitudes and making it more difficult for AFP planets to rise up against the criminals running that government. I mean, they would have arrested you for violating their ridiculous sexual laws had they known you were involved with Ambassador Polli."

Temar didn't answer even though he suspected the AFP wanted supplies enough that they would have overlooked the relationship. Morals, even sick and twisted morals, were one thing—having a shortage of supplies was another. After a week, he only knew one thing for sure—these people all thought they owned the moral high ground. When Shan woke up, he was going to love lecturing all of them about Christ and forgiveness. Temar caught Shan's hand in his, rubbing this thumb against the back of Shan's hand.

"Did you make contact with Livre?" Green asked.

"They're grateful that you're offering medical services."

"Of course. You and Ambassador Polli are the victims caught in the middle of all this." Green offered a look of sympathy that left Temar unsure as to how to react. The fact was that the Planetary Alliance was at least partially to blame for the entire universe's general state of chaos. However, Green didn't want to hear that, so Temar remained silent as he waited to find out why he'd come to Shan's room.

"The captain wanted to let you know that we've rendezvoused with the *Sunkissed*. Representative Fields is here to negotiate the terms of the trade deal you alluded to, if you're still amenable."

Temar nodded absentmindedly. Too many people and too many names had left him unwilling to try to keep names and requests straight. Captain So-and-so thought this. Officer So-and-so wanted to know about Livre culture. Representative So-and-so wanted to trade. When the person cared enough to stand in front of Temar and talk to him, then he'd care about their requests. Until then, he let the words flow over him, not disagreeing but not going out of his way to cooperate.

"Ambassador Melton's replacement sent a formal statement of gratitude that your partner tried to save the ambassador."

Temar nodded. More useless information. Words were an addiction with these people. Green eased farther into the room.

"I wanted to broach the subject of immigration."

Temar looked up. This was a new topic.

"I respect the fact that your people don't trust words. We have a saying: 'Actions speak louder than words.'"

Temar raised an eyebrow and continued to use his thumb to stroke the back of Shan's hand. Considering how these people loved their words, the saying was more than ironic.

"Normally, immigration files are private, but the government would like to offer your council a chance to review confidential documents. It would permit you to consider allowing immigration for people whose files show they take the sort of actions that would allow you to accept them."

"Your government is concerned we don't have enough people to mine," Temar summarized.

Green gave him a wry smile and shrugged. "I'm sure that's one consideration. Another is that the planet was always scheduled for open immigration."

"It's not now," Temar said, reminding Green again that the Planetary Alliance had defaulted on their terraforming agreement, negating all previous treaties. He was starting to understand why the AFP had declared war, although Temar wasn't a fan of their hatred and discrimination either. "And files are nothing more than words."

"So, you won't allow any immigration?" Green frowned.

"I've seen Verly Black put his life on the line for a plan he himself gave a 20 percent chance of success. I saw Natalie Aral and Rula Lish handling a terrorist attack while never losing sight of protecting a stranger who didn't understand what was going on. Those are actions I could endorse."

"So, you're limiting immigration to three people?"

Temar shrugged. "Maybe. I told Ambassador Melton that *we* say the truth is finer than sand. You have to carry it in a bag for a while to see if it's going to escape through the mesh."

"So, wait and see?"

"That sounds like a plan," Temar agreed, his eyes going to Shan as Shan's fingers twitched. "Shan? Hey, can you hear me?" Temar stood and leaned over the bed. Shan's eyes pressed closed even tighter. "Coward," Temar teased. "You never do like to open your eyes in the morning."

"Because there's always too much light," Shan managed to say in a weak voice.

"I'll get the doctor," Green offered before vanishing out of the room.

"Well, you had the good sense to wake up in the middle of the night shift, so most of the lights are off."

Shan cracked one eye open a tiny bit. "My throat hurts."

"I'll get you the medicated ice they left here. Hold on." Temar hurried to retrieve the cup from the refrigerated cubby where the nurses kept it. When he returned to Shan's side, Shan's eyes were closed again. Taking a smooth piece of ice, Temar brushed it against Shan's lips.

Both Shan's eyes came open. "What is that?" he asked, struggling to raise his hand.

"Water that's so cold it turns hard."

"Ice," Shan said blearily as he made the connection.

"Yep." Temar put the ice up against Shan's lips, and this time he opened his mouth to suck it in. He sucked on it for some time while Temar stroked Shan's arm, feeling the warm skin and letting himself bask in the pure joy of believing that Shan would be fine. Oh, the doctors had said it often enough, but seeing Shan wake up meant more than all their promises.

"Gary Pentalia?"

"He died in the rescue," Temar said softly. He could see the pain in Shan's eyes, and Temar felt a sprout of guilt. He'd done the right thing, but Shan would try to save the universe. It was in his nature. "He murdered Melton."

Shan gave an abortive nod and groaned. "I feel like he did a good job of trying to kill me."

"You took some hits," Temar admitted.

"Ambassador Polli, it's nice to see you awake," the doctor said as he came into the room, checking all the machines before he turned to Shan himself. "Do you have any pain?"

"Only everywhere," Shan said.

"I don't doubt that. You have more stitching in you than my wife's entire closet," the doctor joked. Temar really didn't appreciate the humor, since it was so true. "Does anything in particular hurt more? Any sharp pains?"

"No, just a dull, aching everywhere."

"That's normal. Part of the healing process is pushing the body's own regenerative abilities, and pushing that tends to make the entire body hurt, even parts that weren't injured. Pain pills will slow the recovery, but too much pain can cause additional damage, particularly to the heart. Do you need any pain medication?"

"I've hurt worse after falling off my bike," Shan said.

Temar leaned closer and searched Shan's face. "Would that be the time someone was shooting at you and you got a third-degree burn on your leg after laying your bike down in a hidden rock valley?" he asked.

"You've heard the story?" Shan asked with a strained sort of humor.

"Idiot," Temar said softly, but he held Shan's arm tightly.

"You've been hanging out with Naite too long."

"I saved up all my insults for when you woke up. After scaring me so badly, I figured you deserve them."

Shan had such sad eyes. Even when Shan had been a priest, back in the days before all this started, Temar always wanted to do something to make Shan smile so that it reached his eyes. "I'm okay," Shan promised weakly.

"You will be." Temar leaned close and let his lips rest against Shan's, a soft imitation of a kiss that wouldn't strain anything.

"That's the best medicine of all," the doctor said. "I'll be on duty until shift-end, so call if you need more medicated ice or if you need pain medicine."

Temar pulled back and smiled at the doctor before he left.

"Um, Temar, why did the uniforms change?" Shan asked.

A laugh slipped out before Temar could stop it. It wasn't that the question was funny as much as a sort of giddiness that Shan was awake enough to realize he'd slept through all the drama. "Because a lot happened while you were asleep. Welcome to the Planetary Alliance, Ambassador Polli."

"The PA? Really?" Shan looked around. "I didn't expect that."

"Yeah, well, I'm learning to expect the unexpected," Temar said.

"Yeah, me too," Shan agreed, but his voice was already heavy with sleep. Temar stood by his side and rubbed Shan's arm gently while he fell back to sleep.

chapter
thirty-three

SHAN WAITED until the doctors had left to make his grand announcement three days later. That was about how long it took for him to settle into a schedule that allowed him to stay awake for longer than an hour at a time. "I feel disgusting." The machinery and tubes that ran under his blanket suggested that he wasn't getting out of bed soon. He didn't even want to think about where some of the bits were stuck. Machines should be things people used or rode on, not things stuck in them. "I'm dirty and I need to shave."

"You're clean. They used that vibrating-waves thing." Temar stood by his bed, looking odd from this angle. Shan didn't normally have to look up at the bottom of Temar's chin. Shan considered his lover. There was a hard edge there that Shan hadn't seen since they'd been running from Ben. The return of that look worried him more than his own unresponsive and sluggish body or rough beard.

"Are you okay?" Shan asked quietly. He didn't want to share his concerns with any of these people. He didn't like or trust any of them.

The hardness fell away, and Temar rested a hand against Shan's arm. "You scared the life out of me," he admitted, his fear showing through his eyes.

"I'm indestructible," Shan bragged, and after the number of messes they'd been through, it might be true. Either that or God spent a lot of his time looking out for two fools in particular. "I really need a shave, though. I feel dirty, even if I'm not." Shan added that last when Temar opened his mouth to explain again how they'd used some machine to clean him. Machines should not do some things.

"You're not getting up," Temar said firmly, a little of the steel back in his expression.

"That's fine." Shan held both of his hands up, and one arm had a silver sleeve thing from his wrist to his elbow, four tubes running down to the side of the bed. Shan looked at it in mild disgust. Never in his life had he felt such a longing for the double moons of Livre and the heat rising up from the sun-warmed sands at night. These people might think the citizens of Livre would pay any price to get rescued, but Shan couldn't imagine any of Livre's people coming up here. If they tried tying Lilian to a bed, the woman would rip out every tube and wire she could find with her bare hands and then walk out of the room to die in peace. As much as Shan wished for some other outcome, some miraculous medicine she could drink to save her, he knew she wouldn't trade her life on Livre for this sort of a mechanical miracle.

For a second, Temar stood next to him, their fingers threaded together as Temar stared at the arm. It took some time, but he shook himself free and stepped back. "I'll see if I can find some shaving supplies."

"Thank you."

With a brisk nod, Temar turned and headed toward the exit. Shan leaned back against the bed. His body didn't hurt or even ache anymore, but it felt strange. He was tempted to lift the blanket and look underneath, but he didn't want to see machines hooked to his body.

"So, you're Shan." A man walked up, tall with wide shoulders and light brown hair. He had a hard look to him, even though he was smiling. "Lieutenant Commander Verly Black," he offered, holding out his hand. Shan shook it.

"Nice to meet you." Meeting strangers when flat on his back left him a little uncomfortable, but it seemed rude to say so.

"We met before. I carried you out."

"Oh." Shan straightened up. "Thank you."

"I'm glad I could help. I wanted to meet the great Shan Polli myself after hearing about you from Temar. He was very worried, and when Temar's worried, he does tend to make the rest of the universe miserable. I figured if you weren't okay, I'd transfer to another station." The smile grew a little wider.

"Temar...." Shan let his voice trail off. He had no idea who Lieutenant Commander Verly Black was talking about, but that didn't sound like Temar.

"I'd give a lot to have someone love me that much, and feel free to tell me to shut up if I'm out of line, but you may want to avoid the AFP planets after that show. They're not a very tolerant bunch."

"And your people are?" Shan asked suspiciously. If this was some attempt to get them to side with a particular alliance, he didn't want to deal with it until he could stand on his own two feet.

"No, we really aren't," Black admitted, which surprised the snot out of Shan. "My people tend to look down on anyone who doesn't fit their definition of civilized."

"Like us," Shan guessed.

Black shrugged. "Could be. But they'll deal fairly with anyone who has something they want." With that, he gave Shan a quick nod. "It's nice to see you looking better. And let Temar know that I'm sorry I missed him, but I have to get to my duty station. Some of us can't afford to lie around all day."

Turning around, he headed out the door, leaving Shan to wonder if that was some attempt to warn them or manipulate them. He didn't know enough about Black or about what had happened to understand. He could only stare at the ceiling and hope Temar had these political maneuvers in hand. He'd grown used to trying to protect Temar. He was actually uncomfortable that he couldn't do that now. He couldn't even stand on his own feet and shave himself.

A man in the ubiquitous light blue uniform came and checked the machines without a word to Shan himself. Shan didn't know if he was a nurse or a doctor or even a mechanic. He was certainly more interested in the wires than Shan. It wasn't the sort of behavior Shan was used to when injured. He missed Hannal's hands over his leg, calling him names for not getting his burn treated sooner. Of course, he couldn't have, given that at the time he'd been trapped in the deep desert, trying to walk out before the sandrats got him. However, he associated doctors with warm hands and questions and unhappy glares when you did something stupid. This man who tended Shan's bed certainly didn't match that image. He left without a word, and Shan was left to think about how strange these people were until Temar returned.

"Hey, look what I found," Temar said from the doorway. Shan smiled.

"Please tell me you found whatever strange machine they use for shaving."

"Better," Temar said with a smile. "I found an actual razor. The doctor tried explaining how to use their thing, that does this thing with hair follicles, only he kept explaining how improper use can lead to damage of the dermal layers." Temar grinned. "I think he saw the look of horror on my face at the idea of basically burning your face off."

"I think I'd rather avoid more injuries."

"Yeah, I told him I'd rather have a razor." Temar came over, balancing a thick bowl with wisps of steam rising from it and a bag hanging from one wrist. "They're going out of their way to accommodate our odd choices," Temar said with a wink.

"Odd choices? I take it they don't approve of us?" Shan hadn't been awake long enough to make any odd choices, and Temar was usually quiet enough to avoid really catching anyone's attention. Shan frowned as he thought of Black's description. Maybe that wasn't entirely accurate.

"I get the feeling that they're a little amused by us."

Shan hated the idea of Temar being alone with people who laughed at him. The man was so intensely private he didn't even want to deal with his own sister's emotional spillage, so he shouldn't have to deal with random strangers. "I'm sorry I'm leaving you to deal with all this," Shan offered, helpless to do anything else.

"Hey, I'm fine. If they annoy me, I start talking about how strange it is to have bowls and containers that aren't made out of glass. It's killing them that we have so much glass that we let school children play at glassblowing."

"Not with optic-quality glass, we don't," Shan pointed out.

"I might not have mentioned that," Temar said with a shrug. "They may have all the fancy machines, but we still have something they want, and we aren't going to give it up easily."

Shan sat up a little more and studied Temar. He was different. "You're enjoying this."

Temar had been taking things out of the bag and setting them up beside Shan's bedside, but he stopped at that. "I think I am," he said slowly, almost as if he wasn't sure. "It's like blowing glass, watching for the signs that you're applying too much heat or letting the piece cool too much, only instead of fire, you have to find out what heats or cools these people."

Temar's glass, the pieces he'd done in school when most students turned out blobs of shapeless glass and uneven rough cups, had incredible balance and grace. If Temar could see these people in terms of glass, Shan suddenly wasn't as worried. "Then I have faith that you know how to keep the temperature right," Shan said. Temar gifted him with a bright smile.

"Thank you."

"For what?"

"For being able to say that without any doubt at all."

Shan took Temar's hand. "I love you, I trust you, and I really want to shave, so hand over the supplies."

Temar laughed. "Oh no. You are going to lie there while I do the shaving. You just about got yourself blown up, and one twitch at the wrong time and you're going to slit your own throat with a straight razor."

"I'm not that injured."

Temar made an impolite noise and went back to sorting his supplies. Shan realized he'd lost the battle. He wasn't sure how, but he clearly had. He settled back into the bed. If Temar wanted to do this for him, that was fine. Temar had made it more than clear that he enjoyed initiating touch, and Shan was more than happy to indulge that particular preference.

Temar put a cloth into the bowl and pulled it up, dripping with water. "You know, they don't think anything about me taking this much water out of a slosh stall." Temar paused. "Shower," he corrected himself.

"We come from different worlds." Shan rested his hand against Temar's arm.

"We do. I miss home, but I have you, which makes it a lot easier to put up with the rest of them." Temar dunked the cloth in the water again, carefully wringing most of the hot water out before he leaned over and curled the towel around Shan's face. Shan closed his eyes and let the heat soak into him. At home, they had all the heat they needed, but no one heated water. Hot water created steam, and that led to water loss. The hot water against his skin was a new sensation, one he enjoyed. He liked it better than ice, which made his mouth hurt if he sucked on it wrong.

"Feels good," Shan muttered. He hadn't realized his shoulders had been tight, but now the muscles relaxed.

"I'm glad." Something clinked rhythmically, like a spoon in a bowl. Shan was tempted to raise the towel and look, but he was enjoying the heat and he didn't like the way his body felt when he moved, like things were pulling tight and he couldn't really feel them. It was like when you sat on your foot too long and you had to look at it to make sure it was actually still there.

A hand ran up his bare arm, and Shan sank into the feeling of Temar's warmth against his skin. The towel had started to cool, but when Temar took it away and dropped it back into the steaming bowl, Shan still missed the heat. He never thought he'd be so hungry for heat, but his body craved it. Well, most of his body. Even though Temar leaned against the bed so that Shan could see the angle of his shoulders and the curve of his jaw, his cock was not reacting. His cock always reacted to Temar.

Temar brought his hand up to Shan's cheek, white foam covering it. The soaplike foam smoothed across his skin. "Smells like…." Shan stopped, not sure how to describe the scent. It was spicy and warm, nothing like the stinging scent of Livre soap.

"Like Mittel Jones's cooking and the desert at night," Temar offered, and it was a good description of the soap. Temar's hands stroked up Shan's cheeks and then down to his neck, rubbing the foam into his skin. Shan tilted his head back to give Temar more room.

Temar lightened his touch, a finger tracing over Shan's lip and then up to the tip of his nose. Shan smiled and cracked one eye open. He was fairly sure his nose didn't need shaving. Temar followed the bridge of Shan's nose up, the slick soap leaving a cool trail where Temar touched. "I want to wash all of you," Temar whispered. "I want to touch every inch until I'm sure you're really here."

"Okay," Shan agreed, not entirely sure what had brought that on.

Temar paused, his palms brushing against Shan's shoulders, leaving streaks of soap behind. Leaning to the side, Temar grabbed a second towel and wiped his hand. "I'm going to hold you to that as soon as you aren't connected to every machine in the room."

"It's a date," Shan agreed. Temar took a deep breath, his hands almost shaking for a second, but then he turned a bright smile toward Shan.

"Scared yet?" Temar teased as he held up the straight razor.

"Nope." Closing his eyes, Shan relaxed back onto his pillow. If Temar couldn't get control of the hand shake, he'd stop. Shan knew that.

Shan lay still as Temar rested one hand near his ear and then slowly pulled the razor's edge down his jawline and down to his neck.

When Temar pulled the razor back, Shan lifted his chin more. Temar's fingers brushed over the newly shaven skin, and Shan shivered as his skin tingled from the touch. He made a little humming noise, and Temar ran a thumb over the skin again before the razor swept down his neck. The warm cloth brushing over the sensitive skin startled Shan, and he opened his eyes to watch Temar. He had an intense look on his face as he got more soap foam from the small jar and stroked Shan's cheek before running the razor down the next bit of his face.

"They may have too many machines, but they do know how to make a good razor," Temar said as he wiped the extra soap off on the towel, wasting the moisture. Moving in again, he angled the blade and drew it gently down, the familiar rasp ending as Temar reached his jawline and pulled away. Shan let his eyes drift closed again. Despite all the sleep, he was still tired. More than that, Temar had things well in hand. Temar pressed on the underside of Shan's chin, and Shan obliged by angling his head. Temar took the razor down over his neck, and then he laid the warm, wet towel against the sensitive skin.

"You scared me," Temar said, his voice low and soft. Shan might have tried to answer, but the razor returned, moving down his neck in a way that made talking dangerous, so Shan stayed quiet. "I thought I was going to lose you and I was so angry and afraid."

Temar flicked the razor away and shifted the towel onto the newly bare skin.

"Do you have any idea what I would do if you left me?" Temar stopped, putting the razor to one side before he leaned forward, one hand on Shan's shoulder and the other braced against the edge of the hospital bed. "Promise you won't leave me." Shan could see the emotions starting to leak out, and he caught Temar's hand and held on as tight as he could.

"Even if something did happen, I would still be watching you, loving you," Shan promised. He had no control over insane terrorists or freedom fighters or governments. However, he did know he would always love Temar.

Temar had a storm of emotion in his expression. "That doesn't make me feel better."

Shan pulled the towel off his face and tossed it aside before tugging Temar closer. "I don't have answers or promises. I can't give you what I don't have. But I'm here, Temar. I'm fine." Fine was an exaggeration, but Shan had survived.

"They all wanted me to make the decisions." Temar bent until his forehead rested against Shan's shoulder. "That's not true. They were all trying to make decisions, only their decisions were less than helpful, so I started making better ones, but I was so afraid I would pick wrong. I was so afraid you were going to die on me."

Shan reached around and offered an awkward hug. "We survived. I survived, and I don't mind telling you, I wasn't sure I would. I was pretty sure I was going to die in that room with Melton's brains staining my shirt."

"I was terrified," Temar whispered.

"You were terrified and you did well." Shan summed it up. He didn't say anything else, but Temar's back started to relax, the hard muscles slowly yielding as Temar rested against him.

"I hate being the one out front. I don't like it when I have to make the decisions. I hate it even worse when I have to live with the decisions other people make." Temar muttered the words against Shan's shoulder, and another day Shan might have pointed out the illogic. If you didn't want to make decisions or live with others making decisions, that didn't leave a lot of options. Today he didn't feel any need to point that out. Besides, he suspected Temar already knew that. Temar took a deep, shuddering breath and then pulled back.

"Don't ever come that close to dying again," Temar said more firmly as he grabbed the discarded towel and put it back in the steaming water.

"Yes, sir," Shan agreed with a smile.

Temar gave him a hard look. "Don't start with the sirring. I've been ordering these military people around, you know."

Shan thought about Black's comment, that when Temar was unhappy, entire universes suffered. "I hear you were quite good at keeping them all in line," Shan said. A flicker of confusion crossed Temar's face. "Lieutenant Commander Black stopped by," Shan watched as Temar's face pinked. "Temar?"

Temar cleared this throat. "I might have threatened him once or twice."

Shan's eyebrows went up. "That would explain his offer to transfer to another station or another universe if you were unhappy."

Temar's blush deepened.

"And he seems to genuinely like you," Shan added.

"I think I threatened the people from the AFP more than I threatened him, which is an odd place to start negotiating treaties, but…." Temar shrugged.

He picked up the razor again and looked at Shan before he put it down and got more of the soap out of the jar. He stroked the soap over the unshaven skin, and Shan settled down to watch the emotions slowly calm in Temar's gaze. The man was a storm front, shifting suddenly and powerfully from one emotion to another, but the ragged edge had dulled some. Clearly he was upset, but something had taken away that sharp need Shan could never understand when it crossed Temar's face.

Temar stroked the blade over Shan's face, wiping the blade between every pass and pausing every now and then to run a thumb over the shaven skin. Every single time, that touch made Shan shiver. Eventually Temar finished, putting the razor aside before getting the warm towel out of the water. He curled it around Shan's face, and the heat soaked into the skin. Shan moaned in pleasure. Shaving himself had never been so pleasurable. Temar waited until the towel had cooled before pulling it off and then carefully wiping Shan's face.

His movements had turned sure and steady as he opened a metal bottle and poured a small bit of gel onto one hand before rubbing his hands together. He brought both hands up and smoothed the cooling balm over Shan's cheeks and neck. Clever fingers stroked over his skin, tracing the small lines at the corners of Shan's mouth and trailing down to Shan's neck. Leaning closer, Temar offered a chaste kiss. They'd shared passionate and desperate kisses, but this one was softer, needier in some way.

Shan brought his hand up and stroked Temar's hair. "Are you okay, really?" he asked.

Temar nodded. "I had to take charge, and it worked out okay. No one yelled at me." He frowned. "No one whose opinion I care about yelled at me, no one I tried to save died, and none of the many, many broken pieces has anything to do with me."

Shan wondered if Temar was mentally comparing that to a certain night where he hadn't taken charge—he'd followed someone else, and that had almost ruined his life.

"It sounds like you did great," Shan offered.

"I kind of did. However," Temar said, his voice growing sharp, "you are not allowed to get kidnapped, shot, or blown up ever again."

Now probably wasn't the time for the lecture about what humanity could or could not control. Shan nodded. "Got it."

"Are you okay? Really okay? Verly said that Pentalia would probably torture you until he got you to apologize for giving the AFP supplies."

Shan closed his eyes and felt helpless regret rush through him for a moment. "He was so angry, and I tried to talk to him about making the morally right choice, even when other people didn't. Christ himself lived in an immoral world."

"You gave him a sermon?" Temar sounded surprised.

With a shrug, Shan admitted, "I think I did, but at the time I thought I was just talking to him. He wasn't an evil man, but he was hurt and angry and so very confused. But he never did hurt me. Unfortunately, I had the feeling he had every intention of killing me, and himself." Tightening his fingers around Temar's hand, he held on tightly. It would be a long time before he forgot Melton's body falling to the ground, the warm splatters of blood across his skin. However, Shan didn't have regrets. He'd done everything he could to save both Melton and Pentalia, save them physically and morally. God had chosen a different path for them. "I would have died if you hadn't showed quite the talent at taking charge of the situation."

"Am I allowed to completely hate the fact that I had to take control of the situation? Hate. Loathe. Detest."

"But you did it well, even while you were hating it," Shan pointed out. He suspected Temar probably did better than he might have. When he was in charge, his big plan had included charging after Ben and his whole group with no weapons, no backup, and no actual big plan. Looking back, Naite had every right to yell at him. Loudly. "You did it well, and you're proud of your work," Shan said, sure he was right.

Temar's earlier blush had faded, but now he got pink again.

"So, how long am I stuck in here? Any chance of you using your newly found powers of intimidation and getting someone to let me out?"

"Consider yourself lucky to be alive and stop complaining." Temar started cleaning up his supplies.

"I wasn't complaining," Shan complained. "Much. Was it really that bad?" Temar paused to give Shan an incredulous look. One look at Temar's face told him the truth. It had been. Shan looked around at all the machines quietly beeping and the flashing buttons. He might love his God, but he wasn't ready to meet him, and he was suddenly struck with the realization that he might have come closer than he'd thought. He brought his hands up and started to feel along his oddly numb chest and abdomen.

Temar intercepted his hand, holding it tightly. "Don't." Temar's voice broke, and he went silent for a moment before giving Shan an insincere smile. "But hey, the good news is, you got me to pray."

"You prayed?" That surprised Shan. He had faith that God listened to every prayer, and he even had faith that God understood and loved Temar despite his lack of faith. However, he never thought Temar would find solace in prayer.

"I prayed that he wouldn't take you away. I guess I have to believe in God now, because he gave you back to me."

Shan tightened his hold on Temar's hand. "God doesn't work that way," he said gently. "God won't prove he exists. If he answers a prayer, he does it only because he knows what's best for you."

"Then I guess God thinks you're good for me." Temar looked away, his eyes bright.

"I hope so," Shan agreed. "And I'm here now, so you can stop worrying."

Temar's face was still heavy with fear. Distress swirled around them, and that wasn't what he wanted to feel. Not now. He was alive and they were together, and in the end, that mattered more than whatever dangers they'd faced. They were okay. "So, I guess you won't be ambushing me soon," he said, putting on his most mournful expression.

For one second Temar simply stared, as if his brain hadn't quite processed that comment yet. Then a rough bark of laugher burst out. Temar still might be physically on the small side, but his personality had somehow grown. He laughed loudly, not even trying to quiet himself. "Oh, I can still ambush you. We'll have to go slow and easy. I can't exactly sneak up on you until you heal."

"So, it's going to be a slow and easy ambush with a lot of warning?" Shan asked.

"Yep," Temar agreed.

Smiling, Shan curled his fingers around Temar's smaller hand. "Deal," he said.

chapter
thirty-four

SHAN DRIFTED in and out of consciousness with such regularity that he suspected something in the machines made him fall asleep every time the ship's vid system started showing the daily report of ship status. Shan wasn't entirely sure he understood why everyone would want rows upon rows of numerical data that ranged from oxygen levels to weather on distant planets that Shan would never see. Hopefully. At this point in his life, he wasn't willing to make any more bets. If he had his way, he and Temar would settle in for a quiet life on a farm where he could fix a lot of machinery and rediscover the joy of cursing. Maybe he could even figure out how to talk to Naite without wanting to hit him and then needing to go to confession.

"Ambassador Polli?"

Shan looked up to see two men standing just inside his room. The sudden burst of discomfort that blossomed in his gut surprised him. Pentalia had done that—stood between him and the door. Shan pushed himself up a little higher in the bed and tried to rein in his emotions. He couldn't go around assuming every government official wanted to blow him up.

"Yes?"

The older man smiled. "Ambassador, you are looking much better. I'm Representative Fields of the PA. I had hoped we could discuss treaty rights. After all, we can't allow the terrorists to stop us from conducting the business of the day, can we?"

Shan raised his eyebrows. From the little bits he had gleaned from Temar, his partner had grown quite competent at handling negotiations. After his total failure with Pentalia, Shan had decided to give up on trying to use persuasion. He was better with a wrench.

The other man cleared his throat. "I'm Commander Green. Perhaps Ambassador Gazer has mentioned me."

"No." Shan took a little satisfaction in seeing how that annoyed them. Considering that he'd been nearly blown up by a terrorist trying to support the PA's political position, Shan was petty enough to want to hurt them a little bit.

Representative Fields took a step forward as though cutting off any response the commander might have. He had to be nearly as old as Lilian, but he had a softness to him. Lilian was a third his size, but Shan would wager she could take him in a fight. "I'm sure Ambassador Gazer has focused on your health, keeping you from the bulk of the negotiations."

"I haven't really asked about them."

The two men exchanged glances. "I won't bore you with details," the representative said, moving closer. His face was lined deeply, but there was a pink tone Shan associated with children—a freshness adults generally lost about the time they started working outside for any length of time.

"Sandrats chew only one corner at a time," Shan answered. He honestly didn't care about negotiations. He cared about getting the machines out of his body and going home.

Oddly, the representative smiled. "Your planet does have a colorful way of communicating. The linguistic shifts are fascinating, especially since only three or four generations separate Livre from PA space. So, a sandrat is one of the local predators and a corner is clearly as small piece of the whole, so I am guessing that you are suggesting that the devil is in the details."

Shan looked at the man, not understanding the other man's overly friendly smile.

That smile slowly faded. "We do have business to conduct. Your planet needs water, technology, medical equipment, and medicine. The fatality rate for simple accidents and childbirth is terrifyingly high. We can help with all that. We can benefit each other."

A bit of scripture popped into Shan's memory. "Today or tomorrow we will go to this city or that, spend a year here, carry on, and make a little money," he intoned. Div would have come up with a better quote—one that didn't potentially insult his host since the rest of the quote cast aspersions on people who put business ahead of God.

Again, a flash of confusion crossed both men's faces. "I'm afraid I don't know that quote."

"It's from John." Shan paused. "Or James... I'm better at remembering the quote than remembering where it's from." Since he wasn't a priest anymore, he didn't need to keep his books of the Bible straight.

His visitors developed matching sour expressions. The AFP might take religion too far, but Shan believed too strongly to like the thought of people who were so quick to dismiss the Bible. Naite's attitude about God certainly annoyed Shan to no end. And considering how well Shan did talking to his brother, he figured he should probably avoid any conversation with these guys. He couldn't figure out why Lilian and the others had sent him at all. Other than flirting with a woman who had no interest in him, surviving the cold of space, and recovering after a chunk of metal cut through his guts, he hadn't really done much.

"We were hoping to discuss some numbers."

"With me?" Shan asked Representative Fields.

"You are an ambassador."

"So is Temar."

Commander Green shifted, and Shan suspected the negotiations had turned more contentious than Temar had told him. Shan's body twinged with pain. If these people wanted to play dirty, Shan couldn't even get out of bed. It wasn't a good feeling. A heavy fear settled in his guts, and for the first time in his life, Shan wished he had a gun in hand. Getting blown up had changed his outlook on violence, that was for sure.

Fields gave Shan a conspiratorial look. "We had hoped that you would be more reasonable. You must admit that Ambassador Gazer is young and perhaps untested in diplomatic waters. The world is not quite as black and white as he would assume."

"Wait. You think I'm going to be less... what? Less rigid with my morals?"

"Morals? No." Representative Fields recoiled from the word the way another man might from a slap to the face. Honestly, these people made no sense. "We would never ask that someone violate their moral values. Ambassador Gazer simply needs some help to understand that negotiations require give and take."

"So you think I'll be...." Shan let his voice trail off as he invited them to explain exactly what they were talking about.

"Perhaps more flexible." Fields got that smile on his face again. He wasn't going to be smiling in a second because Temar stood in the open door behind them with a look on his face that reminded Shan of Div on a truly bad day. When Pelip had admitted that he had not only broken his vows to his husband but that he had gotten a woman pregnant, Div had this disbelieving shock crossed with a cold fury that made Shan want to hide in the next room. He had never expected to see that look on Temar's face.

Shan smiled, truly amused now. "So, Temar isn't flexible? Why do I suspect that means that he isn't giving you what you want?"

"Your planet needs supplies. We were hoping as the older of the two diplomats you could get him to understand the need to compromise in difficult situations."

"I think I already understand your definition of compromise," Temar said coldly.

Both men spun around amusingly fast. Perhaps it was unkind, but Shan couldn't keep from grinning. It was so nice to watch someone else flail for a change. "Ambassador Gazer," Commander Green said with an unctuous smile.

Temar's response was decidedly cold. "Commander."

Representative Fields moved closer, his movements small and cautious. "Ambassador, I do apologize for any breach of protocol, but we felt that both of you should be advised of the reasonable offers we have put on the table."

"So, calling Livre to try to circumvent me wasn't enough?" Temar might not be a large man, but sometime in the last few weeks, he had developed a glare that could sting like a nettle.

"They called Livre?" Shan asked, surprised he hadn't heard anything about all this conflict.

"They reached Naite," Temar said as he came to Shan's bedside.

Shan cringed. "Oh, that must have gone over well. Please tell me he didn't suggest they do anatomically impossible acts with a sandcat."

Temar grinned. "He might have. He certainly does seem a little obsessed with sandcat genitals."

Shan groaned. Growing up, Naite and his friends seemed to make a contest out of inventing new profanity and stealing the genitals from biology class dissections to stick in other people's faces. Sadly, Naite had never outgrown one of those two habits.

"It could be worse. They could have reached Lilian." Temar gave him a conspiratorial wink.

"Oh yeah. If they want to see inflexible, we should introduce them to Lilian. That woman would bend the universe before she yielded one inch."

Temar perched on the edge of Shan's bed, his hand resting against Shan's thigh. "She scares me, and not much scares me anymore. I think Lilian and the sight of you getting blown into space—that's about it."

"I'll try to avoid any more assassination attempts," Shan promised, and for a second, they gazed at each other, and the reality of their near loss seemed to press closer so that Shan wanted to cling to Temar—to hold him and reassure himself that they had come through one more disaster alive and together.

Then Representative Fields cleared his throat. "We only want what—"

"What will benefit the PA," Temar interrupted. His voice was low and soft, but it had a power behind it. "You think we will trade our world away for water—water we can get from any number of worlds, or maybe we will trade with the AFP for an ice mining ship. You betrayed my world once, and now you want to pretend that didn't happen."

Fields stiffened. "The war necessitated many sacrifices, and we have accepted that you now have every right to renegotiate a new treaty, but if you plan to join the AFP, we will move to intervene."

Temar gave a humorless laugh. "Do you think we would join an alliance that would outlaw homosexual marriage? Our people wouldn't put up with that, but we aren't nearly as desperate as you seem to think for your trade. You may have water, but we have optic glass and minerals. We have rare metals, and we have trade goods you haven't even considered. We have a drought-resistant corn species that only requires a hundred and ninety pounds of water per crop acre. We can bring in millet at almost half that and rye at just over three hundred pounds of water. How much is that worth? How much time could you save in terraforming with those sorts of seed varieties?"

Temar stood, and the power shifted in the room. Temar had clearly done his homework because the two PA men were utterly still.

The shock was a near palpable force that rolled through the room. As much as Shan had felt quickly repressed shivers of desire when Temar had shown up in the back of his church, that paled in comparison to the desire he felt now. This was a strong man who didn't need protecting. Temar wasn't someone to be sheltered, someone Shan had to protect or worry about hurting. This Temar could take care of himself while verbally gutting anyone who got in his way.

"I think you'll find that Temar is the most reasonable person on Livre because I wouldn't have even offered those crops," Shan said mildly, not mentioning that he wouldn't have known enough to recognize their value. "You can negotiate with him or you can give up all rights to our minerals and our seed crops."

"Those *are* valuable trade goods," Representative Fields said slowly.

"And if you try to circumvent me one more time, they are trade goods that will go to the AFP," Temar interrupted. "I may hate the AFP on general principle, but you are annoying me to the point where I might start hating you more. Now Shan needs his rest, so I suggest you two leave." Temar crossed his arms. The room grew silent and taut, and Shan waited, not sure what he could say or do to back Temar's position. Luckily, he didn't have to. The two PA officials glanced at each other, and then Commander Fields held out his hand toward Temar.

"Ambassador, I am sorry for interrupting your evening."

Temar took his hand. "Don't repeat the mistake," he suggested in a tone that made it clear he wouldn't forgive so easily next time.

Commander Green headed for the door with a simple, "Ambassador," and then both men left, closing the door to Shan's room behind them. The second the door clicked shut, Temar sagged, leaning on the bed and Shan's good leg.

"Well, you've been having fun," Shan commented. The glare Temar gave him could have cracked glass. "I take it that the negotiations you never want to talk about aren't going that well."

"You don't have to worry about it."

Shan studied Temar. "I don't worry about it because you can handle yourself and them. You're doing better than I would have. But I'd like to hear about it."

Temar's gaze softened. "You aren't upset that I left you out?"

Shan had grown so used to worrying about Temar that it had become second nature. Was he pushing too hard, too fast? Would Temar get hurt if he talked to Natalie? Naite had warned him about respecting Temar, but looking back, Shan could see he had already spent too much time thinking of Temar as a victim. Now that he'd been the one held captive and threatened—now that he'd faced death, Shan could see one truth. It didn't change him. And Ben's evil didn't prevent Temar from turning into a sharp-tongued negotiator who could go toe to toe with Lilian.

"I'm not upset at all. So, is there anything I can do to help you? Do you need anything?"

Temar smiled and reached up to brush his fingers over Shan's cheek. "Do you want to look up crop figures for the five planet agricultural belt and download them into a spreadsheet comparing natural rainfall to irrigation to crop yield? I think the drought resistant crops might be a good bargaining chip here, and I would like to have some more ammunition, but I'm already in the middle of researching industrial uses for yttrium."

Giving an exaggerated sigh, Shan looked up at the ceiling. "I offer him my body, and he wants me to research water use and crop yields. I think we've reached boring old married couple status before the wedding."

Temar answered him with a soft punch in the arm.

"Do you have a datapad I can use?"

"I'll get you one," Temar said, and he started to go, but Shan caught his arm and pulled him back to the bed.

"In a second. Payment first, research later." Shan pulled on Temar until he was close enough that Shan could reach up and curl his fingers around Temar's neck. Smiling, Temar obliged by leaning closer, and Shan parted his lips, kissing his lover passionately enough to make him forget about crop yields and yttrium—whatever the hell that was.

chapter
thirty-five

SHAN DIDN'T realize he'd fallen asleep for the millionth time in the past few days until he drifted toward awareness. Temar sat in a chair next to his bed, one foot braced on the corner of the mattress, and all his attention on a datapad. Sometimes during sex, Temar would get this expression, as if he knew exactly what he wanted to do and exactly how he wanted to do it. He'd move with this surety that never followed him outside the bedroom. That same surety seemed to cling to Temar now. He scrolled through the datapad without looking around the room nervously or shifting in the chair. In all the years he'd known Temar, he'd never seen this quiet in him, but it was a look he carried well.

Shan rested his hand on Temar's foot. Immediately Temar set the datapad aside and leaned forward to take Shan's hand in his. "Hey, how are you feeling?"

"Ready to be ambushed," Shan lied. His body still had traces of that foreign numbness that made him feel disjointed.

"They must have better medicine here than back home, then," Temar said. "And speaking of, right now we are officially in orbit over Livre. However, your doctors turned several colors of green when I suggested shoving you in a skip, shuttle, airship thing and taking you home."

"Skip, shuttle, airship?" Shan asked with a smile. That was an interesting description.

"You know what I mean." Temar poked him in the arm.

Shan swallowed and mentally prepared himself before asking his next question. "How long, then?"

A shadow crossed Temar's face. He didn't answer immediately. "You were really injured. I thought we were going to be up here for months, but the doctors said you can start walking today, and after a week of the machines speeding the healing, they'll send you home."

"Oh, thank the Lord," Shan breathed. "I don't know what makes me happier—the idea of getting to walk after days in this bed or the promise of going home." Shan smiled at Temar. "Of course, one thing could make me happier." Moving slowly, so that Temar would have time to stop him, Shan reached for his lover's arm and tugged him closer. Temar moved so he was right up against the bed, and when Shan kept tugging, Temar got an amused expression as he climbed up next to Shan.

"Look at that," Shan said with feigned surprise. "I'm in bed with my lover, who I have desperately missed." The numbness in his body had faded over the past few days, and now Shan's cock was warming nicely to the close quarters.

"Just me and my critically wounded partner with the serious internal injuries." Temar pointed out.

"Doctors… they all exaggerate injuries to make you feel more grateful that they could heal you."

"I saw your internal organs being noninternal," Temar pointed out dryly.

"So no ambushing?" Shan asked sadly. Temar rolled his eyes.

"Your manipulative powers are not in the same league with Lilian's," he pointed out.

"I wouldn't even try to compete, but can we please put Lilian on that list of people who we do not talk about while trying to have sex?"

"Is that what we're doing?" Now Temar was teasing. Shan could see from his expression.

"Hopefully. I haven't been ambushed for a long time."

"So, you're asking me to ambush you?"

"Yes." Shan came right out and said it. Temar smiled, and he moved like he was chuckling, even though no sound came out. There was an ease in Temar now, a shift that meant he didn't pull back anymore. Shan reached up to stoke the back of his finger along Temar's cheek.

"I'm leading. You'd try to do something energetic, and with our luck, we'd be hanging from the chandelier when you tore out stitches and all these doctors came running."

"Hanging from the chandelier?" Shan frowned. He'd never heard that saying. He wasn't even totally sure what a chandelier was, although he seemed to remember it was a light.

Temar cleared his throat. "Verly gave me a book… as a get-well gift for you."

"And it had chandeliers in it?" Shan was seriously confused.

The deep blush that spread over all of Temar's face and down onto his neck and shoulders confused Shan more.

"What?"

Temar put his hand on Shan's chest. "I promise I will show you after you have all the stitches out, okay?"

"Is this the sort of thing that's going to make me track Verly down and hurt him?"

"No. You might, however, buy him dinner. So please, maybe we could drop this."

Shan opened his mouth to try to pry more information out of Temar, but Temar leaned close and kissed him gently. Their lips pressed together, the heat making Shan forget everything else as he parted his lips in invitation. Temar's fingers caressed Shan's neck, and Shan stroked a thumb over Temar's smooth shoulder, sucking Temar's lower lip in while Temar made a small whimper.

Temar shifted closer, and Shan slipped an arm under him, pulling them tightly together. Then, midkiss, Shan grunted in pain. Immediately, Temar pulled back.

"Are you okay?"

"I'm fine," Shan said.

"You grunted."

"I just had a twinge."

"A twinge." Temar pinned him with a look far colder than Shan had ever seen on Temar before.

"A twinge. It means a little, tiny pain." One of Shan's arms was still under Temar, so he held up the hand with the medical cuff on it and showed how very small the twinge had been with a finger and thumb. "Tiny," he repeated.

"We shouldn't do this."

"Temar." Shan tightened his arm, not above begging at this point.

After a half second, Temar relaxed back into Shan's embrace, and only then did it occur to Shan that he'd been physically restraining Temar. He stopped breathing and searched his lover for any signs of distress, but all he could see was a sort of amused exasperation in Temar's face.

"We are so going to get caught by the doctors, and I am not going to explain how you pulled stitches."

"It'll be worth it." Shan pulled Temar close enough to kiss again and ran his hand over Temar's backside and down to a well-formed ass.

Temar pulled back no more than an inch, so they were nose to nose, Temar's breath warm against Shan's skin. "Just lie there. No moving, no damaging internal organs that haven't completely healed."

"Still. Got it," Shan agreed. Slipping his hand between Temar's legs, Shan slowly stroked Temar's hard cock through his pants.

Throwing his head back, Temar groaned. "Oh God, yes." Temar was two groans into a very good time when he reached down and caught Shan's wrist, pressing it down to the bed and holding it there. For several seconds, Temar panted as he clearly tried to get control of his lust. It felt good to make a lover that needy, although it'd feel better to finish him.

"I thought you were going to lie there," Temar finally said, his voice still breathy.

"Just offering a hand."

"You are bad. You're also going to be stuck here longer if we do this wrong."

"I don't think there is a way to actually do it wrong."

Temar blushed again, and Shan had the feeling he had so totally missed something. Before he could ask, Temar was pushing the sheets down, revealing Shan's cock pressing up. Shan hadn't seen his body before; his midsection was encased in a silver cocoon. However, his cock stood proudly at attention. Temar's hand slid down over his chest, and then Temar moved below the wide band of metal encircling him.

"Let me touch you," Shan begged in a whisper. He wanted to. He wanted to feel Temar come under his hands, and if he got a few twinges, he could live with that. Instead of granting permission, Temar let his hand rest on Shan's hip, an island of warmth that made his cock twitch with need.

"You want to touch me, even if you hurt yourself doing it?" Temar asked. He slipped his fingers under the waist of his own pants and arched his back. The hungry noises Temar was making were enough to make Shan come right there. Temar fondled himself with this look of ecstasy on his face. "I love the way you smell, the heat when we lie close, and the feel of your hands against my skin," Temar whispered.

Shan groaned with need, and his machines clicked out a merry tempo, recording the accelerated heartbeat. "The doctors… they'll hear," Shan suddenly realized.

"I told them we needed privacy," Temar admitted wryly, and Shan's cock was even harder at the thought that Temar had made arrangements for all this. Temar definitely needed to be the plan-maker in the family. Shan slipped his hand under Temar's shirt, stroking his back, and Temar's groans grew louder. Squirming with need, Temar pulled his hand out and slowly pushed his pants down to his thighs, his cock now visible. Shan reached down, his medical cuff trailing tubing as he stroked the hot flesh, feeling the muscles twitch under his touch.

Temar was breathing faster now, and Shan's breath sped up, his injuries a faint annoyance as he stared at Temar's hand around his own cock. The pants slipped farther down so that Shan could see the darkening shaft, the head of the cock slipping out of the foreskin, the slit slick. Temar pressed against Shan's side, and Shan wrapped his fingers around Temar's cock, pushing Temar's hand to the side, but Temar captured his wrist. Leaning close, he whispered in Shan's ear. "You're injured. Let me do this."

Shan licked his lips, but he let his fingers open as Temar moved Shan's hand up to rest against Temar's hip. Temar started stroking his own cock faster. A tiny line of moisture appeared at the slit, and Temar arched his back and cried out, coming on Shan's hip, the white catching in the tiny, dark hairs of Shan's body. Then Temar's whole body went limp. He lay with his forehead pressed against Shan's chest, panting and radiating heat. Shan's own cock jutted up unhappily, but Shan couldn't repeat Temar's performance, not when the medical band around his center made it hard for him to reach between his legs.

"Now there's no more reason for you to be squirming around to try to reach me," Temar finally said.

"I don't need a reason. I happen to like touching you," Shan pointed out.

"Well, this is my ambush, so lie there and take it like a seriously injured man," Temar advised him. Shan laughed.

Temar slowly leaned in. Shan had leaked some precum, so when Temar pulled the sheet to cover him, it made a small, dark spot on the fabric.

"Is someone coming?" Shan asked, checking the closed door. If someone was, Temar's bare butt was still fully exposed.

"Nope," Temar said before he bent down and mouthed the dark spot. The featherlight pressure against his hard cock and the feel of fabric across the sensitive head made Shan gasp. He tried to thrust up and get more pressure, but Temar braced his hands on Shan's hips, holding him down.

"My ambush. Lie there and be injured."

Shan panted, his cock aching with need. "I can't. Oh God, I need more," he finally gasped out.

Temar sucked harder, right through the sheet. Shan gasped as the pressure started building, painfully fast. Then Temar started a soft hum, the vibration of it traveling through Shan's cock.

"I need to come," Shan cried out, not caring if some random hospital person overheard.

Temar's hands shifted, stroking down Shan's legs and pushing the sheet to the side. Shan pressed his head into his pillow and grabbed the sides of the mattress while Temar explored down his inner thighs and then up to torture his balls with a gentle stroke, no more than a feather against his skin.

Shan cried out, the need erasing everything else. He squirmed as Temar teased the head of his cock, a finger running along the slit. Then Temar took Shan in his mouth, his cheeks hollowing as he sucked at Shan's hard shaft. When Temar started lowering himself, taking more and more of Shan into his mouth with each stroke, Shan had to close his eyes before he came right in Temar's mouth. But that made the rest even more intense. In the darkness of his closed eyes, he could feel the wet heat as Temar worked him, sucking and sliding and denying Shan the very ability to breathe as his tongue explored the vein on the underside of Shan's cock. Temar's hands rested against Shan's hips, so even though Shan tried to thrust up, he was caught, unable to do anything except feel as Temar teased him until the world grayed out at the edges. He wanted this moment to last forever, and he wanted it to end, to come right now.

Shan got dizzy, and he forced his body to suck in air as Temar teased him. "Temar, please," he pleaded, his brain fogging with pure lust. Temar pulled off, nestling close to Shan's side as he wrapped fingers around Shan's shaft and gave the fast, purposeful strokes that let Shan slide away into oblivion. It took several strokes, but then Shan came, a strangled cry wrested from him as his whole body jerked and then settled back into pure bliss.

Shan panted, his remaining brain cells scattering to the four corners of the world. That was fine; Temar had sucked most of them out, so there weren't all that many to scatter.

Temar settled down next to him and rested on Shan's shoulder. The sounds of the hospital slowly started reminding Shan that a nurse could come in any time, and considering that they were two ambassadors carrying the dignity of their world, they looked... well, they looked like they'd just had really, really good sex. Temar had a blurred, satiated look on his face that Shan could only imagine mirrored his own. With a happy little hum, Temar reached down and caught the sheet, pulling it up.

For a long time, they lay in silence, their bodies slowly cooling and the machines clicking and whirring around them. Shan wondered if some nurse was watching the machines count out his accelerated heart rate and fever-hot body. If so, they had the good manners not to mention it.

Shan was drifting off to sleep before Temar asked softly, "If Ben had gotten this far, do you think he would have come back for the rest of us?"

That wasn't the sort of question to answer blithely, and Shan fought back some of the lethargy to really consider his answer. "I don't know. I like to think he would. The easy alternative would be to tell them that we were dead and to leave us to die out. If he had come back, they would have asked some difficult questions."

"Like how he stole water from the planet," Temar agreed. "Somehow, after seeing the way they live, I'm not sure they would ever understand what that meant to us."

"Probably not," Shan agreed. Livre would trade with these people, but they wouldn't be able to live with them, not most of them, anyway. In a hundred years, something fundamental had changed, and Shan was so very grateful that he had ended up on Livre's side of that divide. "And considering how well Ben could tap dance around the truth.... I doubt he would have gotten into much trouble over that. They might have written it off as a bold move by an insightful leader."

"Yeah, they might. They'd love Lilian, if they didn't kill her first."

Shan laughed. It was true enough. However, most of Livre wasn't like her. Most of them never wanted more than existed beyond the farm and family, and the longer they were away, the more Shan realized those were the only two things that did matter. "They wouldn't have forgiven his other sins," Shan said softly, not sure if this was a particularly appropriate time to bring up the subject, but asking about Ben and not bringing it up felt a lot like avoidance.

"Raping me," Temar said quietly.

"That's not something civilized people easily forgive," Shan pointed out. He suspected the PA would be less brutal in their punishment, but they wouldn't simply forgive a rape.

"I know."

"What are you thinking?" Shan ran his fingers through Temar's hair. At the part it was slightly darker, where the sun hadn't yet had a chance to bleach it.

"I'm wondering if Ben even knew what he was doing."

"If he…." Shan frowned. "What do you mean?"

"He used to talk to me… talk playfully, like he expected me to share a laugh with him. It was like he had this switch in his brain and he could convince himself that I wasn't really hurt… that he was taking care of me. God, I sound crazy."

Temar pressed his forehead to Shan's shoulder. Shan wished he could pull all these feelings out and burn them in front of Temar, erase them so they would never exist again, but he couldn't.

"No, no, you don't sound crazy. You have a right to feel what you feel."

"I felt so scared and then angry and then scared and angry, and I guess I'm settling on something between disgust and pity." Temar shifted so he could look up at Shan, and Shan waited through the silence. Silence and time were the only gifts he could give Temar. "He was a sad little man who acted big. He acted like he had power, but real power is Lilian, who can sit in a room with someone strong and know she's still a lot stronger. Power is you doing what's right even when you don't know how it's going to turn out."

Shan stroked a hand over Temar's cheek. "Power is you not wanting to step up, but doing it and doing it well because you know it's the right thing to do."

Temar smiled. "What he had was an illusion, and to feel powerful, he had to make everyone else weak. That's sad. Not scary, not evil, just sad." Temar blew out a breath and tried to sit up, but Shan wrapped Temar in a hug and held on. "I'm saying it wrong," Temar said miserably. "I'm making it sound like I'm okay with it, and I'm not."

"You're saying it perfectly, Temar. My father was the same way. I don't think he ever understood that he'd hurt Naite. If he did, if he knew that he'd ripped Naite into emotional shreds, he would have known why Naite kept striking out. But he didn't. When Naite got slaved out to Tom, our father was so confused and angry and hurt." Shan remembered his father's face when he would stare out over the fields like he expected to see Naite out there, working. His father would get drunk and go up to sit on the boulder high above the house, and Shan always thought it was because he could see the top of Tom's house from that spot. He'd watch that house and drink until Shan had been sure he would fall down and break his neck on the rocks. "He was hurt," Shan admitted. "He didn't understand how people could betray him, and he never understood that he'd betrayed all of us first. The first lesson Div taught me was to forgive. We all sin, and some of us more than others, but the important thing is to forgive ourselves first and to forgive others second."

"No sermons. You already got me to pray once, so let's call that a spiritual success and move on."

Shan gave a huff of laughter. "Deal. No sermons. And no feeling guilty for being a strong enough man to leave the fear and anger behind you. He's gone. He's not worth being angry at."

"Naite would call us both idiots."

"Yep."

"He will call us idiots if he hears us talking about this."

"Personally, I plan to never let him hear this conversation."

"Good plan."

"Every once in a while I do have a good one. The rest of the time, I'm leaving it up to you to make the plans." Shan wasn't even kidding on that front. Temar might not like to take charge, but he did it a good deal better than Shan ever had. Shan cringed as he remembered getting in fights with Naite right in the middle of council meetings. That wasn't the way to inspire anyone to listen to your arguments fairly.

"And if my plans involve going back to our quarters the second you can walk without twinging so I can slowly and carefully ambush you again?"

Shan smiled. "Now that sounds like a good plan."

"Doesn't it? I'm thinking some of this oil that works like gakka and the lights on low and me on my back with my legs over your shoulders and maybe afterwards, a long soak in a hot tub of water."

Shan's eyebrows went up. "Your legs over my shoulders?"

"Problem?"

"Oh no. I like your plans. Your plans work out so much better than mine. So, oil, legs over shoulders, a soak in a tub… I can work with that plan. I'm feeling better already."

Temar rolled his eyes. "Oh no—this time the plan is to wait for the doctors to clear you before the ambush, and no more ambushing me to demand an ambush."

"You mean, the ambush you'd already made plans for and warned the doctors about?"

Temar blushed, and Shan had to laugh. "We're going to be okay," he said.

Temar shifted some and settled in with his head on Shan's shoulder. "Yes, we are."

Keep reading for
an exclusive excerpt from

Desert World Immigrant

Desert World: Book Three

By Lyn Gala

Lieutenant Commander Verly Black is ready to leave the atrocities of war behind and immigrate to the planet of Livre, where he can build a future away from the ghosts of his past. He doesn't expect to find a kindred spirit in councilman Naite Poli—a man with secrets as dark as Verly's own and bearing the scars to prove it. Both men have done what was necessary to survive—Verly in battle and Naite in defense of his family—and they're haunted by memories that leave them wary of trusting others. As they circle each other, the political maneuvering around them grows more dangerous, with the outer worlds trying to force Livre into one alliance or another. Some still view Verly as a killer and a spy, and they're determined not to let him forget what he's done. Others fear the implications of a military officer sharing the bed of a councilmember. When the rebel alliance moves beyond threats, Verly and Naite must push through the pain of their pasts and stand together to fight for the future of their world.

Coming Soon to
http://www.dsppublications.com

chapter
o n e

VERLY HELD the edge of his seat, feeling the machine struggle through the air. The seat vibrated and rolled just a little left and then banked to the right before evening out for all of two and a half seconds before repeating the cycle. Verly understood the irony of a pilot bothered by the bucking of a shuttle as it fought its way through air, but normally he was the one in control. He trusted his own flying more than Lieutenant Gilson's.

"How's it going?" he asked.

"Not much longer, sir." Gilson managed to sound almost respectful, but Verly had seen the sneer when Gilson had first heard his name.

Sometimes Verly wondered how he would handle an entire planet of people who didn't recognize his name, assuming he could really call Livre a planet. Today, the Planetary Alliance would never allow colonization or even mining in such a fragile environment. The planet had huge mountain ranges that interrupted deep deserts with and an underground water supply that had too many poisons for human consumption. That led to a relatively limited range of flora and fauna.

Back before the civil war and before ships could carry people to countless systems, humans had put boots down on planets that could barely sustain them. They terraformed and carved out niches in places where no human should go. Most of those colonies had failed, but against all odds Livre was still here. And now Verly was going to make this one small planet his home—his refuge from the past and the mistakes that still haunted him. Step one had been learning all about this new home of his.

Honestly, Verly had studied the biology out of a desire to avoid ending up a meal for some carnivorous plant or rodent, which Livre seemed to specialize in. He'd fought in space for most of his life… fought the dirty war of terrorism and bombs that had followed the official end of the Alliance War. So dying with his foot in some pipe trap while rat-sized mammals ate him… that was not an option.

Of course, thirst posed as much of a danger as the plant life or the local predators. Naturally occurring pure water was too rare for human survival, but huge tankers had once landed on Livre carrying water to begin the terraforming. That had been before Verly's birth. He hadn't even heard of Livre before its two rather eccentric ambassadors had negotiated an interesting treaty that put Livre off-limits to all but pre-approved applicants on official business.

Verly had one of those rare visas.

As a planet, Livre left a lot to be desired. He wouldn't find cities or long rails for aircars or shuttle launches. He wouldn't live in sealed buildings or even walk manicured natural spaces with carefully controlled ecosystems. This was a border world like Verly had never seen before, and he wasn't sure of what he could expect to find.

Dust.

People as odd as Ambassadors Gazer and Polli.

Citizens who didn't look at him oddly the moment they recognized his name.

The shuttle did an odd little hop as it passed through a column of hot air. "Final descent before landing," Gilson said, and then Verly could feel the engines shifting into a lower gear, the bottom jets firing to keep the shuttle from dropping too fast as it slowed.

White sand interrupted with streaks of yellowed land and red and brown rocks rose up under them. The lack of actual landmarks was disorienting for someone who'd grown up in a jungle of buildings where the skyline always told you if you were north or south of the river—east or west of main landing. And the sky back home on Diamond was always streaked with the trails of planes and shuttles. Here the cloudless blue stretched out to the edge of the world.

Eventually, he could see a line of ragged mountains in the distance—young rocks just pushing up from below the surface with all their sharp edges pointed up to the sky.

"Are we going over those?" Verly asked. He didn't bother defining "those" because any pilot worth half a credit would have an eye on those mountains. Those were the sorts of formations that could chew through every safety feature and turn a shuttle into a steaming pile of junk if they got too close.

"Yes sir. We're staying well above them and landing in the dunes on the far side. Most of the settlements are on the west side."

"Great."

Verly kept his eyes on the land as the shuttle screamed through the heavy air of the low atmosphere. The shuttle bucked like a great beast and then it finally scraped its belly along the ground, landing gear useless in the fine, white sand. Great clouds of dust rose up. The shuttle actually seemed to slide against Livre, slipping to the right until it finally settled, an enormous cloud of sand swirling around them.

"Any idea how long until the dust settles?" Verly studied the glow of the sun through the sandstorm.

"No idea, sir." Gilson didn't sound very interested in having any sort of conversation because he started reading off shut-down procedures. Pilots never had to read those things out loud, not after their first dozen flights, but Verly let the man retreat into his administrivia. It took at least thirty or forty uncomfortable minutes before the sand slowly settled and Verly got his first look at his new home. If things went well, he'd be here for years. If things went poorly, his commanding officers would lose his paperwork and leave him here a whole lot longer.

"This is shuttle Zulu requesting permission to disembark," Gilson requested.

"Sure, come on out," the radio answered. The Planetary Alliance was not a fan of informal procedures, so that voice coming through the official PA radio sounded very odd. At least Verly had the advantage of having worked with Ambassador Gazer, so he'd been prepared for less than orthodox people. Gilson actually looked over at Verly as if looking for some sort of reassurance. Turning his seat around, Verly busied himself with his personal belongings while Gilson cracked the side door open.

The smell of heat hit Verly like a storm front. He hadn't even realized heat had an odor until this moment, but he sneezed several times.

"That's an interesting scent," Gilson said quietly, but then he cleared his throat. "Sir, after you," he offered stiffly.

Verly gave a nod and hiked his bag's strap over his shoulder as he strode down the metal planking to his new planet. His first impression was that it was bare, and then he started sneezing again, and Verly realized he didn't have a cloth. He was in danger of making a snotty mess out of himself. That would make for a great first impression. Wiping his face, he tried snuffing, and that just made his eyes water as the heat seemed to invade his head.

"Here," a gruff voice offered, and a man shoved a cloth toward him. "Rula had the same reaction. It makes me wonder what sort of air you have up there."

"Thanks." Verly took the cloth and blew his nose before checking out his savior. His first impression startled him so much that he took a step back. The man was a warped mirror image of Ambassador Polli. He was an inch or so taller—tall enough that he nearly reached Verly's own six-five—and he carried a lot more muscle, but the two men shared the same prominent nose and dark eyes and dusty skin. Honestly, they were both exotic and beautiful the way a sharp-edged weapon was. He had angles that were simply interesting to look at.

"You got more stuff?" the man asked with a disgusted look at the shuttle. Usually the disgust was focused more on Verly.

"Nope. This is it," Verly held out his hand. "Verly Black," he introduced himself.

This sharp-edged man with his wide chest and shoulders eyed Verly for a second, and Verly drew himself up to full height, which came damn close to this guy's impressive six-two or six-three. They were a matched pair, although Verly didn't have as much muscle. Piloting didn't provide much of a workout.

The guy finally took Verly's hand. "Naite Polli."

"Ambassador Polli's brother?" Verly guessed.

Naite gave a snort and turned toward a cluster of low buildings so far away that you could have landed a shuttle before hitting them. "At least you didn't bring armfuls of shit," Naite commented before he started striding across the sand.

Clearly Naite was as unconventional as his brother. That was fine with Verly. Leaving the shuttle and the surly pilot behind, Verly blew his nose and set off across the blowing sand. He made it less than half the distance before he had to slow down. His eyes watered and his cheeks ached from squinting, but still the sunlight seemed to reflect off every speck of white sand. Worse, his lungs ached from the heat, and the sand dragged at his feet.

Stopping, Verly closed his eyes and tried to shut out the stabbing sun for a second as he caught his breath. He'd been on a dozen alien worlds, but none of them had felt alien. Every world had trees and rivers and square buildings rising toward the heavens. Some world required more effort to get those pieces all in place, but the Planetary Alliance had a firm policy of not allowing any planet to suffer from a lack of terraforming. But Livre was truly alien.

Verly opened his eyes and started as he realized that Naite had returned. The man stood a foot away, arms crossed over his chest.

"Are you planning on throwing up?"

"No, I can safely say I'm not," Verly said. The frown on Naite's face made it pretty clear that he questioned the veracity of that statement. "The sun is much brighter and the air much hotter and drier than I'm used to. I just need a second to catch my breath."

"Well hurry up so we can get out of the heat. We're fools for standing out here."

If Verly had the energy, he would have danced for joy. If the heat made Naite miserable, that meant they were headed someplace cooler. That thought gave Verly the strength to wave Naite toward the building. "I'm good."

One dark eyebrow twitched, but Naite turned and headed for the building. The low squared sides still showed the tool marks from the drop ship's claw. This was the first settlement. Verly had been to first settlement on Diamond. Most schoolchildren did visit the place and walk in the steps of the colonists as a memorial to those first humans who had braved Diamond's vicious swamps and poisonous wildlife. However, this place looked like people still used it.

Naite clamored down a ladder with more grace than Verly had expected from such a large man.

"Are Ambassadors Gazer and Polli here?" Verly asked as Naite pulled a heavy blast door open. The stamped metal suggested it'd been scrapped from some colony ship. This place was like stepping into a historical reenactment.

Naite gestured for Verly to head into the slightly less hot interior of the building, which he was only too happy to do. Waiting until after he'd pulled the door shut leaving them in an artificial twilight, Naite answered, "Shan and Temar are over at Blue Hope trying to talk some sense into come folks who don't have any to start with."

"Well I'm sure Ambassadors—"

"Don't call them that," Naite cut him off as he headed across a narrow room.

"Call them what?"

Naite stopped and eyed Verly up. If they'd met in a bar, Verly definitely would have assumed Naite wanted to have some very hard and very fast sex. If Naite had been a superior officer, Verly would have assumed that look meant an upcoming demotion. Naite had this odd combination of sexual heat and personal aggression—of carnal looks and suppressed anger. Maybe it was Verly's self-destructive streak showing up, but he really found himself wondering whether Naite bedded men. "Don't call them ambassador anything. They're just plain Shan and Temar," Naite said firmly, and Verly realized that he was in danger of losing track of the conversation.

"I don't want to be disrespectful," Verly said carefully.

Naite snorted. "And I don't want you giving those two an overinflated sense of their own importance."

That surprised Verly. The Planetary Alliance was full of difficult people who all knew that their beliefs were the only correct beliefs for anyone to hold. The ambassadors had navigated political waters that would have sunk lesser men, and they'd done that after giving the breakaway worlds a run for their money. As far as Verly was concerned, those two could have some fairly large heads without overinflating anything. They deserved a few bragging rights.

However, Naite's expression made it clear that Verly did not have permission to argue. "Okay," Verly said slowly. "So, they're talking to this other city?"

With a small nod of approval, Naite turned and headed through a door into another identically sized room, only this one looked like someone lived in it. "Hopefully Temar's doing the actual talking," Naite said. "Shan's version of persuading people usually involves large amounts of guilt and God, two subjects that plenty of people have a rather uncomfortable relationship with."

Verly frowned as he realized that he had misunderstood Livre's political scene. He hadn't expected the leaders to inspire such resentment. Usually Verly saw that on much more developed planets, not small worlds with scattered settlements that had to work just to survive. "I suppose I don't have a very clear impression of Am…. Shan. He was injured most of the time I knew him," Verly admitted.

Naite stopped near another door and really studied Verly. "Huh. That's right. You're the one who saved him, are you?"

Verly gave Naite his widest smile. When he was sixteen, he'd spent an embarrassing amount of time learning how to give potential partners a crooked, devilish smile, in part to make up for the fact that he had a rather austere expression with a square jaw and prominent chin that seemed even more noticeable with his fair skin. He had a manly face, a face that the military had once chosen to put on the front of an advertisement for pilot training. But he'd intentionally developed a boyish smile.

"The official reports actually say that I'm the one who put him in danger. Luckily, Temar gave a direct order, so very little of that blame fell on me or I might have been dropped back another rank."

"It's hard to see Temar giving orders." Naite opened the door, and the brutal heat of the planet once against pushed against Verly's skin.

"Actually," Verly said as he squinted his eyes, "Temar threatened to bring me to Livre and let the sandcats strip the flesh from my screaming body if I double-crossed him or didn't follow orders."

Naite's mouth fell open. "He what?"

"That's not a threat a man forgets soon," Verly pointed out. "I get the feeling that Temar is very attached to your brother and a little overprotective."

"Obviously more than I knew. He really said that?"

Verly nodded. When Naite's angry exterior dropped, he looked even more like Shan, although Verly wasn't fool enough to say it. Naite didn't seem like a big fan of his brother.

"Well you're lucky it wasn't the other way around with Shan making the plans and Temar in danger. Shan's plans are downright suicidal. So, since those two are off doing whatever they're doing, you're stuck with me. Shan suggested that I show you around, but I have work, so I figure I can show you the working end of a dig-stick. Unless, that it, you have some problem with putting in a day's work." Naite crossed his arms again, clearly waiting for Verly to make a protest.

"No problem at all, at least not as long as you keep in mind that I have no idea what a dig-stick is."

"It's a stick. You dig with it."

Verly smiled. "I had gotten that far in my analysis of the term. I just don't actually know what to do with one, and you really don't have to suggest that I dig."

Naite grunted and closed the door to the silent base behind him before setting out for a newer and much less level building. This one seemed to be made of native twigs and a cargo hauler of some sort waited in the shade. Climbing up into the driver's seat, Naite waited as Verly got up into the passenger side. The vehicle had two ovals of plastic right in front of the driver and passenger seat, but it didn't feel like enough protection. Verly felt a little like he was perched on top of some teenager's version of a bootleg motorized vehicle. Naite started it, and the machine yanked itself into motion with an uneven lurch. Verly grabbed at the nearest stable point as he tried to not fall. He grabbed Naite's arm.

Naite looked down with a barely veiled humor. The edge of his mouth twitched. "Problem?"

"Old machines and worse, old machines that I'm not driving."

"Do you even know how to drive a hauler?"

"Nope. But pilots are all the same. We don't do well if we're not steering."

Naite gave him a long look. "I generally prefer to steer," Naite said, and his voice had an edge that almost sounded like an invitation. Almost. However, it'd been so long since anyone had invited Verly for a quick tumble that he wasn't sure whether he could trust his judgment. Perhaps he only wanted that invitation so much that he imagined Naite's interest.

"You need a sand veil," Naite said, his voice suddenly businesslike as he pulled a white cloth out of his pocket. It looked like burn gauze with heavier strips of white fabric on either side, trailing off into long tails. "You tie it around your face to makes sure you don't breathe in too much dust. If you do, you can get sand pneumonia."

"Charming." Verly took the veil and started tying it around his mouth and nose. Naite tied his own sand veil around his face, the white of his fabric already grey with dust.

"That's never going to stay." Naite half-stood and leaned over to roughly tug the veil into place. Reaching around, he tied it around the back of Verly's head, but that left him so close that Verly could smell his musk. The scent reminded Verly of barracks and men pressed close together, of dirty little moments stolen between drills and hand jobs in corners. Verly's cock was already starting to ache with need, but Naite finished arranging the veil and then sat back down in his seat.

"We'll get to the valley in an hour or so," he offered as he put the hauler into gear and made the machine lurch forward again. Either it had been far too long since Verly had gotten laid or this trip to Livre might prove more interesting that Verly had expected. Maybe both.

LYN GALA started writing in the back of her science notebook in third grade and hasn't stopped since. Westerns starring men with shady pasts gave way to science fiction with questionable protagonists, which eventually became any story with a morally ambiguous character. Even the purest heroes have pain and loss and darkness in their hearts, and that's where she likes to find her stories. Her characters seek to better themselves and find the happy (or happier) ending.

When she isn't writing, Lyn Gala teaches history in a small town in New Mexico. Her favorite spot to write is a flat rock under a wide tree on the edge of the open desert where her dog can terrorize local wildlife. Writing in a wide range of genres, she often gravitates back to adventure and BDSM, stories about men in search of true love and a way to bring some criminal to justice... unless they happen to be the criminal.

BRANDON WITT

SUBMERGING
INFERNO

MEN of
MYTH

http://www.dsppublications.com

http://www.dsppublications.com

the **prince**
and the
program

aldous
mercer

http://www.dsppublications.com

For more
great fiction
from

DSP PUBLICATIONS

visit us online.

WWW.DSPPUBLICATIONS.COM

www.ingramcontent.com/pod-product-compliance
Lightning Source LLC
Chambersburg PA
CBHW051538260626
47170CB00003B/986